DESCENT

By Ken MacLeod

DESCENT

Ken MacLeod

www.orbitbooks.net

ORBIT

First published in Great Britain in 2014 by Orbit

A CIP catalogue record for this book
is available from the British Library.

ISBN 978-1-84149-941-3

Typeset in Goudy by Palimpsest Book Production Limited,
Falkirk, Stirlingshire
Printed and bound in Great Britain by Clays Ltd, St Ives plc

Papers used by Orbit are from well-managed forests
and other responsible sources.

MIX
Paper from
responsible sources
FSC
www.fsc.org
FSC® C104740

Orbit
An imprint of
Little, Brown Book Group
100 Victoria Embankment
London EC4Y 0DY

An Hachette UK Company
www.hachette.co.uk

www.orbitbooks.net

To the memory of Iain M. Banks

0.1111 Recurring

The trouble with my job is that far too often it lets me lie late in bed, watching my ex-fiancée. I don't blame the job, you understand. I blame myself, even while I'm doing it.

Especially while I'm doing it. This is an activity so futile, so self-destructive, so time-wasting, so unethical and unprofessional and unproductive and downright *unsafe* that I hate myself for indulging in it, as if I were addicted to some harmful and expensive drug (I am, to several) or fixated by a kink so innocuous yet ridiculous that it doesn't have a porn site let alone a pride march to call its own (that, too) or obsessed with a conspiracy theory so elaborate yet so tenuously supported and so self-centred and self-serving that I'd blush to outline it (but you're ahead of me, right?) or . . . ah, fuck it. Compared to all the other things I have to be ashamed of, what I'm doing right now is a foible.

1

So, here I am at, let's say, eight thirty on a Tuesday morning, leaning back against the headboard of a bed in a flat near Haymarket in Edinburgh and hovering over a Kelvinside canyon of sandstone tenements in Glasgow. I have tree-top-height line of sight on a door at the top of a dozen worn stone steps, cast-iron railings on either side, man-high weeds sprouting from between the flagstones of the carpet-sized front yard.

The door opens. Gabrielle steps out and closes it behind her. Her red hair flicks as she turns. She's pert and petite. Her belted coat looks a size too big for her. I'm not getting much in the way of sound other than road thrum and beep but I fancy I hear her boot heels tick as she skips down the steps and sets off up the street towards the main road. I zoom after her, lose resolution, and for a moment consider renting some time on the drone and sending it drifting after her. Then I decide this might be too risky and I just let the app flick and a new view pops up, this time face-on and from lower down, probably from a traffic cam at the junction.

God, she's pretty. Bright wide eyes and big wide lips in a small face. Not perfect: she has the brow-ridge, barely notice-able except in profile, and the slight fleshiness about the nostrils that trace her descent and, to the discerning, mark her kin, but these make her all the more beautiful and fascin-ating to me. Her eyes and lips are narrowed at the moment. I wish I knew what she's thinking about. Probably work. It's less than ten minutes' walk from the steps of her flat to the swing doors of the biology building. Lucky her that she has such a brief and brisk commute. Lucky me that I can follow her all the way.

I watch her until she disappears into the ground floor foyer. Another moment of hesitant consideration, this time of linking to drone cameras that can see her through the ninth-floor windows. I've done this once or twice – well, seven or eight times – over the past few months, and I've got away with it so far, but for today I decide not to push my luck. If she ever found out she could call the police. Well, maybe she wouldn't, all things considered, but others might. Then, whatever the outcome, the least that would happen is I wouldn't have the job. End of problem. There are times when I think this would be a solution.

But I do have the job, and with it a big and busy day ahead. I catch up on the news, knock out a few instant reactions, then take the iGlasses off. I consider visiting a few of my favourite sites, then – to compensate for my earlier indulgence – decide not to, and to get up. I have to be at Holyrood for ten thirty, and I want to be there early or at least in good time.

Just before ten, any day in the middle of May, the street at the top of the Mound is crowded with men in black. This disturbs me less than you might think. They're ministers of the Church of Scotland, here for the General Assembly.

Men in black, I think. Ha! The thought makes me smile.

In my early teens, after I got into all the flying-saucer

rubbish and – as I thought at the time – out of it unscathed and unsullied, I read science fiction on my father's old Kindle. I'd outgrown kids' books, YA was embarrassing, and the classics prescribed at school were boring and about girls. The SF novels on that antique device with its red leather case were labelled 'classic', but my father persuaded me not to let that put me off.

This is why, as I walk up the Mound and down the High Street, the alternative Edinburghs I distract myself by calling up in rapid succession on my glasses aren't just the standard historicals, entertaining though it is to stroll the main drag of Hume's and Smith's Athens of the North and watch the chamberpots tipped from upstairs windows to splatter heads below, or to scroll the city's growth from Neolithic settlement to modern capital, or let the smoke of Victorian lums and Edwardian slums rise to swamp the streets and then, with quite surprising suddenness, disperse the miasma with a wave of the Clean Air Act.

I play with overlays of alternate pasts and possible futures, with steampunk and cyberpunk, utopia and dystopia. Looking down towards Waverley Station, I replace its long sheds with the Nor Loch, stagnant and stinking. I swing by the Victorian eminence of the Bank of Scotland and see it blazoned with the banners of John MacLean's 1919 Workers' Republic. The vista along George IV Bridge gets an instant make-over as a Blackshirt mob storms the National Library, then I time-shift the street to the metropolis of concrete, glass and steel the agitators fancied themselves fighting for. Before I turn into the Royal Mile, past the verdigrised statue of Hume with its pilgrim-polished toe, the whole fascist facade crashes under USAAF bombs, and I smirk in smoke so thick it almost makes me miss my footing and so vivid I can smell it.

The view, now downward to the sea, is of the High Street in yet another unlikely mash-up of possibilities. The houses and shops and churches retain their higgledy-piggledy sandstone granularity, but beyond the Old Town new towers rise, spindly, improbable constructions of materials that suck sunlight and burn breezes, lively as trees. The flags that hang from poles jutting over hotel and shop doorways are the saltire of St Andrew and the cross of St George, Europe's star-circled banner and Ireland's starry plough, the Maple Leaf and the Stars and Stripes, and the red flags of the workers' republics (unimagined by and unimaginable to MacLean) on whose trade and tourism and tat the street relies. Above are, of course, the airships without which any such alt-historical scenario would be incomplete – no lumbering gasbags these, but silver-skinned streamlined shapes that bore through the air with drill-bit determination. Between the airships' altitude and rooftop height the air is speckled with the dots and flashes of drones occluding or reflecting light.

As above, so below: form follows function in every outré retro style. Nothing is ironic, nothing tips a wink to the past. Men's broad-brimmed hats shield from unforgiving sun or lashing rain, and block surveillance from above; dandy shirt-fronts, long flapping coats and wide lapels soak energy from the air and information from the ether. The face-framing, profile-hiding visors of the poke bonnets affected by fashionable young ladies are transparent from within, opaque from without, giving augmented peripheral vision on the inner surface, and conferring privacy to and from the sideward glance as well as shade; floor-skimming full skirts might look like clumsy crinolines in a still picture, but in the moving image they balloon and glide, hems rippling autonomously like the lateral fins of flatfish to avoid toes and heels, obstacles and dirt, and their extravagant yardage of sun-drenched or wind-stirred fabric powers that motion as well as warming or cooling threads and a panoply of coms with every flounce; lacy parasols uplink to satellites and drones, and dainty handbags encompass libraries by default.

Vehicles on the street whizz by silently but for the whir of rims on cobbles, powered by legs and light, solar battery and hydrogen tank. Urchins scamper unhindered through the throng, watched over by the automated benevolence of the distributed panopticon stare and protected by loitering overhead drones like time-shared guardian angels poised to pounce. Layered in and imbricated with the new, of course, are the strata of earlier looks and times: diesel-belching buses, petrol-burning taxis, trouser suits and short skirts and jeans and skip caps and bare heads and bare legs, airliners coming in with metronomic regularity above the North Sea and then the Firth to sink above Cramond and touch down at Turnhouse, or still climbing from far to the south to head out over the Atlantic high above the airships, and so on and on, but here it is nonetheless, an iffy skiffy future like none I would or could have imagined in my teens.

Oh, wait. That's reality.

I've never had a problem with reality. I've had a problem with dreams. Sometimes I think I still do.

I have a recurring dream. The details vary, but it's always the same dream. It's so vivid it doesn't feel like a dream. It feels real at the time. I told it once to a man who knows about these things, and he told me what it means. It means they'll stay with you, he said. They'll always be with you. You'll take them with you to the stars.

This is how it begins.

I'm falling out of the sky. All I can hear is screaming. How much of it is from the air and how much from the other hundred-odd passengers I can't tell. We're hurtling straight towards the ground, at free-fall speed from twenty miles up, in a needle-nosed, narrow-winged arrowhead. From the window I can see a blue curve, an arc of a vast circular target whose centre is dead ahead. It's impossible, at some primal level of my primate brain, not to be convinced we're going to hit.

At such moments your life is supposed to flash before your eyes. It does, if you're flicking back and forth through decades of visual capture on your glasses. The rational layer of my mind is as terrified as the monkey module. I'm not afraid of dying. I'm afraid of judgement.

A shudder goes through the craft, and the screaming is drowned out by a steady roar as the ramjets ignite. I'm pushed against the back of my seat. We're still going straight down, no longer free-falling but accelerating. The scream's pitch and volume rise above the roar, which continues unabated. My weight's axis swings, pressing me down hard on the seat then again and more strongly back as the spaceplane swoops its hairpin turn around the end of its drop and begins to climb on a course that is not vertical but feels like it. The sky goes from blue to black as the blood returns to my eyes.

I look out, over the slanted sliver of starboard wing. We're climbing above the ocean. Far below us, pillars and castles of cloud are lit and shaded by the early sun. Not far to the west, a huge brightly lit sphere rises on a parallel course, gradually falling behind: it is the balloon that carried us up and from which we dropped a couple of minutes ago.

It passes out of sight, and I continue to stare out. A smaller, dimmer light rises from below us, overtakes, then drops back into view and paces our ascent for a few seconds. No one else seems to notice. I can't look away. It dances, then darts off, dwindling to a point, then nothing.

I blink and replay the past ten seconds in my glasses, zooming the view. In close-up, it's evident what the source of the light was: a fragment of fabric from the now burst balloon, caught in an updraught and then in our slipstream until a random gust whipped it away. I'm unconvinced. Some code in the spectrum of its colour taunts me and tells me I've seen that light before.

The ramjets choke off as the air thins and there's a second or so when I feel as if I'm falling, as indeed I am but on an upward trajectory, then the main engine kicks in for the final push to orbit. For a few minutes I'm pressed back harder than ever, and then without warning or transition we're in free fall. In the sudden silence I hear fellow passengers gasp or squeal with delight.

I have no time to share the thrill or enjoy the view. For me, this is judgement day. Within a few hours, I have to justify my life. What I'm searching for, in the back captures and the memories they evoke, is anything that will serve as explanation, as exculpation, as excuse.

PART ONE

1

The thing is, we weren't supposed to be on the hill. Our parents thought we were at Sophie's with Ellie and Aiden, revising for our maths exam. Sophie and Aiden had a grip on topics the rest of us flailed for, and improved it by matching wits with each other and us. Also, helping classmates counted for Social, so they offered. Incentive problem right there, you think. But they were too competitive towards each other to play tricks.

About half past two Calum leaned back from the table and stretched. He looked out of the window and then he looked at me.

'Cut?' he said.

The Cut is a walk, along the bank of an obsolete aqueduct that follows a contour around the hills, from the loch and the reservoirs to the town. Out of nowhere, my legs ached for it.

I shook my head. 'My dad'll kill me.'

Calum nodded down at the table. His phone and mine lay with the others', sustaining the trigonometry problem that shimmered in the midst.

'OK,' I said, standing up.

Ellie gave Calum a look. He smiled at Sophie.

'Fresh air,' he said, chair scraping. 'Back in a bit.'

Sophie said nothing, Aiden didn't notice as usual. Ellie pouted. Then all three heads bent again over the five phones.

I followed Calum through the hallway and out. He closed the front door with barely a click, then capered down the steps and clanged the gate. Across a quarter mile of descending rooftops we looked to the moor and the hills.

'Wa-hey!' Calum said.

'It'll do us good anyway,' I said.

'Aye,' said Calum. '*Mens sano* in whatsitsface, yeah?'

'Yeah,' I said.

(The experience began, I think, between the moment we both wanted the walk and the moment we decided to leave our phones behind. That's how it always begins. You wanted a walk. It was a wet afternoon and you fancied a drive. The night was vile and you were minded to check on the cow.)

It was a Saturday afternoon in May, the air damp under bright low cloud. Gorse on the hillside opposite blazed like surrogate sunshine. A faint smell and haze of burning tyres hung in the air. The smirr gave us a good excuse to have our hoods up, which was handy just in case our parents were relying on more than our phones to keep tabs on us. We

14

walked down to the main road and over the footbridge, barely looking down at the stalled traffic, then over the railway bridge at Branchton and up the foot-worn zigzag path through gorse and bramble to the Cut. I glanced each way for thoughtless mountain bikers, took a step or two across the broken tarmac and looked over the Cut's bank. The past week's rain had raised the water level, but the flow was still sluggish, barely stirring the clumps of algae upon which froglets and tadpoles pulsated, blobs of black jelly with a double sheen from their skins and from their surface-tension meniscus cloaks.

We set off to the right, westward, facing a view out along the Kip Valley across the Firth of Clyde to the hazy hills beyond. The weather had kept all but the most determined of the usual weekend walkers and cyclists away. Old folks in singlets and shorts, grimly power-striding past us; lads and the odd lass on mountain bikes, spraying us with gravel. A police drone drifted around the shoulder of the hill, then turned away over the valley. Along the same flight path a few seconds later came a smaller civilian drone, swooping close enough for us to see the solidarity sigils on the underside of its wings. The smoke column from the blockade on Inverkip Road wavered into the air in front of us. As we drew level with it we could see the burning tyres heaped across the middle of the road, bracketed by oil-drum braziers at the kerbs. The narrow passages left for vehicles to snake through guaranteed each driver an earful of harangue along the way. A police car parked on the verge, blue light flashing, meant that the cops intended only to sit and watch.

'Wonder what it is this time?' I remarked.

Calum grunted. 'Disnae matter, it's all the same.'

We mooched on, agreeing that the country was in a terrible state and that something should be done about it. In the light of what was to be done, and so soon, you might imagine us quivering with radical zeal. You would be wrong. Sixteen years old, smack in the middle of the pissed-off mid-to-late teens demographic, our generational rebelliousness consisted of a yearning for order. We'd had years of what seemed like its endless, pointless opposite.

'Bet you the revolutionaries are behind it,' I said.

'Aye, nae doubt there's one or two in there. They're aye stirring things up.'

'They wouldn't have anything to stir up if people didn't have legitimate grievances,' I added, trying to be fair, 'like not getting paid for weeks on end.'

'All very well tae say that,' said Calum. 'But people have legitimate channels tae take up that kindae thing. No need tae make things worse for everybody else.'

I laughed. 'Except the revolutionaries – for them it's a case of, "The worse it gets, the better"!'

We shared dark chuckles and knowing looks. We thought ourselves wise to the ways of the revolutionaries because we knew all about their claptrap, dangerous, discredited ideology and cynical tactics from school assemblies and from the news services. As good sixteen-year-olds we treated these with about as much respect as we gave the likewise pervasive warnings about smoking, drink and drugs, but even so the exposures

16

had an effect. We'd seen the revolutionaries' leaflets and their irregular bulletin, *What Now?*, and we'd even occasionally seen revolutionaries themselves, handing their agitprop out at railway stations and bus stops, but like most people we ostentatiously binned the sheets unread. I had secretly read one once in the school toilet and found it so boring that I'd been tempted to use it as bog paper.

Despite their manifest unpopularity the revolutionaries seemed like an invisible army of tens of thousands, and their hidden hand was seen behind every strike, road blockade, power cut, net outage, traffic snarl-up and workplace occupation in the country. No one caught actually involved in any of these had ever been proved in court to be a revolutionary, and the only thing the police could nail the overt revolutionaries for was littering.

'If the filth are nae up to the job,' Calum expounded, 'it's time they made way for the army.'

'Aye, right,' I said. 'And if the soldiers aren't—?'

Calum glanced sidelong at me, and jerked a thumb over his shoulder at the blockade. 'A few good blokes with spanners and tyre irons could scatter that lot.'

'Like your dad's three mechanics and two apprentices, you mean?'

'Maybe not, but guys like them. Well, like them but . . .'

He waved his arms and shrugged at the same time. We both laughed.

'Ah, fuck all that,' said Calum. 'So long as the fucking teachers aren't on strike for the exams.'

'Watch it,' I said. 'My mum's a teacher, and she'd never go on strike.'

'Ease off, man, you know what I mean.'

At a shoulder of the hill, we came upon a beam of wood thrown across the Cut, just downslope from the ashes of a recent small fire and a clutter of empty cans. A microwave mast broke the skyline. Calum turned and marched across the narrow bridge, arms outstretched, pretending to slip and sway. I followed, less ostentatiously. By unspoken consent, we set off up the hill. The summit wasn't far, and we reached it after a few minutes' walk through soaking heather and long grass. We stood by the square of barbed wire around the mast and gazed around at the moorland behind the hill and the expanse of sea and shores below.

Calum took a long breath. 'Feels cleaner up here.'

'No stink of tyres,' I said.

My face felt chill and damp. I looked up. The cloud was low enough to make the top of the mast indistinct. Within a minute, mist had descended on us. Visibility dropped to ten metres.

'May as well go back down,' Calum said.

I shrugged and agreed. But going down the slope wasn't as easy as coming up had been. We couldn't walk straight down, and turning this way and that to cope with hummocks and terraces meant that we weren't entirely sure which way we were facing at any given moment, and that a downward course wasn't necessarily taking us straight back to the Cut.

'We should have reached it by now,' I said, stopping.

Calum peered into the now pervasive and swirling whiteness.

'Aye, maybe wait till it clears.'

We stood still. The fog seemed to be rolling downhill. Before long we were suddenly under open blue sky, above the layer of cloud that had now settled over the Kip Valley. Looking about, I saw that the microwave mast was in a quite different direction from where I'd thought it was. We'd worked our way down the hill all right, but into a saddle between two summits.

'Fuck,' said Calum. 'Trust this tae happen when we don't have our fucking phones.'

'You wouldn't have a compass about you, by any chance?' I asked, mimicking an English accent.

'Why the fuck would I have a compass?'

'On a keyring, or a knife or something?'

'Nope.' He shook his head.

'Not to worry,' I said. 'Sun's in the south and west, just keep it behind us and we'll be going in the right direction.'

Calum gave me a sceptical look. 'We'll be lucky to dae even that with fog all around us.'

'Yeah,' I said. 'Like in that physics thing about diffusion.'

'Like common sense.'

I shrugged. 'Best we can do, unless you want to just wait it out.'

'Nah – folk's'll be worried. Cannae go far wrong anyway.'

I glanced up and to the side just to check where the sun actually was in the sky, and saw a pinprick of light at the zenith.

'Look!' I said, pointing. 'What's that?'

Calum saw it too.

'It's getting bigger,' he said.

The light became a bright sphere, shimmering and expanding.

'Weather balloon,' said Calum.

'Why's it coming down?'

We gazed up at the now silvery sphere for a few more seconds as it became bigger and – I suddenly realised – far closer than I'd thought.

'Fuck, that's no a—' Calum grabbed my arm. 'Come on, it'll be right on top ae us!'

We sprinted pell-mell across the heather. I remember a moment when the hillside in front of me was illuminated brighter than the day, then a moment when I could see nothing but white light.

2

My back hurt in several places. There was bright light in my eyes and something gritty in my nose. I sneezed, then moved my arm to shield my eyes. The knuckles of my right hand had black stuff on them. The light was just the white cloud of the overcast sky. I sat up, to find myself in the middle of a circular patch of burned heather about three metres across. Calum lay on his back alongside me, eyes closed. His arms and face were carelessly smeared with soot. At my anxious poke he went through the same startled awakening as I had. For a moment he looked frightened and perplexed, then with a visible effort he composed his features into a puzzled look.

We stood up, pointed at each other's faces, and brushed at our clothes. The soot and ashes were dry, although the grass and heather all around were beaded with moisture. We were on the hillside, a couple of hundred metres away from the route we'd taken up from the Cut.

'What the fuck!' said Calum, with a shaky laugh.

'Do you remember the light?'

'Of course I fucking remember the light. It was just a minute ago. Must have been ball lightning or something.'

'How could it burn all this and leave us . . .?'

'Easy,' he said. 'It burnt aw this, and knocked us out at the same time, and we fell onto the patch that got burnt.'

'But the burnt patch would still be hot, so why aren't we burned?'

'Aye, you've got a point.' He walked out of the black circle, and I followed. Fine black powder puffed underfoot like moon dust. I sneezed again. As I wiped the back of my left hand across my upper lip I caught a glimpse of my watch, and yelped.

'What?'

'It's half past five.'

'Jeez. Best be heading back, then.'

I stayed where I was. 'When we saw the light . . . it can't have been later than half three.'

'Four,' said Calum, frowning at his own watch. He sounded as if trying not to worry.

'Whatever,' I said. 'So what happened in the last hour and a half?'

He headed down the hill, and again I followed.

'I suppose,' he said as I caught up, 'the . . . ball lightning or whatever knocked us out, and we just sprawled there.'

'Somebody would have seen us.'

'No while the fog was still down.' He waved a hand to the left, toward the crude bridge we'd crossed, and the patch of burned heather near it. 'Anyway, even after it lifted, we'd just look like a couple ae drunk lads sleeping it off where they'd made a fire.'

This didn't sound likely to me.

We took flying leaps across the Cut at a section where the banks had collapsed, then scrambled down and washed our hands and splashed our faces. Back on the path, we bashed black dust out of our hoodies and swatted at the backs and seats of our jeans. After a mutual check we assured ourselves that, while still a mess, we wouldn't actually get stared at on the street. This turned out not to be the case, but we made it back to Sophie's flat without incident. By now it was after six, and Sophie and her parents were at their tea, as her father pointedly told us when he let us in.

'What happened to you?' he asked.

Calum replied before I could.

'We were walking round the Cut,' he said. 'Went up a hill and got caught in fog on the moor. Couldnae see where we were going. We kind ae blundered about for a bit then after we both tripped and fell onto a patch of burnt heather we reckoned it was best to wait till the fog lifted.'

Sophie's dad looked at us sceptically.

'Well, that's no the kind of tripping you look like you've been daein,' he said, baffling me. 'Wait a minute.'

He came back with two objects, one for each of us. For a

moment, I held a slab of bevelled black glass in my hand and couldn't for the life of me remember what it was.

'Phone home now, the both of you,' he said. 'You got calls about half five, parents wondering where you were. After that – do you want to stick around, have a bite?'

'Uh, no thanks,' I said. 'I think my tea will be in the oven.'

This was not exactly true, but I didn't want to sound posh.

Calum nodded. 'Aye, mine too. Best be off. But thanks. Say hello tae Sophie for us.'

Outside, we each duly phoned home. I repeated what Calum had said, and got an earful in reply.

'Sorry, Dad,' I said. 'I'm just on my way now.'

'As long as you're all right,' he said, in a relenting tone. Then he added, 'You *are* all right, aren't you?'

'Yes, I'm fine thanks. Just a bit grubby from the ash.'

'OK,' he said. 'See you soon.'

Calum had rung off a moment earlier.

'Everything OK with your old man?' I asked.

'Aye, sure, he said my ma was a wee bit worried but no much.'

'Same here, more or less.'

Calum grinned. 'Aye, yours hae more imagination.'

'Why didn't you say what really happened?'

'Tae Sophie's da?' Calum looked surprised. 'He'd have thought we were making it up, and he'd wonder why. Yi heard what he said about "tripping". If I'd said we'd got knocked out by a strange light from the sky, he'd have thought that for sure. That or us having it off wi' each other.'

I laughed. 'Oh, give me a kiss!'

'None of that,' said Calum, in a tone of mock severity.

'None of what?'

'Homophobic mockery, and that. I could knock six points off your Social.'

'Ooh, get her.'

We went through another round or two of this, laughing louder each time, then clapped each other on the shoulder and went our separate ways.

My way home took me through a maze of housing estates and over the Lyle Hill, a rocky rise straddling the border between Gourock and Greenock and overlooking the Firth. As I hurried up the long slope of Lyle Road, I found myself gazing at the anchor and double-barred cross of the Free French war memorial on the hillside ahead. The gorse, grass and whin on the summit behind it pulsed yellow and green in the westering sun as if lit from within by flickering neon. The sculpture itself seemed more solid than usual, a shape rather than a symbol, weighty and enigmatic as a megalith. Two or three people stood on the platform, ignoring the memorial, attention fixed on the view. I glanced over as I passed, trying to see whatever it was they were looking at. Just sea and hills.

Over the top and walking downhill, past the golf course with its club-clicks and cries and curlew calls and smell of mown grass, I saw Greenock and Port Glasgow spread out before me, a song of sandstone and cement, and thought I could see into every house and block, like an app, and at the imagined sight of tens of thousands of people having their evening meal or working late or getting ready to go out I was overcome by a wave of wonder at how much good was going on, and how you heard about the bad things that happened so much that you overlooked the immensely disproportionate majority of other acts done to the real benefit of self and others without which none of this would be here at all, and the vast exercise of virtue, of skill and thought and care that had gone into the very buildings, literally built in, what though some of them were built on foundations of slavery: of capital coined from cotton, tobacco and sugar lashed from sunburnt skin in plantations far away and long ago.

A little further along and down the side of the hill I came to myself and felt I had been walking for hours. I looked at my watch and no, it was six thirty-two and forty-one seconds and I was about ten minutes' brisk walk from home. So I walked on, fast, and the first thing I thought was: why am I thinking like this? The second was: what happened?

I didn't think that whatever fell on us – or just beside us, if Calum was right – could have been ball lightning. The heat that had reduced grass and heather to ash must have been intense and local. The object had been bright, but not glowing, therefore reflecting not radiating. Our impression that it was a weather balloon had been contradicted only by the speed of its descent. Its appearance had remained solid and substantial.

We'd had an encounter with an unidentified flying object.

I turned over the phrase in my mind. It was literally true. I was quite careful with myself – I didn't jump to the conclusion that the unidentified object *was* identified – and as an alien spacecraft, at that.

No. Looking back, and taking into account my state of mind, I was still thinking rationally. But like anyone else I had the default UFO template in my head. In my early teens I'd explored the topic in enough breadth if not depth to make its tropes indelible, however much I now disdained them. Aliens crowded in, all oval heads and almond eyes and long, probing fingers. I pushed them away. This was easy to do, actually, because my thinking had become mercurial, and quite different from the stubborn, dog-with-a-bone worrying that was habitual to me at that age – and still is, come to think of it.

The road passed the side of the golf course and my route swung into a long street of low houses and bungalows, a locally limited surge of the same suburban-style sprawl that had covered the hills at the back of the town where I'd just walked from. On grey gravel spilling from driveways I crunched over broken stems of crinoids. Small children scooted about on bikes or kicked footballs across the quiet road. At the end of that street was another abrupt transition, to the older West End of Greenock, laid out like Edinburgh's New Town on an Enlightenment grid. The slab-concrete and picture-window dwellings of third-division footballers and call-centre middle managers gave way to the more substantial red or buff sand-stone villas of doctors and ministers, of well-paid workers and the well-off retired. No change, however, in the proportion – about a tenth – of houses whose windows were boarded up.

I turned sharply up the street that marked that boundary and then into our own street, diagonally across from the clubhouse at the eastern end of the golf course. At the foot of the steps up the short steep slope of green to our house I stopped to get my story straight. Sweat stuck my shirt to my back and chilled under my armpits. My heartbeats boomed on my eardrums. Blood moved grainily in my veins, the tickle of its trickle like sand falling on skin. I had evidently been walking very fast, almost running, and I couldn't understand how I could have taken so long to get from Sophie's place to mine.

I looked at my watch and saw that the time was six forty-four and twenty-seven seconds. Twenty-eight. Twenty-nine . . .

Six forty-five and twenty-five seconds. I'd been standing at the foot of the steps for almost a minute. It had felt like longer. I pulled myself together, unlocked the gate, locked it behind me and bounded up the steps. I unlocked then locked behind me the outer and inner doors, after a minute of bafflement as to what I was doing in the narrow space between them.

The hallway smelled of the polishes for wood and brass. I walked through it towards the smell of cooking. The table was folded out and laid in the living room but dinner hadn't started yet. In the kitchen beyond, down a step into the back of the house, my father stood over the cooker, stirring a vegetable curry. He looked up.

'Ah, there you are, Ryan. Good of you to drop by.'

'Aw, c'mon, Dad, I told you what happened. Sorry I'm late. We just went off for a walk.'

He rested the wooden spoon against the rim of the pan and straightened up.

'I don't mind you going off for a walk, even if you did say you were going to be studying. I do mind you leaving your phone behind. That's just childish.'

'OK, OK.'

'You had what could have been a serious accident.'

'We just tripped and fell.'

He nodded. 'Exactly. You should know better than to blunder about in mist, too. If you'd had your phone, you could have called home, told us not to worry, and sat tight till it lifted.'

'OK, OK,' I said again, despising myself for how teenage and petulant I sounded but unable to think of anything better to say.

My father grunted and gave the curry another stir, then sucked a smidgin from the spoon with a slurping noise that revolted me.

'Make yourself useful,' he said. 'Chop some coriander.'

'Good to know you trust me with a knife,' I said.

'Don't push it,' he said.

I wasn't pushing it, but I refrained from correcting him on this point. Instead I manoeuvred round him, rattled about in the cutlery drawer, and scissored a clump from the coriander pot on the windowsill. I rinsed it under the tap and got busy with a knife and chopping-block on the work surface beside the cooker. All the while I was timing my actions in seconds, anxious not to drop into another missing-time dwam.

'You've chopped it fine enough,' my father said, in an amused tone. I passed him the block and with the edge of the blade he scraped rather than tipped my efforts into the pot. Five seconds it took him.

'Why do you keep looking at your watch?' he asked, stirring again.

'I'm . . .' My first impulse was to deny it. Then I'd had enough of evasion and plunged boldly ahead. 'I'm trying to keep track of how time feels and compare it to time on the clock – subjective and objective time, you know? Because I'm noticing how different they are when you get absorbed in something like just now when I was rinsing the *dhania* under the tap or you let your mind drift like when I was walking home and looking at the town and thinking about how much is going on in it right now and all the historical and geological time that's piled up in every stone and that we see at every moment piled up again in, in –' I recalled a phrase from something I'd read '– the light-world of our eyes.'

My father almost dropped the spoon. He laid it carefully on the chopping-block and turned to face me. I had seen him almost every day of my life, but never as he seemed at this moment: heraldic, monumental, archaic. I had to remind myself who he was. His name was Richard Sinclair and he was forty years old. He was an accountant, currently and precariously if lucratively employed by one of the local Healthcare Trusts. He had a dozen visible white hairs amid various shades of brown, and three low-amplitude, long-wavelength lines across his forehead. These lines moved closer together and their fissures deepened.

'Ryan,' he said, 'are you on drugs?'

'No,' I said. 'I'm not.'

Something darkened around the light-world of his eyes.

'I'm not sure I believe you,' he said.

His words felt like heavy stones added one by one to a rucksack on my back. My knees almost buckled. I rallied a smile.

'Oh come on, Dad,' I said, with a laugh, 'if I was on drugs, my pupils would be dilated.'

Suddenly he looked normal again. He frowned and stared at me.

'They are dilated.'

'I'm sure it's just the light,' I said, then giggled because this was accidentally true.

Dad frowned and shook his head.

'Go and wash yourself.' He sounded disgusted.

Upstairs in the bathroom, I saw why. My face was pale, making the remaining streaks and flecks of ash stand out. My irises were narrow rings around solid circles of glossy black, like annular eclipses of a blue star by an obsidian moon. My clothes were more than just a bit grubby. Soot was all over them. I had carbon footprints. I stripped off my shirt and jeans and threw them in the laundry basket. I washed my face and arms and neck and considered shaving, then decided I didn't have time. I nipped across the landing and along a narrow corridor and up the stair-ladder to my attic bedroom where I pulled on fresh jeans, an old T-shirt and worn-out trainers.

In these I padded downstairs and back to the living room. My father and my mother, Lizbeth, were at the table as was my sister, Marie. Two years older than me, Marie was in her first year at Glasgow University. She didn't like living at home, but couldn't afford to rent so much as a shared bedsit in Glasgow.

All three looked at me as if they'd just stopped talking about me. I sketched a wave.

'Hi, Mum, Marie.'

'Hello,' they chorused, giving me glassy smiles and then looking away to exchange significant glances. I sat down.

We all helped ourselves to vegetable curry, brown rice and nettle aloo. I resisted the impulse to gaze in wonder at the detail of the soggy leaves, or to watch the rainbow colours the overhead light made in the rising steam. I let the conversation swirl around me, contributing no more than the occasional nod or monosyllable. Every so often I glanced at the television above the fireplace, running in the background as usual and showing the evening news. The Russian, British and American navies had ships on the move on a variety of convergent courses that criss-crossed the Atlantic in a confusing manner. A map came up and I thought I could see a pattern that eluded the talking heads whose speculations flitted as subtitles. Then it eluded me too, and I glanced away and returned my attention to the conversation. As I did so I found myself comparing my present behaviour with memories of how I normally behaved at the dinner table. They seemed to match. I didn't usually have much to say. Situation nominal.

'What do you mean, nominal?' Marie asked, giving me a quirky smile and tilt of the head, fork halfway to her mouth.

How much had I said? Had I been prattling away without realising? I tried to remember what my family had been talking about. Something about something in the news, I seemed to recall.

'Oh, just the situation,' I said. 'The general situation, that is. It's nominal, in the mission-control sense, if you see what I mean.'

'I'm afraid I don't,' said Marie.

'Well, you know,' I went on, waving my hands about, 'when the engineers at Baikonur or Canaveral or that place the French have in South America or the Chinese or, anyway whatever, when they're in a countdown and they're giving a systems check and everything's OK and working as it should they say it's nominal.'

'Put down your fork and knife,' said my mother. 'You'll have someone's eye out.'

This was such a Mum thing to say that I spluttered with laughter as I complied.

Dad frowned. 'If that's what you mean, the situation is far from nominal.'

'The general situation?' I asked.

'You could say that,' he said, with another significant glance at Mum and Marie.

'Yes, that's what I am saying, and I see your point but my point is . . .'

I'd forgotten what it was. Fortunately my mind was working with mercurial speed and laser precision again, and I immediately understood what I'd been trying to articulate and continued: 'My point *is*, right, that this crisis we're all talking about is just what happens every day and we live from day to day without knowing what's going to happen tomorrow or even what's just happened unless we check our phones every few seconds we don't know if another war has started or the ATMs have stopped working again or the revolutionaries have made another cyber attack or the EU has collapsed or everybody except you know the responsible people like us has gone on strike or the army has taken over but we all know any of these could happen any time or something I haven't thought of and anyway what is actually holding everything together and keeping us going from day to day is the knowledge that it could all end tomorrow or like I said has already ended since the last time we checked the news and all the time we think of it as something we're waiting for and will watch when it comes and therefore we don't feel it as something that could happen to us or is happening to us right now so in that sense as I said the situation is nominal.'

At this point my mouth was a bit dry so I took a sip of water. I had by no means finished my discourse but Dad, Mum and Marie took my pause as a conclusion and started talking about something else entirely. The television moved on to a nature programme, and my mother turned up the volume. A man climbed a high ladder into a tree, and lowered a cylindrical box to a woman waiting below. She placed the box in a big transparent plastic bag and removed the lid, to reveal a drowsy dormouse. As she lifted it out and placed it on the bottom of the bag, the little creature awoke and scurried around. The woman passed a wand under the bag, peered at a read-out, and connected a bell-jar to a gas-filled bladder. She popped the dormouse under the glass dome and puffed gas in. The dormouse rolled over. She picked it up gently and pinched the skin on its back, then injected a microchip, poked the tip of the injector into yet another device, and laid the little rodent on a scale. The dormouse recovered after a few seconds, and was placed back in its bed in the nesting box, which was duly closed and hoisted back up the tree.

'This is the twentieth generation we've tracked like this,' the woman explained. 'It's probably the last, actually. A few years ago we noticed a trend for the dormice to become less stressed from handling, and to have a better adult body weight, and we puzzled over it until we looked back over the stats and realised that it was the result of natural selection – the individuals least stressed by being chipped had bigger litters, and so on. So in studying the population we were inadvertently changing it.'

After dinner I offered to wash up but Dad said pointedly that perhaps it might be a good idea for me to catch up with the revision I'd missed that afternoon. I took the hint and a mug of coffee and went upstairs.

3

Sitting at my desk in a corner under the sloping ceiling of the roof-space attic bedroom, I stared at a geometry problem in the maths textbook on my tablet. No matter how I tugged the lines around I couldn't make the angles add up. The room darkened. I switched the desk lamp on, and was about to try another solution when I became distracted by the minute, complex shadows cast by the grain of the wood on the surface of the desk.

After some time I sipped at the coffee (black, instant, expensive) and found it cold. I swallowed it all. It may have been the caffeine surge that jolted me out of my odd mental state. I stood up and stepped to the skylight window and looked out at the rooftops and lights of Greenock.

What the *fucking fuck* is *happening* to me?

Did I just fucking say that out loud?

I listened for echoes and concluded I hadn't.

I texted Calum. He rang back in less than a minute.

'Evening, Sinky.' Somehow less than cordial.

'Hi, Duke.' Calum's nickname was better than mine, derived by some primary-school playground word-association daisy chain that went: Calum, CalMac (the ferry company), Rothesay, Duke of Rothesay, Duke. You had to be there and seven years old. 'You OK?'

'Uh . . . aye. Fine. Hunky-dory. You aw right?'

'I'm not sure.'

'What's up?'

'You're not having any . . . weird things going in your head, like?'

'What kindae things?' Baffled, guarded.

'Uh . . . like, uh, time slowing down then speeding up? Finding yourself rattling on? Mind racing away like . . . like something fast racing away?'

'Naw. Nothing like that. Is that what's up wi you?'

'Aye,' I said.

'You ever done any ae that stuff?'

'What stuff?'

'Acid, an' that. Magic mushrooms.'

'Of course not! I'm no a fuckin' eejit.' Lapsing into his accent, I noticed.

I heard his breath across the mike of his phone, and interpreted this as a sigh.

'Ah . . . well, Sinky old pal, I got a wee confession tae make . . .'

37

'You slipped me one!'

A moment of offended silence. 'For fuck's sake, Sinky! That's the paranoia talking. My wee confession is that I was an eejit a couple years back. Tried the old magic-mushroom trip.'

'And you didn't invite me along? Jeez.'

'I was wi another crowd at the time. Fucking wasters. Anyway. Haud the horses for a wee second and listen to me. What you're describing sounds like what I went through on my trip. It's no that scary when you know what's going on, see what I mean?'

I rallied my rationality. 'That, Duke, is the problem. I don't know what's going on. I am in an interval of ludicity. Lucidity. And ludicity, come to that. And I am unable to account for my unaccustomed loquacity. Given that I did not partake of any drugs.'

Another long pause. 'Uh, man, can you be absolutely sure ae that? I mean, we were knocked out for an hour or mair, and—'

'An hour or mair or more on the moor in a mare's nest.'

'Will you fuckin' stop *daein* that? What I'm trying to say is, you could have picked up magic mushrooms or something while we were both out ae it, we couldnae know.'

'Nae know nae know nae know . . . Allow me to repair to a separate interface, hold the line please, an adviser will be with you shortly . . .'

I dropped the phone, scribbled with a shaky fingertip on a scratch pad and peered at the result. I picked up the phone again.

Calum had rung off. I rang him back.

'You aw right?' Calum asked.

'Of course I'm all right. I told you to hold.'

'You were babbling about interfaces or something, and then there was this crash and I thought you were fuckin' deid, man.'

'I appreciate your concern.' I paused to remember what it was I'd been doing. 'Ah yes, according to Professor Internet here psychoactive mushrooms are out of season, so . . .'

'So, that disnae mean—'

'So, that means a direct effect of the encounter we are both so not talking about, or some episode of somnambulistic fungivory upon the psilocybin genera, or . . .'

'Or what?'

'Or somebody slipped me a mickey.' I thought about this possibility. 'You bastard!'

'Wisnae me, that's for sure, and yi ken that fine.'

'Oh,' I said. 'Yes. We've been over this already. Hm. So back to some direct effect of the funny light on the brain. Ah. Speaking of brain . . .'

'Aye?'

'That lucidity I mentioned?'

'Uh-huh?'

'I can feel it going.'

'You seeing things? Hearing voices?'

I looked around, and listened carefully.

'No. Well, I'm seeing my room and hearing you, but that's real. I think.'

'It's real aw right. Listen, mate, you might hae concussion. From when we fell down, like. Stay where you are, call your ma or da, call a doctor, get yirself tae hospital.'

'I know about concussion,' I said. 'This isn't concussion.'

'You could be coming down wi meningitis or something.'

'Same again,' I said. 'Different symptoms. Look, Duke, my parents have drilled into me what to watch out for. Whatever this is, it's not that.'

Long pause, or perhaps another time-warp.

'OK,' Calum said. 'OK. I've just gone and looked these up, and you're right. Maybe you better just get some sleep.'

This seemed like good advice, until I took it.

To understand what follows, you have to think about where my bed was. Imagine, if you will, climbing the steep, creaking stair-ladder to the attic. You emerge in a vestibule with an overhead light. The ceiling slopes behind you, making you duck as you take the final step. Old books are stacked against the wall facing you. To your left is an open door to a room that occupies one side of the roof space. It could be a bedroom. Right now, it's a cluttered box room, as you can see by the light cast from a small, locked skylight window set in a continuation of the same sloping ceiling.

To your right there's a half-open door. Stepping through, you almost bump into a desk chair and desk facing a corner lined with bookcases under the ceiling slope, against which you almost knock your head. Pictures and photos – some still, others moving – are tacked to odd spaces on the wall and ceiling. There's a keyboard and docking station on the desk, a recent-looking tablet, and a couple of scratch pads as cheap as the paper notebooks and school exercise books they lie among. An empty coffee mug, an angled lamp (switched off), toy robots and other small action figures, desktop detritus.

You turn now to the main part of the room, which is dimly lit by a long skylight window that juts from the roof. One pane of it is propped open a few inches – the built-in stopper won't let it open further – to let in the night air (and nothing much else, a cat at the unlikely most). Nothing overlooks that window – it faces the blank gable end of the house next door, and it needs no curtains. Above it, the sloped ceiling gives way to another ceiling low and flat, just high enough to be comfortable for an adult of normal height. The wooden walls are half covered with posters – bands, football teams, female rock stars – many of which move in silence through loops of stereotyped action: a sweat-flying-off guitar thrash, a penalty shot to the back of the net, a smile and a sweeping flick of the hair. A small bookcase, stacks of electronics, a guitar leaning on the wall; clothes, boots, shoes, dusty old toys strewn across the worn carpet. The floorboards creak underfoot at the lightest step.

Along the wall facing the window, up against the far corner, is a single bed with a small bedside table. An adjacent wardrobe with clothes hanging on the outside from pegs and from the top of the half-shut door, takes up most of the remaining space beside the little table.

On the table is a glass of water, an old radio alarm clock, a watch, a torch and a phone.

And in the bed, under a duvet, there's me, asleep.

OK, you get the picture. There's no feasible way into the room, except up the creaky stairs and across a creaky floor, littered with trip hazards.

You're not there. You're in my imagination.

I woke at 03.35 by the clock radio's red, fading LEDs, and gazed at the ceiling. The night was still dark, though light from streetlamps and sky-glow came from the window. A scatter of fluorescent star and moon and flying saucer and rocket shapes, stuck on the ceiling about ten years earlier, glowed faintly. I found myself suddenly wide awake, but undisturbed. For the first time since yesterday afternoon, my mind ran clear. The only discomfort I felt was thirst. I rolled to one elbow and sipped water, then put down the glass and settled my head, hands clasped behind it, back against the pillow.

The array of tiny five-pointed stars, crescent moons, rockets with portholes and fins, and flying saucers with flanges and rivets, made me feel a slight pang for childhood, now so far – six years, seven – in the past. There were more wee toy stars than I remembered. Surely I couldn't have stood on this bed, and patiently peeled them one by one off their waxy backing-paper and stretched out to stick all these up! No, my mother had helped, I remembered: it was she who'd done most of the patient peeling and sticking, from sheets and sheets of shapes.

There were a lot more of them, and brighter and more various than they'd seemed at first. Funny that. They only glowed for a while after the light went off. Perhaps my eyes were more dark adapted than usual, what with the distended pupils that my father had so embarrassingly noticed.

Across that childish starry sky, something moved. I blinked hard. It was still there, a crawling dot of light, moving at the exact speed and course of a satellite crossing the real sky. For a moment I thought, absurdly, that some exotic firefly had found its way to my room. In another moment – a beat, a pause before a punchline – everything resolved. I realised, with a chill as cold as if the ceiling and roof had really lifted and exposed me to the night air, that I was looking at the real stars, in the real sky above Greenock, and watching a circumpolar satellite. Shifting my gaze a little, I could even see clouds coming in from the west.

Then I thought: Oh, shit. I'm having actual hallucinations now.

I didn't feel frightened. I felt that very adult impatience and resentment that's been so well expressed by Dorothy Parker: What fresh hell is this? I thought I was shot of whatever had warped my brain the previous afternoon and evening. I thought I'd slept it off, and woken clear-headed and none the worse. A fury arose in me. I was going to dispel this illusion. I made to sit up, intending to rise and touch the now invisible but undoubtedly still solid and present ceiling.

I couldn't move anything but my eyes.

43

In the shock that shot through me at that realisation came another: I was not alone in the room.

Someone, or something, was standing at the foot of the bed.

With petrified reluctance I tore my gaze from the real or imaginary stars, and looked. I was not surprised to see black, lidless, tilted, almond eyes look back.

Terrified, but not surprised. The creature was a cliché, your average working alien, a bog-standard Grey. About four and half feet tall, with a big oval head, skinny torso, spindly limbs, a ditto of nostrils and a lipless little em-dash of a mouth.

It stretched out an arm towards me and extended a long finger, then raised its arm to point slowly upward. And up, floating, I went, into the starry sky above. I'd been lying naked under the duvet. The duvet didn't come with me and I didn't feel it slipping off, but this discrepant detail didn't seem a pressing problem at the time.

You have to remember that I knew I was hallucinating. I even had a clear understanding of the processes involved. As well as having read or watched many tales of just this kind of scene, I'd read their sceptical, scientific debunkings. I knew, or firmly and with good reason believed, that I'd woken up, and that, while gazing at the starry ceiling, I'd drifted into sleep without realising. What I was experiencing, then, was a classic falling-asleep hallucination along with sleep paralysis, its content pathetically predictable from conscious and unconscious worrying about my strange encounter, and the associated images of UFOs and aliens with which my mind was as well stocked as anyone's. I knew, from my sceptical reading, that artificial electrical stimulation of the brain could induce bizarre mental states. I knew of the speculations that some baffling UFO encounters could be accounted for by some poorly understood natural atmospheric or geophysical electrical phenomenon which could induce experiences interpreted as alien communication or abduction.

The apprehension I felt, which was enough to have made me quake if I'd been capable of even involuntarily moving a single skeletal muscle, was that of someone sliding helplessly into a nightmare that they know is a nightmare but that they know, too, will take its inevitable course to its unpleasant end.

As I rose toward the rapidly growing disc of dark against the stars above me, I could already imagine the quasi-medical scene awaiting me within: the bright sourceless light, the examining table, the invasive procedures, the metallic implants, the probe up the arse. I could imagine the scenario as vividly as you can. I'm still proud, in a way, that I was prepared for all that.

I was not prepared for what happened on the ship.

4

What happened on the ship was this.

As I came close to the underside I glimpsed structure – radial ribbing, perhaps circumferential pipework – and a central circular area that opened like a camera iris. It was just wide enough for me, still lying horizontal, to rise through. It couldn't have been more than a couple of metres across. As I passed through it I screwed up my eyes, expecting a flood of bright light. None came. Warily I opened my eyes wide. In the dim, reddish lighting I could see a low, domed ceiling above me, with some kind of thin, curving radial struts, rather like the inside of a yurt made from taut Mylar and bicycle spokes.

My upward levitation stopped, and was replaced by a movement sideways then down. I felt my normal weight pressing me against a flat, slightly yielding surface that might have been stretched canvas. Like, say, an operating table.

Uh-oh. Here it comes.

Then I found myself sitting bolt upright. My mouth opened and I yelled. It was as if my body were completing the action that the sleep paralysis had prevented. In the confined space, the scream rang in my ears. I took a ragged gasp to fill my empty lungs, closed my mouth, then drew up my heels to my crotch and my knees to my chest, clasping my arms around my legs. As I did so I found I was no longer naked, but wearing the clothes I'd worn on the hill, all as clean as they'd been before I'd fallen in the black ash. I stared in shock at what I saw in front of me.

A man and a woman, tall, good-looking, stood between the foot of the bed-table and a sloped shelf or bank of flickering lights and instruments that seemed to encircle the craft's interior. Their clothing reminded me absurdly and predictably of *Star Trek* Starfleet uniforms (original series, at that – the woman's outfit was a long-sleeved flared mini-dress that skimmed her hips and then stopped). Both had dark complexions and black hair: the man's cropped like an astronaut's; the woman's wavy, trimmed to just above the neckline of her brief tunic. Their features, fine and regular, seemed to come from some attractive melange of every human race. They were looking at me with expressions of compassion and concern.

'There's nothing to be afraid of,' the woman said.

Her voice was warm, and more finely modulated than any voice I'd ever heard. She had an accent that was likewise new to me. But in a sense I recognised her, and the man. I'd encountered their like in the UFO rubbish I'd read when I

47

was young and naïve. In the first bright dawn of the flying-saucer delusion – the early 1950s – before people started meeting or being abducted by sinister Greys, they met tall, blond, silver-suited, Nordic-looking folk they called Space Brothers, who spouted theosophical rubbish. The two people facing me were obviously an updated, multi-racial version of these half-forgotten visitors. I was on the point of saying something defiant, secure in the knowledge that this was a dream from which I would awake, when I realised what having my clothes on meant.

This might not be a dream. I could be reliving a memory of what had happened already, on or above the hill. I had survived that, but with no idea of what had happened or what had been done to me, and I was about to find out.

'Where's . . .?' I looked over my shoulder. The Grey – or a Grey, anyway – stood with its back to the instrument panel behind me and to the right. It raised its right hand, palm open. Three fingers and a thumb, all long. The entity was naked, and had no visible genitalia. Its skin seemed to have fine scales, like a small lizard. There was a pulse at its throat. I could read no expression on its face. I turned away with some unease.

The craft's two human-seeming occupants were still looking at me, now with friendly smiles. Their teeth were perfect.

My mouth was dry. I summoned spittle, and swallowed.

'I'm not afraid,' I said. I clutched my legs harder to stop them shaking. 'I know this is a dream or a hallucination. I know what caused it. I know what's going to happen.' I put

48

my hands on the bed beside me and let my legs relax, to straighten and splay. 'Ah, fuck it, go ahead. Do what you have to do. Get it over with.'

They both laughed, politely, like the peals from a light and a heavy bell chiming in harmony.

'That's an unusual reaction,' the man said. His voice was a mellow bass; his tone suggested some unshared reason for amusement.

'What do you expect us to do?' the woman asked.

'Oh, the usual,' I said. 'The medical examination. The probe.'

Defiantly, knowing this was a dream or a memory, I stuck up my middle finger at her.

Her face clouded a little.

'There's no need for that,' she said. 'And there's no need for an examination in your case.'

'Or in most others,' the man added, hurriedly, with a glance to my right. 'There's been a change in policy.'

Of course, I thought. The dream-logic was working itself out, giving me some reason to avoid the traumatic scene I'd dreaded.

'So what are you going to do?' I asked.

'We are going to give you our message for humanity,' the man said.

Of course they were.

'If you have a message for humanity,' I said, 'you can give it to humanity, on every channel and network on Earth. You don't need me.'

'Oh, but we do,' the woman said.

Of course they did.

'Why?' I asked, wondering what my subconscious mind would come up with.

'Those you call the Greys could have given their message directly to the whole of humanity,' the woman went on, 'at any time since we became human. They chose not to, because our culture would then have become merely another part of theirs. Our distinctness is valued by them, and by others. That is why they work through human allies, like us, and why we in turn seek to persuade those such as you. We can show you the path, but you must choose it yourself and walk it in your own way. That is how and why we have always worked through teachers. I need not name them, but your name may one day be counted among them.'

Not bad, I thought. A bit New Age and Von Daniken, but not bad. At the same time I was trying hard not to giggle, because 'teachers' to me meant not saints and prophets but primarily (so to speak) people like my mum.

'So what's this great message?'

Wait for it, wait for it . . . the importance of wisdom, love, and peace; the dangers of climate change, nuclear weapons, genetic engineering . . .

'You must rely on reason and science,' she said, 'and be guided by a likewise rational ethic of human concern. You must do your utmost as individuals to improve your under-standing, ability and compassion. As a species you must maintain and extend your presence in space, and from that vantage do what you can to repair the Earth. Whether or not you succeed, you must never give up.'

'That's not what I expected,' I said.

'But it's true,' the man said.

'It's not what you used to say, or what the teachers you claim to have worked through said.'

'Ah,' said the woman, 'their message was for their own time. This is the message for yours. And for you.'

They stood looking at me as if expecting something: thanks, probably. No way, Space Brother, Space Sister, no fucking way.

'That's it?' I said. 'Can I go now?'

The woman and the man looked at each other, and this time both glanced to my right, toward the Grey.

'We still need your genetic material,' the woman said.

Of course they did.

'DNA?' I opened my mouth. 'Take a swab.'

The woman smiled.

'I meant gametes.'

'You can make them from stem cells,' I said. 'Even we can do that.'

'We prefer to get them directly.'

'Oh,' I said.

She drew a finger from her collar down to her midriff. The top of her tunic fell open, and she shrugged out of it. Then she stepped out of it, and stood to the full height of her lithe beautiful naked body. She didn't look away from me the whole time.

51

She stepped forward, placed her hands on the end of the table, and deftly jumped up to kneel facing me, just in front of my feet. I pulled my legs up again and scrambled into a kneeling position, aware that I wasn't getting out of my clothes in anything like as dignified and graceful a fashion.

'Go ahead,' she said. 'Do it.'

Her face was close to mine; her nipples brushed the sparse hair on my chest. Her breath smelt sweet and her eyes were violet.

'You want me to have sex with you?' I asked, unbelieving.

She rocked back a little, with a look of surprise.

'No,' she said. 'I want you to have a wank.'

'But . . .' I looked around. The Grey and the man had gone. Or become invisible, what did I know?

I reached out to touch her shoulder.

'Don't,' she said. She leaned away further, then placed cool fingertips vertically across my lips, as if asking me to be quiet. I felt a small shock, a tingle like tonguing the terminals of a low-voltage battery. She glanced down, then up, and smiled. 'You can do this.'

And I did. Just before I came she reached to the underside of the table and brought out a small container, which a moment later, I filled.

Then, banal as it sounds – and was – she capped the container, put it back where it had come from, and handed me a tissue.

'Thank you,' she said, and hopped off the table and climbed back into her uniform and closed it up.

Flushed, still panting, I stared at her.

'Why do you need . . . that?'

I wondered what rationalisation my mind would come up with, and I wasn't disappointed.

The woman laughed. 'Not for human-alien hybrids, as some in your position have thought. We're as human as you. Our ancestors came from Earth. We have no wish to become a separate species, so we take every opportunity to interbreed with the parent stock when we can, as now.'

'Haven't you heard of sperm banks?'

She shrugged. 'This is the simplest way.'

Of course it was.

While we spoke, the man and the alien had returned without my noticing how.

'Everything all right?' the man said.

'It's all fine,' said the woman.

The man turned to the Grey.

'Take him back,' he said.

'Wait,' I said.

But there was no waiting. The Grey gestured with its hand. I found myself involuntarily stretched out and unable to move; and, seconds later, watched the craft dwindle as I fell.

Then I was in my bed, naked again under the duvet, with the Grey looking at me as before. It raised a hand, waved, and was gone. The time, to my complete lack of surprise, was 03.36.

The next I knew was morning.

*

07.30, and the sun well up. I rolled out of bed and padded to the window. A fine Sunday morning with a haze just rising from the Firth of Clyde. I stuck my face in the skylight opening and took a deep breath.

When I remembered, I almost banged my head on the edge of the window. Shaken, I stepped back and sat down on the bed. Jesus. What a weird dream. But I didn't recall it like a dream. It had none of a dream's evanescence, or its combination of awkward transitions and scraps of vivid, unnecessary detail. It was as if everything had literally happened. Yet there was no evidence. I turned back the duvet, and found no trace even of a wet dream. Dried blood on the pillowcase showed I'd had a nosebleed in the night.

I remembered the Grey at the foot of the bed, and looked over my shoulder with an uncanny dread, as if it might be behind my back. It wasn't. I leaned sideways and peered over the end of the bed. The floor where I'd seen the Grey stand was stacked with old books and magazines, dust-furred outgrown trainers, and the jutting corner of a cardboard carton of old toys. There was no way anyone or anything of the creature's apparent height could have stood there. I wasn't sure this was a relief, but at least it confirmed that whatever had happened in the night had not happened physically.

If, of course, that distinction meant anything any more.

I stepped into slippers, pulled on my dressing-gown, and went out on to the little landing. As I turned to back down the stair-ladder I had another moment of dread, and turned round more sharply. Nothing, of course. I backed down the stair-ladder, glancing twice over my shoulder, gripping the handrail hard. In the bathroom mirror I saw that I had dried blood across my upper lip and left cheek. As I washed it off I remembered the Space Sister's chill fingertips touching my mouth, and wondered with a shudder if the tingle I'd felt had been of some device being slipped surreptitiously into my nostril. The delusion, or memory, of small metal implants was common in the abduction accounts I'd read. I hated the thought of being hag-ridden, of being haunted and afflicted for life as so many were, by that obsession.

After I'd washed, shaved, gone back up to the attic, and dressed, I checked on my phone that Calum was awake and online. He was, so I gave him a call. He responded within a couple of seconds, pinging that he'd keyed to visual. I took the phone from my ear and looked at the screen from which Calum peered at me, bleary-eyed.

'You're up early, man.'

'You look like you haven't slept,' I said.

'Naw, I slept fine.' Calum rubbed his eyes, then frowned at me. 'You over yon trippy thing fae last night?'

'Far as I know, yes,' I said. 'Had . . . a bit of a weird dream, though.'

'What was it about?'

'Uh, I dreamed about . . . some kind of alien abduction scenario, sort of thing.'

Even on the small screen, I could see Calum's momentary start. Then he gave a short hoot of derisive laughter.

'Little green men an' that?'

'No. It was grey. A Grey. You know, the usual. Then two who looked human.'

'Did they dae the usual probe?' He sounded more amused than concerned.

'No,' I said.

'So what happened?'

'They just – talked. About the importance of reason and compassion, something like that.'

Calum rubbed his chin, rasping stubble enviably darker and more abundant than the chin-fluff I'd just soaped and scraped.

'Did it aw feel like it was real?'

'Uh, no,' I said. This wasn't true.

'Well then,' he said. 'Say what knocked us out was ball lightning or something. That could affect your brain, right? And we all have these ideas about UFOs and aliens and that, and—'

'Yes,' I said, interrupting. 'That's just what I was thinking myself.'

'Aye, well, good.' Calum smiled. 'And if what it got you dreaming was peace and love hippy shit instead ae a probe up the arse, it says tae me you're in good mental health. Much as it pains me tae admit, Sinky. And you look like you're none the worse for it. So let's just keep quiet about this, right?'

'Oh, aye,' I said. 'No point talking about it, is there?'

'None at all. I'll no tell if you won't.'

'OK.' I made the lips-sealed gesture. 'See you tomorrow.'

Calum nodded. 'Aye. Unless you get taken away in the meantime.'

'I don't think the aliens actually take people away,' I said.

'I didnae mean them,' he said. 'I meant the men in white coats.'

'Ah, fuck off.'

'You too, mate.'

We grinned at each other and rang off.

I set up my tablet and searched online. The first thing I checked, of course, was whether anyone else had seen the light in the sky. No local UFO reports that I could see, though across the country there had been the usual dozens of sightings that day. As my search widened, I found myself back in the old familiar online network of rabbit holes. Abduction accounts had peaked way back in the 1990s, but the steady trickle in the decades since then were more than enough to bewilder. I narrowed the search by setting high credibility parameters and rigorous semantic parsers to screen out irrelevancies, rubbish, and speculation. Still overwhelming. Sifting that flood of hits by the specific features of my own experience – the light in the sky, the appearance of the occupants, the uniforms, the embarrassing sexual encounter and the secular humanist platitudes – returned nothing.

I relaxed the criteria a bit, and found enough to keep me reading for hours. Fortunately for my state of mind, I didn't have hours. Shortly after I plunged into the morass of claim and counter-claim I was startled by my mother's voice calling from below: 'Ryan! Do you want a Sunday breakfast?'

'Yes! Thanks, I'll be right down.'

'Get washed and dressed first,' she said.

'I am,' I called back.

Hastily I closed the search and locked the screen, then swung down the stair-ladder, to land with a thump just in front of my mother. She was dressed for church, the main reason the rest of the household didn't get much in the way of a Sunday lie-in. I planted a morning kiss on her surprised cheek and left her to try to rouse Marie.

Dad was in the kitchen, grilling bacon, a weekly treat we could now barely afford, but a kind of compensation for our early rousing. He looked well-slept, fresh-shaven, bright-eyed from a brisk walk to and from the shop.

'Good morning,' he said, with a wary smile.

'Morning, Dad.' I clapped an arm across his shoulders. 'Anything I can do to help?'

'Butter the rolls,' he said.

I could see him eyeing me as I opened three warm rolls with the breadknife. (Marie was in a vegetarian phase and would be having cereal with soya milk.)

'What?' I said, picking at a corner of foil on the butter.

'You all right?' he asked. 'Better this morning?'

'Fine, thanks.'

He turned off the grill, and busied himself with kettle and tea.

'Sleep all right?'

I put down the table knife and looked straight at him.

'Not too well,' I said. 'Had some weird dreams.'

'Huh!' His scornful snort was followed by a smile, more normal this time. 'I'll bet! Still, no harm done by the looks of it.'

He glanced around the side of the dining-room doorway, checking that Mum and Marie weren't down yet.

'Between you and me, though, don't do it again.'

'Do what?'

His eyelids pinched.

'Don't act it,' he said. 'I'm talking to you man to man. When I was . . . a bit older than you, in my last year at high school I think, I mean the summer just before I went to uni, I dropped some acid.'

He looked like he expected me to be impressed. I had no idea what he was talking about.

'What do you mean, "dropped acid"? Like, an industrial accident?'

He shook his head, then glanced around again. 'Swallowed a tablet of LSD.'

'Ah!' I said. 'What was it like?'

'I think you know damn well what it was like.'

'Like last night? I mean, yesterday evening.'

'Uh-huh,' he said, in a now-we're-getting-somewhere tone.

I found myself scratching the back of my neck.

'Um, well, if you want to know it was something like that . . .'

'Aha!' he said.

'But it wasn't, uh, that.'

He looked disappointed. 'So what was it?'

'You might find it hard to believe,' I said.

'Try me.' He didn't sound keen to hear it.

I took a deep breath. The dining-room door opened.

'After breakfast,' Dad said.

5

Sunday breakfast together was one of these odd family traditions that you grow up with and are later embarrassed to discover aren't shared by your friends' families. We sat on stools round a shoogly little table in the kitchen, ate bacon rolls – or, in Marie's case, sulkily munched cereal – and drank tea. The conversation was likewise predictable.

'So,' Mum said brightly, 'who's going to church with me this morning?'

That was how she always said it: 'this morning', as if there were Sunday mornings when any of us did come with her. I had dim memories of sitting beside her in an oaken barn of multi-coloured light and a smell of peppermint breath and perfume and elderly ladies, watching a bearded man in a green and gold cloak say incomprehensible things accompanied by elaborate gestures from behind a carving of an open book on a stick. I also remembered playing with other small children in a corner of the church, around a big low table covered with white plastic and well supplied with scrap paper, felt-tip pens and blunt-ended scissors. None of this, nor even the biscuits and orange juice, had been enough for me to want to continue going, as soon as I was old enough to understand that I didn't have to. Marie had stopped going about the same time as I did. There was no conflict over it: our mother's Scottish Episcopalianism hadn't driven her to object when it became plain that Marie and I had more in common with our father's no less genteel agnosticism. If anything, Dad had seemed the more disappointed, not surprisingly as our withdrawal from divine service meant he had us on his hands every Sunday morning.

'Not today,' said Dad.

Marie mumbled something negative around a mouthful.

I looked at my mother. Diffused, refracted sunlight from the kitchen window lit up her face and made her hair a halo. She was wearing a neat grey trouser suit and a high-necked white blouse with a small silver cross on a silver chain glinting on its front. A glance down at the table showed the mugs, stained with the unavoidable minute dark dribble from each drinker's lower lip, and the half-eaten rolls on side-plates on the scuffed Formica, lit as if from within and suffused with Eucharistic significance and the binding energies of sub-atomic interactions.

At the same time I was suddenly so overwhelmed by the contrast between what I was seeing and what I remembered from the previous night, the sinister, sordid, sticky squalor of it that so belied the soothing scientific-minded words the Space Sister had mouthed, that I felt about the prospect of church like I might have felt about a bath or a shower.

I looked up again at my mother and said, 'Yes, I'll go today.'

She blinked. 'Really? You don't have to, you know. Are you sure?'

She sounded almost worried. I smiled, both to reassure her and in amusement at how very Anglican it was that her first reaction to my unexpected response to her stock invitation was to try to talk me out of it.

'Yes, I'm sure,' I said. I looked sidelong at Dad, who chewed his roll and sipped his tea and looked straight ahead. 'Uh, it's not that I'm suddenly interested in church per se, so to speak, as that I, like, had a bad dream, I mean a really bad dream last night and it sort of creeped me out and I just suddenly there had the feeling that going to church would help to clear my mind, sort of thing.'

At this point everyone was giving me worried looks.

'You sound just like you did last night,' Marie said.

'No I don't,' I said.

'Are you sure you're all right?' Mum said.

'I'm fine,' I said.

And really, I was. I knew I wasn't in the same glissade of thought as I had been the previous evening. My mind felt fine, and under my control.

'I'll see you after you come back,' said Dad. 'I still want to talk to you.'

I drained my mug of black tea. 'No probs, Dad.'

I sat through the service entranced. The congregation had changed since my childhood, or perhaps my childhood memories were distorted – it could hardly have been all elderly ladies even then, what with the number of small children that also featured in my recollections. Now, though statistically middle-class, middle-aged and white, it included a score of people who looked like they lived on the street, and rather more members of the Pure Race – all, even the handful of obvious refugees, very respectably dressed – than you'd normally find in one place anywhere else in Greenock, as well as a couple of dozen people around my own age, who seemed to know all the hymns and responses, and fortunately didn't know me.

'Well, what did you think?' Mum asked me, as we walked back from Union Street up through the sloping streets of Greenock's West End.

'I didn't think,' I said, feeling awkward. 'I just sort of let it . . . wash over me.'

'Cleared your mind of the bad dreams, then?'

'Yes!' I said. 'I feel better. A lot better.'

'So,' she said, wryly, 'you got some benefit from it.'

'Yes,' I said. I looked down, and realised I was mooching. Any moment now I'd be kicking a pebble, like some surly kid. I straightened my back and took my hands out of my pockets. 'That doesn't mean I've started believing in it, though.'

Mum sighed, in part theatrically. 'Up to a point, you know, you can benefit without believing.'

'How?' I asked, in a tone more belligerent than I felt.

This time, it was Mum who looked down, slowing her pace as she thought aloud.

'Well . . . there's the social aspect, and the psychological element of being taken out of yourself and caught up in the ritual, just like watching a performance on stage is mentally refreshing in a way that seeing it on screen isn't. I suppose you would agree with me there, so far.'

'Uh-huh.' I wasn't sure where this was going.

'But there's also, as I and almost all of the rest of the people there would see it, the spiritual side, the presence of God among us, which precisely because it's real is bound to affect you whether you believe in it – in him – or not.'

'Oh, Mum!'

'What?'

'That's such a . . . you could say that of any religious service, in any church or mosque or synagogue or whatever.'

'I'm sure you could.' She sounded amused, but firm. 'You might even be right – in fact, you almost certainly would be. Surely you don't think we expect God to work only on Sunday, and not stretch to cover Fridays and Saturdays at the very least!'

This threw me a little.

'But that's so wishy-washy!'

She lifted her head, straightened her back, and quickened her pace.

'Not at all,' she said. 'It's Christian. Whatever you come to think or believe, Ryan, don't make the stupid, ignorant mistake of thinking that any believer who is not a fundamentalist is *soft*.'

I could hear in her tone that something rankled more than my lazy jibe. Looking back, it's obvious now that she'd heard more than enough of that accusation in the controversies that had roiled the Anglican Communion for decades. But I had no idea of that at the time, never having paid the slightest attention to church affairs. I decided to try a different angle.

'But there's no evidence for any of it, anyway.'

'That's what your father says, yes.'

'And he's right, isn't he?'

'Oh, sure,' said Mum. 'If you mean *historical* evidence – that, say Jesus rose from the dead. How could there be? History's about probabilities, and that's a very improbable story.' She laughed. 'As improbable as it gets, actually!'

'So why do you believe it?'

She looked at me sharply. 'Because of experiences like you've just had.'

For a moment I thought she was referring to the experience that was on my mind. I almost tripped. Then I realised what she meant.

'Like feeling better for having been in church?'

'That, and others. If you don't feel like church again anytime soon, you can always join me for a stint at the food bank.'

For me, my mother's Wednesday evening good works and occasional social activism were even more incomprehensible than her religious observances. As far as I was concerned, the best thing one could do for the poor was to not add one's self to their number. The notion that one might get some spiritual benefit from associating with them disgusted me.

Something of that must have shown on my face.

'Oh well,' my mum said. 'Just keep your mind open to the possibility, all right?'

We'd reached the junction at the bottom of our street, where the sandstone tenements gave way to sandstone villas. Ahead of us, on the outer curve of the street just as it began to slope up and to our right, was a stand of ancient beech trees on the steep side of a small hill, atop which one could just make out through the green spring leaves the cupola of a mausoleum. As a child I'd often enough squeezed through a gap in the rusty railings to play in the bouncy beech-mast floor of that coppice, which continued over the hilltop to merge with the wooded areas of Greenock's vast cemetery. I'd climb onto broad boughs and venture outward until they bent, or straddle their groins with my back against the trunk and stare out through the dapple until my head swam.

Now, as we waited to cross the road while a police column trundled past, I looked at the trees and found myself struck by the thought of death. This may have been the first moment in my life when I realised that death really was going to happen to me. All possible paths from this moment, however long, however winding, would end in the same black hole.

We looked both ways and hurried across the wide, cambered road.

'Mum,' I said, 'if I don't go to church, will I go to hell?'

'Oh, for heaven's sake, Ryan!' she said. 'Can't you take this seriously for once?'

We walked the rest of the way home in silence.

'Ryan –'

'Yes?' I turned from giving my lunchtime soup mug an ineffectual cold-water rinse.

Dad gave his head an upward jerk, his eyes an upward glance and his eyebrows an upward twitch. From this I guessed he meant us to go upstairs. I left the mug in the sink, and slouched after my father to the main front room of the first floor. Nominally the master bedroom, it did indeed have a double bed, but its main use was as Dad's home office and (I suspected) chill-out room. A desk with an old computer and an Anglepoise stood in one corner, between the guest wardrobe and the wall. Bookshelves overhung the mantelpiece above a fireplace long since blocked off and occupied by a radiator. The big bay window overlooked the roofs of the West End and afforded a broad view over the Firth to the Holy Loch and the hills and beyond them to the mountains.

Dad sat down on his desk chair and swivelled it outward.

'Have a seat,' he said.

There were no other chairs in the room. I sat on the edge of the bed.

'So,' Dad said, 'you were going to tell me what happened yesterday.'

I took a deep breath. I felt an irresistible impulse to slide the palm of my hand across the back of my neck, as if I'd just had a haircut.

'What I said, me and Calum going for a walk up the Cut, the fog and that,' I said. 'That all happened but I left something out.'

'Go on.'

'We were up the top of the hill, by the microwave mast. The fog came down, and we tried to walk downhill, then we saw we weren't getting anywhere, so we stopped. And the fog kind of rolled down below us, so we were above it. I looked up to see where we were, and we both saw a light in the sky.'

'In the bright, blue sky?' Dad sounded sceptical.

'Yes,' I said. 'Very bright, and round, like a silver balloon. That's what we thought it was, then we saw it was coming down fast, right on top of us. So we ran.'

'Uh-huh. Sensible. And?'

I rubbed the back of my neck again. 'The light . . . seemed to fall on top of us. That's all I remember, a white light all round us. Next thing I knew, I was lying on the ground in a big circle of ash, and so was Calum, and it was an hour or more later. The fog had lifted and we could see where we were, not far above the Cut.'

'A circle? Like, a ring?' He outlined one in the air with a fingertip.

I shook my head. 'A filled-in circle, about three metres across. We had ash all over on our clothes.'

Dad tipped the seat of his chair back and forth a few times.

'I saw it,' he said. 'I put them in the wash this morning. More like soot than ash.'

'Yes.'

'Did anyone else see this light in the sky?'

'Not as far as I know. I checked the news. No other reports.'

Dad looked sceptical. 'That's unlikely, isn't it?'

I shrugged. 'We were above the cloud, and most people who might have seen it were below.'

Dad compressed and twisted his lips. 'Hmm. Possible, I suppose.' He stood up. 'Well!' he said, smacking his palms together and rubbing. 'That circle should still be there. Think you could find it again?'

'Uh, sure.'

I wasn't sure at all, but how hard could it be?

Our bikes were out the back, in a low brick bunker that still had fragments of coal in its dark corners. When I was about twelve I'd blunted a good penknife blade carving lumps of the stuff into approximations of comic-book characters. Dad ducked half inside and wheeled out my bike, then his. We took our helmets from the handlebars and made our way down the path by the side of the house, brushed by wet branches of overgrown bushes, through the garden gateway and down the front steps.

The front gate clanged behind me as I swung my leg over and settled in the saddle. Down the street I free-wheeled, slewing the bend, and stopped at the junction as Dad caught up.

'Take it easy,' he said.

Another downward ride, around a roundabout and out along Inverkip Road. From the flow of traffic, I guessed that the blockade had been lifted. We zigzagged through back streets and up a steep slope to the Cut, then pedalled sedately along the path's long curves. More people were out than there had been yesterday, drawn by the brighter day. We passed the school, then Branchton. Beyond it, down on the road, the tyres had been cleared, the fires were out. But the oil drums stood on the grass just back of the pavement, cylinders of tyres stacked beside them, ready for the next time.

I looked over my shoulder. 'A bit along from here,' I called. Dad waved acknowledgement. The bike wobbled as I slowed to eye the hillside. I could see the microwave mast on the skyline. On a bit, a couple of hundred metres before the plank across the Cut . . . that was where it had been. Just around the side of the hill . . .

The sound of an engine wavered on the air, becoming louder as I followed the bend around. A thickening and slowing of the path's traffic made me weave in and out among walkers, wheelers and parents pushing buggies. Some delay in front, I guessed. I glanced up and to the side. Just ahead was the crumbled stretch of the banks where Calum and I had crossed on our return. Now it was bridged by a pair of flanged tracks, with a red-striped plastic barrier on trestles across the nearer side. From the far side, two parallel strips of chewed-up grass and heather marked the way to where, high on the slope above, a small yellow caterpillar-tracked JCB digger was busy tearing up turf and stacking sods into the skip of a small dumper. The two drivers, in hard hats and hi-vis jackets, were on their own up there.

My wheels spat gravel as I braked. Dad drew level with my shoulder and dismounted.

'Is that where it was?'

I nodded. I couldn't speak.

'How bloody convenient,' my father said.

I didn't know if he was being sarcastic.

He dismounted. 'Hold the bike, will you?'

And with that he was off, scissoring his legs over the barrier, pacing across one of the metal tracks with his arms out to balance, and striding up the hill. He approached the vehicles and waved his arms. Engines coughed off. I saw him talking to the drivers, and peering into the dumper's skip. He loped back down and returned to my side, shaking his head.

'What's going on?' I asked.

'They're fae the Cooncil.' He mimicked the local dialect. '"No idea, pal. Just a job. Something to do wi' drainage."'

'Did they say anything about the round black patch?'

'Yes, they said it was ash from a fire some idiot had made

71

with lighter fuel or such. I could see the stuff in the skip myself.'

'Well,' I said, 'at least that confirms –'

Dad sighed. 'Doesn't confirm anything, I'm afraid. But as it happens, Ryan, I don't think you're lying.'

'Gosh, thanks, Dad!'

'You're welcome.'

He took his handlebars, and turned his bike round. As I followed suit, he glanced back up the hill and then at me.

'Not exactly the Roswell debris field, eh?'

'You know about that?'

'Doesn't everyone? I'm more surprised that you do.'

'I used to read that stuff,' I said, 'when I was thirteen or so,' I added, in a tone of disdain for foolish youth.

Dad snorted. 'So that's what was on the sites you used to tab away from as soon as you saw me or your mum coming?'

'Yes. Well, usually.'

'It'll make you go blind. UFO stuff, I mean. Don't start again. And don't say anything more about it.'

I was about to protest this blatant collusion with the great UFO cover-up when Dad swung his leg over the saddle and pushed off. I followed, fuming at first, then gradually cooling down.

At least he didn't think I'd been on drugs.

6

'You fucking bastard, Sinky!'

Monday morning, and I was just off the bus to school. Calum, having arrived by a different bus, had waylaid me at my stop, about fifty metres from the school entrance. He'd met my good-morning grin with a furious look, followed by furious words as he fell in beside me.

'What's up, Duke?'

'Don't gie me that. You know fine well what's up.'

'No, I don't.'

'You telt my da.'

This sounded so primary school I almost laughed. 'Did not.'

'Some cunt did.'

'Oh, fuck.'

'What?'

'It was my dad.'

'Why the fuck d'yi have to tell him?'

'Come on,' I said. I glanced over my shoulder. The pavement behind us, as in front, was crowded with pupils, in clumps and couples and alone, but no one was closer than a few steps away. 'You know. He thought I was tripping on LSD or something on Saturday night. Couldn't let him think that, could I? That would have got us both into trouble, right?'

'Aye, I suppose.' Calum sounded grudging.

'So I told him about the light. And the weird dream. I don't think he believed me, but he went with me up to the Cut and—'

'Saw the circle?'

'No, saw it being dug up with a JCB.'

'What?'

'Yes,' I said. 'Anyhow, he must have called your father, because I sure didn't. What happened?'

'Gave me a right grilling. He sounded dead worried. Wanted aw the details I could remember. Speed and size ae the light and that. He was very anxious tae know if I remembered anything from after it knocked us out.'

'And did you?' I asked.

'Like I told you, and I told him – no. Then . . .'

We were just entering the school gates. As we paused to hand our house keys and fistfuls of change around the metal-detector, we were no longer out of earshot. Calum waited until we were halfway across the front playground before continuing.

'The funny thing is, he started asking me about what

state my head was in, like if I'd noticed any weird feelings or if my sight had gone funny just after or if I'd had any nightmares or anything. It's like he knew exactly what had happened to you.'

'Well, he probably did,' I pointed out, 'my father might have told him.'

Calum scratched his head. 'He didnae mention you. Didn't even ask if I'd spoken tae yi. Went through other things and aw, stuff you hadnae said anything about. High temperature, rashes and that. Sair glands. Stuck his thumb under the side of my jaw, wiggled it about, asked if it hurt. That didnae come from your da.'

'That's odd,' I admitted, 'but—'

'Aye, aye,' said Calum. 'He couldae just hae been guessing about radiation or something. But that's no the really weird thing he said.'

'What's that?'

We were in the crush through the main door.

'Tell you later,' Calum said, over the heads of a mob of first years surging about us at elbow level. 'Meanwhile, when you get a minute, take a wee look on your phone.'

In maths class, of course, looking at our phones was legit. I took the opportunity of being a little ahead in working out a problem to surreptitiously shrink my page of algebra scribbles and open the latest message from Calum. It was a picture – or rather, it was a picture of a picture, a photo of what appeared to be part of a page from an old book, though the background looked too white to be old paper. I unfolded my phone to see it life-size. Around the borders were what looked like incomplete sentences of print – or of precise handwriting – in two columns cut off by the edges of the photo. The script was unfamiliar to me, the language unknown, and would in any case have been made almost impenetrable by the uncial font, its elegant parallel uprights and stately curves entangled with curlicues and serifs. What grabbed my attention, though, was the woodcut in the centre, around which the columns flowed, narrowing to half their usual width on each side.

The picture was captioned by Roman numerals: IX VII. It was, in outline, unmistakably the head and shoulders and raised right hand of a Grey. The oval head, the almond eyes, the dotted nostrils, the slit mouth, the pencil neck, the four-fingered hand. In detail it was something else. The top and back of the head, and what might be called the cheeks, were shielded by a mask-like helmet encircled by a jagged tiara. Antennae sprouted from the forehead. The eyes were faceted and convex. The chin was a closed pair of laterally aligned mandibles. The neck was segmented. Behind the neck, wavy vertical lines suggested something like coils of wire hanging from under the back of the helmet. The fingers had barbs along the inner surface, like the distal portion of a locust's leg, and the hands had no palms.

I felt my own palms sweat.

*

At lunchtime I tracked Calum by his phone location to behind the bicycle shed, where he and a dozen other fourth and fifth years were sucking on (to all appearances) the hollow tips of retractable ballpoint pens and meditatively puffing out vapour. At the sight of me he stuck his fake pen in an inside pocket and joined me in a mooch around the playing field. The sky was overcast, the odd spit of drizzle enough to keep most people away from that particular stroll – apart from young-love couples, which no one (I hoped) would suspect we were. We exchanged a few jokes about the previous night's episode of *Anachron*, a cult programme to the high school cognoscenti of the day, then I asked, 'Where the fuck did that picture come from?'

Calum cast me a smug glance.

'Gave you a fright, did it?'

'No,' I lied. 'But it's fucking weird.'

'Not what you saw, though? In your dream, like.'

'Nope.' I shook my head, with an uneasy effort at a dismissive laugh. 'I saw the standard model Grey. Reptilian, I guess – I remember scales on its neck. That thing in the picture looks like some kind of insect.'

'Fucking hell!' said Calum, smacking fist to palm.

'What?'

'Just had a thought.'

'I can see how that would be a surprise.'

'Insects, right.'

'Uh-huh.'

'They're like . . . good at mimicry, right? Remember that mole cricket we saw in the museum up at Glasgow Uni.'

77

'Vaguely,' I said.

'And the leaf grasshoppers and that?'

'Aye, sure, I've watched the odd David Attenborough in improving childhood moments.'

'Well, there you go,' said Calum, 'there could be insects that mimic Greys.'

'Fascinating,' I said. 'You still haven't answered my question.'

'Oh, aye. Well. Like I was telling yi. After my da gave me the third degree and the medical, so tae speak, he hoiks me out of the house and down to the garage. I swear if I'd been a wean he'd have dragged me by the lug, that's what it felt like. Raging, he was, but scared wi it, know what I mean?'

'Yes,' I said, although if I'd been more honest or less tactful I'd have said I had no experience of my own father in such a mood. I'd seen him angry with me, but never raging, and certainly never scared. In fact, I couldn't easily imagine it of Calum's father. Although a bit of big lunk – like his son was fast growing towards – with alarming beetle brows and a broken-looking nose, and hair on his swarthy face from chin to cheekbones whenever he forgot to shave, in my few dealings with the man from childhood onward he'd struck me as fair-minded and even-tempered, albeit with the sort of right-wing views one might (if one was as incurably snobbish as my sixteen-year-old self) expect from and make allowances for in a self-made small businessman who still got his own hands oily and fingernails broken in the repair pits.

'The garage is closed on Sundays, unless there's a special

job on, which there wasn't yesterday. Old man has the codes, of course, so in we go. Naebody's around. He takes me to the office around the side of the main garage. On a shelf above the desk there's stacks ae they file boxes, you know, the ones that haud the papers wi a spring clip? Old and greasy and dusty, doubt they've been looked at for years. Labels turning yellow and that. He hauls one down and blows the dust off it. He opens it and it's bulging wi papers, dockets and tax forms and the like, fucking ancient. The spring can only just hold them in. He clicks it back and under a wadge ae papers there's this big thick heavy book. Leather binding, kindae frayed around the edges. Tiny flecks ae gold at the top of the spine, but nae title left tae read.

'So he opens it and the pages are aw white-looking, and its full ae tiny writing or printing and wee drawings, swords and battles and kindae Gandalf-looking geezers wi robes and beards. And he flicks through tae near the back and there's dragons and burning cities and then there's this picture.

'"Whit's this," I says, looking down at it, "some kindae Grey alien?" And the old man gies me a smack upside the head – no hard like, it's his way ae showing affection – and tells me that's what the gadgies call them, but we should show more respect, so we call them the Fine.'

'The Fine?' I pronounced it 'feenih', suddenly feeling clever. 'Meaning "the people", like in the Gaelic?'

'No,' said Calum. 'Like in the English. Fine, as in fine folk.'

'Wait a minute,' I said. 'If he said "the gadgies" then . . .'

I didn't quite want to say it.

'Oh, aye,' said Calum. 'There's a bit ae the travelling folk in us Williamsons, nae doubt about it, though it's generations since we settled down. That's no a secret, though my ma tries to keep quiet about it.'

He looked at me curiously. We'd done almost a circuit of the field, and the bell would soon ring. 'You never knew?'

'To tell you the truth,' I said, 'if I ever thought about it I sort of vaguely assumed there was a touch of the Pure Race in your family, maybe a Black American soldier or African sailor or something, like Sophie's great-grand-dad or whatever.'

Calum clapped my shoulder. 'That's touching,' he said. 'Nah, we're tinks, way back. Anyhow, like I say, no secret. What my da told me might be, though. In fact it is. He damn near swore me to secrecy, though maybe not quite, so I'm going to fucking swear you before I say any mair.'

I laughed. 'What do you want me to swear on? The Bible? *The Origin of Species?*'

Calum looked as if he were considering this carefully. 'Aye,' he said. 'That'll do.'

'OK. I swear by God and Darwin I won't repeat what you're going to tell me.'

(I'm now of course breaking this oath, but I expect God and Darwin will forgive me. As Roy Batty might have put it, it's nothing that the god of evolution would keep me out of heaven for.)

'He telt me the book was handed down through the family from way, way back, hundreds ae years like, from when the Romanies were in Romania, or wherever the fuck they came fae. He's no saying *we're* Roma, by the way. Our branch ae the Williamsons are unquestionably tinks fae Ireland, surviving camp-followers ae Bonnie Prince Charlie's army according tae family legend, but beyond that there's some Spanish connection, via a shipwrecked Armada sailor as the story goes, back tae where some Romany rover had his way. So there's just a wee drap ae authentic Gypsy blood in our ancestry, which I can believe well enough. And the book, handed down in secret.'

'Why secret?'

'He said in the old days folks could get burned if they got caught wi it. Naebody kens any more what the book is. Naebody kens what language it's in, or how tae read the funny lettering, or even what the lettering is. Couldnae make head nor tail of it myself. Maybe in the old days they could read it, or somebody they kent could, the family itself having aw been fucking illiterate until some time after the 1872 Education Act. They must hae hung on tae the book wi' nae clue as tae what it said. Some ancient work ae magic or lore or whitever, that's what he reckons it is.'

'And he keeps it on a shelf in the garage?'

'Safest place for it. Who's going to steal old receipts?'

'Point,' I admitted.

Calum shook his head impatiently. 'Anyway, that's no the important thing. No the big secret. The big secret is why they kept it aw these years, aw these centuries. It was because ae that picture. The thing is, they kept it because they *recognised* it. They've known about the Fine for a long time, for a long,

long time even before that picture was made. And, my da told me, they – we – see them for whit they are. The gadgies see angels or devils or aliens out ae science fiction, but we see them as they are, they scary fucking insect things.'

'Who's "we"?' I asked. 'Roma? Travellers?'

'No exactly,' said Calum. He hesitated, glancing around. 'Our people. A people who kindae travel alang wi the travelling folk, that was how he put it.'

'You're having me on,' I said.

'I am no!' Calum snapped. 'Christ, man, I'm taking a risk just telling yi. I'm damn near betraying my family. I wouldnae make this up.'

'So where did these mysterious people of yours come from?' I asked, still sceptical of what he was saying. 'Egypt? Asia? Atlantis? Outer space?'

Calum licked his lips, and looked around again.

'Nowhere,' he said. 'We've always been here. We were here before . . . the other people. Before the ice.'

'I always suspected your old man was a Neanderthal,' I said.

Calum laughed. 'Many a true word, an' that.'

'And these Neanderthals know what the Fine are up to?'

'Oh aye,' said Calum, suddenly confident again. 'They watch. They've been watching us all alang, my da said. Probably aw the way back tae Africa, he said, though he admitted that was speculation. Since before the ice, he said, that we know for sure. Now and again, the Fine snatch someone, examine them, mark them and let them go. It's like ecologists daein capture and release. Putting rings on birds, and that.' He laughed. 'I must say, that part ae it does make sense.'

I recalled the item about ecologists microchipping dormice that had been on television at dinnertime on Saturday, and wondered if Calum had seen it too.

'I still don't believe you,' I said.

'Explain the picture, then.'

'Explain how you got it,' I said.

'Pretended tae get a call fae Sophie, pulled out my phone, took a snap while my da was politely looking away.'

'Oh, aye,' I said. 'Pull the other one.'

'Please yourself,' said Calum.

He didn't sound hurt. He sounded as if he didn't care whether I believed him or not.

The bell rang. We ran.

That evening, after I'd done my homework, I sat at the desk in my bedroom and set about taking Calum's strange picture apart. I began by zooming in to the highest resolution my phone was capable of. Peering closely at lines and letters, I could just make out a spidery tracery of ink in the fibres around them. So far, so good: unless Calum had used some specialised and expensive rendering software, this was a genuine photograph of part of a page. Of course, he could have written and drawn the page himself: as I recalled, his primary-school exercise-book cover doodles had always shown a disturbingly precocious grasp of perspective and anatomy, though these days he seemed to hide any artistic or graphic talent he might have under the bushel of O-level technical drawing, at which he excelled.

I zoomed back out and isolated images of individual letters and pasted them to a side column. There were sixteen distinct symbols, plus the Roman numerals. I ran searches on every one of them, and found no matches. Relaxing the criteria and looking for resemblances to every known script returned nothing, though it did tell me more than I needed to know about alphabets. An image search on the apparent woodcut predictably brought up Greys and insects, but nothing close to the original.

The only comprehensible marks on the picture were the Roman numerals. I searched on them, and predictably found lots of stuff about Roman numerals.

IX VII meant nine and seven, so I searched on that.

'9 7'

Again, lots of nothing to the point.

I sat back and let my eyes go a little out of focus as I gazed at the picture. What did it most look like?

'9 7 Grey'

'9 7 alien'

'9 7 insect'

Narrow the search, I thought. What *kind* of insect? The one that had come to mind at first glance was a locust, and some of the results of the image search had been locusts.

'9 7 locust'

Bingo.

I called Calum.

'I know what your old book is,' I told him.

'Oh aye?'

'Do you have the photo handy?'

'Just a mo – aye.'

'Look at it and listen to this: "And the shapes of the locusts were like unto horses prepared unto battle; and on their heads were as it were crowns like gold, and their faces were as the faces of men." Revelation, chapter nine, verse seven. Next verse: "And they had hair as the hair of women, and their teeth were as the teeth of lions." What your father showed you is a Bible!'

'No,' said Calum. 'The pages were that thick, if it had been a Bible the book would have been a lot bigger than it was, and it was big enough.'

'Well, the New Testament, then.' I thought for a moment, then a detail clicked into place from a historical novel I'd read a year or two earlier: Umberto Eco's *The Name of The Rose*. 'The pages are thick and white because they're not paper – they're vellum. What you've got is a manuscript of the New Testament, in some language and alphabet that's not known any more, at least not online.'

'Been searching on it, have yi?'

'Of course I have.' I told him how I'd found my clue. 'I'm surprised you didn't,' I added.

'Huh!' he said. 'I believed myself, didn't I?'

'There you go,' I said. 'Scepticism works.'

'So why,' Calum asked, 'would anyone keep it a secret?'

85

'You said it yourself,' I told him. 'Well, your father did. People could get burned for having it, he told you. Back in the old days, the Roman Catholic Church was dead suspicious of translations of the Bible into local languages. I guess your Gypsy-rover ancestor wasn't too keen on explaining to the Spanish Inquisition what he was doing with one. If he didn't know what it was, that made it even more risky. Could have been full of black magic or heresy or whatever. Especially if it was in a language no one spoke and letters nobody could read.'

'Why would it be like that in the first place, though?'

'My guess,' I told him, with all the authority of a ten-minute trawl through online resources on alphabets, 'is that it's a script invented by some medieval monk or whatever, like St Cyril's supposed to have invented Cyrillic, to translate the Testament into some obscure language in Eastern Europe. And you know what that means?'

'I know all right,' said Calum. 'It means it's worth a fucking fortune.'

I laughed. 'There's that, aye. But it's worth even more to scholars, to the Church, to science – well, linguistics . . .'

'Nae doubt,' said Calum, grudgingly. 'But as far as I'm concerned it's staying right where it us, until such time as my old man passes it on tae me.'

'You could tell him what I've told you – heck, you don't even need to mention the photo. Just say you searched on what you remembered, the Roman numeral and a description of the picture—'

'No,' said Calum. 'He'd still be fucking livid. He'd never trust me again.'

I thought about this.

'OK,' I said. 'Let's leave it. But . . . I hate to say this, but I trust you a bit more now.'

'Ha-ha! Gee, thanks, old pal.'

'You know what I mean.'

Calum sighed. 'Aye. Well, let's leave it at that.'

And we did.

7

On Wednesday evening, about 7.30, I sat at the living-room table, refried slices of Sunday's nut roast and sweet potato heavy in my belly, and struggled with *Jane Eyre* for English homework. Mum was down at the old container port, ladling out soup to the destitute. Dad was working late. Marie was in Glasgow, working the early evening in a bar as usual through the week.

I highlighted a passage that puzzled me, searched on it, and consulted Calum, to find him as baffled as I was. We exchanged a few messages with Sophie to help us distinguish wheat from chaff. I don't know what Calum made of it, but I went on to read the first critical discussion that Sophie recommended and found it very helpful indeed. In the midst of my effort to avoid using that discussion's wording in my own, someone rang the doorbell. I thumbed to the door camera and saw a man in a black suit standing at the top of the front steps. Holy shit! I thought. A Man in Black! Then I smiled at my own silliness as I noticed the white clerical collar above the black shirt-front.

Rather glad of the interruption, I folded the phone and went and opened the door.

'Hello?' I said.

The man was young, slim and pale, with broad, muscular shoulders. He stuck a fingertip inside his collar and slid it back and forth for a second or two, then desisted and stuck out his hand. I shook, finding it cold.

'Good evening!' he said, in an unexpectedly deep and resonant voice. He glanced down at a phone in his left hand. 'You must be . . . Ryan Sinclair?'

'Yes,' I said.

He smiled, his teeth as white as his collar. His right arm twitched, as if he'd been about to shake hands again and had thought better of it.

'James Baxter,' he said. 'Pleased to meet you.'

His accent was Scottish, but educated. He might have been from Edinburgh.

'Likewise,' I said.

'You'll be wondering why I'm here.'

'Yes,' I said.

He hesitated for a moment as if wondering the same himself.

'Ah!' he said. 'Yes. I'm from the church.'

He fished from the breast pocket of his jacket a laminated card and held it up to my face, and coincidentally to the door camera. The card showed a photo of himself, with his name and the name and logo of the Church of Scotland. I waved my phone in front of it and confirmed the card's authenticity.

'Yes, I see, but . . . my mother's not in, and anyway she goes to the other – uh, the Episcopalian church.'

'Oh, that's fine,' said Reverend James Baxter. 'We local ministers all work together, you see. And I'm not here to visit your mother – I'm here to visit you.'

I took a step back. 'Why?'

Another toothy smile. 'I understand you went to church last Sunday for the first time in several years,' he said, 'and, as part of the parochial pastoral ecumenical outreach initiative, I've been asked to pop by and see if there's anything you'd like to discuss. In confidence, of course, if you like. Or with your parents present, if you prefer.'

'Oh, no!' I said. 'Uh, not with my parents and not, uh, at all actually, I'm fine, and as it happens I'm quite busy at the moment, homework and that, you know, and . . .'

As I spoke his countenance became more and more disappointed and dejected.

'Are you quite sure?' he asked, in a concerned voice. 'I got the impression you might be . . . troubled in some way.'

'How?'

He gave me a direct, knowing look. 'I'm only ten years older than you, Ryan, and I remember very well what it's like at your age. All kinds of personal problems and perplexities can weigh on your mind – they certainly did on mine!

Are you sure there's nothing you'd like to get off your chest?'

'I didn't mean how was I troubled,' I said. 'I meant, how did you get the impression that I was?'

'Your vicar noticed,' he said. 'Connie's quite perceptive about these things.'

The easy familiarity of his tone, and my rush of embarrassment at the thought that Reverend Connie Jameson had observed me from the pulpit, left me feeling I had little choice. I also had a strong suspicion he might elaborate on the discussion right here on the front step.

'Well, come in then,' I said.

As I closed the door he stood in the hallway, peering around then looking up the stairs as if expecting to be invited up there.

'Uh, in here,' I said, opening the door to the chill, formal front sitting room with its sofas and armchairs and big bay window. 'Can I get you a cup of tea?'

'Ah . . . yes, thank you, but coffee would be perfect.' He twitched up his eyebrows. 'If I may?'

I thought of the quarter-full jar of precious instant. But he was a guest.

'Yes, of course.'

'Thank you. Black, no sugar.'

'I'll bring it through in a mo,' I said. 'Uh, make yourself comfortable, Mr Baxter.'

'James, please.' He smiled and went in.

When I returned bearing coffee in a cup and saucer for

him and a less formal but more generous mug for myself, he was lounging cross-legged in one of the pair of armchairs on opposite sides of the fireplace.

'Thank you, Ryan.'

I sat down facing him, then searched for and found a coaster for the mug, which I carefully and rather pointlessly placed on the glass-topped coffee table between us.

'Well,' I said. 'James.'

Baxter fixed me with a penetrating gaze over the rim of the cup as he sipped. He sighed appreciatively. As he replaced the cup on the saucer, which was balanced on his crooked knee, he seemed to notice for the first time a clamshell on the fireplace's tiled surround.

'Ah!' he said. 'An ashtray! I haven't seen one of these in a long while. How very civilised!'

He picked up the shell in a darting movement of the arm and put it on the coffee table. The cup and saucer on his knee didn't wobble. He took a lighter and a gold-coloured cigarette packet with no visible health warnings or scare-pictures from the side pocket of his jacket, tapped a cigarette out and lit up. I watched open-mouthed. I hadn't been in the same room as a lit cigarette in my life. The air instantly filled with the acrid odour.

'I hope you don't mind?' he asked.

'Not at all,' I said, though I did, quite a lot. The room was going to smell like my mother's clothes usually did when she came back from helping the poor. I would have some explaining to do.

'Now, Ryan, as I was saying. When I was your age, and just beginning to take my nominal faith seriously, after' – he flashed a smile – 'the usual bout of adolescent atheism, I found myself worried over matters that weren't really very important at all. For example – I know this might be embarrassing, but bear with me – ah, to be blunt, erotic dreams and fantasies. They're nothing to feel guilty about.'

'Oh, I don't,' I said, wishing I could curl up in a ball. My bizarre abduction dream hadn't recurred, but the past couple of nights I'd wanked myself raw reliving its climax.

'Very good, very good. There are pamphlets, you know, the church's youth website is very helpful, with online confidential counselling if you feel the need, so to speak.'

'Uh, well, I might look into it.'

'Another common pitfall,' he went on, after sucking hard on his cigarette while frowning at the ceiling, 'is untutored Bible reading.' He raised a hand, his fingers in the exact position of a priest's when blessing a congregation, except that the priest isn't usually holding a cigarette between his upraised fore and middle fingers at the time. 'Not that we wish to discourage personal Bible study – quite the reverse! But focusing on random passages from the scriptures, without understanding their context, can lead the unwary reader very far astray.'

'Well, to be honest,' I said, 'I haven't read much of the Bible for myself, and, uh, if I wanted to I'm sure I would ask Reverend Jameson for a study plan or something, or my mum, but as it happens I'm very busy studying English literature right now, so I'm not sure I have time to . . .'

93

'Well, of course! That's your duty for the present, though you will find the Bible very useful even for English literature, so do consider some . . . properly guided reading, if you wish to explore the scriptures further. Again, the church website has excellent resources for the young inquirer.'

'I'll check it out,' I lied.

'And I'm sure Connie would be happy to enrol you in a Bible study group – a sort of Sunday school for adults, so to speak. I believe it meets on Thursday evenings.'

'Well, maybe, but . . .'

He tapped ash into the shell. 'I see you're looking puzzled. Allow me to explain. The Churches, the established Churches that is, as well as the Free Church and even our Roman Catholic friends, have noticed recently a rather unhealthy preoccupation among, ah, certain lay people with End Times prophecies, as they're called. Not surprising, really, when you consider the times we're living in. Wars and rumours of wars, and so forth. Earthquakes in diverse places.'

'Oh, don't worry, sir,' I said. 'I'm not interested in anything like that.' This came out not quite as I'd intended. 'Not unduly interested, I mean.'

'The book of Revelation,' Baxter continued, as if I hadn't spoken, 'is a highly symbolic and deeply obscure work, as no doubt it was intended to be. Have you read it?'

'I've . . . glanced at it, I suppose,' I said.

'If you were to take it literally,' he said, 'you might come away with the impression that Christians expect to spend eternity praising a dead mutant infant sheep inside a giant glass cube from outer space.'

The slight shock I felt at this crudity must have shown on my face.

'Ridiculous, of course,' Baxter said, with a smile. 'But even people who would flinch at these words, like you just did, and regard them quite rightly as a grotesque, malicious, village-atheist caricature of our hope, can still be found earnestly and fearfully expecting someday soon to see – to take an instance at random – locusts with human faces, women's hair, and lions' teeth swarming from a huge hole in the ground.'

He stubbed out his cigarette, shook his head, and gave me another challenging look.

'Nothing like that troubling you?' he asked.

'No, no,' I said.

'You sound alarmed. You look worried.'

'No, I'm fine.'

'Any dark thoughts on your mind?'

At that moment, I had a few, thanks to him.

'No,' I said.

'You're definitely not worrying over the book of Revelation?'

'Definitely not,' I said. 'Uh, I really should be . . .'

'Of course, of course,' Baxter said. 'I'm forgetting my manners.'

He stood up, catching the now empty cup and saucer on the fly as they fell and laying them on the table in one smooth swoop. They didn't even rattle.

'Thanks for the coffee,' he said, 'and the hospitality of the ashtray. And thanks for listening, and for being so open.'

If I'd been open, it wasn't by intent, but I had an uneasy feeling that I had been more open than I'd intended. I saw him out, returned his wave as he sauntered down the steps, and shut the door. Resisting the temptation to lean back against it and breathe out, I nipped to the downstairs toilet and took a spray-can of air freshener to the sitting room. Only after I'd rinsed the shell and the cup and mug and left the sitting room with the door open for the smells of tobacco smoke and jasmine to fight it out did I sit down at the living-room table and breathe out.

Had I just encountered a Man in Black? Or was Reverend James Baxter merely an eager and socially awkward young minister, who had mentioned by sheer coincidence the very verses from Revelation that had been on my mind since Monday? I didn't know, but I knew how to find out. I opened out my phone on the table and selected the footprint of the minister's ID card. It was there all right, but inert, with no trace of the authentication I'd seen earlier, and no warning either. A hasty visit to the local Church of Scotland site, the local *Yellow Pages*, and then a wider trawl, found no minister of that name. Nor was there any such project as the parochial pastoral ecumenical outreach initiative.

Holy shit, it seemed, had been the right response in the first place.

Naturally, I said nothing about the strange visit when my parents came home. My mother didn't notice the cigarette smell, having no doubt been desensitised by her stint at the relief centre, but my father did.

'Don't add smoking to your liabilities, Ryan,' he told me, and said no more about it.

'That's funny,' Calum said, when I told him about the visit at first break the following morning. 'My old man was up tae high doh last night, poking about on his phone and checking his taxes and VAT and payroll and all sorts. Said a wee nyaff in a black suit and waving a Cooncil card had been nosing around the garage, asking aw kinds ae questions about use ae unauthorised machinery. Da was sure it was some kind ae fishing expedition tae find some excuse tae shut him down. Yi ken what the fucking Cooncil's like, aw Reds and Nats and Greens, nae friends ae the car driver or the sma' business man. Or woman,' Calum added, politically correcting himself. 'So he was dead chuffed like when I suggested checking the cunt out, yi ken, by seeing if the Cooncil card was real by tapping it on my phone. And guess what? It wisnae! Nae fucking trace ae the fucker anywhere.'

'Must have been quite a relief.'

'Well, no exactly – after he's convinced the guy's no fae the Cooncil, he decides tae dae some work in the garden, even though it's getting dark and there's a bit ae a smirr on. Asks me to gie him a hand wi' some tomato frames he wants tae shift. So out I go, and he tells me very quiet like that after seeing one ae they strange lights in the sky it's no unusual tae

97

get a visit like that, best thing is tae say nothing and they stop hassling you.'

'Come on,' I said. 'We haven't said anything anyway.'

'We talked on the phone. You telt yir father. He talked on the phone tae my da. That could be enough.'

I shivered. 'You mean we're being watched?'

'Aye, and our calls and our web searches monitored. How the fuck else wid yir phony minister guy ken yi were thinking about yon verse in Revelation? And we'll only stop being watched if yi shut the fuck up about it fae now on.'

'Who's doing the watching? The Fine? The MoD?'

'Both, my da reckons. Think the MoD disnae know about things like what we saw? They track everything that moves in British airspace. Somebody behind a screen in a bunker somewhere knows what happened tae us on Saturday, and they send someone around tae check what we're saying about it.'

'That's stupid,' I said. 'Why send someone around with a strange manner and a cover story and ID that anyone can see through afterwards, instead of, say, an RAF officer or someone from the Ministry with proper ID, to have a quiet word?'

'Ah,' said Calum. He tapped the side of his nose. 'Deniability. Name ae the game. They dinnae want tae admit they're interested, see? So they stick tae the tried and tested MiB routine. Bit ae bizarre behaviour, hint ae menace, black suit, transparent cover story. That way, nae fucker will believe yi if yi tell them about it. Nae doubt they have a good laugh about it back at the office.'

'Well, speaking of the office,' I said, 'we've both got his picture on our phones, right? We can search on his name, and on his face—'

Calum frowned. 'And get loads ae false positives, nae doubt.'

For a moment I wondered if he really did have a Council ID card on his phone.

'All the same, it'll narrow it down.'

Excited, I took my phone out and retrieved the ID that Reverend Baxter had given me. Calum laid a hand on my arm.

'Gonnae naw dae that,' he said.

I looked up, surprised. 'Why not?'

'They—' He stopped, shrugged, went on. 'The MoD, GCHQ, NSA, whitever . . . they can aw track our searches. And even if we found who the guy wis, whit the fuck wid that accomplish except show the fuckers we're still curious? Leave it be, man. Dinnae gie them a reason tae try something heavier next time.'

I was still not sure I believed anything that Calum had told me – about how he'd got the picture, about what his father had told him, and even about the visit the previous day. Just because he was my best friend, I knew him too well not to suspect him of an elaborate prank, or at least of opportunistic exaggeration. And the explanation he'd just given was, in its free-wheeling circular logic, a small but perfect example of the paranoid style into which thinking about UFOs seemed to lock so many people. But my encounter with the bogus minister had shaken my confidence.

So, to spite Calum and to spike his ploy, I did exactly what he'd suggested.

I shut the fuck up about the whole thing.

8

Of course, I didn't stop thinking about the whole UFO thing. For at least two weeks afterwards I was obsessed with the topic, in a different way from my younger naïve fascination and the (as I'd naïvely thought) hard-nosed, seen-through-all-that scepticism that had hitherto replaced it. This wasn't just because of my own two (or three, if you count the dream) direct experiences of aspects of the phenomenon, but because – in the three or four years since the last time I'd got lost in that wilderness of mirrors – one particular explanation had gone from a minority to a majority view among the less dogmatic believers and sceptics alike. This was known in the jargon as the Defence Technology Hypothesis, abbreviated to DTH by way of deliberate contrast with the conventional Extra-Terrestrial Hypothesis, or ETH.

According to the DTH, the tiny fraction of UFO reports

that remained genuinely inexplicable after you'd ruled out hoaxes, camera glitches and misidentifications of the Moon, Venus, Jupiter, satellites, meteors, spacecraft re-entries, balloons, birds, conventional aircraft, lighthouses, etc., were quite likely to be of encounters with top-secret, advanced aircraft (including drones), sometimes combined with radar jamming and spoofing. Furthermore, the stories that the US and other governments were covering up their knowledge of UFOs, and that secretly these governments were in contact with the aliens already, and had a stash of crashed saucers that they were reverse-engineering, and/or alien bodies or captives that they were extracting information from, and all the rest of the UFO mythos, had originated from or been cunningly reinforced (through planted rumours and faked documents) by various government agencies and armed forces, or at least by specific groups and individuals within them. The evidence for this included detailed, documented confessions by former insiders.

In short, the canonical *X-files*-type government cover-up story was *itself* a government cover-up story, and what it covered up was advanced aviation technology. Far better that any civilians who happened to glimpse the latest black-budget breakthrough should attribute it to aliens rather than to the USAF. And as sheer disinformation, having your enemies unable to entirely shake off the suspicion that you were in a secret concord with immensely powerful aliens was quite a coup, if you could pull it off. Even more neatly, when the other side – the Russians or the Chinese, say – had figured it out, seen through it, and themselves become convinced of the DTH . . . it meant they had to keep taking all UFO reports seriously, because any of them could be an indication of a genuine unknown, but earthly – specifically, American – threat.

A good example of how the myth was kept rolling along is a story that had roiled the believers around about the time I'd first become interested – in fact, if I remember right it was an echo of that very commotion that had drawn me in. The website of a long-standing UFO investigation group in Alberta had received some tantalising emails, swiftly followed by a mysteriously delivered stash of documents that showed every sign of being authentic to the last molecule, from the age of the paper to the font and ink of the typewriter to the remaining faint but detectable traces of the typist's perfume, all of which dated the first tranche to the mid-1950s. A second tranche, from the mid-1970s, was just as minutely authenticable in every way.

The documents told a remarkable story, one that turned several aspects of the traditional UFO mythos on its head. In this version, there was indeed a long-standing ET presence in the solar system, and in the late 1940s one of their craft had crashed in the United States. Two of the entities within (Greys, naturally) had survived. An ultra-secret, top-level committee of various agencies and armed forces of the US government had held the luckless occupants hostage until regular communication was established a couple of years later, and the aliens had fessed up in exchange for the captives' safe return.

They were scientists. They had a base under a crater on the far side of the Moon. They had come from a solar system twenty-seven light years away, about a million years ago, and (rather as Calum's father had allegedly told him) they'd been observing us ever since, out of the pure scientific interest that was the main motivation of their unthinkably long lives. They had travelled between the stars in a vessel that had a speed of, oh, about 1 per cent of the speed of light. Their short-haul craft, the classic flying saucers, had been seen and interpreted in various ways, throughout history. In the twentieth century, and particularly during and after World War Two, their observation sorties had been stepped up in response to humanity's increasing mastery of rocketry and nuclear energy.

They were no threat, really, and they'd always expected that we'd discover them some day.

Pressed to give details of exactly how they'd been observing humanity, they'd explained their technique of capturing random individuals, implanting tracking and monitoring devices in their bodies, wiping or muddling their memories of the encounter, and releasing them back into the wild.

At this point the representatives of the secret intelligence agencies had pricked up their ears.

Was there any chance, the spooks had asked, that you could do some of this for us? To, uh, some not so random individuals? Ones we select for you?

Well, said the aliens, that's a big ask. It would disrupt our careful, controlled, scientific observation programme, and we're not quite finished with it yet. Besides, we have ethics.

We have guidelines. The folks back home check up on us. There are committees and everything.

The spooks, shocked by such scruples, had been left at a loss. At this point, the man from the US Navy had leaned forward.

Suppose we could give you an incentive, he said. Suppose we could make you an offer of something so worth having that your supervisors would forgive you a little, teensy-weensy deviation from the guidelines?

Well, replied the aliens, it'd have to be one heck of an incentive.

How about, said the Navy man, anti-gravity, space warps, and faster-than-light travel?

That puts rather a different complexion on things, said the aliens. Tell us more.

At this point the USAF, the Army, the Government, and the CIA representatives had requested a brief adjournment. The aliens had duly trooped out, back to their cells or pods or whatever, and everyone had turned on the Navy man.

What, they wanted to know, the fuck was he on about?

Oh yes, he'd said. The US Naval Laboratory had stumbled on space warps in 1943, while working on some crackpot scheme for making ships invisible by bending light around them. The Navy's scientists had taken the experimental results to Einstein, he'd done the math, and it had all checked out.

So why, everyone demanded, the fuck don't we know about this?

That's above my pay grade, said the Navy man, but my

guess it's all about security. I mean, you don't want the Reds to know we have bases around Alpha Centauri, do you?

Alpha Centauri? yelled everyone who knew what Alpha Centauri was.

Sure, said the Navy man. Sending a ship to Mars or the Moon would be hard to hide from the Russkis, whereas no telescope on Earth could see planets around other stars. And anyway, with faster-than-light travel and all, why the heck not?

Wonderful, said the USAF guy. With anti-gravity aircraft, we could really sock it to the Russkis!

Nu-uh, said the Navy man. Who said anything about aircraft? What we have are *ships*!

What about the flying saucers? They're aircraft!

Yes – *naval* aircraft, because they take off from ships.

What! This is—

Let's leave that till later, gentlemen, said the man from the Government. We can sort that out when we've made our arrangement with the aliens. Our most pressing need isn't better aircraft than the commies'. We already *have* better aircraft. What we don't have is reliable intelligence about what the commies are up to. If the little grey guys can give us that . . .

So the deal was struck. The aliens carried out abductions, implants and tracking for the CIA, in exchange for advanced space technology from the US Navy. They were pathetically grateful to have regular, rapid travel between the solar system and their planet around Zeta Reticuli. They were happy to

106

have teams of scientists and military personnel accompany them, and more than happy to show them around the home world (physically largely desert, socially boringly communist, overall as exciting as a kibbutz in Utah). By now, there were US and allied colonies – officially, naval bases – dotted all over the sky, to about a hundred light-years out.

The USAF, meanwhile, had to be content with getting the aliens' obsolete, pre-anti-gravity flying saucers to reverse engineer from, out at Groom Lake. They'd fumed about this, but the Navy had been adamant that starships were *ships*, dammit, and therefore their own flying saucers were carrier-based aircraft. Anyway, the USAF had got the Stealth bomber and God knows what else out of the deal, so in the end they'd accepted the situation, albeit with ill grace.

It took the aliens until the 1970s to fine-tune the spatial distortion tech to the point where they could lift people straight out of their beds from under the covers and space-warp them directly aboard the saucers without regard for material obstacles. After this breakthrough abductions went, so to speak, through the roof. From then on there was no stopping them, and nothing to stop the CIA finding out everything it wanted about anything and anyone on Earth.

The documents were a work of art. Besides the apparent physical authenticity of the forgeries, plenty of rabbit holes for the conspiracy minded were scattered unobtrusively in the text. For instance, the documents alluded to the Philadelphia Naval Shipyard, and hinted at the involvement of Aleister Crowley, Robert A. Heinlein, Isaac Asimov, and L. Ron

Hubbard, all of whose names appeared in transparently disguised form. There was a passing reference to the (in 1943) young naval officer John F. Kennedy, as being in on the truth but a possible long-term security risk because of his (in 1955) political ambitions. There was even a brief mention in a footnote of a plan to build a trans-Atlantic guidance system concealed inside tall twin towers on Manhattan Island.

Within months, the whole preposterous farrago had been debunked. In the meantime, according to some in a position to know, the rumours about it, and the hard, public evidence of frantic efforts by the US authorities to recover the documents and suppress and discredit the story (thus, of course, multiplying its credibility) had wound up the Russians and Chinese something wonderful, to say nothing of what it did to the French.

I finished reading the most recent summary of that particular story one midnight. After I'd closed the site I found myself wondering how much of it I'd known before. A quick scan back through my data stash confirmed that in my embarrassingly naïve pubescent fumblings with the UFO mythos a few years earlier I'd encountered an earlier draft of the tale from before its dubious provenance had been exposed. Thinking back, I recalled being particularly excited by the idea that human beings were already out there among the stars, some of them riding in our very own starships, others perhaps taken there centuries or millennia ago by the real aliens, the Greys.

I'd even seized on the latter possibility as an explanation for the Nordic-looking 'Space Brothers' reported by the early-1950s flying-saucer contactees.

Was this, then, the origin of some of the details of my dream? It seemed all too plausible an explanation. I shut down my screen and pushed my chair back carefully so as not to wake anyone. I backed down the stair-ladder for a final pee before turning in, pondering all the while. As I crept back up the creaking steps with the sound of the re-filling cistern like a torrent in my ears, I had a sudden thought that made me freeze at the top of the landing, then scurry to the illusory shelter of the duvet with a shiver between my shoulder blades.

What if the story were true? What if it wasn't disinformation at all, but perhaps an unwittingly leaked truth hastily covered up by making it *look* like disinformation? In that case, my experience might have been more real – and more deceptive – than I'd thought. The Space Brother and the Space Sister might just be US naval personnel, and their tale some bizarre psychological ploy. The detail that I'd found myself wearing my clothes when I was in the ship indicated that the experience couldn't have been entirely as it had seemed – or did it? If they had technology that could warp me from under a duvet and through a solid ceiling and roof, surely they could warp me into my clothes as well!

At this point I told myself very firmly not to be ridiculous, and went to sleep.

*

On subsequent late nights of fruitless research the disturbing thought returned, but by and large I kept my thinking rational, and well within the bounds of the Defence Technology Hypothesis. The DTH made a lot of sense to me, as did the distinct but compatible – and likewise well-supported – hypothesis of ESB: electromagnetic stimulation of the brain.

In laboratory settings, magnetic fields had been shown to induce a strong sense of invisible presences, feelings of limbs being tugged, and religious and spiritual experiences whose content depended very much on the subject's prior expectations and beliefs. Some UFOs did seem to be natural plasma phenomena less well understood even than ball lightning, and it was quite possible that encounters with such things could induce the sort of weird hallucinations that go down in UFO lore as 'high strangeness incidents'. It was also possible that some of the advanced aircraft and drones postulated by the DTH had strong electromagnetic fields of their own, so they too could generate high strangeness episodes during or after the encounter.

This, I reckoned, was what had happened to me. I could even explain to my own satisfaction why I'd had a weird mental state and a disturbingly real dream afterwards and Calum hadn't. I didn't quite believe his tale about his forebears, but I did suspect it had a grain of truth. Most people whose ancestors moved out of Africa in prehistoric times have a few per cent Neanderthal, Denisovan and other not-quite human genes in their DNA. One thing we can be fairly sure of about Neanderthals: they didn't have much in the way of religion.

They buried their dead in ways that can be interpreted as evidence of a belief in an afterlife – a handful of flowers, a smudge of ochre – but that's all. They left no trace of worship: no shrines, no images, no sacrifice sites. They didn't have the god gene. There's a part of the human brain, the temporal lobe, that is associated with religious experiences as well as with epilepsy, and it's the same part that responds to electromagnetic stimulation with hallucinations, often of good or evil presences.

If Calum's paternal ancestors happened to have more than the usual share of Neanderthal genes – and one glance at him or his father was enough to raise the thought, even with a smile – then perhaps he was missing the god gene, and therefore the brain module that it usually built. His temporal lobe would be less likely than mine to respond to electromagnetic stimulation from a close encounter with a UFO – natural or artificial – with trances, dwams, hallucinations, moments of religious mania and strange, vivid dreams.

So far, so rational. I could have left it there. I should have. I didn't.

Instead, I worked out my own conspiracy theory in that obsessive couple of weeks. My very own paranoid explanation. My way to make sense of what had happened to me, and what hadn't happened to Calum.

It was this.

The DTH, it seemed to me, needed to be given another

twist, taken to another level. The twist was that if the US and its allies had aircraft and UAVs that stimulated the god module, then they must know that they did. They could hardly *not* know. And in that case, wasn't it possible that they didn't just write it down as a sometimes useful side effect, but they actively exploited it?

Perhaps having a UFO experience wasn't, by a long way, the commonest response to an encounter with a UFO. Over vast areas of the world, people who got an electromagnetic kick to the god module wouldn't meet *aliens*. They'd meet angels, or demons, or departed saints, or, for that matter, gods or God. These same vast areas were precisely the ones over which the US was striving to maintain its influence. Most of the opposition to that influence was articulated as religion where it wasn't articulated as godless communism. Quite possibly, having prophets and visionaries pop up with new and disruptive revelations in, say, Iran or China, was very much a win for the US.

Something similar might be going on, or at least being tried out, in the secular West. Right across Europe and North America, we'd supposedly been on the brink of revolution for as long as I could remember. Somehow we'd never gone over that brink, nor had we stepped – or been pulled – far back from it. The crisis had never been resolved. It just went on and on. The revolutionaries did their worst, and every now and then there would be riots or marches or general strikes, and then it all fizzled out until the next time.

What if the US and other Western governments were

experimenting with inducing religious and/or UFO experiences in their own populations? As a distraction, perhaps, or as a way of dividing their populations before they could unite against the endless depression? It seemed a risky tactic, I had to admit, but then so was arming jihadists, and they'd been doing that for decades, blowback be damned. The real beauty of my conspiracy theory was that it took the riskiness into account: some elements or factions within whatever agencies were behind this scheme were worried about the dangers of religious or cultist extremism, and were subtly subverting the project, perhaps by varying the electromagnetic effects to stimulate other parts of the brain than the god module.

That was why my encounter had induced a vision (rooted, perhaps, in my earlier speculations) of a Space Brother and a Space Sister in old style *Star Trek* uniforms with a message to match: rationality, science and secular humanism. They'd said that message was for me. For all I knew, they could be right. I might be the only one it had reached.

I suppose I already had a wish to believe, despite daily evidence to the contrary, that some at least of the rulers of the world were rational, knew what they were doing and meant well. I conjured a romantic image of a cabal of beleaguered liberal humanists under deep cover in the deep state, a secret band of brothers (and sisters) who strove to use their power for the greater good.

With the world to choose from, they had chosen me.

Why they would have chosen a sixteen-year-old schoolboy to be the great teacher of the stunning revelation that we needed no revelation was a question that, to my credit, gave me pause. Rather less to my credit, it didn't give me pause for long.

I figured they knew what they were doing.

That embarrassing conspiracy theory I mentioned earlier – elaborate, tenuously supported, self-centred and self-serving?

This isn't it.

9

Working out my own conspiracy theory took less time than you might expect, but more than I could afford in the run-up to my Highers. In the fortnight after the encounter, I stayed awake far too late every night, even after I'd gone to bed, exploring the endlessly branching warren of UFO rabbit holes on my phone. My nightly reimaginings of the sexual element of the abduction experience didn't help. Nor did the false awakenings, in which I relived the terrifying presence of the Grey in the room. The second Saturday after the encounter, I woke in mid-morning light to see a looming figure in the bedroom's shadowy doorway. For once, I wasn't immobilised by sleep paralysis. I sat bolt upright, hands out in front of my face, with a dry-throated scream. My mother yelped as she slopped the mug of hot tea she'd carried upstairs for me.

'What's the matter with you?' she asked, putting the mug on the table and dabbing at her wrist with a tissue.

'You woke me from a bad dream,' I said.

'Don't say that like it's my fault.'

'Sorry,' I mumbled. I sipped the tea. 'I didn't mean it that way.'

'Hmph! Just doing something nice for you, and I get yelled at. You scared me.'

'I didn't know it was you,' I said, sounding more whiny than I could stand.

She put her lips to her wrist as if to kiss herself better. 'I'll have to run this under a cold tap.'

Her steps sounded heavy on the stair-ladder. I sat in bed, hands around the mug, feeling sorry for myself, then got up. I spent the rest of the morning studying, and clomped down for Saturday lunch – another odd family habit – when my mother shouted up the stairs about one o'clock.

Marie was not long back from Glasgow for the weekend. My dad was in from the back garden, having picked the early greens that went into the pitta breads my mum had made and that lay steaming in a heap in the middle of the table by the potato and nettle soup tureen, fragrant with coriander. I mumbled hellos and munched away, keeping half an eye on the television above the fireplace. The sound was off and I followed the scrolling subtitles. Nothing much was going on in the world, I was relieved to see. Iranian terrorists had just wiped out a US patrol in Tehran. Heavy rain was forecast for the coming Tuesday. The fallout count was not expected to rise as a result. The Russian and US naval build-up in the Caribbean was the highest since the Cuban missile crisis; likewise in the North Sea, the Mediterranean and the Gulf, with French and British ships adding to the maritime traffic jam. The European Central Bank was into its second week of talks with the International Monetary Fund. There was going to be a general strike. The latest batch of exoplanets found had edged the known total to over ten thousand. I smiled to myself at the thought of US naval bases on scores of them. What could the Iranian resistance do about that?

'Honestly, Ryan!' my mum snapped.

I chewed and swallowed. 'What?'

'You didn't hear what I said?'

'Sorry, no.'

'I'm fed up with the way you're acting more and more like a lodger.' She glanced sideways at Dad, looking for support.

Dad nodded. 'You should make more of an effort, Ryan. You haven't seen Marie for a week and you haven't said a word to her.'

'Not that I'm complaining,' Marie said.

I ignored this.

'Sorry, Mum, what did you ask?'

'I asked what you're doing this afternoon.'

'A bit of revision,' I said.

'And this evening?'

I grimaced and laughed, shrugging. 'A bit more, I suppose.'

'No, you're not,' said Mum. 'This afternoon you're going to

help your father in the garden, and this evening you're going down to the Westender to meet your friends.'

I stared at her. 'Why? You're always telling me I need to buckle down and revise for my exams.'

'Yes, but not when you're turning pale and silent and sullen. You need to get out and relax a bit. You haven't even been out to share revision work for weeks.'

For two weeks, in fact, but I wasn't going to point that out.

'I thought you liked visiting Sophie's,' added my mum, with a sly look. 'You haven't even had your pal Calum drop by for ages.'

I met Calum at the bus terminus about eight. The evening sky was clear, its blue shading to lemon in the west. The forecast was for a dry summer. A drought summer. After tea my mother had insisted I have a hot shower, though I'd already had my weekly one on Thursday. If this was a consequence of helping my father in the garden of a Saturday I could get used to it. Clean faded jeans, fresh-pressed shirt, bomber jacket. Calum wore much the same but, as I recall, carried it better on his bigger frame.

'How're you doing, Sinky?'

'Aw, fine. You?'

He shrugged, falling in beside me as we headed for the covered shopping area at the town centre. 'No bad.'

Inside the roofed street, Calum grunted something and took a sharp right along a passage where all the windows

118

were boarded and half the lights were out. Discarded freesheets – the local *Greenock Telegraph*, the fashion weekly *Style/Content*, the revolutionaries' occasional *What Now?* – lay underfoot. Pigeons murmured on overhead pipework and pecked at insulation. Ads cycled through obsolete products, months-gone expos and cancelled gigs. Every camera lens had been spray-gunned. There was a stink of piss.

'Wait here,' he said, and disappeared around an even darker corner. Five minutes later he came back, looking jaunty. He half opened one side of his jacket to flash the top of a clear plastic bottle, then uncurled one hand to show a brace of inch-long, light brown cylinders, like cigarette cartridges.

'Sorted,' he said.

'I thought your brother got these for you.'

'They're no nicotine,' he said, sounding scornful. 'Pure hash oil, man.'

'Fuck,' I said. I hadn't known he toked.

'Naebody cares,' he said.

We returned to the main drag, bright windows or decent shutters, lights, background tracks, ghost wafts of perfume and bread. The Westender had been a pub before the drinking age went up to twenty-one (and later became a pub again, for the converse reason). In the interlude that so annoyingly coincided with the very years we could have benefited most, it was a café and juice bar, and the favoured hang-out of our peers.

Decor: brash. Lighting: bright. Ambient noise: loud conversation, music audible only as a beat. Smell: teenage sweat

119

overlaid by scent and deodorant; coffee, vanilla, coffee breath, an acetic tang of fruit juice.

I scanned the big main room as the doors swung shut behind us. Our own gang stood around a tall round table towards the back, near the dance room: Aiden, Ellie, Sophie, Matt, 'chelle and the rest. Sophie turned as we shouldered through the roar. For a second or two, from about ten feet away, I was caught in the full beam of her smile. She was more glam than I'd ever seen her: hair up, face made-up, dangly earrings. She wore a top that was either a short dress with a small flipped-out skirt or a long blouse with a big frill around the hips – the feature, I later learned, is called a peplum – over shiny black leggings and high platform shoes. Her silhouette matched that of the Space Sister in her flare-skirted *Star Trek* mini-dress so closely that I was hit between the eyes.

Her gaze locked with mine, her smile widened and lips parted a tiny but detectable increment, and I felt an immediate, autonomic jolt of lust for Sophie, out of the clear blue of a hitherto straightforward liking and admiration for a smart school-friend who happened to be a girl and pretty. Then her look flicked a fraction to the side and she stepped forward and greeted Calum with a hug. They swivelled together, arms around each other's waists, to face the familiar crew, leaving me to figure that I must be the last to learn they were an item, and to get them and myself drinks.

I returned from the bar with two iced coffees and a fruit-juice cocktail, and sat down with Calum on my left and – after she'd shifted sideways and patted a stool – 'chelle on my right.

120

She was in the year above and I didn't know her very well, though she was in our crowd.

'Anybody's drink too hot?' Calum asked, after a bit.

A chorus of ayes and yeses and exaggerated wincing sips. Calum produced the clear plastic bottle and unscrewed the top.

'Wee drop ae cold water, that's what we need.'

'Yeah! Good man, Duke!'

'To the rescue!'

'Capful each should be enough, I reckon,' said Calum, passing the items to Sophie. She did as instructed and passed them on. When they reached 'chelle she let the cap run over a little, and licked the tips of her forefinger and thumb afterwards. I poured more carefully, and returned the bottle to Calum, who replaced the cap and disappeared the evidence.

The hooch made little difference to the taste of my iced coffee, but I could feel the kick in my throat and the heat in my gut as the sip went down. A short while later, Calum remarked that the conversation was so lively somebody should take notes. He took what looked like a pen from his shirt pocket, unscrewed the barrel and screwed in one of the cartridges he'd bought. He put the pen back together and sucked on the tip, looking thoughtful, then passed it along. Sophie shook her head, so it went to Matt, then Aiden and Ellie and a couple of others. I watched as a smile followed it around the table, spreading like a shared secret that gave folk the giggles – the joke from the toke. 'chelle grimaced as she took the pen, then gave me a challenging look and took a long draw, then passed it to me while still holding her breath, face reddening by the second.

I turned the pen over in my fingers, and sipped now slushy coffee. I'd never so much as vaped before, let along toked. Vaping was then illegal at our age, toking illegal at any – but as Calum had implied, and immediate circumstances confirmed, enforcement was haphazard and lax. I didn't want to show myself up in front of 'chelle, a girl for whose opinion of me I'd hitherto had not the smallest regard. So I toked, taking small puffs with plenty of air on the side and between. Calum gave me an approving nod as I handed the pen back.

'You look like you know what you're doing, Sinky.'

I exhaled, slowly. 'Yeah, I should by now.' Having read so much about it, I didn't add.

'chelle (that really was how she spelled her name, with an apostrophe and lowercase 'c') had a sudden fit of coughing and laughing, and grabbed my elbow for support, and swung me around.

'So what's been eating you, Ryan?' she asked, head cocked. 'Havni seen you around for like ages.'

'Aw, just studying,' I said. 'Head down and that.'

'You're getting that peelly wally.'

'That's what my mum said.'

'Did she inaw? Gottae dae summin aboot it naw?'

'Aye, I suppose . . .'

I noticed Matt's and Aiden's ironic eyes across the table, and mentally told them to butt out.

'No way tae talk, Sinky,' said Matt, looking offended.

Amazing, I thought. Who knew that dope could give you telepathy? 'chelle, for some reason, laughed. She slid off her stool, dragging me.

'See's a bop, Ryan.'

I knocked back caffeinated and alcohol-laced slush, and let her haul me to the next room for a dance. The single on the speakers was something I forget. The floor wasn't crowded. We circled each other, my hands moving like slo-mo kung fu, then like giving origami instruction for the deaf. She wore something long, which she held off the floor in one hand, and with the other hand sliced and diced the bouncing air. Vapour and dry ice swirled in flickering fans of low-watt laser beams.

For a moment, though 'chelle was nice enough and cute in her way and giving me most encouraging smiles when our eyes caught, I heard a voice in my head saying, 'Yi fucking eejit Sinky, yi've got aff wi the wrang lassie!' It sounded like Calum, but that couldn't be right. Calum had got off with the right lassie as far as he was concerned, and it was just my bad luck that I'd been suddenly smitten with Sophie seconds before finding out she was with Calum. And 'chelle, it seemed, had decided to get off with me. Moreover, as we went on bopping she didn't seem the wrong lassie at all. The track ended. Trinity Valentine's first big smoochy slow-dance number came on, but we weren't anywhere near there yet, as we mutually acknowledged with a smile and a shrug. We went back to the table, had another drink enhanced from Calum's clear plastic bottle, and another puff from Calum's pen. Around

123

about ten 'chelle announced she had to get home, and I offered to walk with her.

Her family lived in one of the high flats up the back, and on the way there the lights went out. 'chelle took a wrong turning, and was lost, or so she said, and when I checked my phone I saw the net was down too, at least locally. I blamed the revolutionaries, on the basis of sheer probability. 'chelle took another turning, said she'd found the long way back, and then tugged me down a side street and into a close. She put her handbag on the ground, hitched up her long skirt to the waist and jumped me. She had her arms around my neck and her thighs clamping my hips and her heels behind my knees before I knew what was going on. I was unprepared, but she wasn't: she let go with one arm and pressed a condom into my hand. I felt her legs and lips and her warm, fast breathing but when I closed my eyes I saw Sophie's long legs and flippy flirty little skirt.

After that it was just a Bad First Sex Scene, though possibly more so for 'chelle than for me. Or more of the bad and less of the first, I don't know and I didn't ask. I walked her the rest of the way home, and we kissed each other good night beside the bin cupboards and bike racks, but though I saw her at school and around often enough after that she never mentioned our brief encounter again. I have no idea why she did it – did me – at all. I put it down to some kind of subconscious imperative on her part, explicable perhaps by genetic calculation – subverted by consciousness and a condom, but no less powerful for all that – to get herself pregnant before all the young men went off to the war. Some of the fifth year girls, perhaps less canny or more impulsive, actually did get pregnant around the same time. In those weeks of late spring and early summer we all felt the same way: febrile, unsettled, knowing something big was coming down but not knowing what, and defaulting to the usual catastrophes of sinister premonition. Or maybe 'chelle just wanted to get a shag in before the exams.

Anyway, that's how in one evening I lost my virginity and acquired a thing for bared or closely-clad legs and flared skirts imprinted by countless erotic re-imaginings of my encounter with the Space Sister and now locked in place by the grip of 'chelle's naked thighs and the memory of that sudden sexual sight of Sophie's silhouette and the electric shock of her smile.

Bare legs, short skirts – I ask you. Talk about bad timing.

PART TWO

10

The morning of my Modern Studies exam I checked the news with the vague thought that it might be useful for last-minute cramming and saw that all the big stock exchanges – Wall Street, the Dax, the Footsie, Cac 40, the Nikkei, Hang Seng, RTS and lots more – were closed for the day. The main headlines were about an urgent financial reform that had been rushed through legislatures – Congress, Senate, Diet, Dáil, Parliament, National People's Congress, whatever – in a rolling thunder of rubber stamps that had followed the sunset around the world the previous night and was now chasing the dawn. The new law was called the Howard-Minsky Act in the US and had likewise local names elsewhere – at Westminster, the Banking and Financial Services (Miscellaneous Provisions) Act, at Holyrood the same words in a different order – but reports and comments had converged on calling it the Big Deal. The details came across as numbingly technical even on the main news but the gist was explained as 'defusing a hidden time-bomb under the world economy'.

As this was the third time in as many years that an overnight crisis bill had been more or less globally passed, and just as comprehensively made no discernible difference to the flat-lining economy of said globe, I thought nothing of it and went off to school to face the two papers and an essay.

I walked out of the school just after three. The exam hadn't gone too badly, and it was my last. Unless I had to go back next year, I never had to set foot in the place again. I looked sidelong at the other released fifth years beside me and gave a whoop and started running. Others joined in. Most halted at the bus stop but I kept going, then slowed to a walk. At the Barr's Cottage junction there was more than the usual holdup – road works years incomplete, traffic lights permanently on the blink – and half a dozen people who looked like office workers were taking advantage of the delay by handing out freesheets to stuck drivers and random passers-by. As I drew closer I noticed an odd thing about the distributors: they all wore running shoes with their suits.

One of them shoved a paper in front of me. It was the latest issue of *What Now?*, the barely licit rag of the revolutionaries. The top half of the front page was:

THE BIG DEAL –
Who's buying?

I took it, startled and curious, and was about to say something cutting when the guy I'd taken it from looked past me and stuck his fingers in his mouth and whistled. The running shoes came into their own as the revolutionaries scarpered, scattering in all directions, chucking handfuls of their papers into the air to come down in fluttering flocks as they fled. A siren and a blue light came a minute later, and a minute too late to catch anyone. By then I was a hundred metres further on, stealing glances at the front page.

I stuffed it in my pocket as another patrol car went past. When I got home I tore off my tie, made tea, and took the mug and the paper to my bedroom table. The lower half of the page, laid out in successive solid blocks of small print, began:

Not us, that's for sure. It's not that we think it won't work. It will work – if we let it. Nationalising the banks and privatising everything that isn't nailed down has worked before, and it'll work again. It worked in China, and it'll work here.

If we let it.

The next hours and days are critical. This is a moment of weakness for the bosses and their system. They've been forced to lop off what they see as the cancer of finance capital – and with it, a big slice of the ruling class itself.

The aim of this high-risk operation is to save the patient, not kill it. In the long run – not so long, for us – the system will get back on its feet. A good thing, you might think, until you remember on whose shoulders those feet will be standing. State capitalism may solve some of our problems. All sorts of schemes of participation and democracy may be tried out to tie us in to it. Some will even call the result socialism, and rail against it or rally to it. We'll all learn better eventually. Why not now? Do we really have to go through all this one more time?

For the moment – for days, for weeks at the most – capitalism is in intensive care, kept alive by the state machine. This is our chance to strike. We don't necessarily mean walking off the job. Instead, let's walk on the job – and stay there. Let's talk to our workmates, our colleagues, our neighbours, and decide what to do.

It's not difficult. We have the numbers. We know the drill.

If you think you don't know the drill, take a look inside.

And I did, appalled. It hadn't crossed my mind that the Big Deal would make any more of a difference than previous emergency measures had. From what little I knew of the revolutionaries, I might have expected them to decry it for that very reason. To see them argue that it would work and that the best hope was to cause so much disruption that it would fail struck me as monstrously perverse. How could such people have, as they claimed, the best interests of everyone, or at any rate the majority, at heart? It seemed to confirm the conventional view of their cynicism, and that they indeed held that 'the worse it gets, the better'.

Almost despite myself, I found the reports and think-pieces intriguing, and I wanted to find out more of whatever ideology lay behind them. There I drew a blank. There wasn't a website address on any of the pages. No physical address either, which didn't surprise me, but – not so much as a PO Box? I searched online and found plenty of sites about the revolutionaries, but none by them. Weird, I thought, but then realised it made a strange kind of sense: word of mouth communication, face-to-face organisation, and distribution by hand of printed paper all kept their activities off the net, and thus below the radar of the state's search engines and algorithms, imposing the higher costs of face-recognition trawls through surveillance-camera recordings, and no doubt also of police shoe leather, the wages of agents and infiltrators, the slush funding of bribery and blackmail . . .

The front door opened and closed. I hid the paper at the back of a bookshelf and went downstairs. My mother had just dropped her shoulder-bag on the table and sat down. She looked tired.

'How did it go?' she asked.

'All right,' I said. 'I think.'

'Modern Studies,' she said. 'I should bloody hope so.'

'Well, yes,' I said.

'So that's it over.'

'Yes,' I said. 'Yay! Freedom!' I put my hands behind my head and leaned back, closing my eyes and stretching.

'No doubt,' Mum said, dryly. 'Meanwhile, I could really do with a cup of tea. And when you've done that, there's nettles out the back need cutting for this week's soup.'

I took the hint.

While working away with the pruning knife and my dad's leather gardening gloves with the holes at two fingertips that I had to be wary about, I found myself turning the revolutionaries' bulletin over in my head. I was at the age when you don't just dismiss anything you read that you disagree with or that questions your view of things. That's an adult skill, which most people find all too easy to acquire. No, I had to take it seriously, to try to fit it in with what I already knew about the world or – if that proved impossible – revise what I knew. All very scientific.

The very scientific hypothesis that I came up with was that, if the revolutionaries were right and the Big Deal really was a big deal, then I was right about the secret cabal of rational people inside the US Government and/or the global ruling class. The same people who had planted the rationalist message in my head had taken over – or at least (because, I told myself sternly, I had to be cautious here, and not let my imagination run away with me or anything like that) had their policies adopted. That they couldn't be all-powerful, I understood. I knew enough about the seductive nonsense of conspiracy theories to dismiss as ridiculous any thought of Bilderbergers or Illuminati or some such pulling the strings.

I took my bundle of nettles into the kitchen. My mother was by the cooker, minding a large pot of water coming to the boil while watching the news on her phone.

'Look at this,' she said.

In Monaco, French soldiers tramped along boulevards. Belgian tanks nosed through back streets in Luxembourg. US marines, laden with kit, splashed ashore on Bermudan beaches, parachuted into Panama. Royal Marines stormed St Kitts and blockaded St Vincent. The Russians had landed in Dubai.

'What's going on?' I asked, alarmed. 'Is it the war?'

Mum snorted. 'Not exactly. Just a crackdown on tax havens. Every last one, except Switzerland.'

'Why Switzerland?'

'Read up on Swiss defence policy,' she said, peering into the pot. She looked up as I reached for my phone. 'Not now. Give the nettles a rinse.'

A lot of things happened that summer. Some of them were connected, but I was too busy joining my own dots at the time to see the lines. I passed all my Highers, and was offered a place at Edinburgh University – on the BA course because, rather to my surprise, I did much better in English, History, French and Modern Studies than I did in Maths and Science. Calum applied for and got a place at Strathclyde, in Aerospace Engineering and Business Studies. In the meantime, I'd taken a summer job – several short-term openings had come up, for the first time in five years, in the local supermarket. Marie received a letter from the student loan company, informing her that her loan was suspended but that she should apply for a grant instead. She almost had to look the word 'grant' up in the dictionary. I applied to the new funding authority and got a student grant for my first year.

There was uproar, rising as far as riots in London, over the Golden Parachute scandal: the government had handed out billions to top banking and financial executives, by way of compensation for losing their jobs or taking a massive pay cut – an offer conspicuous by its non-occurrence in millions of earlier cases of rather less well-paid workers who'd had to make the same choice, when they'd had a choice in the matter at all. My mother came home early one Wednesday evening in August, to report that the soup kitchen and the refugee centre had almost run out of people to help. The old container port was about to re-open, and every able-bodied person, including illegals, had been offered a job clearing the place up, and the definite possibility of work at the port when it got going. My parents got a letter from the building society, informing them that the mortgage payments had been over-calculated for decades, and the loan had in fact been paid off five years earlier. The overpayments had been credited to their joint bank account.

The gigantic Firth of Clyde Tunnel construction project was announced, and the consortium began hiring immediately. The abandoned computer factory on Inverkip Road was retooled and reopened as a biotech plant, and required in the first instance hundreds of unskilled workers, all of whom had the prospect of training for technical work over the next couple of years as production came on stream. Thousands more got employment on what were called upgrade projects: the high school, for example, was refurbished entirely over the summer, a railway line reopened, and the parks regenerated. Retired, disabled, or part-time workers were in huge demand for information collection, machine supervision and auxiliary tasks. Those still on various doles and schemes suddenly found their money went further, as prices and rents unaccountably began to drop. Small businesses opened or re-opened all over the place. The smell of burning tyres left the air, to be replaced by that of fresh-poured concrete. And that was how it was in Greenock.

If you're old enough, you remember. It was much the same where you were.

At the Freshers' Fair I joined the Humanist Society, the SF Society, the Geology Society and the Archaeology Society, then wandered along the stalls. There were a lot of cultural societies for overseas students, and a slightly smaller number of wildly diverse religious societies among which the Union of Muslim Students and the Christian Union looked like voices of moderation. At each I helped myself to armfuls of free literature, nodded politely, and strolled on. I did the same at the stalls of the few political societies for the mainstream parties, and at those for two or three left-wing groups, whose stalls stocked Marxist literature that had long outlasted the states in which it had been printed and whose stall-keepers hawked tabloid newspapers with red mastheads and big black headlines like **FIGHT THE CUTS!** and **GENERAL STRIKE NOW**. The sellers looked as bemused as I felt. I picked up some dusty Marx pamphlets and – cheaper and more useful for my coursework – a shiny memory stick of the Marx and Engels *Collected Works*.

At the very end of the row of tables was one with a stack of copies of *What Now?* and a heap of memory sticks. A young guy in the now predictable smart suit and tie stood behind it, flicking through his phone with a bored expression. I looked down at the front page:

GOODBYE, AND GOOD LUCK

We failed.

The crisis is over. The revolutionary moment has passed. Power has shifted from financial to industrial capital. The working class, atomised by generations of neoliberalism, has turned down its fleeting but real chance to make a bid for power. Although the free market in labour power has not been restored, the decades-long campaign to do so has pushed down wages and social provisions to a level compatible with industrial profit. A new cycle of accumulation has begun, and with it a new upsurge of the capitalist economy, at the expense of further distortions of the market. The new boom may be expected to last one decade at least, probably more, before it in turn goes into crisis. Just as radioactive decay passes through a series of unstable isotopes, some of which may last some time, so does a declining system. We never claimed to know in advance the half-life of capital.

No revolutionary organisation can outlive the revolutionary situation. If it tries to do so, it becomes at best a caricature of itself, at worst counter-revolutionary. Almost all previous revolutionary organisations have made this mistake. We do not intend to repeat it.

This is the final edition of *What Now?* The question posed by the title remains, but the answer has to change. What the former revolutionaries can do now is learn the lessons of the past few years, and analyse, without illusions, the present as it unfolds in order to prepare the struggles of the future. To do that, they need full freedom of thought, discussion and action, not the discipline of the revolutionary organisation, which is hereby dissolved.

If you want to find us, don't come looking. We'll find you.

And so we say goodbye . . .

UNTIL NEXT TIME

I picked up a copy of the paper.

'Uh . . .'

The guy transferred his attention from the phone to me. He still looked bored.

'Yes?'

'That's not true, is it?'

'What?'

'About the revolutionaries not being able to outlive the revolutionary situation. The Russian revolutionaries failed in 1905, and the Chinese revolutionaries were nearly wiped out in 1927, but they kept going, didn't they? And they won.'

If I'd expected this snippet of Higher-level Modern Studies wisdom to impress him, I'd have been disappointed.

'If you call *them* revolutionaries and *that* winning,' he said. 'Anyway, the *conditions* for revolution still existed in both cases. These societies remained in crisis. This one' – he waved a hand around – 'not so much.'

'You really think the Big Deal's going to work?'

'It's already working.' He made it sound like an answer to a very stupid question. 'It's what Gramsci called passive revolution. The revolutionaries failed to unite enough people around them to overthrow the system, but the crisis didn't go away. Society was at an impasse. The *necessity* for revolution didn't go away. So the ruling groups are going to carry out some of the necessary changes, which together add up to as much of a revolution as is compatible with their remaining in power. A revolution from above, that keeps the people at the top *at* the top. The reforms add up to what most people who *said* they wanted a revolution really hoped for from a revolution. Peace, jobs for all, green tech, saving the planet . . . all that sort of thing. It's a lot less than what we wanted, but it'll stave off the revolution for another generation. We're snookered.'

'So you lot are – just going to go away?'

'No point hanging about, is there?'

'I guess not,' I said, still puzzled.

He nodded down at the stack of papers. 'I'm not kidding. This is my last gig for the revo. Take a copy while you can, because you won't see any again. Consider it a collectable.'

'How much is it?'

'It's free, as always.' He shrugged. 'The memory sticks have the complete run. Help yourself.'

'Thanks.' I stuck a stick in my pocket and the paper in my Student Union freebie bag.

'Have you read it before?' he asked, as I straightened.

'Once or twice.'

'What did you think of it?'

'Not a lot. It just seemed a bit, you know, negative.'

He snorted, but said nothing. His continuing bored expression goaded me.

'Still,' I said, 'it's something to admit the revolutionaries are going out of business.'

His expression changed from boredom to pity.

'"Out of business"?' he jeered. 'We're going *into* business.' He returned his attention to his phone.

'OK, well, bye,' I said.

He didn't look up. 'Until next time.'

I was down the stairs and out on the rain-wet cobbles of the Pleasance before I thought of the perfect parting shot. I played the dialogue in my head.

'So you're offski,' I would have said.

'What?' he'd have replied, still supercilious, but with a dawning suspicion.

'Offski. You know, the famous Russian revolutionary?'

Well, it made me laugh. You had to be there. Except I wasn't.

11

I was sitting in the Library Bar, marking paragraphs of extracted Derrida in the *Norton Theory* on my phone, turning half the screen a provisional yellow between lunch and the 4 p.m. seminar. The room's furnishing was exactly what you'd expect from its name: old books on shelves behind glass around the walls; seats, benches and tables, niches and nooks, a big bar with carved posts and a fret-worked canopy. Mercy Fuck's 'Warriston Crematorium' on the PA, for like the hundredth time. Someone sat down beside me. I saw, out the corner of my eye, legs in black leggings visible through a thin pale pleated skirt that went down to the ankles of likewise visible long black boots.

'Oh, hi, Ryan.'

I looked sideways. A bonny lassie in a black leather jacket, half turning to face me, a glass of orange juice in her hand.

Her hair was deep black, crinkly and long. Eye make-up. Musky perfume.

'Sophie! Oh, heck, I didn't recognise you for a sec.'

She smiled. 'It's been two years.'

'Aye. Jeez. How're you doing? What are you doing?'

'Fashion and Fabric Technology at the College of Arts,' she said.

'Hence the, uh . . .'

'Stylish look? Yes.' She flicked her hair.

'I always thought maths was more your thing,' I said.

'Oh, I'm doing that too,' she said. 'I'm over at Informatics today.'

'Must be quite a disconnect.'

'Oh, they're connected,' she said. 'It's the new materials.'

'New materials?'

'Look.' She took out her phone and flicked to a catwalk show. Models did their bold bouncing stride in frocks so elaborately flounced, embroidered and embellished that they looked like those seahorses that mimic seaweed. Colours flashed from jewels, flowed through fabrics and glowed around edges. The music changed and suddenly the models did front-flips and cartwheels and rolls, then sprang up – ruffles, so to speak, unruffled – and sashayed off to applause.

'Hmm,' I said. 'Not very practical.'

Sophie plucked at a pleat. 'I made this with an offcut.'

She stuck out a foot and tipped a gulp's worth of orange juice on her skirt, splashing it down her shin. The fabric

144

soaked it up, unstained. She wiped the glass on the side of her knee to mop the dribble, with the same result.

'Practical, yes?'

'Uh-huh.'

'This is going to be big. I'm thinking of going into the biz, maybe do an MBA after I graduate. And I'm fine. Enjoying uni. What about you?'

'English, Sociology and Philosophy,' I said. 'I did Geology as an extra last year.'

'I meant, how are you?'

I leaned forward and took a sip of cold black coffee to hide my reluctance to tell her the embarrassing truth. I was miserable, and I had no right to be. I knew I should be happy. The only rational reason I had for being unhappy was the dreams, the nightmares and false awakenings, and the occasional full-on alien abduction experience. I knew they were unreal but it wasn't helping my sleep. No amount of reading refutations and arguing about the paranormal and the supernatural with any of their proponents who crossed my path seemed to make any difference. Apart from that, I knew I had nothing to complain about.

'I'm fine,' I said. 'I'm sharing a decent wee flat near Tollcross with two engineering students who I don't see much of anyway, I go home about once a month, I get enough fresh air and exercise on excursions with the Geo Soc and the Archaeology Soc, and I go to the Humanist Soc sometimes and the SF Soc and Skeptics in the Pub for drinks and chat and that, and I've got plenty of time to study, so I'm doing all right in the assessments . . .'

Sophie regarded me with amused, half-lidded eyes. 'That bad, huh?'

I had to laugh. 'I know it doesn't sound very exciting,' I said, 'but I'm doing what I want.'

She looked away, then back. Maybe she frowned a little in between. 'What *do* you want?'

'What do you mean?'

'You haven't said anything about your social life so, OK, you're busy studying – fine, I can see that, but what's also a bit revealing is you haven't said anything about what you're studying *for*.'

'Well, you didn't ask,' I said, trying not to sound as if she'd touched on a sore point. 'I'm studying for a humanities degree.'

'And then?'

I shrugged. 'Go for a PhD in philosophy, then further research if I can get a position and the funding. If all else fails, get a proper job.'

Sophie gave me an impatient look over the rim of her glass. 'What are your *dreams*, Ryan?'

'Dreams? Jesus!' I flailed. I had a moment of horrible suspicion that Calum had told her about my abduction experience. I could feel myself blushing, to my shame. 'I mean, what the fuck kind of question is that? A bit personal, isn't it?'

'I'm not asking about your *wet* dreams, Ryan,' she said, witheringly, not at all taken aback by my vehemence, unembarrassed and unamused by my embarrassment. 'I'm asking – what are your ambitions? What do you want to achieve in life?'

146

Aye, there was the rub.

'Oh, that,' I said. 'Well apart from all the usual personal stuff I want to be a humanist philosopher.'

I fully expected Sophie to laugh in my face. A *humanist? Philosopher? You?*

She looked puzzled. 'Why humanist? I mean, isn't that a bit wishy-washy? Like a sort of none-of-the-above thing?'

'No . . . well, yes, it is a bit. But it doesn't have to be. Think what we could be like if we took our real situation seriously.'

'This is the only life we have, and all that?'

'Yes, that, sure,' I said, 'but more important I think is to take seriously that we're just at the beginning of history, that humanity might well have millions of years still to come. We've just about got over the idea from the Bible that we've only had a short past, a few thousand years, right?'

'Half the Americans haven't got over it,' Sophie pointed out. 'Plus there are lots of Muslims who seem to be taking it up.'

'Tell me about it,' I said, laughing. 'Look at this.'

I swung my rucksack onto my lap and hauled out a small stack of books and pamphlets, which I flicked through to show Sophie how I used them: a battered, black-bound, copy of the Authorized Version of the Bible, with verses I'd highlighted and annotated in four different colours of ink to cross-reference contradictions, unfulfilled prophecies, absurdities, and atrocities; Marmaduke Pickthall's translation of the Koran, in which I'd been careful to mark pages only with variously coloured tabs; a paperback *Origin of*

Species, with the passages marked that were most often truncated in creationist quote-mangling; several copies each of booklets from the Royal Society and the National Academy of Sciences, explaining evolution and the age of the Earth in the simplest possible terms for the benefit of creationists; *The Counter-Creationism Handbook*, conveniently indexing and debunking creationist claims; and a few other books and pamphlets doing the same for alternative medicine and UFOs.

'I've got lots of similar stuff on memory sticks too,' I added, reaching to the bottom of my bag and fishing out a fistful. 'Quite often when I'm arguing with Christian Union or Islamic Society types they'll take a memory stick when they won't take a pamphlet.'

Sophie looked at me somewhat askance. 'You do a lot of this?'

'Well . . . I stop by the stall on my way to lunch, sometimes. Or when these people turn up at Humanist events, it's always good to have refutations handy.'

'Seems a bit of an . . . odd hobby.'

'Maybe it is,' I said. 'Anyway, it isn't my main thing. Like I was saying, my point is that even people who've got over the idea of a short past are still stuck in the idea of a short future, which also comes from Christianity – from the opposite end of the Bible, in fact, from Revelation. That we're living in the End Times. We just have secular versions of it, like global-warming catastrophe or nuclear war or the final crisis of capitalism all being imminent in this century.'

Sophie smiled. 'Some might say there are good reasons to think any or all of them are.'

'Yes, but—'

She raised a hand. 'Wait. I think I need a coffee.'

'I'll . . .' I half rose.

'No, I'll,' she said, waving a card. 'You?'

'Black, no sugar.'

'OK. Mind my bag.'

While she waited at the bar I looked her up on my phone. She had an open-ended CV on a network that consisted of everyone else doing the same – brusque and business-like; a photo album of dress-design sketches, family and landscape pics, with the odd close-up of architectural detail; and the usual Splatter trail of thousands of cryptic remarks. I wasn't surprised: like me and most of the more thoughtful of our cohort, she'd evidently acquired from older, sadder and wiser relatives an early wariness about online self-exposure. Were she and Calum still a couple? I didn't know, and her online footprint showed no traces either way. I could have asked her, but it would have felt awkward.

Something buzzed past my ear as I put away my phone. My head jerked reflexively and I saw a camcopter the size of a bee, hovering above the next table for a second or two, then darting away above the bar and zooming out of the open door to the patio. I saw an arm swipe above a head, heard a laugh. Usually the little buggers moved too fast to see properly, let alone to swat. In the glass tower of Informatics, no doubt, some engineering student was having a laugh.

Sophie returned, balancing cups on saucers. She sat down with them still in her hands, in a smooth movement that vaguely disturbed me because I found it sexy and because it reminded me of the actions of the mysterious minister.

'You were saying. Millions of years?'

'Billions,' I said. 'In fact, it's more than that. Trillions. Look. We all know there's a deep past, right? But we're still thinking about it in the wrong way. Stephen J. Gould or somebody' – I resisted the impulse to look it up – 'came up with a nice image for the past. Do you ever smooth your nails?'

She waggled her fingers and gave me a look.

'OK. If you were to stand on tiptoe or' – I glanced at her boots – 'in high heels, say, and stretch up your arm as high as you could above your head, and we take that as representing the age of the Earth, then you sit down, I guess, and take the end of the nail of your middle finger and give it one swipe across with the, uh . . .'

'Emery board?'

'Yes. Then you've just wiped out what on that scale is the whole of human history.'

'Cool,' Sophie said, leaning forward and blowing on her coffee. 'Sort of puts things in perspective.'

'That's the idea, yes,' I said. 'Or there's the other example with the whole four and a half billion years represented by a twenty-four-hour clock, and our history is all in the last second or the last tick or whatever. But that's all wrong. I mean, it's right as far as it goes, but what people usually take from it is like "Oh, we're so insignificant!", because they forget what it leaves out.'

'Ah!' Sophie said. 'Yes! It leaves out the scale of the changes we've made.'

I was momentarily thrown. I hadn't thought of that.

'That's a very good point,' I said. 'But it wasn't the one I was thinking of. What the tippy-toes and the clock things leave out is *the future*. All the ages to come, in the immense future of the universe. That's the real deep time, and on that scale four point five billion years is a very small thing.'

Sophie laughed. 'So we're even *more* insignificant!'

'No, no,' I said. 'Don't you see? We're just at the beginning of things. There's no reason why we couldn't – as a species and as our successors, whatever they are, machines even – survive into a very distant future and affect it.'

'But we're so small.'

'Yes,' I said. 'But . . . but, look' – I was waving my arms, I was trying not to raise my voice – 'the scale of the universe is so unimaginably immense, in space as well as in time, and in all that we're the only thing that even knows it's there. There this . . . this enormous, practically endless expanse of mindless matter doing its meaningless thing, gas contracting and fusing and exploding and all that, over and over, and here we are, a tiny, almost infinitesimal flaw in it all. A tiny, tiny crack of meaning and purpose and mind in an endless plane of meaninglessness. In fact, a crack is . . . You know what happens when a single atom is out of place in a crystal?'

151

'Yes,' said Sophie, with the look of someone trying hard not to laugh. 'I'm doing materials, remember? Any force that's applied to the crystal gets concentrated on that atom, and soon there's another atom out of place, and so it goes on. That's how cracks get started. And once they start, they propagate. That's how scissors work and fabric rips.'

'Exactly,' I said.

'I don't see what this has to do with our significance.'

'Well,' I said, 'if even one atom out of place in a sheet of glass, say, can end up cracking the whole pane, just because we're small doesn't mean we can't have big effects.'

'You want us to crack the universe?'

'Yes,' I said. 'Or maybe, thinking about it as fabric, cut it into a shape more suited to ourselves.'

Sophie's cup rattled as she put it down. 'I see where you're going with this,' she said, looking me intently in the eye. 'If there are all these billions of years and lives to come – my God! It's like God! If you weigh it up like that greatest happiness of the greatest number thing—'

'Utilitarianism?'

'Yeah, OK, if we were to count in the happiness of future people, and we do . . . Jesus fuck.'

'What?' I said, slightly shocked. I'd never heard her swear.

'It means anything we do to make sure humanity survives into this far future is right, no matter what so long as it works. Jeez.' Her smile glowed, as if from the back-light of trillions of happy future faces in the sky. 'I mean, even if ninety-nine per cent of the human race got wiped out, as long as there were enough left to have all these descendants, it would be worth it.'

'No, no!' I said, alarmed. 'I wasn't thinking that at all, you can't go sacrificing lives in the present for the sake of the future—'

'But we do,' she said. 'Well, states do. All the millions the US and UK and their allies killed in the war – all right, most of them not directly, so let's say caused to die if you want to be picky – and all the thousands of their soldiers who died, it's all justified in terms of reduced infant mortality and increased life expectancy and girls in school and women with jobs and cars and all that, right?'

'Are you winding me up?'

'It's what you believe, right?'

'Well, not—'

'You supported the war, didn't you?'

I had, much to my embarrassment and shame now. I couldn't even blame my parents: they'd always been opposed to it, in a passive, resigned way that had annoyed me and provoked me to my mid-teen pro-war pose. Only now, as a result of supplementary reading around my Sociology and Philosophy courses – the Ethics module had been gruesomely specific on torture, terrorism and the supposed justifications for both – had I come to see how deep and bloody was the pit from which we had so recently begun to climb.

'Oh come on,' I said. 'I was just a kid.'

'Fine,' she said. 'So what's your mature, considered view?'

I shrugged. 'Now that it's all over? I don't know. I wouldn't justify it in these terms anyway. Maybe self-defence—'

153

She laughed in my face.

'Let me *finish*,' I said, testily. 'That was how it was officially justified in the beginning – against nuclear and chemical and terrorist threats and so on. All I'm saying is that if they'd been telling the truth, they'd have had a point. All the humanitarian justifications came *after* it turned out they weren't.'

'All the same,' Sophie said, 'that's how it's justified now, isn't it? And the Second World War, too. So I'm not going out on a limb about how your idea about humanity's vast and glorious future might let us off all sorts of moral hooks now.' She gave a wry smile. 'Even if that justification turns out to be only made after the fact.'

'Yes, you are,' I said, feeling more secure. 'Out on a limb. Honest, Sophie, you've got even utilitarianism all wrong. Well, maybe first-order . . .' I stopped and sighed at the thought of re-treading the first-year Ethics module. 'Anyway, look, the point is—'

'No,' said Sophie. 'You look, and let me tell you what my point is, OK, Ryan?'

'Yeah, yeah, I'm not—'

She took off her black leather jacket with a sinuous shrug and leaned forward a little, a movement that set the shiny material of her sleeveless top quivering. I made a polite and belated effort to keep looking at her in the face, which was itself fascinating enough, her dark-outlined eyes bright.

'The question I asked to start with,' she said, 'is what you want to achieve in life. You haven't answered that and to be honest I think you're evading it. I mean, all this stuff about the glorious future of humanity is all well and good but what's it got to do with the future of you?'

She said all this in a light, friendly tone. I found myself frowning, and opening and closing my mouth a couple of times.

'Well, all right,' I said at last. 'It's . . . important to me because . . . everything we do or don't do matters a heck of a lot because we're at the beginning of things, the ground floor so to speak, the foundation or maybe just the hole in the ground. And we've got all that responsibility – it's terrifying. But instead of living up to it and realising we're building this vast civilisation and maybe making ourselves fit to be part of it, whether we live into it or not, we're still squabbling about stupid shit like whether evolution happened or the climate is changing or which religion if any is true and so on.'

'No, we're not,' said Sophie. 'That's just the bloody nonsense of American electoral politics and in countries where Islamism is still a problem. Religion just doesn't come up anywhere else, and certainly not here, apart from a minority of students. So why does arguing about it matter to you?'

By now it was mid-afternoon. The coffee was cold, the Library Bar had gone quiet.

'Well,' I said, feeling painfully self-conscious, 'I think religion and cults and so on are being artificially stimulated in a very deliberate way to distract people from the economic crisis and all that. And I think my . . . what I want to do is fight that, help make people see what is really going on.'

'Artificially stimulated?' Sophie looked interested. 'How?'

'I think some of the UFO phenomena are secret aircraft

and UAVs and so on, and that they have some kind of electrical effects that stimulate the temporal lobes – the parts of the brain that can give people religious experiences.'

She just stared at me. 'That seems a bit . . . far-fetched,' she said, in a tone that suggested she was keeping careful control of her voice. 'And a bit redundant as an explanation, seeing as the social and psychological reasons why some people have these weird beliefs and experiences are . . . pretty much well understood, you know?'

'Uh, yeah, but—'

'And anyway,' she added, 'even if it *is* happening, what makes you think *you* can do anything about it – by arguing with spotty-faced fundy students at stalls on your way to lunch?'

I opened my mouth, then closed it again. I didn't know what to say.

This wasn't because I didn't have an answer. I had one, right on the tip of my tongue. It was this: because the Space Brother and the Space Sister told me.

Don't get me wrong – I knew very well that the Space Brother and the Space Sister were figments of my imagination. But my private explanation of those figments seemed, now that I was on the verge of uttering it, even more bizarre: they were planted there by a secret faction of the rational elements of the secret rulers of the world.

Jesus H fucking Christ, I thought. My one-man mission to promote rational thought against religion, pseudoscience and the paranormal was rooted in a UFO encounter, a single vivid dream that still seemed real in a way my frequent nightmares and abduction experiences didn't, a phone-camera pic alleg-edly of a page in a conveniently inaccessible book, and a conspiracy theory that curled up and died on my lips out of sheer embarrassment the moment I found myself about to expound it.

Suddenly the whole thing stank with the squalor of the occult.

'Well, now that you mention it,' I said, with a half laugh that I hoped sounded self-deprecating, 'it does seem a bit disproportionate, doesn't it? And my UFO theory – well, it's not just mine, and I think it's worth looking into, but you do have a point. I mean, if something like that was going on, the best thing I could do would be to encourage people to wear tinfoil hats.'

'Tinfoil hats,' Sophie said. 'Yes, that just about sums it up!'

'Oh, well,' I said. 'Fancy another coffee? Let me get it this time.'

Sophie shook her head. 'Nah, thanks, but I've got a lecture in half an hour, and I need to nip into the library first.'

'Aw, right. I owe you one, then.'

She shrugged into her jacket and gathered up her bag and books. Just before she left she turned to me and said, 'You look after yourself, Ryan, OK?'

'OK,' I said.

'I mean that,' she said. 'Look after *yourself*. Stop worrying about saving the human race. Get a bit better acquainted with a few more of its members, right?'

'Right,' I said. 'I see what you mean.'

What she'd said sounded like good advice. It would be easier to take than most such, because she'd just pulled the rug from under my entire sense of purpose in life.

She looked at me quizzically for a second or two, blinked, shook her head slightly, then smiled and left, leaving a faint trace of her scent and a nagging sense of a missed opportunity and a missed point. Had she been suggesting that I get better acquainted with her? For a minute or two I contemplated running after her, catching up with her before she'd walked the hundred metres to the library, and asking her . . . what? Out for a drink? And what if she turned me down? And what if she were still with Calum? And what if . . .? By the time I'd war-gamed the possibilities in my head, the moment for the action in reality had passed.

I looked at my watch. The time was a quarter to four. I had a seminar on *Middlemarch* at four in the David Hume Building, less than five minutes' walk away. I had made extensive notes for it on my phone.

Fuck you, George Eliot, I thought. I needed time to think. I strolled to the bar and ordered a double single malt.

'Let me get that,' said a voice behind my shoulder. 'And the same for me, please.'

I turned, and saw a man a few years older than myself wearing a black suit with an open-necked blue denim shirt.

'Good to see you again, Ryan,' he said, sticking out his hand. As I shook it, he grinned and added, 'You look a little perplexed. Perhaps you don't remember me.'

'Oh, I remember you all right, Reverend Baxter,' I said.

12

'Call me James,' said the man in black.

He waved a card to pay, and took his turn with the glass jug of water, tipping a careful quarter measure into the double. Then he fingered a cigarette packet from his pocket and nodded towards the door to the patio.

'Shall we?'

'I'll just get my bag,' I said.

I stuffed the books into the backpack, feeling his eye on me as if he could see every scornful, sceptical scribble in the margins of my King James.

The patio was below ground level, a long draughty roof-less room furnished with rough, weather-greyed wooden benches, rougher tables, rusty umbrella poles and dusty saplings. Tiny camcopters hovered and darted like un-seasonal wasps. I followed Baxter to a vacant table and sat down opposite him, taking care to be on the side of the exit steps in the far corner.

He raised his glass. '*Sláinte.*'

'*Sláinte.*' I sipped.

He lit up, keeping his gaze fixed on me through the Zippo flare and the first puff.

'I reckon I owe you an apology,' he said.

'What for?'

'The last time I met you,' he said, meditatively blowing smoke in my general direction, 'I was extraordinarily rude and gauche, even for a newly ordained minister.'

'Were you really a minister?' I asked.

He raised his eyebrows.

'Indeed I was,' he said, with a sort of forced joviality that in itself almost vouched for his claim, 'and I still am, despite having got rid of the dog-collar, for which relief much thanks! That's because, in fact, I'm the Church of Scotland chaplain here. Why do you ask?'

'Because the local churches had no trace of you, and neither did the Church of Scotland.'

'You checked up on me?' He sounded amused, as well as bemused.

'Yes,' I said. 'As soon as you were out the door.'

He waved a hand. 'Go ahead then – check up on me again.'

I did. I went to the university website on my phone, and there he was.

'This isn't what happened last time,' I said, looking up.

'Oh dear,' he said. 'I can see how that might have been a

bit disturbing, especially in the, ah, troubled conditions of three years ago. I can only assume there was some problem with the Church's websites – apart from the revolutionaries and all their monkey business back then, I know for a fact that our IT was, and still is come to think of it . . . well, pretty much what you'd expect from an outdated institution in terminal decline.'

'That's what you think the Church is?'

'Oh yes,' he said. 'It's dying on its feet. That's not just my opinion – it's the conclusion of the Church and Society Council's report to this year's General Assembly.' He gestured vaguely over his shoulder, I guessed towards the Mound about half a mile away, where the Church held its annual synod. 'Plenty more where that came from. Anyway, that's what I wanted to talk to you about.'

'Talk to me?'

'Yes,' he said, stubbing out his cigarette and lighting another. 'In fact, I came into the bar especially to have a word with you half an hour ago, but you seemed to be deep in conversation, so I bought myself a pint and waited.' He smiled knowingly. 'I thought it best not to interrupt. Nice girl, by the looks of her. Close friend of yours?'

'I knew her at school,' I said, irritated. 'Have you been keeping an eye on me, or what?'

He waved his hands cross-wise. 'Not at all, not at all. Your name came back to me, from an argument you had with a student who later came to me in some confusion. And of course I remembered you from Greenock. You were such an intense young man that you were hard to forget, especially since the recollection was so embarrassing to me. Smoking in the sitting room, accepting a cup of instant coffee as if I didn't have a clue what it cost in those days. And now, here on campus . . .' He shrugged. 'You've built up quite the reputation – pillar of the Humanist Society, eloquent debater, fire-breathing rationalist, scourge of the fundamentalists.'

'Really?' I said. 'I'm flattered.'

'Yes, really,' he said. 'And I'm delighted. Those fundamentalist dingbats are the absolute bane of my life, let me tell you. Most of them are engineers, you know. Have you *seen* the posters they stick up? A picture of a Bible with "When all else fails, read the instructions". One of them even ran off copies of the same poster with "RTFM".'

I'd seen the first, but not the second.

'What does that mean?' I asked.

Baxter leaned forward a little, and spoke in a low but vehement voice: 'It's an old programmer joke. Stands for "Read the Fucking Manual". God help them if that's how they see the Bible! Nit-picking, pluke-faced, world-building nerds – they'd be better off in the SF Soc, if you ask me, applying their exegetical skills to the *Silmarillion* and *The Lord of the Rings*. If you can prise them out of their literal-minded stupidity you'd be doing their souls a service.'

I had to demur. 'The only people I've had any effect on with that sort of thing, and it's only been one or two, have ended up becoming atheists. Surely not what you want, is it?'

'Obviously I'd prefer that they didn't, but they do a lot less harm as atheists than as supposed Christians. And in any case, who am I to say? Atheism may be part of their spiritual journey.'

I laughed. 'That's what my mother tells me!'

'A wise woman, indeed.' Baxter leaned back, regarding me with lowered eyelids. 'Have you ever considered studying for the ministry?'

'What?' I nearly splashed my whisky.

'I'm quite serious.'

'So am I,' I said. 'And I'm an atheist.'

'Well, that needn't stop you taking a degree in Divinity. And your study might give you some grounds to reconsider. It's merely your current opinion, after all. You were baptised, were you not? As far as the Church is concerned, you're still in the fold, albeit as an Anglican.'

I laughed. 'I can see how that would be more of a problem!'

Baxter acknowledged the jest with a tight smile, and then frowned. 'What I see in you, Ryan, is a young man who takes these matters seriously. From what I hear, you evidently know the Bible very well; you've obviously read up on apologetics, theology, biblical criticism, history, archaeology, philosophy . . . you'd be off to a flying start at New College, ahead of most of the actual candidates for the ministry, frankly. And what's more, you're genuinely interested in these subjects.'

I shook my head. 'I'm flabbergasted.'

'You should be flattered.'

In a way, I was. Having just lost my main ambition, inchoate though it was, the prospect Baxter dangled before me was oddly tempting. A postgraduate degree from the theological college could open up a wide variety of academic careers, quite aside from any question of belief. And I knew, from my mother's way of thinking as well as from the occasional liberal Christian I ran into in my sceptical evangelising, even belief could be nuanced and finessed.

'No,' I said. 'Well, let me think about it. Let me get a round in.'

'No, let me,' said Baxter, rising. 'Now, now, I still owe you for using that ashtray, as well as for the coffee. Same again?'

'A beer this time, I think. Whatever the guest beer is.'

'Good idea.'

He disappeared inside. While he was gone I found myself wondering if he was the same man as I'd met at home a couple of years earlier. He was so much more relaxed, fluent and assured than his younger version that he might almost be that Baxter's not-so-evil twin. More probably, I thought with a wry smile at this lapse into paranoid thinking, he'd just matured. People could. I knew I had.

'Took the liberty of ordering a plate of nachos,' said Baxter, as he sat down with the pints. 'Ah, here they are.'

'Thanks,' I said, to him and to the waitress, as the smell of hot melted cheese took over my brain.

There was a minute or two of silence as we noshed in.

Baxter wiped the back of his wrist across his mouth.

'By the way,' he said, 'when you checked and couldn't find me, back in Greenock – what did you think I was? I mean, I can see the point of a bogus meter reader, or a bogus social worker – but a bogus *minister*? What on earth did you think I was up to?'

I looked away for a moment, then sighed. 'This is so stupid,' I said. 'I thought you were a Man in Black.'

'But I was a man in—Oh, I *see*!' He laughed. 'Like Will Smith in the movie? Good grief. What gave you that idea? Had you recently seen a UFO, or something?'

'Well, as it happens, I had,' I said. 'Oh, don't get me wrong, I didn't think it was an alien spaceship or anything. Just something weird. A light that fell from the sky and knocked me out, one day when I was up in the hills. At the time I thought it was ball lightning, maybe, but, well, you know how it goes.'

'Oh, I know how it goes,' said Baxter. 'The brain does play tricks on us sometimes, eh? This ball lightning – did it leave any physical traces?'

'Burned a neat circle in the grass, which—'

'Let me guess,' said Baxter. 'Was dug up the following day, quite coincidentally?'

'Yes!' I said. 'How did you know?'

He put his elbow on the table and leaned forward and raked his fingers through his hair, then propped his chin on his hand and gave me a weary look.

'How do you think?' He straightened a little, running thumb and forefinger up and down his larynx, as if confirming with relief the absence of the dog-collar. 'We men in black, ha-ha, that is to say men of the cloth, and women too, of course . . . we hear stories. We're *told* stories. People come to us with their problems, even non-religious people, as if we were some kind of spiritual Members of Parliament – and about as much use, come to think of it! I've heard everything – if not personally, then from older colleagues. I myself was once asked to perform an exorcism. An exorcism! Imagine. I've heard tell of ghosts, angels, saints, the Blessed Virgin Mary – that was from a nice old Catholic lady in the street who thought I was a priest of her confession – and, oh yes, grey aliens and flying saucers and all the rest of it. And you know what, the physical evidence always, always is missing or ambiguous when you go back and check. The picture was overexposed, the footprints have melted, the claw marks in the wallpaper were . . .'

He shook his head, or perhaps shuddered. 'Anyway, I wouldn't worry about it, whatever you saw. And I don't want to know any more about it. Just put it out of your mind, Ryan. Rest assured, it's a more common experience than you'd think.'

'Yes,' I said. 'That's pretty much how I see it.'

And at that point, I think, it was. And I'll say this for him, and for Sophie – that night, and many hundreds of nights after it, the dreams didn't come back.

We seemed to have finished our pints.

'Another?' I said.

Baxter stood up, rubbing the palms of his hands together, with a 'the night is young' gleam in his eye.

'I was wondering,' he said, 'if you wouldn't like to have a pint or two with some New College students. See what they're like, maybe get an idea of the sort of courses on offer, you know?'

'Hmm,' I said. 'I'm not sure. I mean . . . aren't theology students likely to be a bit . . . quiet?'

Later that evening, standing under a fine drizzle on the tiny, crowded, raucous patio of the Jolly Judge, a pub down some steps from the Royal Mile, I found myself clutching my eighth pint and shouting something about Karen Armstrong's misreading of Karl Barth's introduction to Feuerbach into the ear of a biker in black leathers who in turn was trying to make herself heard above the voice and through the pipe smoke of a bearded American Calvinist in a red T-shirt displaying a Guevara-style portrait of the famous Belgian Marxist economist, Ernest Mandel.

'Total depravity,' the American kept saying. 'Total fucking depravity. You gotta hang onto that, man.'

'Will you fucking shut the fuck up about that,' said the biker, as if tested beyond endurance, 'or I'll stick a fucking tulip up your arse, and that stinking pipe of yours after it. Now,' she went on, turning to face me and lighting one cigarette with the end of another, 'what you atheist fuckwits don't get about the apophatic tradition, see, is that it's not some kind of ad hoc rescue hypothesis, like some kind of fucking Thomas Kuhn epicycle thing, no that's not right but you know what I mean, right? But is in fact, in fact, completely in line with . . .'

I forget what it was in line with. I do remember that later still, sitting inside and stuffing my face with crisps to try and give the alcohol something more to soak into than the now distant memory of half a plate of nachos, I mumbled to the biker that I really owed James Baxter for introducing me to such a brilliantly entertaining crowd.

'Who?' she said, swaying slightly over a glass of red wine.

'Baxter,' I said. 'You know – the Church of Scotland chaplain. He was here earlier.'

She was experimentally making sucking noises by placing the heel of her hand across her eye socket and jerking it away. With the other eye – what would later be known as 'her good eye', if she made a habit of this tic – she gave me a funny look.

'No, he's not,' she said. 'The chaplain.' She carefully removed the end of a fall of her hair from the glass and sucked the wine off the tips, then tucked the hair behind her ear, from where it fell again. 'I am.'

I checked on my phone. She was.

'Fooled again,' I said. 'Fuck me.'

'Is that an invitation?' she said, tossing back her hair and striking a pose, then falling off her chair. She climbed back and added, 'Then you're out of luck. My wife wouldn't stand for it.'

'Total depravity,' said the American, loftily passing by, somehow carrying five pints in two hands. 'Total fucking depravity.'

'Irresistible grace!' the biker shouted back, over her shoulder. 'Perseverance of saints!'

She fell off the chair again.

13

I stood on the steps in front of the Scottish Parliament and looked out over a sea (well, a loch) of marquees, tents, booths, bothies and benders that spread from the plaza across the green and, to my right, over the other side of the road, lapped against the first steep slopes of Holyrood Park. Above it floated banners, blimps and balloons, amid a thin haze of smoke from fast-food stalls, communal braziers and individual sticks of weed. Camcopters of various sizes buzzed and darted, making wireless connections to similar encampments in the Meadows and St Andrews Square and to other venues across town, and then onward and outward to the phones and screens of a million or so remote participants. My ear-phones skipped through a spectrum of hot-spot music channels, from which I selected a faint fiddle sound as a suitable backing track to my wait for Calum.

The late-July sky was blue, the morning heat already rising. The Scottish Futures Forum was well into its first full day, a Saturday. The theme for the week-long event – a Scottish Government initiative, projected as a creative mash-up of corporate trade and recruitment fair, social forum and nostalgic Occupy re-enactment – was The New Improvement. Its end would segue into August and the Edinburgh Festival kick-off, in the hope of pulling and retaining international visitors. Judging by the numbers of Asian, South American and African delegates and tourists I'd seen going in and out of the Parliament, the languages in conversations I'd overheard, and the colours of the crowds below, this was working.

With my third-year exam passes and distinctions under my belt, I was in a hopeful mood and frame of mind, looking forward to checking out future employment or postgraduate funding opportunities. Relieved (in every sense) of my aspirations to be a humanist philosopher, I'd decided on English Literature as my final-year subject. I hadn't decided what to do after that. I vaguely contemplated getting funding for a PhD, or taking a journalism course where I could leverage my interest in and knowledge of science (not a strong point with journalists, in my view) into some preparation for a career in reporting and commenting on all the exciting developments that already accompanied the economic recovery and that were further projected under the Forum's rubric of a new Improvement. The first Improvement, harked back to here, was the transformation of Scottish agriculture and industry in the eighteenth century in the course of Scotland's original passive revolution, an apt and curious template for the slow upheaval that the Big Deal had enabled.

'Hi, Sinky!'

Calum came bounding up the steps. We clasped hands and clapped shoulders.

'Good to see you, man,' I said.

We eyed each other with wry smiles – this was probably the first time we'd seen each other in a suit and tie. Like me, Calum was keen to check out the Forum, and he'd vaguely mentioned a family occasion in the evening. After a minute or so of catching up and checking that no one close had died or anything we turned to business and made our way down the steps and into the crowds. I hadn't decided where I was going, but Calum had – the recruitment stall of a satellite-manufacturing company – and was navigating us there by phone.

'This is insane,' said Calum, after we'd picked our way through a crocodile of high-school students, all of them talking loudly.

'What is?' I said.

'All this,' he said, with an encompassing sweep of his arm. 'I mean, this is supposed to be how the country's gonnae decide its technology strategy! Out ae the debates here! They're going to make a plan for the next five years – a five-year plan, aye, right, we get the message. It's socialism, Sinky, that's what it is.'

'Socialism?' I said. 'When was the revolution?'

'While we were busy doing our Highers, I reckon,' said Calum.

'The Big Deal?' I laughed. 'Prevented a revolution, more like. It actually *saved* capitalism. The banksters and all the other rich bastards were totally fucking up the capitalist system with their outright fucking bare-faced criminality.' I added what was by now a well-trodden joke: 'The authorities went after them for tax evasion, but had to settle for getting them for the St Valentine's Day Massacre.'

'You can laugh. State control ae finance! We might as well be in fucking China, man.'

'You been listening to your da again?'

'Aye, well.' Calum shot me a slightly abashed smile. 'Maybe *you* should listen tae him sometime. Nae loans or grants for business expansion coming his way, I'll tell yi that.'

We ducked into a big marquee on the first green. Inside was mercifully cooler and quieter than outside. The camcopters were few, small and silent. Scores of stalls stood in long rows, between which people mostly our age drifted, or clumped around some particular attraction. Flat screens suspended from the marquee's roof cables seemed to be the thing, but their effect was to cancel each other out in an eye-straining clamour of colour and movement. Calum headed straight for the nearest space company stall, above which a bunch of thread-tethered ten-centimetre cubical balloons bobbed. I followed him, and selected from the stacks of leaflets and memory sticks and company-logo gewgaws (a pen, a key fob, a sheet of card that folded into the cube-sat's shape, an LED torch) while he talked earnestly with the young man and woman behind the table. The conversation ended with him handing over his CV, which the woman uploaded to her phone and handed back.

'How did it go?' I asked him as we wandered on.

'Fucking great,' he said. 'Practically a job interview on the spot. If I keep my head down and nose to the grindstone and that, this time next year I'll be working wi them.'

'Aye,' I agreed, solemnly, 'doon the spaceship yards of the Clyde.'

'Well, that's mair or less what they are,' said Calum. 'Plenty to choose fae and aw,' he added, heading for another space company – this time a still-speculative asteroid mining venture – and repeating the process. This time, I didn't bother picking up knick-knacks but instead scanned other nearby stalls. One that caught my eye had a banner on two thin poles diagonally across it. The banner read 'Fabrications', in a font and on a background that continuously varied, in yet another variation of the locally de rigueur assault on the eye.

Sitting under it, behind the table with another young woman, was Sophie. It took me a second glance to recognise her: she had her hair up and she was wearing a high-necked blouse under a fitted pinstripe jacket with a matching long skirt. When Calum had finished his pitch and got yet another encouraging response I nudged him and nodded. We walked over. The table was spread with what looked like fashion brochures, with artfully scattered pads looping through catwalk shows. Sophie was fiddling with a swatch of material that looked soft but held sharp creases wherever she folded it.

'Hi, Sophie.'

'Oh, hi, guys!' She stood up, stepped out from behind the table, and gave us both quick air-kisses. I smelt her perfume, heard the tinkle of her earrings. 'Good to see you, Calum, Ryan. Hunting for jobs?'

'Yeah,' I said. 'Looks like you've found one.'

'Just an internship for the summer.' She flashed a smile at the other woman. 'High hopes, though.'

'It's kindae funny,' Calum said, 'seeing you looking so formal.'

'Well, same to you! It's part of my job here,' said Sophie. She parked herself on the edge of the table and leaned back, arm out, striking a car-show eye-candy pose for a moment, then sat up straight. 'Anyway, this isn't formal. This is smart casual.'

'What's the difference?' I asked.

'Casual is with a petticoat. Smart casual is with lining or a slip.' She tugged her skirt at the knee, raising the hem, to demonstrate. 'Formal is with hoops.'

My gaze swung as helplessly as a compass needle to her ankle and then back up, to lock on her knowing smile.

'Hoops?' I said, baffled.

Sophie gestured downward and outward curves.

'Oh yeah,' said Calum, glancing at the displays. 'The lamp-shade look.'

Sophie nodded. 'That's the one! It's becoming a thing, isn't it? And one that works great with our fabrics, as it happens – no actual hoops, no dragging or catching, no inconvenience.

But that's not all we do, it's a tiny part of the possibilities. We have tons of new ideas, menswear and everything. Come and have a look.'

She flipped to pages and tabbed to shows with a very different focus from the catwalk's formality and frivolity. Guys – and gals, to be fair – took sport, outdoor and leisure gear through its paces, demonstrating fabrics that stiffened on impact to ward off and absorb blows, that changed colour to camouflage faster than a chameleon, that water rolled off like sea off a surfacing submarine, that made the wearer almost invisible, that powered every handheld device short of an electric drill just from storing energy from motion and light, that you could wade waist-deep through a bog in and emerge with your boots shiny and your trousers looking freshly washed . . . Then there were garments of a more experimental cut and shape for everyday wear: jackets and shirts with jutting shoulders and high turned-out collars, jodhpur-style trousers, long flared coats, and in general a look that combined evident lightness with apparent bulk.

'Can't see myself wearing that,' Calum said.

'It's all about maximising surface area,' Sophie earnestly explained. 'For the movement and sunlight, yeah? With sports and outdoor you don't need so much, but day and evening, well, you see the problem. It's not so bad with women's, because you have skirts and frills and stuff to work with, but men's suits and casual wear and so on, well . . .' She sighed, then brightened. 'Lots of interesting design ideas for these from the eighties, though.'

'The eighties?' I said. 'As in, the *nineteen*-eighties? The decade that taste forgot? Honest, Sophie, ask your granny. Ask mine, if you like. She'll tell you the only good thing about it was that the internet and phone cameras weren't invented, well hardly anyway, so most of the awful photos are lying out of sight in drawers and shoeboxes.'

'Good point,' said Sophie, ostentatiously tapping out a note. 'Must do a hard copy source search. Charity shops, museums, eBay. Also, ask my gran.' She looked up, smiling, one hand playing with a dangling earring, the other on my elbow for a moment. 'Thanks, Ryan. Maybe you could switch from philosophy to fashion, eh?'

'Nae chance,' I said. 'And anyway, you put me right off philosophy.'

My voice sounded more accusing than I'd intended. Sophie withdrew her hand and cocked her head, frowning a little.

'I did?'

I rubbed the back of my neck. 'Last year, remember?'

'Oh, yeah.' She looked away, then back. 'I didn't mean to put you off.'

'No probs,' I said. 'Honest, it was just a . . . not very good dream. Like, you burst a wee bubble, right? I'm doing English now and having a great time, and looking for a job or training in science journalism.'

'Ah,' said Sophie. 'That sounds . . . up your street.'

'Speaking of jobs . . .' said Calum, shuffling his feet a bit.

'Oh! Yes, of course, guys. And I've got to get on with mine.'

There were, in fact, one or two more people peering at the stall than Sophie's colleague could deal with by the looks of it. Sophie sat down again behind the table and saw us off with a hasty wave.

'What was all that about?' Calum asked, when we were further down the aisle and out of earshot.

I pretended more interest than I felt in a model tidal turbine. 'Uh . . . just a chat I had with Sophie last year. It was nothing she said, just that telling her about my ambitions I realised how vague and unrealistic they were and sort of focused a bit more after—'

'I'm no talking about *last year*,' said Calum. 'I'm talking about the now.'

'What?' I said.

'You didnae see it?'

'See what?'

He stared at me, and shook his head. 'Disnae matter.' He puffed on an ornate little electronic pipe – he'd come a long way from his old fake pen, as had the habit, prohibitions battered down by Chinese waves of imports – and nodded towards the next row. 'Come on, there's a solar-sail company along there I want tae check out.'

We finished trawling the marquee and wandered around other stalls. Now and then we sat in on a discussion, in a tent or on the grass. Calum accumulated space company contacts and prospectuses; I did the same for tech magazines and news sites.

About five we found ourselves back at the plaza in front of the Parliament.

'Thirsty?' Calum asked.

'Parched.'

Calum scanned the refreshment stalls scattered around the plaza, weighed up queue length and beer quality, and optimised. We headed.

'First's on me,' I said.

By the time I returned with two chilled bottles of Innis & Gunn, Calum had found seats and a table.

'Cheers.' We clinked bottles.

'Ah, that's good.'

'Aye,' said Calum. 'Any plans for the evening?'

'Not particularly,' I said. 'Maybe grab a bite somewhere, then take a wander over the Meadows and check out if there's been any new creative developments exploring technological possibilities through agitprop skits, drum circles and the medium of interpretive dance.'

Calum chuckled. 'That keen, eh? I've got a better idea. This family do I mentioned. It's just up the road, in the Skandic. Starts about six.'

'What kind of a do?'

'It's an after-wedding-reception bash, informal, maybe a ceilidh band and a buffet, kindae thing. It's not exactly family, more like distant rellies. My da and ma are invited, and I'm included. Want to come along?'

'Will I get in without an invitation?'

'Dinnae wory about that. I know enough people going on

the basis ae nothing stronger than hints on the family grapevine, third and fourth cousins and that, like, that even wi you alang it wouldnae exactly be gate-crashing if we were tae drop by, scavenge the buffet table, make free wi the free bar, and join in a dance or two. Plenty ae lassies, that's for sure, some ae them unattached and on the pull.'

'Young, naïve, half-pissed and all dolled up?' I said.

'Got it in one,' said Calum, rubbing his hands and miming a leer.

'Sounds like a plan.'

I relaxed, sprawling as much as the plastic bucket seat would allow, and idly surveyed the plaza. Crowds were still coming and going, in and out of the Parliament building. Good place for people-watching, I thought, if conversation should flag. My gaze slid past then clicked back to a face seen in profile: a man talking to another man, just under the big awning by the door. James Baxter, the man in black, though not in black now, but wearing an open-necked loose shirt over jeans.

'Calum,' I said, leaning forward and not looking away from my target, 'don't look round. Take out your phone, set it on some Not Looking, Honest app, and keep it on me. Oh, and mind my drink.'

'Uh-huh,' said Calum. 'Whatever you say, boss.'

I got up and strolled over. It was an effort not to sprint, especially as Baxter was shaking hands and saying goodbye to the man he was talking to. I intercepted Baxter just as he turned away to step towards the entrance. It was definitely him, a recognition reinforced by the nametag hung from a chain around his neck.

'Hello again, James,' I said.

Once, making my careful way back from the buffet on a London train, I caught sight of a guy I knew from the SF Soc – not a close friend or anything, but someone I'd drunk and talked with dozens of times. He was sitting at a table reading a science-fiction magazine on his pad. I'd said hello, and he'd looked up with the same look of complete bafflement and non-recognition that Baxter was giving me now. A moment's conversation had established that I'd made a mistake. Different name, different voice and accent, different guy entirely. So there are doppelgangers – completely unrelated people who look virtually identical. This was like that.

Baxter frowned, then stretched a smile. 'Have we met?'

'Yes, the last time just over a year ago, when you were claiming to be the Reverend James Baxter, whereas now . . .' I peered closer at his nametag, and made a theatrical blink and recoil. '"Jim Baxter, MSP". Well, well.'

He was still giving me a fixed, strained smile, very much the politician, and shaking his head.

'I'm sorry, I really don't know what you're talking about. I've never been a minister, God knows! So to speak!' He stuck out his hand. 'But, seeing you're here, let's get acquainted. You are?'

I shook his hand, without enthusiasm. 'Ryan Sinclair. You know me. You bought me a pint in the Jolly Judge last year when you were claiming to be the university's Church of Scotland chaplain.'

He glanced round, and made a gesture like patting the head of an invisible ten-year-old.

'No need to raise your voice, Ryan. Please. Honestly, I've never been a minister and never claimed to be. That's a criminal offence, you know, impersonating a minister of religion.' He put two fingers in his shirt pocket and fished out a card. 'I'm a list MSP for Edinburgh West, for the Renewal Party. I came in with two others at the last election back in May. Before that, I worked in defence avionics – you'll find all my details here, my platform, my CV, everything!' His eyes creased, his smile became more genuine. 'But no evangelical or pastoral experience, sorry.'

I took the card, turning it over as if I could read its contents.

'Defence avionics?' I mused aloud. 'That's interesting.'

'Yes, it is actually!' Baxter said. His voice and manner hadn't changed a bit since he'd posed as a minister. For a moment the thought flashed that it's possible, however unlikely, that there are separated identical twins who, by pure coincidence, have the same name. 'I miss it sometimes, to tell you the truth.' He glanced at his watch. 'I'm afraid I must be off – I have a meeting in five minutes. Do make an appointment to see me any time, and sorry about the mix-up, however it was caused.'

'I have to say I don't believe you,' I said.

He gave me a half-amused, half-irritated look. 'Well, go ahead, check me out.'

'Oh, I will,' I said. 'Just like I've done twice before.'

He shook his head. 'Really?'

'Yes, really,' I said. 'So who *are* you?'

With a snort of barely restrained annoyance, he brushed past me and hurried into the Parliament. I watched until the glass doors closed behind him, then walked back to the table.

'Did you get that?' I asked.

Calum put his phone down and flicked back and forth. 'Aye, got it. Looked like you were having quite a barney. What was that all about?'

I told him, briefly, finishing the story – or stories – along with the beer.

'Weird,' said Calum. He fiddled with the screw-on stem of his electronic pipe. 'You're sure it's the same guy?'

'Of course I'm sure. Unless I have completely false memories.

'Aye, well. Speaking ae memories. See's that card.'

He tapped the card on his phone. Little stylised gears tumbled like snowflakes across the screen – transfers were that slow, back then. Calum handed the card back and began poking around. After a minute or so he passed me the phone and the card.

'Knew I still had this somewhere,' he said. 'The card my da got fae *our* Man in Black.'

On the screen was a reproduction of a much more basic business/ID card, issued by the Environmental Health department of Strathclyde Regional Council. It clearly showed a hologram portrait of the man I'd just spoken to, with the name 'James Baxter' and a string of details and a flurry of logos underneath.

182

'That's the one that turned out to be fake?' I said.

'Aye, it did. Like you found when he was a minister.'

I stuck Baxter's latest ID card in my pocket. 'And this one too, no doubt. I'll check it later.'

'No, hang on, I can check it right now.'

Calum spread out his phone, thumbed up a search, whistled at the result, and slid it over. *Edinburgh Evening News*; BBC and STV; the Scottish Parliament's site; the Renewal party news site; even the house magazine of British Avionic Systems: they all confirmed Baxter's claim to be one of the new intake of MSPs, in a small new party too thinly supported to win a seat outright, but with enough votes across the country to have three candidates on its list duly elected under proportional representation. Until then, he'd been a bright young engineer, climbing the pay grades for the past ten years in BAS's factory at Crewe Toll in Edinburgh. I closed my eyes and shook my head.

'This happened last time,' I said. 'I checked the university site, and it confirmed him until a few hours later, when he was gone. I think he has some way of spoofing the systems. I'll look again tomorrow.'

'Fuck looking tomorrow,' said Calum, standing up. He gathered up his stuff and stalked off to the Parliament entrance. I followed him, pausing just through the doors as he strode up to the security barrier. There was a bit of a queue, but the processing was fast. He vanished through to the reception area and a few minutes later returned to flourish glossy papers under my nose.

'It's aw there,' he said, as we went out. 'Cunt's name's on a printed list under the desk, which they hae as back-up in case the electronics go down. Baxter's name and office number's up on a big board ae they wee alphabet tiles, same reason. And here's his mugshot and bio, in hard copy in Yir Wee Scrote Vistor's Guide Tae Yir Fucking Elected Fucking Representataes. I paraph'ase slightly, yi unnnerstaun, Sinky, I cannae stand the fucking patronising affectation ae scribin' official communications in Synthetic Fucking Scots. Anyhoo. Whitever. Yi can also find his bio and pic in the Standard English and Urdu and Polish and you name it leaflets, and nae doubt in the ones in Teuchter and Gaelic and Tinker fucking cant an aw.'

He seemed somewhat disproportionately exercised by the linguistic equality policy, but I let it pass.

'Hard to fake, that,' I acknowledged.

'What I don't get,' said Calum, 'is if he's using false IDs, and he is at least sometimes, why the fuck does he use the same name every time?'

'We don't know that,' I pointed out. 'Maybe he just does it with us. He could be using other names with other people.'

'Why, though?'

I shrugged. 'To fuck with our heads. Or with my head.'

'You're getting a bit paranoid, Sinky.'

'I am that,' I said. 'Come on, let's go seek out squiffy young ladies and spicy chicken wings.'

PART THREE

14

I like to tell this story as the one about how I went to a wedding ceilidh and fell for the woman in the white dress. It's not quite as tragic as it sounds.

Calum strode confidently in front of me into the reception rooms of the Skandic Hotel, showed his invitation to the guy on the door, waved to a guest already inside and hustled me along for an introduction before any question could arise about my being included in the invitation. We plunged into a small crowd of wedding guests – smart suits and big dresses, flower crowns and fascinators – in the midst of which Calum hailed his parents; his father said hello and pumped my hand, his mother pecked me on the cheek and remarked on how I'd grown. Calum quickly strategised finding seats and drinks, and sent me off to grab somewhere quiet with a view.

'Say this for our Sophie,' said Calum, upon returning with a brace of pints to the corner of the small and currently almost empty side room with two rows of tables, the rearmost of which he'd selected as our base of operations, 'she's in the right business. She's got an eye for a trend, aw right. Out there it's carnage, man, lampshade ladies bouncing aff each other like dodgem cars.'

'I noticed,' I said, after a sip. 'And the colours – God! My eyes are still hurting from what I saw in the corridor. It's like in first year when I wandered into a steampunk do in the Student Union, except instead of black it's full-spectrum Victorian vulgar. Like an explosion in a dye factory.'

'Goths discover pastels?'

'Aniline,' I corrected. '"Pastels" just doesn't do it justice.'

'Poof.'

'Explain, my man, or I shall demand satisfaction.'

'Only lassies and gay blokes know stuff like that.'

'High school chemistry, old chap, no suspect knowledge of costume history required. But just to be on the safe side, let us agree to characterise the mode of the moment as "goths discover garish".'

Calum gave me a long look of mock dubiety. 'So long as you dinnae know the names ae the colours,' he said, 'I might let yi aff.'

At some point, I knew, he was going to revisit our latest encounter with the Man in Black, but I didn't want to go there right away. Since my previous encounter with Baxter, and my conversation with Sophie, I'd had more than a year of not having nightmares, and not thinking much at all about the experience that had started it all off, and I had a qualm that raising it again might bring them back.

'Speaking of Sophie,' I said, changing the subject rather deftly, I thought, 'what was it you said I didn't see?'

'Didnae say anything about what you didn't see,' said Calum.

'You said I didn't see something.'

We were sitting side by side, backs to the wall, keeping an eye on the room and the door, not quite ready yet to plunge in but alert for any possibilities that drifted our way. Calum regarded me sidelong.

'Oh, aye, that.' He rubbed the side of his neck. 'Well, tae be honest Sinky, I'm kindae gobsmacked yi didnae notice she was flirting wi yi.'

'Flirting?' I shook my head. 'You're right I didn't notice. I thought she was just being friendly.'

'"Just being friendly"?' Calum scoffed. 'That's what people say about dogs humping yir leg or jumping up on you.'

'Oh, come on, that's just being—'

'Insulting? Aye, OK, but . . . If she'd carried on like that wi another guy when she was going out wi me, I'd have been well pissed off, I can tell you.'

While recalling our conversation with Sophie that afternoon, my mind went back sixteen months or so to her meeting me in the Library Bar at the Teviot, and as the scene replayed

189

in vivid jump-cut flashback I remembered how close she'd been when she sat down beside me, how intently she'd looked and spoken and listened. I remembered how attractive I'd found her, and her quizzical stare and the slight shake of her head as she'd left.

I smacked the heel of my hand against my forehead.

'Oh, fuck,' I said.

'What?'

'I just remembered. You know I told you about the time Sophie spoke to me last year? Just before I met the mysterious Reverend Baxter.'

'Aye,' said Calum.

'I just realised she might have fancied me then.'

'And you didnae notice at the time?'

'Well . . .' I tried to think myself back to where I'd been. 'I kind of did, but . . . I guess I discounted it, sort of, because I thought she was still going out with you.'

'Maybe she was,' said Calum, thoughtfully puffing on his pipe. 'I mean, I'm no sure if it was before or after we broke up. But even if she had been, I don't see the problem.'

'Well, old chap, I suppose I have to put it down to a certain loyalty to your good self.'

'Ah, the hell wi that,' said Calum. 'All's fair in lust and counter-insurgency.'

'Gee, thanks for telling me now,' I said.

'Oh well,' said Calum, 'water over the dam and that. Anyway, she's wi another man now, or at least she was last time I checked.'

'You checked? How? Has she become a bit less reticent on the old social media front?'

Calum raised his eyebrows. 'You noticed that too, huh? Nah, she's still way careful whit she puts out about herself. Apart fae business, obviously, she's taken tae this Fabrications internship like she's joined a new religion. But I heard it on the grapevine.'

'Ah, I see,' I said, in a sceptical tone. 'Heard about her means asked about her. Sounds like you're still hung up on her.'

Calum took a few more puffs, then put his pipe down, and began turning it over and over, taking it apart and putting it back together. While we'd been talking, a dozen or so more people from the wedding bash had come into the room. A couple of tables had filled up. Conversations were quiet but constant, the laughter polite rather than raucous – most of the guests in here looked like members of the older generation catching up, getting the weight off their feet. A tiny camcopter drifted in and dawdled around just below the ceiling, no doubt taking candid pictures for the wedding album.

'Nah,' he said. 'Honest, Sinky, it's over. But seeing her again this afternoon, and what you said about her bursting a bubble, and the Man in Black business – it's brought back something that's kindae been on my mind. A wee confession, like.'

'Oh?'

Calum glanced around, evidently decided the room was just noisy enough for confidentiality, and leaned forward. 'I ken you stayed a bit mair hung up on that weird thing that happened tae us than you let on, tae me at any rate. Philosophy and scepticism and that, and aw the religion and anti-religion stuff, aw that came out ae it, am I right?'

'Yes,' I said, warily. 'It was . . . realising that was what was behind all these interests that made me drop them, well, not let them fill my mind kind of thing, and it was talking to Sophie or her talking to me that was bursting the bubble – or lancing the boil, more like.'

He grimaced. 'Well, putting it like that's a bit yuck, but . . . Anyway. What I wanted tae confess, right, was that I might have made your obsession wi it worse than it needed tae hae been. Because I lied tae yi.'

'What about?'

'About aw the stuff I said my da telt me, about our family secrets, being descended fae Neanderthals and aw that shite.'

'I'm not sure I ever really believed that,' I said, with an indulgent chuckle.

'And him gien me a wee talk about the Men in Black,' Calum went on. 'Never happened.'

'But surely the visit happened?' I said. 'You showed me the guy's picture just an hour—'

'Oh, aye, yon photie's real, aff the card the supposed Cooncil inspector flashed about. Our mystery visitor, he wis real aw right. And yir old man did ring up mine on the Sunday, and I did get a grilling about whit happened and bit ae an earful about no telling him. And my family really is descended fae Travellers, back tae Ireland and maybe tae the shipwrecked Spanish sailor ae legend. But the rest ae it wis shite I made up tae impress you.'

'Impress me?' I cried. 'Fucking hell, man! Like you ever needed to impress me.'

'Whit d'yi mean?'

'When we were wee,' I said, with the condescension of the third-year student for the fourth-year schoolboy, 'I thought of you as just the coolest dude. A guy I looked up to, and I don't mean because you were taller.'

I shrugged one shoulder, feeling I'd said too much.

Calum laughed. 'You're the one who wis aywis being held up tae me as a good example by my ma and da. "Why can yi no be mair like that nice Sinclair boy, study hard and scrape out the dirt fae under yir nails and be kinder tae yir wee brother?"'

'Well, exactly,' I said. 'Goody two-shoes, moi. Middle class as you can get, son of an accountant and a schoolmarm, for goodness sake. Whereas your dad was, well maybe technically even more middle class, being a small business owner, but he wore overalls and often enough worked with his hands, with metal tools and got oily, and you had the attitude to go with it. So naturally, you were the bee's knees as far as I was concerned. Cool hand Duke, you were.'

Calum punched my shoulder, not too hard.

'OK, OK,' I said. 'It's not like I still feel that way, you understand, so don't worry. What I don't see is why you wanted to impress me in the first place.'

He stared at me. 'Oh come on, Sinky,' he said. 'We both

saw the light, but you got a fucking alien abduction and later on a face-tae-face chat wi an MiB out of it! I wisnae one hundred per cent sure yi were nae making it up, but if you were it wis one hell of a clever stunt. And on the Sunday evening, I wis well pissed aff wi you having telt your da and then him getting the tale back tae mine. So I thought, hah, if Sinky's putting one over on me, I'll dae it tae him right back. Turn it around, I thought, gie him the idea that *no* having an abduction experience wis special. Or maybe, no seeing Greys, or seeing something else . . . then I got the idea ae seeing them as they really are. I made that drawing ae the insect thing—'

'*You* drew that!' I said.

He misunderstood my small shock at having my half suspicion confirmed for surprise at his ability, and gave a self-deprecating laugh.

'Ach, I wis aywis good at drawing, but I wis kindae shy about it. Afraid it wis kindae a poof thing. Never showed it aff tae any ae my mates, except Sophie back in High School. She telt me I should dae mair wi it, and I did raise the question ae daein Art wi my ma and da, but yi ken how it is wi my kindae parents – waste ae time and aw that, never get yi a proper job, et cetera, fucking working-class attitude aw right – so whitever talent I had fae that got turned tae tech drawing instead ae art.'

'That's a shame.'

Calum shook his head. 'Stands me in good stead now, I can tell yi that, in my engineering studies. Anyhow, I already had the idea ae telling yi I'd found it in an old book, and the oldest book I could think ae credibly claiming tae be in the family wis the Bible. Not that we actually had a family Bible, mind, at least none I ever saw. So I went online, ran a quick search on insects in the Bible, found that bit in Revelation and went, Ah-hah! and inked in my final drawing tae fit the description. Stuck the chapter and verse Roman numerals in, nice authentic touch I thought, then I wondered about putting in whit looked like the verses around it. Rummaged about online, considered lifting the relevant page fae the Latin Vulgate, maybe using Gothic script tae complicate matters a wee bit, and then I thought naw, that's too obvious. So I just went tae a game designer freeware site and found a wee programme for generating unique one-off fantasy alphabets and combining the resulting letters intae believable-looking words, for yir in-game ancient prophecies and inscriptions and runes and that. Ran the app, printed random text around the picture, then went over aw the letters wi the same Rotring pen I'd used tae ink the drawing. I knew you'd check it, see, and spot if it wis just printed. I left it up tae you to figure out it wis fae a Bible, because that way you'd think you'd discovered something I didnae ken about the old book, and that's whit wid hook you.'

'And it did,' I said.

Calum grinned and rubbed his hands. 'Aye. You fell for it. Hook, line, and sinker, Sinky!'

Our glasses were empty. I couldn't think of anything to say. I stood up.

'Same again?'

'Aye, thanks. One mair before we hit the dance floor, or whitever.'

Calum did not look at all contrite about his confession. He looked pleased with himself. I left him checking his phone and idly scanning the room for people he knew, and returned from a somewhat dazed trip to the bar to find him talking to a guy about our age who'd dragged up a seat at the end of the table.

'Ryan, Big Don,' Calum said by way of introduction. 'Ryan's an old pal from school. Big Don – not tae be confused with Wee Don, his da – is a, uh . . .'

'Grandson of a great-aunt,' Big Don said, leaning across and shaking hands, imperilling but avoiding the drinks. His suit sleeves were pushed up to the elbows, his shirt sleeves weren't. I vaguely wondered if this was what Sophie would call a thing. His accent was well-spoken Highland, but he looked enough like Calum for you to tell they were related.

'Cousin,' said Calum, simplifying matters. 'We used tae play together on Wee Don's farm up near Alness.'

'Remember that time you got on the tractor, and—'

'Oh, man, don't remind me.'

And they were off, reminiscing about scrapes and adventures and catching up on names that came up. I let them get on with it, savouring the interplay of Don's Highland and Calum's Greenock accents, interjecting an occasional comment or laugh for politeness' sake, thinking it was high time Calum and I went on our projected primeval prowl for food and female company, and people-watching while I waited. The older folks wandered out, younger people ambled in. I could see Calum and Don likewise keeping half an eye on the comings and goings while they talked. They certainly noticed the next arrival.

Two young lampshade ladies came in, evidently from the wedding party because besides the fact that they were wearing ball gowns – one white with a satin top and net skirts with big swirly flowers traced in white thread on the outer layer, the other similar but in reddish purple with gold embroidery – they had their hair piled up and pinned in place with silvery head-pieces. The girl in the white dress had a hanky-sized wisp of veil over the back of her heaped red hair. The other girl – black-haired, taller, looking a year or two older and a kilo or two plumper – was attractive, but the girl with the red hair and – I now noticed – green eyes, was drop-dead gorgeous. Both of them carried tall drinks in clinking glasses, and between that and clutching their handbags and piloting their voluminous skirts they had no attention to spare for us, though we had plenty for them. They sat down facing each other a couple of tables away, with much shifting of chairs and patting down and fluffing out, and began a quiet, intense conversation.

'Windmills are dead in the water,' Don was saying. 'On-shore multi-storey fish farming, that's the big thing now. I'm thinking of going for a diploma in it – you know, to get the practical side. Mind you, the name sounds a bit daft.'

'The name?' said Calum.

Don leaned forward and spoke from behind his hand, 'Pisciculture!'

'"Key-culture"?' said Calum, like an echo.

'No, *pisciculture*.'

'I heard yi the first time. I wis just taking the piss out ae it.'

Don looked puzzled for a moment, giving a convincing impression of the stereotypical slow-on-the-uptake teuchter, then joined the laughter.

'Well, there you go,' he said.

'Take it on the chin, man,' said Calum. 'Any word can be made to sound funny.'

'Space engineering can't,' said Don.

'Spaceship, spaceship, spaceship,' said Calum, sounding more slurred with each repetition, like Sean Connery. 'Shee?'

'Yesh,' said Don. He turned to me. 'What about yours?'

'I'm looking for a gig writing about the sort of thing you guys want to actually do,' I said. 'Can't think how to make it sound funny.'

'Then again,' said Calum, 'it sounds pathetic enough on its ain. You used tae be aw right at maths and that. Then yi were intae philosophy in a big way. Now you're talking about journalism. Where did it aw go wrang for you, Sinky?'

'It didn't go wrong,' I said. 'I just discovered where my real talents lay, and it wasn't in rigorous logic. More in general handwaving and bullshitting.'

'Aye,' said Calum. 'Come tae think of it, you were aywis good at that.'

This banter continued for a time. The two girls we'd

noticed earlier got up and left the room, of necessity walking slowly. They had criss-cross ribbon tapes from the waist to between the shoulder blades, just coming undone beneath their bare shoulders and exposed necks. After they'd brushed one by one through the doorway, Calum and I turned to each other with that tongue-hanging-out face by which young gentlemen express discreet and respectful approbation of young ladies.

'Pervs,' said Don.

'What?' I said indignantly. 'Leching, OK, I'll cop to that, but not perving.'

'They're too young.'

'A bride and a bridesmaid?' I scoffed.

'Yon wee lassie in the white's not the *bride*,' said Don, scornfully. 'She's a flower girl.'

'So you know her?' said Calum, sounding interested.

'Naw,' said Don. 'But I know the bride, Cathy, and that's not her, and I've seen both these lassies in the wedding photies.' He gestured vaguely towards the ceiling, as if to indicate the cloud.

'Speaking of lassies,' I said.

'Aye,' said Calum, slamming down an empty pint glass. 'Time for a wee wander.'

Don nodded and stood up, looming just like Calum. 'Yes, the ceilidh dancing starts any time.'

'Not quite what I was thinking of,' I said. 'But if duty calls, I will face my fate like a man.'

As we filed out of the room Calum picked up the glasses the girls had left and gave each one a judicious sniff.

'Old enough to buy alcohol,' he announced. 'Hence, old enough to—'

'Good point,' I said, before he could elaborate.

'Pervs,' Don said.

Don bought us drinks at the bar and we made our way along a lobby to the main venue for the bash. It was a large room with tables around the sides, a stage at the far end with a ceilidh band, chandeliers overhead, and a clear space in the middle in which a few couples were dancing to fiddle music and a jaunty, jiggy folksong. Most of the guests were standing about chatting or sitting at the tables, talking and laughing and drinking or, in the cases of several of the older people, just gazing benignly at the proceedings or inward to their memories.

As we walked into the room I had a moment of disquiet, which I couldn't quite place: a sense of something out of whack, out of proportion, a generalisation made below the level of conscious thought and struggling to the surface, like a word on the tip of the tongue. Only in the next few minutes, as Calum and I circulated a bit with Big Don as our human shield, did what was odd about the gathering click into place.

It was indeed a disproportion, a statistical anomaly: the men were on average taller, the women on average shorter, than the population mean. The sexual dimorphism extended to facial features: I kept seeing women with small, pretty faces and men with big ugly mugs, all lantern jaws and beetle brows.

Like any such generalisation it had exceptions: we were intro-
duced to Big Don's father, a stocky barrel-chested farmer whose
nickname of Wee Don was both ironic and apt, and I clocked
that the young woman we'd seen moments earlier in the
reddish ballgown, now twirling and skipping on the dance
floor, was of normal height. But taking all that into account,
it was if the yarn Calum had spun me long ago and had just
denied were true, and I'd walked into a gathering of a crypto-
Neanderthal clan, or at least of people with more than the
usual European complement of relict hominid genes.

Calum had exaggerated the prevalence of lampshades –
there were plenty of girls in look-at-me frocks and fuck-me
shoes – but again, a statistical shift was evident; the look was
indeed, as Sophie had said, becoming a thing. Normally I'd
have found my gaze drawn to the mini-dressed lassies, but this
time I had other things on my mind, starting with a heap of
red hair and a pair of green eyes.

The only woman I could see in a white dress here was the
bride – there was no mistaking the bride this time, she was
definitely the one with the flower crown and the big flouncy
white ball gown, like my granny's in her mantelpiece wedding
photo, with puff sleeves to the elbows and lace springing from
every edge and seam. Two girls who looked about eight and
five were also in white, or had been before they'd encountered
the cakes and juice that had given enough of a sugar rush to
set them racing around the dance floor and in and out of the
room.

Then the woman I was looking for came through the door,

chasing after the little girls, catching up and laughing with them. I could see that their outfits were miniatures of hers, down to tiny tiaras trailing tufts of white. She stooped to scoop up the smaller of the children to give her a mock finger-wagging reproof, shooed them both to a table where some adults caught them up, and went out again. I had to hold back from dashing after her.

The fiddlers stopped playing, and the singer stepped closer to the mike and announced that a buffet supper was now available in the next room. Making sure I was well ahead of Calum, I fell in with the throng. In a big bare room with a long table of hot and cold food in the centre and with chairs around all the walls, I found my red-haired, green-eyed, white-robed siren, Gabrielle.

15

We didn't get off to a flying start. She was ahead of me in the queue shuffling sideways along the serving table, and had gone to sit down by the time I had piled my plate. I still had a half-finished pint so I didn't bother picking up a glass of wine. I turned and looked for her, trying not to be too blatant. She was sitting at the wall right behind me. The chairs were filling up fast but there was a vacant one on either side of her. Layers of her skirt overlapped both seats.

'Mind if I sit down?'

She looked up from negotiating a plate and a chicken goujon, chewed and swallowed.

'No, go ahead.'

She put the nibble back on the plate, dabbed her fingers and lips on a paper napkin, transferred a glass of white wine from the chair I was hovering over to the one on her left, and swept a swathe of soft net thigh-ward.

'Thanks,' I said, sitting down.

She nodded and 'mmh-mmh'ed, looking straight ahead. I put my glass on the floor between my feet and got stuck into a drumstick, while looking around as if for people I knew, and stealing the odd sideways glance. The girl seemed about my age, or at most a year or two younger. She was definitely in the small and pretty category of my relict hominid classification. In profile she had a slight but definite brow-ridge, and I'd noticed that her neat little nose spread wide at the nostrils, as if the flesh there were millimetres thicker than normal. Both features were almost undetectable, and irrelevant in the context of her bright green eyes and wide red lips. As she leaned slightly back and forth to eat or sip I glimpsed her bare shoulders and the fluffy hair of her nape.

Beyond her appearance I knew nothing about her, but I'd already fallen for her. That Calum was interested in her too only added to her attraction. His taunt that 'all's fair in lust and counter-insurgency' was still making my ears burn, as was the pang that, thorough stupidity or blindness, I'd missed out twice or thrice in getting off with Sophie.

As I put down the gnawed chicken femur and stooped for my drink I noticed that my plate had a plastic clip on the side for holding a wine-glass stem. The girl's plate didn't.

'Um,' I said, taking the clip off and holding it towards her, 'would this be useful?'

She cast me an impatient look, as if I'd just interrupted

some complicated mental arithmetic. With a tight smile and a brusque nod she took the clip and fitted her glass to it.

'Hmm, that's better,' she acknowledged, once more looking straight ahead.

'My name's Ryan,' I said. 'I don't know anyone here but Calum and his cousin Big Don.'

'Calum?' She looked at me with wary interest.

'Calum Williamson,' I added. 'To be honest he wasn't invited but he knows the family and he sort of dragged me along.'

'Ah, yes, the Williamsons,' she said, sounding slightly above them. Her accent was from one of the sandstone parts of Edinburgh. 'You're not related to them then?'

'No,' I said. 'Are you?'

'Oh, very distant cousins, I suppose.' She flapped a hand. 'You know how it is.'

'Yes,' I said, though I didn't. 'What's your name, by the way?'

'Gabrielle Stewart,' she said. 'Pleased to meet you.'

She didn't look it, exactly, but nor was she quite as chilly as she had been.

'Likewise,' I said, hoping my smile didn't come across as a leer. At this point I wasn't sure what to say. One obvious next move would be to ask her what she did (thus settling the age question in the relevant aspect so tactfully raised by Big Don). Another would be to drop her a compliment. But that might seem obvious and crass. I swithered a moment, then said, 'Uh, that's a very nice dress.'

'Thank you,' she said, returning her attention to the finger food.

'When I saw you earlier I thought you were the bride,' I said, in a tone intended to convey both how easy a mistake this was and wry amusement at myself for making it.

She shot me a sharp look. 'You saw me earlier?'

'Uh, yes, I was having a drink in one of the side rooms with Calum and Don, and you came in with, uh, one of the bridesmaids I think.'

'And you thought I was the bride?' She sounded almost indignant.

'That was before I'd seen Cathy, obviously,' I said.

'Nothing obvious about it,' she said.

'Well, yes,' I said, floundering. I essayed a self-deprecating laugh and added, 'Don said you were a flower girl.'

'Oh, for heaven's sake!' she said, throwing an exasperated exhalation after her words.

'Sorry, I didn't—'

'No, it's not you,' she said, as if I were so far beneath her notice it was a mere impertinence of me to think myself the cause of her annoyance. 'I just knew this would happen.'

'What?'

She turned to me and spoke in a low voice. 'Cathy wanted me in white to match the wee flower girls. I said it's not the done thing and she just kept dredging up royal weddings. I never expected even guys would find it funny.'

'Uh, no, not funny—'

'Inappropriate,' she said. 'Even boys noticing. Jeez.'

'It's not like that at all,' I said. 'I mean, we probably wouldn't have thought about it except we were at the Forum this afternoon talking to one of our friends who's studying fabric technology and interning for a textile company and she was talking about fashion and the big frocks and that and I suppose it was at the back of our minds.'

'The Forum?' said Gabrielle, sounding properly interested for the first time. 'How's it going?'

'Great,' I said. 'Very busy, lots going on. Calum and I were there looking for jobs or scholarships.'

'That's what I was hoping to do,' she said. 'Until I realised that the day my good friend Cathy had me roped in to be her little miss fairy-tale princess was the Forum's very first Saturday. I expect all the good jobs will be gone by tomorrow.'

'No, no,' I said, 'there's still loads. I'll be going back tomorrow.'

'Oh, right,' she said. 'Well, I might bump into you there.'

'That would be good,' I said.

'Not very likely, though,' she said, turning away. 'Seeing it's so big.'

Well, I thought, now or never.

'We could always meet up,' I said. 'What sort of jobs are you looking for?'

'Oh!' She favoured me with her attention again. 'I'm in second year at Heriot Watt, so it's just something temporary.'

'What are you studying?'

'Genetics,' she said. 'Well, and genomics and evolution and all that. I'm looking for work in biotech or syn bio.'

'Brilliant!' I said. 'I saw lots of bio stalls. I could show you.'

'I'm sure I can find them myself, thanks,' she said, but with a smile.

She moved her now empty plate about vaguely as if looking for somewhere to put it down.

'Let me take that,' I said. 'And maybe come back with a refill and a wee cupcake?'

'Yes to the wine,' she said. 'No to the cupcake, thanks.'

'They looked very inviting.'

'Too messy,' she said, making brushing gestures over her lap.

The queue had become a slow-moving swarm. I found Calum on the periphery, clutching a bottle of beer and giving intent attention to the bridesmaid in the reddish dress. She had a hand on his left forearm and was leaning close to make herself heard. Calum broke his eye-lock for the fraction of a second it took for him to twitch me an eyebrow. I nodded and moved on, edging slowly towards the glittering prospect of a table of glasses, rendered remote by hems and toes to not step on.

By the time I came back with white wine for Gabrielle and red wine for me, the seats on either side of her had been taken by an older couple who were talking to her. They fell silent as I approached. The guy had the Neanderthal look, but educated – a gent with the gene – and a polite, closed smile. Gabrielle took the glass with a nod of thanks and a flustered glance. I got the distinct impression – which later turned out to be correct – that the couple were her parents. I also got the impression that they were in the middle of a private conversation.

'Catch you later, Gabrielle,' I said, putting a cheerful face on it.

'Just in case you don't . . .' she said. She took her phone out of her handbag and held it out. I tapped mine against it.

'Thanks,' I said.

'Right,' she said. 'Maybe call me if you're at the Forum tomorrow?'

'That would be great,' I said. 'We could meet for a coffee or something.'

She nodded, smiled, and turned away. I gave a general smile and a vague wave to all three of them, and sloped off.

Wa-hey! I thought. Result!

Later that evening I danced with Gabrielle more than once, but it was in the Scottish country dances so it hardly counts. She always had another partner for the couples' dances – a different partner each time – or was part of a gang of women dancing around handbags and belting out old numbers like they were new, fresh, powerful insights into the human and/ or the female condition. Sometimes I'd catch her glance and she'd flicker a smile back, but she was always somewhere else when I got there.

By the time the hotel workers and waiters were gathering up detritus in the big room and giving people long-suffering looks, and Calum was in the small side room listening to his bridesmaid over what I would bet was the same bottle on his side of the table and not by a long way the same glass on hers, and the room with the tables was echoing and unlit, and the cleaners had crept from their lairs to roam the carpets like trilobites on the floors of Silurian seas, Gabrielle was nowhere to be found.

As you see, it was not for want of searching. I called it a night.

16

I woke on the Sunday morning without a hangover – I hadn't drunk much at the wedding ceilidh, by my standards at that age – but with the uneasy feeling that I'd had some important insight just before waking, one that was now falling out of reach to be lost for good on the cutting-room floor of the dream studio. This was followed by a panic that I'd slept away the day, but the slant of the sunlight from between the curtains told me I hadn't, and a quick check of my phone established that the time was only 11.30 and that Gabrielle was not yet at the Forum. Her actual address was obscured on my phone, but her location was within about a kilometre of mine. Interesting.

With that settled I lay back in bed and stared at the ceiling for a while. The room, one of four in a Tolcross flat converted to multi-occupancy during the depression, was small and self-contained. It even had rudimentary cooking facilities in the form of an unsafe electric kettle, a grease-lined microwave, a parsimonious fridge and a stingy hotplate. None of this had impressed any of the girls I'd brought back, and my wall posters – still heavy on the rock goddesses and sports stars, and now with added sci-fi covers and science and sceptic propaganda – had impressed them even less. The white plaster ceiling had enough cracks and discoloured patches to induce pareidolia, and as I gazed at it I let my mind wander.

The obvious subject of my lost insight was Gabrielle, but although I enjoyed the recollection of her from the previous night and conjured a rather creditable sketch of her from the random marks above, nothing more specific sprang to mind. If I closed my eyes, I could see the swirl of the dance, in one of those curious after-images that seem to reside in the brain rather than the retina. Nothing there, either. I deliberately thought further back, to before Calum and I had—

Yes! That was it!

What had been left to my subconscious to process, like an overnight batch update on an old mainframe, was the conversation in the bar and our encounter with James Baxter. I hadn't hitherto had time or attention to spare for indignation at the deception Calum had confessed. I made up for that now, with a brief red-mist fantasy of throttling him.

But what had really been bugging me was Baxter. How could he be an MSP and former avionics engineer whose back-story apparently checked out, and at the same time

212

have been the man of the cloth whose back-story checked out when he was around, and then vanished as soon as he wasn't?

The answer, it seemed to me, was this. The latest version of Baxter was the true one, and had been all along. British Avionic Systems, I speculated, had had a hand in building whatever black-budget gadget had dropped from the sky on us. Keeping tabs on us and tracing us to our homes would have posed no difficulty for such an eye in the sky. It might even have planted undetectable bugs amid all the ash. James Baxter was the company's man sent to scope out and intimidate any inconvenient witnesses. Posing as a Council official and as a minister to suit the occasion and the target, with just enough oddity to conform to the MiB stereotype, would do the job. He'd never have to put false information about himself on websites: all he had to do was spoof any phone used to check his story. This, I was sure, was well within the capabilities of BAS, let alone the MoD.

Even less electronic trickery would have been necessary for him to spot my interest in Revelation. All that he would have needed was a trace of my online searches, which an agent of the state or of a big company could have for the asking, whatever the legal niceties. The same went for my unguarded phone conversations with Calum. We'd suspected this at the time, but now the speculation seemed more solid.

My second encounter with Baxter in his guise of sinister minister was harder to explain. My subconscious hadn't come up with an answer to that one. But, as I dragged myself out

213

of bed and set about getting washed and dressed, my conscious mind did.

No doubt some low-level, intermittent surveillance of me had continued. My interest in UFOs might have been enough to keep me on the radar. Perhaps, when I'd been seen going from a lunch-time argument with some religious head-banger to a heart-to-heart conversation with my old school friend Sophie – from whose house, after all, our momentous stroll had all those years ago set forth – it had been enough to send Baxter hotfoot from Crewe Toll to the university, a twenty-minute taxi ride. I had an uneasy memory of the little camcopter that had drifted around the Library Bar that afternoon, but even without that he'd have found us easy to eavesdrop. When I'd told Sophie my theory about UFOs, held back only by sheer embarrassment from blurting out the real reason for my interest in the topic and of the encounter itself, Baxter had decided to step in, arriving moments after Sophie had left.

Why he'd urged me to study Divinity I could only guess: for his own amusement, or to distract me from dangerous lines of thought or enquiry. That his intent might have been to counter my mission to preach rationalism did flash through my mind, but I dismissed the notion as the self-aggrandising paranoia that had assigned me my imaginary mission in the first place.

With these questions out of the way, a new one arose.

What was he up to now?

I'd formed an impression from the election campaign that

Renewal was a new party aiming to fill the conservative but sensible slot left vacant in Scotland by the collapse of the Tories north of the border: free-market but liberal, patriotic but culturally unionist, tough-love on social problems but not actively spiteful, more vocal about the poor pulling themselves up than about grinding them down, populist on the land question but happy to see the land sold off to the highest bidder, cannily opportunist in calling for more defence spending while decrying further overseas military interventions, advocating the unwinding of the Big Deal by gradually re-privatising the banks, but not urging anything too precipitate . . . and of course in favour of tax cuts. In short, it looked like an early stab at staking out a centre-right position for the post-Big-Deal world. Few and new though its MSPs were, they were sought-after partners in the current Parliament, in which the splintering of the established parties had left both government and opposition unstable fractious coalitions. If Renewal had existed when I was sixteen, and if I'd had the vote, I might have voted for it myself.

I had no idea why Baxter had left a well-paid and respectable job for politics, of all things, but – I realised, under the shower – I knew how to find out. As soon as I'd towelled myself dry enough to check my phone, I looked up the Forum's programme for the day. Baxter was scheduled to speak in an hour or so, at a debate on economic policy. However, it wasn't at the encampment outside the Parliament, but at the fringe sprawl on the Meadows.

I was wondering how I could fit this in with meeting

Gabrielle when she phoned. It took me a moment or two of staring at her name on the screen before I responded. The phone shook in my hands.

'Good morning!' I said.

'Good afternoon,' she corrected. 'I was wondering . . . do you by any chance fancy a Sunday brunch?'

'Uh, yes.'

'Great! How about that wee place on the corner of the Links?'

'Green Tree? Opposite the big church?'

'That's the one. Full Scottish, mmm.'

I was already smitten. Now I was liking her.

'It's just up the road from me,' I said. 'When?'

'In about . . . half an hour?'

'See you there,' I said.

'The spire of every church,' said Gabrielle, stabbing a sausage and mangling a quote, 'is a dagger aimed at the heart of humanity.' She cocked her head and peered sideways and up, through the café's rain-smeared window. 'Though that one always reminds me of a ray-gun with a grip designed for an alien's claw.'

She straightened up and sat back, hair settling to her shoulders, chewed a bite of sausage, and gave me a 'What do you say to that?' look.

'Couldn't agree more,' I said. I was in love. The black pudding was real Stornoway. 'Alienation, innit.'

Gabrielle nodded. 'Of course they do good too,' she said. 'Like your mum, huh? But still.'

'Uh-huh.'

'I never did get it,' she said. 'We covered this in ELSI.'

'Elsie?'

'Ethical, Legal and Social Implications,' she said. 'Stem cells? I mean, WTF? There was this woman from Anthropology told us religion was like part of human nature, and I said it wasn't part of mine.'

Of course it isn't, I thought. You're one of a secret race that lacks the god gene. That's how you know aliens have claws. I smiled, at myself and at her.

'And then there's my family,' she went on. 'I told her both my parents *and* both sets of my grandparents are atheists, and it might go even further back than that, because my gran says *her* mum never went to church, and her dad – that's my great-grandfather – had a copy of Thomas Paine's *The Age of Reason* that looked so old and battered he might have got it from *his* grand-dad, Seamus the Tink she called him, or Hamish an Duirach sometimes, James from Jura that would be in English, who'd have bought it – if it was his – back when it was more or less illegal under the blasphemy laws or something.'

'What did she say to that?' I asked, intrigued by this talk of another inherited old book as well as inherited atheism, to say nothing of a tinker ancestor.

'She gave me this look and said, "Yeah. there've always been village atheists with their clay pipes and pint pots, but they can't change the village," and I said what about Sweden and China and eastern Germany and Czechoslovakia and Israel and then it all sort of got side-tracked into what counts as socialism.' She was laughing. 'Socialism!'

'My friend Calum thinks that's not funny. He thinks we're living under it.'

Gabrielle dabbed toast in some egg yolk. 'Well, he may have a point there, but it has nothing to do with why religion's dying out, that's for sure.'

'I nearly switched to Divinity,' I said, leaning back and shaking out my paper napkin, scrunching and wiping, feeling replete. The café was brunch-busy, hazy with steam and cigarette vapour, clattering with conversation and cutlery. About half the customers huddled around phones, arguing about the Forum. 'Just for the scholarship, you understand.'

'You should have done it,' said Gabrielle. She sipped sweet lemon tea and regarded me solemnly. 'You don't need excuses.'

'No,' I said. 'English is great and science is still my thing. I want to write about science.'

'English is so *past*,' she said. 'Sure, we need people who can write about what we do, but they don't have to be English graduates. Theology graduates who don't believe any of it – that would be useful.'

'Useful?'

'Uh-huh. For science. For the cause.'

'For you, science is a cause?'

'Oh, God, *yes*,' said Gabrielle. She laughed and shook her head, making her hair flick. 'See what I did? But yeah, it's like . . . what we could have instead of' – she flipped a hand toward the church across the road – '*that*. A big picture we could all see ourselves in. But this time true.'

I stared at her. 'I don't think you need me to write things,' I said.

'Hah!' She swatted at air, but you could see she was pleased. 'You wanna be a hack, be my guest.'

'I'm in,' I said, meaning more than I said.

'Good,' she said. 'I like it when people are rational.'

'So do I,' I said. 'By the way, have you ever been inside a flying saucer?'

She gave this more thought than it deserved. 'No,' she said at last. 'Why? Have you?'

'Just wondering,' I said. 'And no. I've dreamed about it, though.'

'Oh, me too!' said Gabrielle. 'I've always thought it would be great. And you know, we just might really.'

'How do you mean?'

'Airships,' she said. 'The new materials, there's some that can sort of suck in air and blow it out, except it's electrostatic.'

I closed my eyes and swung my head back and forth for a moment. 'That's . . . interesting.'

'We could go and see their stall.'

'What?'

She frowned. 'It was on the site for the Forum. One of the defence companies, British, British, ah . . .' She snapped her fingers.

'British Avionic Systems?'

'Yes!'

'Hmm,' I said. 'If it doesn't take you out of your way.'

Gabrielle looked out at the rain, then back at me. 'No rush. Coffee?'

'Yes, good idea.' I made to get up.

'No,' she said. 'You got the breakfasts.'

'Yeah, but—'

'Sit.' She pushed down on the top of my head. Her hand's light touch felt electrostatic.

'All right.'

I watched her going to the queue. In tight jeans, short leather jacket and floral-uppered Docs she looked very different from last night. And we were getting on a lot better than we had been. I wondered if these facts were connected. She had left her damp, copper-coloured, frilly umbrella hooked by the handle over the back of her seat. While I was waiting, I opened my phone to check on the economic-policy debate panel. I caught Baxter in full flow, standing behind the table, shaking his fist in the air while other panellists looked on with fixed expressions of bemused disdain.

'. . . so ridiculous in my life!' he was saying. 'You've destroyed a huge part of the capital market. You want to replace it with planning – that's bad enough! But is that enough for you? Oh no! You're far too clever for that! Too clever by half, I should say. You already know everything that can be said against *planning*. You read all that can be said on that subject years ago. Hayek, Mises, Roberts, Ramsay Steele . . . all old hat to you. Your mentors dealt with that stuff in a seminar on the roots of neoliberal ideology.' He mimicked covering a yawn.

'You've got the answer to all these hoary old objections worked out. And what is it? We wait with bated breath.' He glared, hand cupped behind an ear, then mimed a start of surprise. 'Oh yes! Crowd-sourcing! Expert systems! Data mining! Distributed algorithms – good Lord, how many of you know what an algorithm is? What else? Oh yes, here we are: dynamically reactive weighted matrix-algebraic optimising!' He turned to the other panellists. 'You do know about that one, don't you? Yes? You do? Good! I'm sure you're all ready to defend and explain it. I'll be very interested to hear what you have to say, because you know what? I just this moment made that one up. Slogans and buzzwords, that's all you have, that's what you're relying on to—'

'Democracy!' someone shouted from the audience.

Baxter affected a cocked head, hand behind his ear. 'What's that? Democracy? You think that'll help? Do "Concorde" and "groundnut scheme" and "British Leyland" not ring any bells? If you've never heard of any of them before – and I wouldn't be surprised – look them up, and tell me if—'

'Who's that?' Gabrielle asked, from behind me. She put a tray on the table and her chin on my shoulder. I wasn't sure I could take another breath.

'Some Renewal MSP.' I peered at the screen caption as if I needed to read it. 'Jim Baxter.'

'So it is,' said Gabrielle, moving away only to haul her chair round the corner of the table and sit beside me. 'A dangerous man.'

'Why dangerous?' I asked.

He didn't look dangerous. On the small screen he looked comical, waving his arms, his rant a squawk from the phone's speakers.

'The *People's* Republic of *China*,' he was saying, random syllables underscored with a pistol finger, 'has taken over the *world* without firing a *shot*. This is *not* even controversial! And *yet*, in all our—'

Gabrielle switched him off, then shifted her chair so that she could face me.

'Don't you realise? He's one of *our* MSPs. We're both in his constituency. And I saw him when he was campaigning. He knocked on our door.'

'He knocks on doors?' I said, impressed.

'Oh yes,' said Gabrielle. 'None of that lazy do it all online stuff for him. He actually said to me, you haven't campaigned properly in an election if you still have the same shoes at the end as you had at the start. Renewal's new, so they have to do things the old way.'

'What was he like?'

'Well, he only had a few minutes, and he started off all affable, talking about freedom and enterprise and so on, sticking up for small businesses and young families, all that. And then . . .' She frowned, as if trying to remember. 'Hard to put a finger on. Something dodgy in the body language. Emphasis on *local* people, young *mums*, hard-working *families* . . .'

I laughed. 'Motherhood and apple pie?'

'Apple pie?' She didn't seem to get the allusion. 'No, but

he did talk about corner groceries, and there was a bit about motherhood, all right, and everything he said was sort of subtly old-fashioned. Like he was appealing to people who've never really got used to immigrants and refugees and working mothers.'

'You mean, the very old?'

Gabrielle shrugged. 'Don't underestimate that as a share of the vote. Anyway – I didn't like him.'

'Fair enough,' I said. I leaned forward to depress the cafetière plunger and I considered telling her what I knew about Baxter, and decided not to.

Later, as we walked across the Links to the Meadows in the continuing rain, I held her copper-coloured girly umbrella over us both, and she put her arm around my waist to stay close and underneath.

And that was us, us.

PART FOUR

17

Gabrielle, tiny beside the standing stone, tinier yet on my phone screen, waved and pointed to something above and behind me.

'Look!' she called out. 'A flying saucer!'

I snapped the pic and turned to the vast Orcadian sky. Low over the low hills came, not a saucer but a bright globe, silent as a balloon, swift as a small aeroplane and about the same apparent size. I gazed at it stupefied for a moment, then tracked it with the camera as it passed over our heads, a couple of hundred metres up, and on out over the sea where it vanished in the glare and glimmer. Gabrielle was doing the same – by the time I'd hurried over to where she stood, she had the UFO identified.

'It's a test flight,' she said, looking up from her phone. 'Says here it's piloted.'

'Wow,' I said. 'British Avionic Systems, by any chance?'

'That's the one,' she said. 'How did you know?'

I grinned and put an arm around her. 'You talked about it the first day we met up.'

'Did I?' she said. 'I'm impressed you remembered.'

'We were going to have a look at their stall,' I said. 'Actually, I don't remember if we did or not.'

I thought back to that day. It had been wet, hadn't it? Yes: Gabrielle sticking close to me under the brolly. The Meadows muddy, some clown on stilts getting stuck, debates under canvas marquees and geodesic tepees, the smell of grilling patties and deep-fried doughnuts, face-painted kids, balloons, buzzing camcopter swarms, huge crowds, arguments, the warm, muggy, sticky all-embracing hug of a popular front in formation. I remembered looking on a phone screen at Jim Baxter's strange rant, but not a visit to the stall of the company he'd worked for before he went into politics.

'Probably not,' I concluded.

'Looks like we missed out, then.' She replayed the video capture, froze and zoomed. 'Look at that, just a silver ball. Heck, look closer.' She worked her thumb, until I could see in the globe's mirror sheen the distorted reflection of her face looking up, and the upraised phone. For a laugh, she zoomed to the highest magnification, to show the reflection of the phone's camera lens and within that a bright pixel or two: the reflection in the lens of the globe itself.

'I mean, how does that work?' she said.

'Reflection of reflection of reflection?'

'No, I mean it looks like a solid polished steel ball, but it can't be. The air's passing right through it, isn't that the idea?'

'Metamaterial,' I said, with a handwave.

'Like that explains anything.'

'I've written about it,' I said. 'Well, them. There's lots.'

'Yeah, yeah. I can't read everything you write.'

'Really? I'm hurt.'

'Come on,' said Gabrielle. 'I don't think *you* read everything you write.'

'Now I'm *really* hurt.'

'Time I took a picture of you, then.' She waved an arm. 'Which stone do you want to pose beside?'

I looked around the wide, incomplete stone circle, sizing up backgrounds of hills, the next field, sea and sky.

'Over there. Maybe take it from . . .'

I pointed.

'OK.'

We strolled off in divergent directions. As I walked up to a slab that seemed to get taller and paradoxically thinner as I approached, I considered whether I should mention my long-ago close encounter to Gabrielle. If I did, she'd be hurt – really, not in banter – that I hadn't told her before. Bewildered, even. I'd had long enough – just over three years, to be exact. She'd wonder what else I hadn't told her. She might ask Calum, and he might brag to her of how he'd fooled me into thinking that he (and by implication, she) was part of a secret race. Calum was a pal, my oldest and closest friend, still was even if we didn't see much of each other, and it was exactly the sort of thing I wouldn't put past him – precisely because he was a pal. He was loyal, but he'd see this as a laugh. Perhaps I should, too.

I laid my hand against the rough stone, and turned.

'Smile!' Gabrielle shouted.

I couldn't not.

'Right a bit, I'll get both stones.'

I moved. She waved. 'Got it.'

I grinned and waved back, then turned to press my hands and forehead against the stone, a tall, neatly split sedimentary slab, probably hacked and hauled from a nearby shore in some feat of skill and cooperation that made me wonder, and made me proud. Beyond that, unimaginably far beyond that, the rock itself, cemented by silent relentless pressure on the floor of a vanished sea from eroded particles of mountains more ancient yet.

'What were you doing there?' Gabrielle asked when I rejoined her. 'Praying to the old gods?'

'Just thinking,' I said. 'About the folk who raised it. Our people. We've been in this land ten thousand years.'

'Yeah,' said Gabrielle. 'Since the ice left.'

I glanced sidelong at her, and smiled, and didn't say that some of us might have been here for longer.

We headed back to the hired car, piled in and drove up to the Ring of Brodgar, then to Skara Brae of the grassy mounds around stone beds and shelves and kitchen sinks and on to the Broch of Gurness. By the time we'd circled Gurness's green ramparts and explored its stone labyrinth it was late afternoon.

We bought paper tubs of ice cream in the visitor centre and dawdled back to the car park.

'Tomorrow, Birsay and Maes Howe,' said Gabrielle, licking sticky fingers and looking at the unstamped sites on our visitor pass.

'Yeah,' I said. 'Today we get stunned by the Stone Age, then impressed by the Iron Age, then tomorrow get gobsmacked by the Stone Age all over again.'

'It's like that, isn't it?' she said. 'Going from Skara Brae to here. You can see at Skara Brae what Gordon Childe saw, where he got this idea of our communist ancestors in their cosy hobbit-holes and then seeing here at Gurness the origin of classes with the walls and the wealth and all the work that must have gone into it.'

'In real life we'd have *smelled* our supposed communist ancestors,' I said. 'From here, probably.'

'Well, their midden heaps, anyway,' said Gabrielle. She wrinkled her nose. 'I couldn't stop thinking about what those mounds of shells and bones must have been like to live among.'

She was in the driving seat. I glanced at her profile as she turned the ignition, and saw again the faint imprint of the strange heritage I'd imagined for her. Like Calum's, her family did indeed trace its ancestry to the Travelling folk, and I'd once regaled her with another romantic notion I'd picked up: that the travellers and tinkers went all the way back to the Iron Age, as itinerant metallurgists tramping the trade routes, making and mending, forging and smelting, giving rise to legends of dwarven mines and of anvils ringing in the deep forest. That she'd found entertaining, if fanciful. Calum's tale of a conscious conspiracy, a genetic and memetic heritage of secret doctrine, would be a different matter. I forbore, again, to mention it.

I forbore, too, to mention something else in this connection, which had been on my mind for some time.

Gabrielle was now a postgrad at the Stem Cell Centre in Edinburgh's BioQuarter; I'd had a string of freelance gigs for science websites. The BioQuarter's energetic biomedicine PR person, Nicola, had her desk in the centre, from which she sent out a steady stream of intriguing snippets about the latest developments. Naturally, I grabbed every opportunity to interview her or pump her for information, partly because she was a good source, but mainly in order to drop by at Gabrielle's desk and have a coffee and chat on the way out. Nicola and I got on well, and I often managed to wheedle out of her some telling detail or curious anecdote that wasn't in the official release. One morning in June, Nicola had trailed the scent of some infertility testing breakthrough, and I'd duly turned up to check it out.

'Hi,' Nicola said, as I put my head round the side of the door of the open-plan office where she worked. She stood up, swept a sheaf of papers and a phone from her metre of desk space, and nodded sideways. 'Coffee?'

I followed her past a couple of proper office doors and into a wide corner with non-glass walls lined with drink and snack machines, and containing a dozen high and low tables interspersed with barstools, random sofas and strategic beanbags. Nicola led the way to a small round table not occupied by a huddle of researchers, left me staking a claim on it, and returned with a couple of steaming plastic cups.

'Thanks,' I said, sipping black coffee. She knew my tastes. We made small talk for a couple of minutes – weather, traffic – then Nicola shuffled her pack and got down to business.

'OK,' she said. 'Very nice development, just out of clinical trials. A non-invasive fertility testing kit. It's a synthetic biology package, with computational properties. You swallow it, it passes through the urinary tract and picks up molecular markers from the sperm and ova, and if your pee turns blue the next day you don't have any obvious fertility problems.'

'What's the advantage? I mean, don't we already have tests?'

'Yes, but tests involve hassle, and embarrassment, and . . . anyway, this will have some uptake. Especially with all the new fertility issues.'

'What new issues?'

Nicola sat back. 'Well, here's one. This is in the technical literature, but for, uh, reasons best known to themselves the researchers aren't too keen on its becoming widely discussed among the general public. At least, not until they've got a line worked out.'

'Really?' I said. 'That sounds like a story in itself.'

'No, seriously. If I tell you, it'll have to be deep background and off the record. If I catch you mentioning it – no more stories from me.'

She sounded serious.

'OK,' I said. 'Deal.'

She mimed shaking on it. 'Right,' she said. 'Well, one of the interesting issues is that some patients are presenting who on all tests seem to be fertile individually, but not with each other. And it turns out – sometimes through various infidelities and divorces and sometimes through consensual arrangements like sperm donation and so forth – that they really are fertile. And the speculation is that some kind of speciation event has taken place without anyone noticing.'

I felt a chill. Speciation. Fuck me.

'How could that happen?' I asked. 'I mean, has it ever been observed in other species?'

'Oh, sure. It was first discovered decades ago in mice when it turned out that certain pairs were infertile with each other but fertile with other partners. What had seemed to be one species – what had always been thought to be one species because they were always found together in the same places and niches and so on – turned out to be two. And something like that may have happened in humans.'

'Now, wait a minute,' I said. 'Mice have, what, how many generations a year? Four? Whereas humans—'

'Yes, it's a theoretical problem,' she said. 'There certainly haven't been genetically isolated human populations since . . .' She shrugged. 'The Neanderthals, maybe?' She didn't see me flinch. 'And they seem to have bred back into the mainstream, as we know. It might be something stochastic – a train of chance events – rather than the sort of reproductive isolation we see in animal populations. But whatever the reasons, it is happening.'

'So the human species is speciating,' I said. 'Just when we thought it was safe to go back in the water . . .'

'What do you mean?' she asked, frowning.

'Just when the whole idea of race is finally just about totally discredited, it turns out there are other actual species hiding inside the human race! Jeez, imagine what someone irresponsible and opportunistic could make of that.'

'I see how that could be a problem, that's why I think it's kept quiet, but I don't see how it could be used that way,' Nicola said. 'There are no obvious physical markers, nor even subtle ones; it's invisible.'

'But they can be found, can't they, with genetic databases?'

'Oh, sure,' she said. 'That's how people get genetic counselling; people can even look themselves up, see if they're compatible . . .'

I stared. 'People do this already? This is a thing?'

'Oh yes. Of course it's not advertised that way, maybe because of that very issue. Just as a personal genetic compatibility prediction.'

'Right,' I said. 'Hmm. Yes, that should make the fertility kits a story of wider interest than I thought.'

'Indeed,' said Nicola, pleased at her work. 'That speciation speculation, though . . . uh, like I said, deep background and off the record.'

'Sure,' I said.

I didn't even mention it to Gabrielle. But every so often, I worried about it.

Back in Kirkwall, we queued for fish and chips, listened to an astronomer in the Peedie Kirk Hall, then repaired to the Reel for local beer, shots of Highland Park, and a clarsach and accordion and an old man's long, strong voice. We fell in with a table of geologists, who talked about stormy weather and the vanished sea of Orkady. That night we slept well in our tent.

In the morning I woke to sunlight stitch-sifted in strings of bright dots, and lay a while before stirring. Yesterday I and Gabrielle had seen a flying object, very much identified, public, known, that matched my long-ago UFO encounter in every respect but size. My hardly original speculation that what Calum and I had seen was some application of advanced secret military technology seemed vindicated. Even the connection with British Avionic Systems, my Man in Black's former employer, was now confirmed. I'd read the excitable tech-press anticipations of this development over the past couple of years, but BAS had kept the thing under wraps until yesterday's test flight. No doubt today's news would be full of it.

I could have looked that up, by rolling over and reaching for my phone. I could have phoned or texted Calum. But I didn't want to. I might get offered a commission to write something about the BAS breakthrough. If I did, I knew I'd pass it up, making some excuse about pressure of other work or lack of expertise (neither of which had ever stopped me writing articles). I even had some expertise, and a continuing low-level interest in UFOs. But the very thought of thinking, writing or talking about the floating silvery globe filled me with dread. As I lay there in Gabrielle's warmth, I tried to understand why.

Gabrielle shifted, stretched, woke. A sleepy smile, a stroking hand.

'Sleep well?'

'Yes,' I said. 'You?'

'Oh yes.'

Somewhere in that brief, phatic exchange, the answer came to me: I wanted to go on sleeping well. I didn't want the dreams to come back.

At Birsay we missed the low tide, and had to be content with a stroll along the shore, where tilted sandstone strata displayed three million years to a single glance, like the riffled pages of an old book. There was a van selling instant coffee, weak and too hot. Then we went to Maes Howe, and in the stone dome followed the guide's words around the walls, peering at inscriptions and Viking graffiti. Stooping in a long tunnel and out into the light, through a stone door whose ton weight had once pivoted to the push of a child's hand.

It was our third September. We were in Orkney for its forty-oddth Science Festival. Out in the Sound the tidal turbines turned. High on the headlands the windmills spun. Lights were on and music was loud. Kirkwall's streets thronged with visitors. Its pubs and halls rang with talk of the New Improvement. Accommodation was nowhere to be had, though we were both on the Festival's programme: Gabrielle taking part in a roundtable on stem cell work, I giving a mid-evening slide-show on – of all things – flying saucers. But we were very minor players: Gabrielle had been chosen as a shining example of what a young researcher could accomplish, and my presence was the almost accidental result of my Sceptics in the Pub evenings at university being remembered by a former fellow student who'd since gone on to great things in the burgeoning sci-com racket. He'd been roped into the festival's organisation, and had a sudden slot to fill due to a bizarre tea-pouring accident that had befallen the scheduled speaker from the *Fortean Times*.

So we didn't have a room in a hotel or a rented house like the big name speakers did. We had our tent, on a campsite just outside Kirkwall. In that tent, on the night before the fourth day of the festival, I asked Gabrielle to marry me.

She looked at me across the pillow, in the glow of a cold light.

'Yes,' she said, smiling, then raised a finger. 'If . . .'

'If what?'

'If I get pregnant.'

I stared at her. 'You want kids?'

'Oh yes,' she said. 'Don't you?'

I thought about it. 'I suppose so.'

'Well then.'

'All right,' I said. 'It's a deal. Is it a deal?'

'Yes,' she said. She grasped my hand, inside the big sleeping bag. 'It used to be called handfasting.'

'Handfasted,' I said, gripping back. 'I like that. So . . . when do you want to start?'

'Now is good,' she said.

And it was, but later that night I woke up and found myself stricken with doubt. I was delighted that Gabrielle had agreed to marry me, but to make this conditional on her getting pregnant took some of the shine off it. The proposal seemed instrumental and somehow calculating. I wondered if she knew of the research Nicola had told me about, and was making some canny advance provision. And yet . . . and yet . . . wasn't she just being honest with me? She wasn't making our relationship conditional on her becoming pregnant, just its legal affirmation. In that light her precondition seemed reasonable enough, even loving – seeking her own advantage to be sure, but suggesting at the same time that what we already had was strong enough not to need formalising.

On the other hand . . . and so it went, a long and inconclusive debate in my head, until edges and seams of the tent brightened, and I fell into a sweaty, uneasy, ill-timed sleep. Over breakfast in a café in the morning we kept laughing and looking at each other and grinning and reconfirming to each other that it hadn't all been a dream. We walked hand in hand around Kirkwall and I totally surprised Gabrielle by marching into a craft jewellery shop and buying her an

239

engagement ring. As soon as she'd put it on her finger and got her thanks and a big kiss out of the way, she opened out her phone and made a big deal of bookmarking a slew of bridal sites.

'We can save a bit of money on all that,' I said.

'How?'

'Well, you already *have* the big white dress . . .'

'Don't,' she warned, 'even *think* about saying that again, or it's all off even if it turns out I'm having *triplets*.'

'Just teasing,' I said.

'I'm not. No way am I going to be anyone's little fairy princess ever again.' She mimed a shudder, then thumbed. 'Hmm, that's more like it . . .'

She pointed to an ivory outfit of slinky trousers and a flared peplum jacket.

'Now that,' I said, hardly able to breathe, 'is a look.'

In my memory that September week in Orkney had more days of sunshine and evenings of song and nights of sex than any objective recording could confirm. I remember it as the last of our good times, not because it really was – we had good times after it, and I do remember them. But they're not what you want to hear about now, are they?

18

I got off the bus just after ten in an April downpour and walked through the long corridor between the front and the back of the hospital that everyone still calls the New Royal. For a few tens of metres from the front entrance there's a display on each side of blown-up, grainy photos and engravings of heroes and heroines of medical history, linked by a once trendy timeline in coded colours. Further on, the corridor widens to a waiting area that's more like a small shopping mall, then narrows again to medical-institutional functionality and opens through glass doors at the far end to the car park at the back.

On the hillside behind the car park, a few hundred metres away by a path across a stream, rises the new BioQuarter. At that time there were six buildings, all newer than the hospital, two of them built in the previous two years. The Stem Cell

Centre, where Gabrielle worked and studied, looks like a scale model of that giant glass cube from outer space in which Revelation, as Baxter pointed out to me on his first visit, promises the righteous a happy eternity.

I swiped my card at the barrier in the lobby, nodded to the receptionist, and waited for the lift, gazing idly up at the slowly rotating suspended double-helix stained-glass mobile that filled the atrium at second, third and fourth floor levels. I'd always thought it spectacular but unimaginative. Not that I could think of an alternative, but that wasn't my job. It was the job of some artistic director who hadn't (in my jaded opinion) done it right.

The lift took me to the third floor, where the labs and offices were – the lower two floors housed the building's machinery and stores. I followed the colour-coded carpet to Nicola's place in the open-plan offices of the floor's outer section, which surrounded the glass-walled inner core that contained the labs. (Maintaining this arrangement as anything but a greenhouse accounts, I guess, for a big part of the ground floor's being entirely turned over to machinery, though the air-conditioning's solar power makes it less inefficient than it sounds.)

As always on my occasional visits to the centre, I wasn't there to see Gabrielle, although I expected to drop by her desk as usual on my way out. I was there to interview Nicola, this time about new developments in sub-dermal tissue regeneration – funding for a major research project had just been announced. Nicola gave me one of her characteristic sidelights on an otherwise routine story: a nugget about some health bureaucrat who'd had an epiphany on the more radical techniques – hitherto regulated with a heavy hand – after a friend had been badly burned in a car crash.

We talked some more, I took the relevant details and we said goodbye. Then I walked to the area where most of the junior researchers and students, including Gabrielle, worked. Here, desks were more cluttered and personal than in the largely admin area on the other side. Gabrielle wasn't at her desk. Her lab coat was draped on the back of her chair.

'Gone to the Ladies,' said a bearded guy at the adjacent workstation. I nodded and waited. After two minutes I began researching more on the story on my phone – not to my surprise, Baxter's name turned up in connection with it. After ten minutes I started to feel awkward. I wandered off and got another coffee from the machine. By the time I strolled back, Gabrielle was at her desk, hunched over a screen.

'Hi,' I said, laying a hand on her shoulder. She started and turned so violently I almost splashed the coffee. Her cheeks were blotched, the skin around her eyes red amid streaky gaps in her make-up.

'What's wrong?' I asked.

'Nothing,' she said, her voice sullen and lifeless, then added in a firmer, brighter tone, 'Nothing to worry about.' She sniffed hard and smiled. 'Hello. Good to see you.'

I pulled up a wheeled stool, laid down the cup, and sat down.

'What is it?' I said, moving closer and lowering my voice.

Gabrielle glared at me. 'Nothing. Like I said. I was just upset about something. It's nothing to do with you. We can talk about it at home.'

I glanced around. 'Some kind of work trouble?'

'Fuck,' Gabrielle mouthed, in a sort of whispered equivalent of a shout. 'No. Just leave it for now, OK?'

'OK,' I said. I took a sip of coffee. I'd never seen her so distressed. I'd seldom so much as seen her in tears. 'Are you sure?'

'Yes, I'm sure,' she said. Another watery smile. 'We can talk about this at home, all right?'

'Are you sure you don't want to just go home now?' I asked.

'For – fuck's sake,' she said. 'No.'

'All right,' I said, 'but—'

'Just go,' she said.

People were beginning to look. Anyone who didn't know about us – at least half the people there at the time – might have thought I was pestering her. I touched her shoulder – getting another flinch – and left.

We had a rented one-bedroom flat in Leith, overlooking a dusty, noisy, through-route street with a view across the rooftops of matching rundown tenements facing us, of abandoned water-front debt-boom developments rising like a gap-toothed row of gleaming teeth spotted with the brown of advanced decay, all now being extracted or drilled and filled by racketing looming cranes day and night. Double glazing, venetian blinds, and air-con made that aspect bearable. We'd made the flat our own and comfortable, furnishing it in the then new New Modern style, and decorating it to Gabrielle's taste – to which I happily deferred, recognising it at once as better than mine.

I settled down on a recliner, propped my opened phone on an angled holder, and continued working on Nicola's story and others in my in-progress file. But I couldn't concentrate, despite a welcome lack of interruptions. Every so often I'd stalk to the window, or make another coffee, or flick to the news or get lost in online byways so far removed from my initial query that I couldn't excuse them as research even to myself, or retrace with any conviction how I'd got there at all.

At about 4.30 I saved my inconclusive work for the day and answered some emails. That done, I went through to the kitchen and started preparing dinner. Like most people who'd grown up in the depression, we had still to get over the reflex of regarding meat as a treat. I took some trouble grinding and mixing spices and soaking brown rice for a vegetable curry, knowing that the actual cooking wouldn't take long. By the time Gabrielle arrived at about six the flat was full of the curry's appetising smell and the rice was almost ready.

She shook raindrops off her coat, kicked off her boots, and without saying a word or looking at me padded to the fridge and poured herself a large glass of white wine. I noticed this because she'd been cautious about alcohol in the past few weeks, saying she needed to be fully alert for her work. The timer alarm went off as she raised the glass and gave me a harsh grin. I smiled apologetically and drained the rice, and before I turned back from the sink I realised what had gone wrong that day.

'Oh, Gabrielle,' I said, opening my arms.

'I lost it,' she said, weeping into my chest. 'I lost it.'

Over and over.

I hadn't suspected she was pregnant, and Gabrielle herself hadn't been certain. She had just got round to thinking about buying a pregnancy test kit. Neither of us had any superstitions about foetuses, but we felt the loss of what we hadn't known we had as a small death. We mourned it, then after a time moped intermittently, then recovered, and tried again.

Nothing happened, not even another miscarriage. We each checked ourselves for infertility. The latest over-the-counter kits gave us blue piss: nothing amiss. Neither of us wanted to visit a clinic. We wanted to try everything less invasive first. By the anniversary of our handfasting we were timing our sex lives to a calendar and a clock. At other times we both drank too much. Whisky is a killer. I love it, I still do, but it's easy to love too much. This was another problem we shared, though we didn't think of it that way. We thought of it as a solution, a ready medicine for the small inhibitions that had infiltrated our every move and touch and word.

19

'You know what our problem is?' said Gabrielle, tipping a splash of water into a fresh-poured Highland Park on the coffee table one of those nights. 'You and me, we're from different species.'

I leaned back into my corner of the vat-grown-leather three-seat sofa – it had been our pride and joy when we'd bought it at Vegan Pelts – and returned her challenging look.

'I know,' I said. 'I've always known. You're a fucking Neanderthal. Look at your dad, it's obvious. Your whole family for that matter.'

I was smiling as I said it, my voice warm to cover the chill I felt inside, the uncanny sense that she had read my mind or independently shared the dark, unavowed suspicion planted in my brain by Calum's thoughtless flight of fancy and Nicola's off-the-record briefing.

Gabrielle shook her head impatiently. 'It's not that, it's

serious. Of course it's possible that my family has a tiny fraction more Neanderthal genes than even your average honky. So what? Everyone who's not of the Pure Race has ancestors who fucked Neanderthals, not to mention all the other hominid relatives we've caught hiding in the genome. That's got nothing to do with infertility. Non-Africans have Neanderthal genes because our ancestors could fucking well *breed* with Neanderthals.'

'That sounds logical,' I said, in my best Spock voice.

'Logical?' She swigged and laughed. 'Yes, this is kind of about logic. It's a pork chop problem.'

I wondered if she'd had a little too much to drink. 'Uh, explain . . .'

She leaned forward a bit, an elbow on a knee, glass in the other hand, the bright-eyed didactic Gabrielle I remembered from what now seemed long ago.

'"Pork chop problems",' she said, 'have nothing to do with pork chops. It's sort of a nickname, because Charles Dodgson – Lewis Carroll to you and me – first posed that kind of problem as a string of banal statements about various different guys who eat pork chops, are running out of money, rise early, and so on and so on. The question is about making some statement about one of the guys that follows from the premises. Stating the problem takes less than a page, but Dodgson confessed he couldn't solve it. Turns out you can solve it with some symbolic techniques that Dodgson didn't have available to him, but that's not the point. The point is . . .' She paused to sip. 'With me so far?'

'Uh-huh.'

'The point is, Dodgson had put his finger on a very general point, which is that there are all over the place, everywhere, sets of facts we already know or can easily see, but which we can't easily see the implications of. I read this in a book by, uh, William Poundstone, I think. There all kinds of truths that might be interesting, if only we could see them. But we can't, even though all the relevant facts are in plain sight.'

'So,' I said, 'there are all kinds of facts we know or could know, but we can't see what *follows* from these facts?'

'Got it.'

I frowned. 'Isn't that obvious as soon as it's pointed out?'

'Exactly. It wasn't obvious until Dodgson pointed it out. Or maybe it was Poundstone who clarified what Dodgson had pointed out, which would be kind of another example of what he was saying . . . Anyway, what all this has to do with species . . .' Her voice trailed off, and she gazed away, as if something interesting were on the blank television screen in the corner.

'Yes?' I prompted.

'Species,' she said. 'And us. And' – her tongue flicked across her lips, and she swallowed hard – 'infertility. Fuck, this is difficult.'

'I know,' I said, laying a hand on her knee. She put her hand across mine, squeezed a little, then shifted her knee and took her hand away.

'Don't make it more difficult,' she said. I felt stung, though I tried not to show it. 'And don't give me that hurt face,' she went on.

'I'm not.'

'You are. Don't tell me I can't see what I see.'

'All right, all right,' I said. I took a small gulp and forced a smile. 'Sorry. You were saying?'

'Yes. What this has to do with species? OK. The human species is breaking up.'

'What?' I closed my eyes tight for a moment, and rubbed my forehead. I didn't want her to know I knew. 'Why do you say that?'

'It's kind of an open secret in genetics,' she said. 'I mean, it's only mentioned in specialist journals and even there it's put . . . kind of cagily, right? Because it sort of opens a new can of worms. The human species, right' – she put down her glass to free both hands for gesticulation – 'has become so big, what are we now? Eight billion? Nine? Whatever. And even before then, even back when we were just a billion or so, we were the most numerous species of large mammals on the planet.'

'Yeah, OK, because by then we'd killed off most of the others.'

'Well, yes, but anyway. There are so many of us and increasing all the time that we're getting instances of reproductive isolation *by chance alone*.'

I shook my head. 'That can't be right. I mean, if various populations had remained separate, like . . . I don't know . . . suppose we – the Europeans, I mean – had never discovered the Americas, or Australia or something, and people had been isolated on separate continents for millions of years, heck even if none of the descendants of those who left had ever gone back to Africa after the migration and no more Africans had ever come out, maybe what people used to call races might have become species. But nothing like that ever happened, and it would have taken millions of years anyway, and people now are . . . um . . . interbreeding like never before, so—'

'This has nothing to do with *races*,' she said, almost spitting the word. 'And it wouldn't have taken millions of years, by the way, there's ten million years between us and the chimps and what is it, I think the latest count is thirty-two distinct hominid species emerged in that time, six or seven in the last million years alone, so . . . Anyway, that's all beside the point because what I'm talking about isn't like that, except it does involve the same mechanism, it's just come about in a quite different way. The mechanism is reproductive isolation – groups that don't breed together, even if it's just because there's a mountain range between them or whatever, gradually become *unable* to breed together. What's happening now is that because there are so many of us, *by chance alone* you're going to find lineages of people whose last common ancestor was way, way back, time enough for mutations to build up and make them reproductively incompatible. It's completely invisible until – until two people from these lineages come together, and, and . . .'

She spread her hands, then put them to her face.

I didn't move.

'This is what you think?'

'It's not just what *I* think,' she said, slapping her hands

251

down to her knees. 'It's a fact, though as I said it's . . . not widely talked about.'

I knew this was true. I didn't want to admit it. 'Even if it could happen to humans, which I doubt, it can't be what's happened to us. Come on, we're both Scottish, we're all Jock Tamson's bairns—'

'Oh, Christ! How many times have I heard that stupid phrase?'

'OK, OK, it's a cliché but that's because it's true,' I said. 'Most of us in these islands are descended from people who came into Europe when the ice went.' I tried a disarming smile. 'Or maybe before, in some cases.'

Gabrielle moved a hand as if swatting at a fly. 'As I said, that's true, but it's irrelevant. I'm talking about a chance thing – in effect it's long chains of genetic coincidence like those long chains of premises in pork chop logic, but with enough people it becomes statistically inevitable.'

'Well how come,' I said, 'the problem hasn't come up before?'

She looked at me as if I were stupid. 'Who says it hasn't? Infertility has been around since forever, and it seems to be increasing, or maybe it only seems to be because it's now seen as a medical problem that can be fixed rather than as a secret shame or a joke or the will of God. Cases of people who were infertile with each other but fertile with other partners . . . well, it's not new or unheard of, put it that way.'

I didn't want to think about the personal implications. I certainly didn't want to talk about them.

'So why isn't this common knowledge?'

'Like I said – the can of worms thing: race and all that rubbish. And of course for quite a lot of people it doesn't matter because they don't want to have kids anyway.'

Now she'd brought it back to where I didn't want to go. Back where she'd started, in fact. Our problem is that we're different species . . .

'But it matters to you.'

'Yes.' She paused and added, 'It matters to us.'

'Oh, fuck,' I said. I refilled our glasses. 'You know what our real problem is?'

'Drinking too much?' said Gabrielle, raising her glass.

'There's that,' I allowed. 'But no. That's a symptom. Our real problem, our problem, right, is that' – I drew a deep, ragged breath – 'you're too focused on having kids, when really we have so much else.'

'Like what?'

'Each other. Our jobs.' I waved around at the room. 'This.'

'Yes, *this*,' she said.

'What does that mean?'

'You're a lazy bugger.'

'What? I work hard, I do my share in the flat.'

'*You* work hard? Hah! You're coasting. Riding the up wave. Recycling press releases for any company whose new shiny you've spotted on your morning trawl. Hell, you don't even need to trawl, you have spider apps to do that for you.'

'Who cares?' I cried, stung. 'It brings in the dosh.'

'Yeah, for now. And enough for a cosy little couple flat. That's what I mean by lazy. If you worked at something where you actually used your abilities, we could afford a proper house.'

'Meaning,' I said, 'one big enough to have kids?'

'Yes, dammit! Yes! I sometimes think you don't want us to have kids. You certainly don't act like you're expecting to have to cope with having kids any time soon.'

'Oh, for fuck's sake!'

'And meanwhile, I'm working my arse off for my PhD, and scraping a bit on teaching and side jobs, all so I can earn more in the future, whereas you're just tarting your knack for glib writing around every high-tech fly-by-night cowboy company that needs its Japanese-robot-written hype turned into proper English. How long can you keep doing that?'

'As long as it takes,' I said.

'No,' said Gabrielle. 'You're a hack, and a flack, and there'll always be younger and hungrier hacks after that sort of job. You're stuck in a fucking comfort zone where you think because right now you earn more than me, and that's enough to furnish a wee poky flat in fucking Leith, that's enough to be going on with. Well as far as I'm concerned it fucking isn't.'

'Is that what this is about?' I said. 'Money? Location, location, location?'

'No, it isn't. It's not just that. You're not contributing all you could.'

'All I could to what? All my money goes on this place and on us.'

'I'm not talking about contributing *money*. You're not contributing to the *cause*.'

'The cause?' I was puzzled, then I remembered. 'Oh, science.'

'Yes, science! The war of knowledge against ignorance, all that, remember?'

'Yes, I remember,' I said. 'And I'm right in it. OK, it's a war and you're a soldier on the front line.' I spread my arms. 'And yes, I admit it, I put my hands up to that one, I'm just a hack propagandist, a war correspondent at best. But come on, be fair. We can't all be scientists, just like we can't all be soldiers. Us hacks and flacks have their place, keeping up morale, entertaining the troops—'

'Yeah,' she said. 'That's you, all right. You're like those big-mouthed pro-war singers and actors who enlisted – oh, how brave of them, knowing full well they'd get sent straight to the rear.'

'That's so fucking unfair,' I said. 'I'm doing what I do best.' I shrugged. 'Sorry that's not good enough.'

'Oh, take your self-pity and stuff it up your arse! Nobody's *asking* you to be a scientist—'

'I thought you just had.'

'That's because you weren't listening. What I'm saying is, you're not using the abilities you *do* have. I know fine well they don't run to doing actual science, though to be honest I'm not sure that isn't another of your lazy excuses for not doing the work when you were at school. OK, so you ended up doing English. You weren't even willing to break out a bit and do Divinity as an open atheist. Now that would have been smart, that would have been a unique selling point in the fucking intellectual labour market. But OK, you get English first-class honours, whoop-de-doo and bully for you. You know where most people with that kind of degree are working? In business and in government, that's where, not in some fucking ivory tower and especially not in fucking dead-end freelance hackwork that any junior reporter could do if they'd paid attention in science class.'

'Well, exactly,' I said. 'They didn't and I did, and that's what gives me an edge, that's what gets me commissions.'

'Yeah, dribs and drabs, which add up to more than I get at the moment but three or four times less than what other people your age with degrees are getting, and five times less than what I'll earn when I get my PhD.'

'Well, I don't see myself doing well in *management*.'

'Don't say it like it's beneath you, your dad's in management and so's mine.'

'A lot of good that did them in the depression!'

'Yes, as it happens it did do them a lot of good! They kept their jobs! The point is, you won't be earning any more in five years, ten years than you're earning now, if you're lucky enough to earn that.'

'Hey, come on, I'm building up a good rep in science journalism.'

'Don't you see?' she said. 'That's only a seller's market at the start of a boom with lots of new tech coming on stream. What about when all that shit is routine?'

She mimed covering a yawn, which set me off on a real one and wishing I could just go to bed.

'Christ, by the time that happens I'll have written a fucking book. Stop worrying.'

'I can't stop worrying. In fact I wouldn't be surprised if it's the worry that's making it difficult for me to conceive.'

'Oh, so all that stuff about separate species was just bullshit, was it?'

'No, it fucking wasn't, but the worry and the tension aren't helping at all, and neither is your attitude.'

'My attitude? Fuck's sake, if I'd known—'

'Known what?'

I didn't heed the warning in her voice. 'Known that you're so obsessed with money.'

'I'm not obsessed with money,' Gabrielle said, 'and I know what you were about to say. Well, if I'd known you were so lazy and inconsiderate, I might not have either.'

'It's not just money,' I said, plunging on. 'It's this thing about kids. I mean, can't we just accept that maybe it's not going to happen for us, at least not without—'

'I am *so* not going through IVF.'

'Oh, me neither, that was my point, but look, what I mean is can't we just accept it then? That there's more to life than having kids? What I said, before we got off on this about money – and you're right, I could look for something more stable and secure, sure, there's loads of jobs. I could find a better job. I'm happy to do that now I know it's worrying you. I'm sorry I was so dismissive about it just now, yeah, I mean I take your point. But the other thing I said, I meant it. We have each other. We *love* each other. Isn't that what matters?'

257

As I said that I leaned towards her, and reached out a hand. She swiped it aside. The gesture seemed to me far more contemptuous and dismissive than Gabrielle perhaps intended. Looking back at it, replaying it in slow motion again and again, all I see is a moment of irritation. It also stung my hand quite hard. In another moment I've revisited many times more than is good for me, I drew that hand sharply back, above my shoulder, poised to swing and hit.

Gabrielle's hand shot forward like a striking snake, grabbing my wrist as she jumped to her feet. Off balance, I rocked back on the sofa. My foot, in helpless reflex, jerked forward, fortunately missing her but kicking the coffee table. Glasses fell and rolled. There was a reek of spilled whisky.

Gabrielle, still gripping my wrist, glared down at me, her face filled with shock and fury.

'You were going to *hit* me!' she cried, as if she could hardly believe it. 'You tried to kick me!'

'No, no,' I pleaded. 'I was just – I pulled my hand back.'

'You raised your hand to me,' she said, in a duller voice, as if coming to terms with something terrible. 'And then you lashed out with your foot.'

'That was just—'

'Oh, I know what happened.' She let go of my wrist, and stepped back, and away. Her eyes welled up.

'I used to love you *so much*,' she said.

She wrenched the ring off and dropped it on the table, where it came to rest in a puddle of whisky.

*

In the morning we had a tearful reconciliation. It was like an inverted image of the morning after our handfasting in the tent on Orkney. We couldn't believe that it all hadn't been a nightmare; that we had said such wounding things to each other. She surprised me by slipping her ring back on. I had such an epic hangover that I felt my relief and pleasure and renewal of hope only as a diminution of misery, still below zero on the felicific calculus.

That night wasn't what ended it. What ended it was all the other nights like that, before and after. One day in October I came home mid-evening from a trek around the syn bio labs of Aberdeen to find her gone. She had taken all her stuff except some opened scent bottles, seldom-worn jewellery, and used cosmetics from the top of the dressing-table; and below it half a drawer's worth of short nighties which she'd seemed delighted with when I'd bought them for her.

PART FIVE

20

'Whole thing sounds like a total bummer,' said Calum, after I'd given him my side of the story a couple of weekends later, over Sunday lunchtime drinks in a quiet corner of a Greenock pub. 'Jeez, man. She seemed so nice.'

'She is nice,' I said. 'More than nice. She's lovely. I'm still in love with her.'

'Yeah, man, I understand. Fuck's sake, man. So what are you doing about it?'

'Apart from trying to contact her so often she's fucking blocked me? And then knocking on her folks' door and getting a severe warning from her old man about the legal penalties for harassment and assault?'

'Assault?'

'Yes,' I said. 'That incident I told you about . . .'

'Yeah, but you didn't actually—'

'I was very firmly told that lifting your hand to someone counts as assault. Following through with it and connecting is battery.'

'So she told her da about . . .?'

'Aye. No doubt her account is a bit more graphic than mine, and no doubt that'll grow in the telling. Plus, her dad's . . . well, he's never been exactly hostile but I can bet he's willing to believe anything bad about me. But honest, Calum, whatever you hear on the family grapevine, I never hit her or even really or intentionally threatened her.'

He closed his eyes for a moment and shook his head. 'Oh, don't worry, I believe you, Sinky. Fuck. I just cannae believe I'm hearing you saying that. That things could get so fucking awful between you and Gabrielle that the question even comes up.'

'Tell me about it,' I said. 'I can hardly believe it myself.'

I hadn't said anything to him about Gabrielle's speciation hypothesis, partly because (despite having found it well supported in the literature, if you knew what to look for and where to look) I didn't accept that it might be applicable to us, and partly because mentioning it would re-open the matter of his tall tale, over which I still felt aggrieved for reasons not then entirely clear to myself. Apart from that I'd told him everything, omitting only some of Gabrielle's more hurtful accusations.

Calum puffed thoughtfully on his electric meerschaum, then gave me a sympathetic look and a clap on the shoulder and got up to order another couple of pints. The pub wasn't one we'd been in before. It was new and so achingly cool it didn't have a television screen (it being taken as read that anyone sophisticated enough to drink there would have a phone and/or iGlasses). Blatantly artificial shapes and colours made it likewise obvious that every piece of wooden furnishing – the wall panels, the tables, the chairs and stools, the bar – was of synthetic wood, and every advertising poster changed every few minutes to make perfectly clear it wasn't paper although was designed to look like paper. In content and style the posters would have reminded my grandparents of TV ads from their youth in the Atomic Age: miracle clothes that didn't need washing; miracle detergents for clothes that did need washing; streamlined electric cars; pipes and cigarettes cool as a mountain stream and healthy as swimming in one; happy families tucking into a fragrant, tasty joint of roast beef that had cooked in ten minutes and had never been part of a cow; longer-lasting batteries demon-strated by genuine footage of dogged little robots marching across the floor of a crater on the Moon . . . Sometimes the anti-irony aesthetic of New Modern or New Serious or whatever the fad calls itself at the moment becomes so self-conscious it flips over into irony, occasioning much self-conscious soul-searching among its more (or less) self-aware practitioners. But then it was all new and exciting, like the pub.

Calum returned with the beers. 'Do you want to talk any more about it?'

'Nah,' I said. I shrugged. 'What more can you say?'

265

Calum nodded. 'Fair enough. Any time you want to talk some more, just call.'

'Thanks,' I said. We both knew perfectly well that I wouldn't. 'How's work?'

'Great,' said Calum. 'Put your glasses on and I'll show you.'

He put his own glasses on, and conjured space in the space between us: a four-sided wedge of vacuum and atmosphere, wide at the top in low Earth orbit and narrowing to a point at the ground.

'At StrathSat we're developing what amounts to real-time Google Earth – well, maybe no exactly, but that's the pitch. It's called SkEye.' (He spelled it out, wincing.) 'There's already enough microsats up there tae give near continuous coverage – orbit's ninety minutes, after all, and there's swarms ae the wee fuckers now. Sae far, sae standard, but the clever bit is integrating and updating the satellite pics wi coverage fae the other swarm we're seeing mair and mair ae, the drones. Micro and nano copters. The idea is, we combine that wi micro and what you might call nano payments – we pay the drone owners a wee slice ae dosh for every minute or second ae info we skim fae them, and our customers pay us for what they see, and a wee bit mair tae take control ae a drone – and a lot mair but still affordable now and then tae an ordinary punter tae take control ae a satellite – and integrate it all together and with existing maps and plans and augments and so on, and we sell it as an eye in the sky for everyone.'

'What,' I asked, 'would everyone or even a significant

fraction of everyone want an eye in the sky for? I'm just not seeing the market for this.'

'Aye, well, tae see it yi need an eye in the sky,' Calum said. 'But seriously – there's the practical applications: traffic, finding yir way around, hyper-local weather forecasting – killer app in Scotland, that – keeping an eye on yir weans out in the street . . . and then there's entertainment.'

'Entertainment?'

'Look.' He threw a demo onto my glasses. 'Keep a haud ae the table.'

I did, and just as well: my POV suddenly rose above the table, through the ceiling and a rendering of the levels above, to soar over the shopping centre and then skyward, to hurtle across the country with the occasional terrifying swoop to rooftop height, all the way past Glasgow and Edinburgh to the North Sea and back to make a graceful descent through roof and ceiling to where I sat. The whole episode took about three minutes.

'Jeez,' I said, taking my glasses off with a shaky hand. The room seemed to be spinning. 'Just as well I don't get motion sickness.'

'Aye, that could be a problem,' Calum acknowledged, amused. 'But you see the potential, right? Make a virtual visit anywhere on Earth – and some places aff it, for that matter. It'll no just be a consumer item, it'll be a market in itself as folks fall over theirsels tae provide guidance tae interesting sites, commentary, tags, augs, stuff I cannae imagine now, that's the beauty of it.'

'You'll need a hell of a lot of processing power.'

'Aha!' said Calum. 'That's no a problem. Two reasons. First, you're still thinking in terms ae virtual reality, whereas this is real time or recent actual images. Second, a shedload ae the processing can be offloaded ontae redundant capacity on the drones themselves, and eventually the satellites.'

'The cloud in the clouds.'

'That's exactly what we're thinking ae calling it.' He rubbed his hands. 'Possibilities there and aw, but I'm no at liberty tae talk about them yet.'

I could imagine them easily enough. Most drones' on-board electronics are off-the-shelf kit. Chips are so cheap they've become a byword. Almost all of those on drones have gigs of memory and capacity to spare. Time-sharing distributed computation across the sky could be a useful little sideline, assuming another company didn't think of it first.

'What about legal problems?' I said. 'Privacy issues, for a start.'

Calum waved as if wafting away vapour. 'Maist ae that's covered by existing legislation on CCTV, drones, et cetera. And after aw, we're only gaein folks access tae cameras that are already out there and up there, so it's up tae their owners tae comply.'

'But this feels different, somehow,' I said. 'All these invisible virtual presences? It would feel like being haunted.'

'Nae mair than's already the case.'

I sensed a stubbornness there, the holding of a line.

'Company lawyers all over it, are they?'

'Aye,' he admitted, with a grin. 'And they'll hae the sma print watertight, nae worries on that score.'

'Oh well,' I said, already bored with the topic. 'They're the experts, I guess. When does this new marvel hit the street?'

'We're going live early in the new year.'

I blinked. 'Fuck. That's fast.'

'Everythin's fast. I'll make sure you get an invite tae the launch party, and a freebie sub.'

'In the hopes of a good write-up?'

'Thought never crossed my mind.'

'Ah, thanks anyway. I need all the work I can get to pay rent on a two-person flat.'

Back on dangerous ground. I gave Calum a fractional head-shake and a toughing-it-out grin. We sipped in silence for a few moments, in mutual tacit agreement not to got here. Calum leaned forward, his face keen again.

'Speaking ae drones,' he said, 'what do you reckon tae the new ones?'

'The silver spheres?' I hazarded.

'Aye.' He tapped the side of his nose. 'No sae new tae us, eh?'

'The thought had crossed my mind,' I said.

Calum chuckled. 'I reckon they've been secretly deployed for years – decades, even. Now the NSA and whit have you has something even mair amazing come out of their black-budget programmes. Something we cannae even fucking see, probably. Nae need even tae disguise them as UFOs. So the companies they worked with are free tae roll out the old stuff as civilian applications aw shiny and new. That's why BAS and rest ae the aerospace defence companies are apparently developing them sae fast – aw the development work's been done awready! They're no just spheres now – there's airships and aw sorts turning up at Farnborough and the like.'

'Yeah, I've seen them in news of air shows.' I laughed. 'Like the old cigar-shaped motherships.'

'The what?'

I filled him in on that ancient piece of UFO lore. He looked round, and grinned.

'Kindae fits in wi the 1950s revival.'

'More like fucking 1850s, some of it.'

'Aye,' he said. He puffed out and contemplated, through a cloud of opium-scented vapour, a nearby seat wide enough for two men or one lampshade lady to sit on. 'Aw this Victoriana. Funny, that.'

'How d'you mean?'

He frowned. 'Well, here we are living under the state banks, and in Scotland we're in the fourth year ae the five-year plan that came out ae yon New Improvement bash. Total fucking road tae serfdom. And yet everything else seems tae be going the other way.'

'It's like they did in China,' I explained, reaching for a half-remembered snatch of revolutionary polemic. 'Nationalise the banks and privatise everything that isn't nailed down.'

'I'm no just talking about the economics,' he said. 'I mean, like, everything else.'

'Ah,' I said, 'I see you are fumbling for the concepts of "culture" and "civil society" and "ideology". Allow me to enlighten you.'

'Thanks but no thanks, Sinky,' said Calum. 'I hadnae planned on an entire afternoon ae drinking. I'll look them up.'

'You do that.'

'It's still communism,' he said, sounding worried. 'It just disnae look like it.'

'Indeed,' I said, wryly. 'The absence of a Party nucleus in every cell of society and of red flags and enormous portraits and slogans in prominent locations might give that superficial impression to the casual observer. And how is your father, by the way?'

Calum gave a slightly caught-out laugh. 'Aye, well. He's still banging on about how it's aw doomed tae end in bread queues and labour camps but he's no doing sae bad outae it. Still cannae get a loan fae the bank but hit on the idea ae raising money by selling shares in the garage online in Nigeria or some such dodgy scheme and he's making it back hand over fist converting petrol and diesel cars tae electric, and fitting solar roof panels and that.'

'Ah,' I said. 'Right. So he's prospering by doing exactly what the government wants him to do, in ways the government hadn't actually approved?'

'That's about the size ae it, aye.'

'Well, there you go,' I said. 'The totalitarian state in action. Sends a shiver down the spine. The dawn knock will be next, mark my words.'

271

We laughed, drank up, agreed it was good to have a serious talk about personal issues now and again, and went our separate ways. I headed up the familiar streets of Greenock's West End to my parents' house, where I'd arrived un-announced the previous afternoon as though I was still a student with the weekly pile of laundry. We'd talked on the phone a lot in the past couple of weeks. Mum had gone from grief at the loss of Gabrielle – whom she'd liked a lot – from her life to cold fury at Gabrielle for breaking my heart. Sunday lunch was over, the table cleared, but my mother had saved a few slices of chicken with rye bread and salad for me, and had just brewed coffee. I ate at the kitchen table, with Dad and Mum sipping coffee and finding as many different indirect ways as possible of asking me if I was all right. I evaded the topic by enthusing about what Calum had shown me.

'That's what you talked about?' Mum asked, crow's-feet crinkling.

I chewed, swallowed, sipped. 'More or less. We talked a bit about Gabrielle at first, but . . .' I shrugged. 'What's to say?'

'Oh well,' my mother said. 'It's good you have an old pal to turn to.'

'Oh, Calum's a rock,' I said. 'Talking to him helped a lot.'

Six weeks later, at a dire pre-Christmas party in the Glasgow offices of a night-soil export company that I was writing puff pieces for, I heard on the Inverclyde High graduate grapevine that Calum and Gabrielle were an item.

*

272

To his credit, Calum was shifty and apologetic when I confronted him about it.

I gave him plenty of time. I went home for Christmas, stayed in Edinburgh for Hogmanay, and in between went to a number of parties where I could reasonably expect to encounter the new couple. They weren't at any of them. Around the sixth of January I decided that enough was enough. That evening, settled back in my recliner, fortified by a half-empty bottle and a full glass of Nepalese whisky on the table beside me, I called Calum.

'Oh, hi, Sinky. I've . . . kindae been expecting tae hear fae you.'

Going by what I could see in his phone and the acoustics of his voice, his flat was bigger than mine. I'd never been in it, but something about the pictures on the wall behind the back of the sofa he was sitting on stirred a vague sense of familiarity, though I hadn't seen them before.

'Happy New Year to you, too,' I said. 'Give my regards to Gabrielle.'

'Next time I see her, aye.'

I waited.

'Look, man,' he said. 'It's no like I stole yir girlfriend—'

'As far as I'm concerned,' I said, 'that's *exactly* what you're doing, old pal. As far as I'm concerned, she still *is* my girlfriend. We're just going through a bad patch.'

'That's no the way Gabrielle sees it.'

'Oh, I'm well aware of that,' I said. 'You got her on the rebound. Good luck with that. But, you know, smart of you to move in on her when she was—'

'That isnae how it wis. No fucking way, man. She got in touch wi me, some time after you saw me in Greenock. I think she'd heard we'd met – I mean, she could figure that out fae yir ain postings and that – and she wanted tae gie her side ae the story. Suggested we meet for a coffee. I thought, fair enough, nae harm in that. Arranged tae meet after work. She came through fae Edinburgh and I met her in Flannagan's by the station. We talked for a bit and time wis getting on so we had a wee bite tae eat, and went on tae a pub tae have a couple of drinks before she went hame.'

'And?' I prompted. 'One thing led to another, was that it?'

'Well, no that night, but we were getting on well and talking away and we agreed we might hae mair tae say so a couple of days later I nipped through tae Edinburgh and, well . . .' He spread his hands. 'Whit mair can I say, man? We just totally fell for each other.'

'You're saying that like it was an accident? Jeez, give me some fucking credit for not having been born yesterday.'

'I knew yi widnae take it well, Sinky, and I'm sorry about that, but I cannae let you being upset stand in the way ae me and Gabrielle being happy.'

Upset? My oldest friend goes off with the love of my life, and he thinks I'm *upset?*

'Oh, I get that totally,' I said. '"All's fair in lust and counter-insurgency" – all right, I get that. What I don't get is, you must know how unlikely it is that Gabrielle's going to be with you for long, seeing as you've got her on the rebound, and

274

how much I'd try to get her back. So you must know that puts you and me in—'

'A bit ae a conflict situation?' Calum scratched behind his ear like a puppy trying to charm after having shat the carpet. 'Well, I'm sorry about that, pal, and I have nothing mair tae say except it's of your making, because there is no fucking way Gabrielle is going back tae yi.'

He was glancing off camera as he said this and I got the impression he was not alone. At the same moment I realised why the pictures on the wall behind him looked so familiar despite my not having seen them before. They were the kind of pictures Gabrielle liked – the kind of pictures that a little over a couple of months earlier had been on the walls of our flat.

'Jesus Christ! She's *moved in* with you! She's right there in the room with you *right now.*'

'No, she is no,' said Calum.

At this bold-faced lie I lost it entirely and said a few things that on sober recollection were probably ill-advised. Calum ended the call before I could say all of them.

21

Calum's response had been so inept that I half-expected him to invite me to the launch party for his employers' flying panopticon in an attempt to mend bridges. He didn't, but early in February I got StrathSat's flood of publicity in my inbox anyway, including a complimentary three-month SkEye trial package. Out of sheer economic necessity I tried it out and wrote up a piece about it, for which I made a couple of hundred pounds and a trickle of sliced and diced micro- and nano-royalties from the reposts on other sites.

I swear it wasn't until a week later, when I was bashing out an article about a new building going up (or growing up, more like, which was the point of the piece) in Glasgow and found myself blinking into SkEye to check how the on-site work was going at that very moment, just as casually as I used Google, that I had the idea of seriously abusing the app for nefarious purposes of my own. (This week-long delay, as we all now know, put me well behind the curve of early adopters.) The nefarious purpose I had in mind was using SkEye to see what Calum and Gabrielle were getting up to.

I finished the article and submitted it, then sat back, holding my glasses in hands that shook a little. Obviously my body was suffering from some drug deficiency, so I topped up the e-pipe I'd bought one dark evening in January with a shot of Focus and took a couple of puffs. The idea of turning the project that Calum was so enthusiastic about against him and Gabrielle made me smile. At the same moment I recognised it as unworthy, unfair, unethical and quite possibly illegal. About ten seconds later I put the glasses on and started searching for Gabrielle.

That wasn't as easy as it later became. I'd unfollowed and unfriended her on all accounts, and she was blocking me from contact. A face search would have taken too long for my current impatience (as would – though I hate to say this – retrieving my pictures of her from the files where I'd buried them to prevent myself continually looking them up). The time was about a quarter to five – she'd be leaving work soon. I zoomed across town to the BioQuarter, swooped on the Stem Cell Centre, and snooped on the public site to find out which room she was in. Her name wasn't on the personnel list. Damn. I dug deeper, searching on her name, and found she'd completed her research at the beginning of December. Since January she'd been teaching undergrads part-time in the Biology Department at Glasgow University to support herself while she wrote up her thesis for submission in the summer. And just as I'd suspected, she'd moved to Glasgow. The site didn't give her address, of course, but I could easily guess what it was.

I flipped my viewpoint forty-odd miles, to the doorway of the Boyd Orr Building, and hovered. I wondered how many other invisible presences hung around that doorway beside me: boyfriends and girlfriends, over-anxious parents, jealous lovers, stalkers . . . Just after five, students crowded out. The POV was partly inferential, its real-time elements pieced together from CCTV, happenstance overflights, passer-by phones. The time ticked on . . . ten past, quarter past. Just as I was beginning to wonder if the spotty coverage had missed her, Gabrielle appeared. She was smiling to herself. My heart jumped like a hooked fish. The doors swung shut behind her. She walked up the ramp to the street, and turned right. I followed her all the way on her brisk brief journey, up the hill past the old university building and down past the library and the Students' Union to the traffic lights. She crossed and walked on, took a couple of turns, and in one of the back streets between the university and the Kelvin river she skipped up a flight of steps to a main door, opened it with a key, and went in. The door closed behind her.

Inside, as I could see from the building's overlay, were three flights of stairs to the door of Calum's flat. No doubt she had a key to that, too. The only view I could get showed a light coming on, but nothing closer was on offer. I dropped back out and took the glasses off. My hands shook even more than they had before I'd put the glasses on. Not with rage or jealousy, but with the sort of slightly shame-faced thrill I sometimes felt while viewing quite innocent ice-skating, dance and fashion-history sites. I found myself wondering what time Gabrielle went to work, and which evenings she and Calum went out.

I heaved myself off the recliner, and went through to the kitchen to prepare my dinner. A tin of mixed beans went into the pan, followed by a carton of passata, a pinch of dried herbs, a few leaves and stalks of fresh coriander and a chopped chilli. While it was simmering I tore off and buttered a chunk of bread, and poured a mug of wine. When the meal was ready I put the pan on the table and ate from it with the wooden spoon while watching the news on my glasses, pausing now and then to wipe off the steam. Replete, I stuck the pan and plate in the sink, topped up the wine mug, and returned to the recliner. I made a careful mixture of Focus and Mellow Yellow – a nifty little combo of cannabinoids, opioids and nicotine from the head shop on the South Bridge that I'd taken to dropping in on – and sat back for a physically relaxed but mentally alert evening of thinking, browsing and watching vapour rings drift apart. After catching up with the rest of the day's news and checking my email and watching a clip of a skate-dancing contest in Kyrgyzstan for the third time that week I found my attention turning back to Gabrielle. With a saving modicum of caution, I resisted the temptation of another virtual visit, but I couldn't stop thinking about her.

She had apparently settled in with Calum. She'd looked

happy to be heading home, light on her feet, smiling, quick up the steps. I'd already seen the touch of her taste in the flat's decor, over Calum's shoulder. I could all too easily imagine the two of them together. They made a couple like those I'd noticed four and a half years earlier at the wedding ceilidh: all the big lunks and gracile lassies. That old Neanderthal sexual dimorphism thing . . .

At this point a thought occurred to me that got me pouring a slug of whisky into the bottom of the now empty mug, and toking Zip, a mixture more potent than Focus or Mellow Yellow. My mind started racing, and I took a swig of whisky to slow my brain.

The thought was this. Remembering the ceilidh, I'd recalled the guarded looks I'd got from Gabrielle's parents the first time they saw me, and their obvious wish for further private conversation with Gabrielle immediately afterwards. Things had continued in the same way after that discouraging start. Her parents had never really taken me to their hearts. They'd been polite enough, even friendly and hospitable, but I'd never been able to shake the suspicion that they didn't rate me as good enough for their little girl.

Was it possible, I now wondered, that Gabrielle's extended family knew, at some level, who was and who wasn't likely to be a good match? That they had some traditional knowledge, even if only in hints and rumours and old wives' tales, of the speciation that Gabrielle had learned of from studying genetics? Calum's now-disavowed schoolboy claim of a secret family tradition came back to me with renewed salience. Of course, he'd said he'd made it up, but when someone says once that they were lying earlier, how can you be sure they aren't lying again?

I could easily imagine family occasions, and weddings in particular, being used as matchmaking opportunities, bringing together cousins distant enough to avoid inbreeding but close enough to be fertile. Was it possible, then, that whoever had invited Calum to the bash had expected him, and not some stranger he'd brought along, to fall for Gabrielle – or at least, for one of the many single ladies there? He'd ended up in deep conversation with one of the bridesmaids, to be sure, but as far as I knew nothing – or nothing much – had come of it. Looking back, I had the distinct impression that Calum had noticed Gabrielle at the same moment as I had, and that the other young woman was very much a second best as far as he was concerned. If Calum hadn't baited me about missing out more than once on Sophie's subtle signalling of interest, might I have been less forward in approaching Gabrielle? Might he have got to her first? Just as he'd got to Sophie first.

Hah. That was, to my surprise, a sore point. Sophie! Every time I'd met her since and including that time in the pub before our Highers I'd missed her signals, misread her situation, put a misplaced loyalty to Calum above the impulse to say something, to do something, to make a move. A sore point, indeed. I decided that probing it further would be like poking at a tooth you already know is going to hurt.

No, what was on my mind and galling me was the thought of Calum being welcomed into Gabrielle's family as the ideal son-in-law. I felt oddly more jealous about that than I did at the thought of Gabrielle in his bed, infuriating and agonising though that was. What if – and it was here, I think, that my most elaborate and self-serving and self-destructive conspiracy theory really took off – Gabrielle's parents had all along intended Calum to be Gabrielle's partner, and had subtly poisoned her mind against me? By hinting or outright saying that I was a waster, a drifter, a man with no future? I couldn't see how I could find that out other than by a direct admission, but that could wait. What I wanted to do, right this minute, was find out if my idea about the wedding and the family had been correct.

Unfortunately for me, I knew just how to do it. My phone, my pad and now my glasses contained all the tools I needed. Some of them were standard apps, others were part of every journalist's kit and therefore on the shady side of legal. I sat up, took a toke of Zip, spread my phone on the table and pulled everything together: Registry Office records of births, marriages and deaths; police and court records; genetic databases; personal searches; consanguinity calculators . . . I started with Calum and Gabrielle, and worked my way back through generations. I soon found the two of them were indeed, as Calum had said, distant relatives. They had a great-great (etc) grandfather in common – that old village atheist Gabrielle had mentioned over our first lunch together: Seamus the Tink, Hamish an Duirach, James the Jura man. From there I began tracing the branching lines forward, through the nineteenth and twentieth centuries and on into the twenty-first. Then I traced other lines back.

By midnight I had a rough genealogy for the clan. In three dimensions it was a multi-node roughly cone-shaped network. I saved it, vaped some Bliss, knocked back a nightcap slug of Glen Pokhara and hit the sack.

The following morning, feeling predictably bleary from the whisky but revived by a shower and boosted by a toke of Zip with my first coffee, I sat at the kitchen table with my glasses on and my chin propped on my hands and watched Calum leave the flat about eight and head down to the Kelvinbridge subway station. I flipped back to the street outside the flat and kept half an eye on it while making and eating breakfast, glancing at the news headlines, and conducting a more careful scan of my science and technology trawl to see if any items worth writing about had been caught in its nets overnight.

Gabrielle left the flat about forty minutes later. I followed her every step on her ten-minute walk to work, and then, in a moment of daring, hitched a floating camcopter to catch a glimpse of her through the windows of the sixth floor. She'd put on a white lab coat and tied up her hair, and she had her hands – fists, going by the muscle tensions – rammed in the pockets as she stared at a wall screen. Then she seemed to relax a little, took her hands from the pockets and slipped on glasses of her own. Quite unaccountably, unless she had the feeling of being watched or the glasses warned of the camcopter's gaze, she turned and looked out of the window as if straight at me. I felt a jolt like electricity, but held the orientation for another few seconds. She blinked hard, gave a tiny headshake and shrug, and turned away.

I dropped the connection and sat quivering. Had she noticed me watching her? Or had she just spotted the camcopter, as a minor flaw in her sight like a floater in the eye? I searched on counter-surveillance apps and found many, several of them recently and specifically developed and marketed in response to the release of SkEye. One or two claimed to be able to show the user the identity of any SkEye user watching them. This gave me a falling-lift moment of dismay, but my experience of tech journalism made me sceptical of the claim. My doubt was confirmed by a quick search on the apps: SkEye itself was advertising counter-counter-measures as standard. The discretion of the watcher versus the privacy of the watched was just another arms race; this one, I could see, would run and run.

But this was no cause for complacency: Calum could easily have given Gabrielle backdoor access to SkEye itself, or for that matter included some usage-tracking software in my trial package. For all I knew, it might not even be a hack, it might be a feature. Maybe I was being a bit paranoid, but . . . I bit the bullet and bought a sub to EyeFly (the name was already in litigation), one of the rival products that had sprung up in the week since SkEye's launch, having been in development for months or years beforehand and hastily readied for market.

That meant it was pretty much a beta release, but I could live with that for the peace of mind.

Unless the tracking software I'd imagined had been left on my glasses . . . No. I stopped that train of thought right there. No need to get paranoid, I told myself, and just to test my nerve used my newly installed app to look at Calum at work in StrathSpace's glass tower on the Clyde. He didn't look back.

Paranoia, I decided, was something I needed to think about. There was a definite danger of my falling into it. It wouldn't do at all to let it get in the way of my investigation into a possible generations-long conspiracy that I suspected had now turned its attentions against myself.

I dropped out of EyeFly and fiddled with my e-pipe, as something to occupy my hands. A calmer toke than Zip seemed called for so I unscrewed that tank and replaced it with one of Focus, to which I added a few drops of Mellow Yellow. After I'd surrounded my nose with a soothing cloud of maple-syrup-scented vapour, I faced up square to my misgivings. Let me try to reconstruct a rapid and at the time rather frenetic process of thought.

What was I worried about? Like everyone else, I'd long taken for granted that the state, and anyone with the relevant resources and connections, could monitor all my online activity. I already knew, or had good reason to suspect, that this had happened to me at least once – when Baxter had traced my search on Revelation – and again more recently when he'd picked up on my conversation with Sophie. But Baxter had no reason to be interested in what I was doing now. I doubted that Calum, or his employers in StrathSpace, had the kind of influence and connections that Baxter and British Avionic Systems had. Nor was this likely of the people whose genealogies I'd roughed out the previous night. True enough, that network of linked extended families demonstrated a thriving lineage, but it was of people who'd done well in the small to medium private sector – business owners like Calum's father, professionals like Gabrielle's, farmers like Big Don's – rather than within the state or in companies cock-in-condom with it like defence. Oddly enough, they were exactly the kind of people Baxter's party appealed to, rather than like Baxter himself.

Baxter . . . something was bugging me about Baxter, some connection I hadn't made. I scribbled his name down, and returned my attention to the main point – that no one I was looking at was likely to be able to repeat his feat, whatever it was he had done.

So I was probably safe enough investigating the supposed family conspiracy. As for watching Calum and Gabrielle, the simple measure of changing to a different app would keep me off the radar of any unconventional counter-measures. That left the conventional ones: if Gabrielle's phone or glasses or just uneasy feelings warned her that someone was watching her, she could call the police with a complaint of stalking, in which I'd be the natural prime suspect. A mention of my name would trigger an automatic trawl of my records, and have me bang to rights.

Well, not over my adventures of the previous night and this morning, obviously, but certainly if I were to make a habit of them. A pattern of behaviour – that's the phrase the lawyers use. I wouldn't go to jail or even be fined for it, unless I'd made actual threats or actively harassed her, which I had no intention of doing. But being convicted of persistent unwanted watching of a specific individual – particularly a former lover – is a good way to get a restraining order slapped on you. And the usual restriction imposed? A software lock on your phone and other devices that leaves you with little more than the capacity to phone your mum or order a take-away. Add to this a legal restraint on your acquiring any other devices or access, and that flags up your name to every business and institution you might approach. There are ways round it, of course, but I'd be barred from any legitimate work in freelance journalism. Even after the order had expired, its record would remain. My employment prospects would be like those of someone whose name had once been on the Sex Offenders Register looking for a job in a nursery.

It might be a good idea to establish a pattern of doing a lot of virtual viewing of other places and other people. There were, after all, many uses I could make of the app in my legitimate work. I just had to be careful, and not watch Gabrielle too often. No more than once a day, say, and only when she was on the street. Or in another public place. Or in a place where she could reasonably expect to be seen. Or in a situation where she had made no provision for privacy. Or . . .

You get the idea.

22

Outside my window, snow wasn't so much falling on Leith as precipitating out of the air, in tiny particles of ice like frozen drizzle. Typical weather for the beginning of April, but enough to provoke a stirring of vague surprise and resentment, which people my age have probably picked up from their parents. It fitted my mood, which was rattled and out of sorts. I'd just come out of my by now daily self-torturing quarter-hour session of watching Gabrielle. I wasn't just watching her on weekdays. For several Saturdays or Sundays now, I'd observed her and Calum doing banal, soppy, couple-ish things, like walking hand in hand in Kelvingrove Park or shopping in Sauchiehall Street or browsing the bookshops and sitting in the cafés of Byres Road or going out to or walking home from an Indian restaurant. The more happy and relaxed they looked together the worse I felt, both about the situation and about my own jealous obsession. Time and again I mentally said goodbye and good luck to them both, waved a wry blessing at their unheeding images, and switched off. Time and again, sometimes after as long as two days, I found myself watching Gabrielle once more.

So now. Oh well. I watched her go to her work, and turned with a certain reluctance to my own. I'd sat up until late the previous night refining my history of Gabrielle's and Calum's ancestral clans, and gone to sleep feeling I had it pretty much nailed down. Now I wanted to dig deeper into it, but that wouldn't bring in any money. Paying rent on a two-person flat, I needed all the money I could get. So much for being out of sorts. What had rattled me, though, was an item that had come up in the overnight trawl.

A space access project, one of several taking shape around the old RAF airbase at Machrihanish on the Mull of Kintyre, had announced the date for its first full-scale test as sometime in the first couple of weeks in May or thereabouts. (There was a reason for this imprecision as we'll see.) The project was one of the many schemes, some on the face of it rather hare-brained, which the Scottish Government had – thanks to the crowd-sourced market-plan hybrid chimeric bastard offspring of the Scottish Futures Forum on the New Improvement – more or less backed itself into backing. We all remember the Sighthill Salmon Ladder scandal, of course, but it's only sad bastards like me who can give you the details of the Spey River Turbine affair, the Moray Firth Delphinarium

290

outrage, the Boat of Garten Wing-Mirror Farm receivership controversy, and so on.

This particular boondoggle involved launching a huge high-altitude balloon which, from high in the stratosphere, would drop a payload strapped to a cluster of ramjets. The ramjets would ignite, the craft would pull out of its powered dive and make a hairpin turn to ascent, and up it would go. The final thrust to orbit would be with a conventional rocket engine, kicking in when the air-breathing ramjets choked off for lack of air to breathe. This being Scotland, the project was called the Rammie, allegedly standing for Rapid-Airbreathing Multiple Motor Innovation Experiment, though I suspected the acronym had been an afterthought to the moniker.

One tiny little technical issue with the whole project was the inconvenient truth that the prevailing wind in Scotland is from the west, as is the jet stream, which likewise inconveniently has a tendency to wander over Scotland quite a lot. This meant that the balloon would tend to drift, not out over the Atlantic, but over the central belt of Scotland, the North Sea and on over Scandinavia and Russia, none of which were used or inhabited by folks likely to take kindly to experimental rockets making a vertical screaming nosedive in their general direction, regardless of how well-tested the 'pulling out in a hairpin turn' part of the plan was.

To this sort of knee-jerk, negative, nervous-nellie, nimby eyebrow twitching the project's participants and backers had a well-rehearsed response, repeated wearily and oft, prominent in the site's FAQ. It was . . . Ah, fuck it, let me just me pull up the quote:

Q: Won't prevailing winds and the jet stream make the balloon drift to the east, over heavily populated territory?

A: No. The balloon we're going to use is made of a new metamaterial which takes in air from one side and expels it from the other, thus moving the balloon. The thrust is small, but steady, and more than enough to counter these air currents. The balloon will only drop its payload over the North Atlantic. Furthermore, there's no intention to set up regular commercial launches from Machrihanish. The purpose of our project is to develop the technology and establish proof of concept. If successful and commercially adopted, any use of the system for scheduled launches is likely to be from the eastern coast of the Americas, or from China. The aim of our project is that Scotland will then have a head start in manufacturing equipment for this new and exciting system of cheap and reliable space access!

As a further safeguard, all our experimental ascents will be carefully timed to coincide with wind from the east, and with the jet stream flowing to the north or south of the flight path.

Not everyone, you may be surprised to learn, was reassured. Disquiet over the project had reached the Scottish Parliament, refracted through the cracked prism of political alignments. The Green Party was in the government coalition, with one junior minister, and its MSPs spoke in support of the project through gritted teeth and with one arm twisted behind them. Plenty of rank-and-file members and supporters of the party were hostile or dubious and backed a small but noisy campaign (predictably called Nae Rammie) against it.

The Renewal Party, as a small component of the official opposition bloc, presented a mirror-image contortion. Party policy and rhetoric derided the New Improvement. Some journalists, however, suspected that Renewal's three MSPs had a sneaking regard for this particular project, it being the sort of wacky optimistic private-sector government-backed space-hype adventure that appealed to them as well as to the party's younger voters, whose free-market principles could always be relied on to take a back seat to a chance to stick it to the Greens. In Parliament two had abided by bloc discipline and voted against it. The third, James Baxter, the opposition bloc's Shadow Minister for Technology, had recused himself on the grounds of perceived possible conflict of interest: the manu-facturer of the self-propelling balloon's engine was none other than his former employer, British Avionic Systems.

It was the sort of story I'd normally avoid, because – besides Baxter – it involved the silver spheres. I was still reluctant to so much as think about the new aviation, despite seeing an increasing number of anomalously speedy balloons and blimps flit across the skies. I'd tinkered with the settings of my tech-news trawls, but now and again something on the subject

293

didn't slip through the deliberate holes in my net. What had snagged this one were two company names that I definitely did keep an eye on.

One was StrathSpace, which had offered to provide the launch with hyper-local weather information and real-time coverage, an offer gratefully received and duly publicised. The other was Fabrications, the company that had given Sophie her internship and her first proper job. Its range had expanded beyond fashion textiles – the division in which Sophie was still employed, and as far as I knew doing well – via outdoor wear to tent, canoe, and microlight-aircraft fabrics, and thence to the new aviation metamaterials. It was flashed up as a sponsor and listed in the background links as the supplier to BAS of the self-propelling balloon fabric, which BAS had developed (ha!) and patented, but which it found more efficient to license out for large-scale manufacture.

Now that was an angle, I thought. It was high time I got over my phobia about the new aviation. Coming at it by way of the new metamaterials might be a gentle route to desensitising myself on the topic. And anyway, I hadn't spoken to Sophie for years.

The time was just after 9.30. I texted Sophie asking for a good time to call, and she replied that she'd ring me back in about an hour. This gave me time for more research, so I got on with that. When the phone rang I threw the call to the wall screen and let her see me too. Sophie sat at a desk, coffee mug to hand, sheets of paper and pads around her, and a wall with tacked-up sketches and swirling white-board arrows behind. She grinned at me. The grin faded as she looked at my room.

'Hi, Ryan. Did you have a party last night, or what?'

'What?' I shook my head. 'No. Why?'

'Bit of a tip you've got there, if you don't mind my saying so.'

'Oh!' I waved as if swatting at midges. 'Yeah, I need to tidy up, I guess.'

'Do that,' Sophie said. 'And yes, I've heard.'

'Heard about what?'

She gave me a look. 'Gabrielle.'

'Oh, yeah, well . . .' I shrugged.

'I understand why you're gutted,' Sophie said. 'But don't let it demoralise you, OK?'

'Well, yeah, I suppose it does seem a bit . . .'

'It does seem a bit,' she said firmly. 'It looks like it whiffs a bit, to be honest.'

I looked at the condition of the front room and saw what she meant. It wasn't obvious squalor: there were no pizza boxes or take-away cartons, because I cooked for myself; no unwashed plates, because I always ate out of pans and left them in the sink; no beer cans, because I didn't drink beer at home; and no whisky bottles, because I doggedly took these to the recycling bins every week. It was just lots of things out of place, an entropic increase in disorder.

'Anyway,' she said brightly, 'I take it this isn't what you wanted to talk about.'

I outlined what I did want to talk about.

'I'm not sure I can help,' said Sophie. 'It's not my area.' She indicated the colourful, slow-twirling sketches behind her. 'I'm still in fashion fabrics.'

'Oh, sure,' I said. 'I know. I just wondered if you could point me to someone who knows a bit more—'

'There's a link here' – she limned it in the air with the tip of her forefinger – 'to aviation fabrics enquiries—'

'Yeah, yeah,' I said. 'I've tried that. Just got the standard stuff, anyone can look at and listen to. I'd like just one sentence from an actual human voice with a name I can quote.'

'Hmm. All right. I shouldn't really do this, but try Jasmine.'

She pushed out the name and I grabbed it, slapping it on my phone before Sophie could change her mind.

'Thanks.' I felt awkward all of a sudden, like having caught myself in a faux pas. Oh yes, I'd been a bit too instrumental and brusque. 'Uh, how are things with you?'

'Fine, thanks for asking,' she said. She sipped from the mug, enjoying my discomfort, knowing I knew she knew about it. 'There's hope for you yet, Ryan. But I have to crack on at the moment.'

'Oh, that's OK, thanks, I understand. Those lampshades don't light themselves, or something.'

'Ha-ha! Not bad, not bad.' Her eyes narrowed. 'And do remember to take care of yourself, Ryan, yes?'

'Yes,' I said. 'You too.'

She snapped her fingers and her face dwindled and vanished, leaving an after-image in my mind if not on my retinae of a fleeting impression of irritation from just before the connection broke.

I called Jasmine, who turned out to be a technical specialist in the aviation fabrics plant. She was wary at first, but relaxed when I mentioned Sophie and, I think, when she realised that like her I was from Greenock. A virtual tour of the plant and running commentary took about fifteen minutes, at the end of which I had plenty of soundbites, quotes, stats, technical details and so forth to cobble together.

'I got to get on wi things, mind,' she said, sounding actually regretful.

'Oh, it's been great, many thanks.'

I wove what Jasmine had told me into other material I pulled in during the course of the morning, fired off the piece, and got a couple of acceptances before I'd finished my lunch. All very well, but picking over my necessarily unused scraps of research I sniffed the potential of something bigger: an analytical article that would get picked up by the serious sci-tech sites, and (if I pushed the right political buttons) even the main news and comment channels, especially in the US where 'The New Improvement: Threat or Menace?' was a perennial talking-head topic of displaced and disproportionate, not to say fair and balanced, debate.

The prospect was tempting. I had the track record, the background knowledge, a good list of contacts and sources, and I was now fully up to speed on developments. The opportunity was mine to seize. Only one thing made me hesitate. There was one politician I could not avoid quoting, and could not pass up the chance of an interview with or off-the-record briefing from.

I sat staring at Baxter's name on the screen for a long time, trying to think of a way I could avoid talking to him. There seemed to be none. Even a news bot wouldn't generate a story about the Rammie debate without some mention of him, and the only way I could get my story past any decent editing software would be for it to be better than anything a news bot could compile. (It's an open secret of journalism that editors fire up news bots and run comparisons on incoming copy.) I leaned back, looking away from the screen, and my gaze fell on a scrap of paper on which I'd scribbled Baxter's name.

For a moment I berated my earlier self for leaving my later self such an unhelpful reminder. Why had I written his name down? Oh yes, I'd been seeking some connection that had eluded me. Some connection – other than the coincidental one raised by my worries about surveillance – between Baxter and the problem of Calum and Gabrielle. And of course other than the obvious one with our encounter all that time ago with a light from the sky that might well have been a smaller and earlier version of the very same kind of balloon as the Rammie project would use. I still didn't get whatever my subconscious had flagged up. I hadn't seen or spoken to Baxter since Calum and I had met him by chance outside the Parliament, just before our far more fateful convergence of paths with Gabrielle. I'd glimpsed him on screen now and again, usually spitting soundbites like he had that time

Gabrielle and I had watched him on my phone while he'd ranted on a panel at the Forum.

The Forum! It was as if a light flickered in my mind. Not the connection itself, but a tiny indicator that I was close to the connection . . .

Then I saw it. I literally jumped out of my seat.

'Fuck!' I said. 'Fuck, fuck, fuck, fuck.'

Half my life suddenly made a lot more sense. I'd never been the person of interest, the focus, the centre of attention. I'd been collateral damage. I'd been played. Well, fuck that for a game of soldiers, I thought. I was a player now, I was going to play Baxter right back, and I was going to play him *good*.

I picked up the phone. I made a call, then wandered through to the kitchen and made a coffee. The time was about 3.30. I decided to give it an hour.

I took my time over the coffee, and crafted a pitch with care. Some journos pitch by buzzword bingo, and you can see the results all over the net, but reputable sites like my first target, *Sci/Tech World*, have more sophisticated editors. You can game these, too, with subtle logical constructions. You'll get the gig, maybe. But your story will get pulled as soon as real people see it (which can take some time, admittedly) and in the long run you have to change bylines so often that you never build up a reputation. *Sci/Tech World*'s front-end editor knows me from way back. It considered my proposal and commissioned the piece in, literally, less time than it takes to tell.

I cheered, celebrated with a toke of Zip, then did a bit more background research while keeping an eye on the clock icon. As soon as the number changed from 4.29 to 4.30 I called Baxter's office at Holyrood, and got straight through. This was unprecedented. I wasn't surprised.

'Hello?'

'Good afternoon,' I said. 'I'd like to speak to Jim Baxter.'

'Speaking,' he said. 'How can I help you?'

I'd already recognised his voice. He had me at hello, I thought. He'd had me at hello from the start.

'My name's Ryan Sinclair,' I said. 'I'm a science journalist, and I wondered if we could meet to discuss the Rammie project. Off the record, if you like.'

'Tomorrow,' he said. 'Ten thirty suit you?'

'Yes indeed,' I said. 'Thanks.'

'I can give you an hour and a half.'

'That's great! Thank you very much.'

'You're welcome,' he said. 'It's just my job.'

We'll see about that, I thought.

'See you then!'

'Cheers.'

He clicked off.

23

'There's a scene in *A Canticle for Leibowitz*,' Baxter said, walking along a window-walled corridor to his office, 'where – have you read it, by the way?'

'Yes,' I said. 'Years ago. On my dad's Kindle, if you can believe that.'

'Kindle, ah,' said Baxter, 'takes me back. Anyway, you may remember a scene where one of the monks has an audience with the Pope, in a very grand room, and afterwards he notices holes in the carpet and dirt in the corners and chips off the gilt and such like. I was quite young when I read that, and it made a lasting impression. My old job took me to all kinds of posh places, as you can imagine. I've been in billionaire's mansions, stayed in hotels in the Gulf States that might as well have been carved out of a solid gold asteroid, and walked through actual palaces, and every time I've noticed rust on radiators, dust on windowsills, that kind of thing – what I've come to call the ubiquity of grot.'

He took me through the front office, nodding to a research assistant and a secretary on the way, opened his inner office door and waved me in. 'The Scottish Parliament,' he went on, taking his seat behind the desk, 'is a fine example, I'm afraid.'

I sat in the visitor's seat, avoiding the draught from the closed window, and had to agree.

'Mind you,' Baxter added, picking up a pen and fiddling with it as if he missed smoking, or handwriting, 'I have to admit – there are exceptions. These minimalist modern hotels – you know: the white rooms where everything is a shelf and you can't see where the light's coming from or the water's going to?'

'Uh-huh.'

'Not a speck. I've looked. They must hose them out or something.' He laughed. 'The kind of place where you could never have an abduction experience, because if you wake up in the middle of the night it's like you're already *in* the flying saucer!'

I forced a smile, genuinely impressed at how skilfully he was winding me up. Of course he knew I'd read *Canticle* – everything you read on a device is recorded somewhere. Of course he knew that scene had impressed me – I'd mentioned it in a school homework essay, its record likewise available. And of course the only reason he'd mentioned it was to bring up, seemingly naturally and in passing, the topic of abduction experiences.

Classy, Baxter, classy. The former MiB and present MSP knew how to dish it out. Let's see how he could take it.

I shifted in the chair, which creaked alarmingly, and took out my phone and pen. Baxter made a face of apology, swivelled his chair, picked up a flask from a recess, poured a couple of coffees and passed me one.

'Now,' he said, 'let's see . . .' He tapped the pen on the desk and pretended to consult a diary. 'Ah yes, the Rammie. What exactly do you want from me about it?'

'Well, on the record, seeing how you recused yourself and that, I was wondering if you'd worked on that project's precursors, and if you had any interesting technical details or, you know, human interest stories you could recount.'

'And off the record?'

'What you really think about it.'

'Ah.' Baxter tilted back his seat, and clapped his fingertips a few times. 'That first. Off the record.'

I nodded. 'Of course.'

'"Sources close to the Shadow Minister believe that privately, he thinks . . ." OK, what I think is – have you ever heard of Cheng Ho?'

'The Chinese admiral?' I felt smug at recognising the name, and thrown off balance by the conversational swerve.

'Yes. Sailed this enormous fleet of gigantic ships to Africa and the rest of Asia and so on. And you know the sequel: the Emperor's decision not to send out any more treasure fleets, to shut down any building of ocean-going ships, and all the rest. China turned its back on the outside world, until

303

the outside world came to it, and not in a good way. That story troubles me.'

'Why?'

'I'm sure you can imagine a future analogy.'

'China shutting out the world again? Stopping trade and all that?' I shook my head. 'I can't imagine it.'

'No,' said Baxter. 'That's not what I had in mind. I can't imagine it either. But what I can imagine, very easily, is China turning its back on *space*.'

'*Space?*' I was even more surprised at this suggestion. '*China* – with their Moon and Mars bases and their space stations and Jovian expeditions and deep-sky astronomy satellites and everything?'

'Cheng Ho fleets,' said Baxter, dismissively. 'They're not turning a profit, not even the orbital hotels when you strip out the cadre reward-holiday subsidies.'

'Asteroid mining—'

'Marginal. Depends entirely on how quickly deep-crust prospecting and drilling become worthwhile. One – not even a technological breakthrough – just an engineering improvement, something as simple as a better drill-bit, and asteroid mining drops off the bottom of the balance sheet. And with all the new materials anyway . . . sure, some of them increase demand for rare earths and so forth, but most of them reduce demand for metals, petroleum, minerals generally.' He spread his hands. 'Bottom line – yes, I can well imagine China under some future government, Communist or not, deciding there were more pressing problems here on Earth, and pulling the plug on all space development outside lunar orbit, give or take a few astronomy experiments and robot probes.'

'All the more for the rest of us,' I said, flippantly.

'No.' Baxter beetled his brows. 'You really don't get it, do you? Soon, sooner than you think, there'll *be* no "rest of us", unless we do something about it. Look around you, man! Everything's made in China, which means that in the long run every decision that matters is also made in China. In fact a lot of them already are. The Big Deal only happened because China threatened to call in its debts, and—'

I held up a hand. 'Excuse me, Mr Baxter, but what has this to do with the Rammie project?'

Baxter gave a self-deprecating chuckle. 'I do go charging off on my favourite hobby-horse sometimes, don't I? OK. What all this has to do with the Rammie project, and others like it, is very straightforward. We can't afford to risk having a single government, whether or not it's formally a world government, deciding to shut down space exploration. I have to admit, in terms of gut feelings that's my strongest objection to socialism – that it makes such decisions possible. So, basically, what I'm saying off the record is that whatever my Party says and whatever my principles might be on the wisdom of pouring public money into such adventures, inwardly I'm cheering the Rammie and hoping fervently that it succeeds.'

'Well, me too as it happens, so . . . yeah, thanks, I'll make sure that view gets forcefully expressed in my article, without attributing it to you.'

'Fine, fine!' He rubbed his hands. 'And the on-the-record stuff?'

'Yes.'

I looked down at my pad, feeling nervous and trying not to show it. When I'd walked into the lobby and shaken hands with Baxter a quarter of an hour earlier, he'd given every appearance of never having spoken to me before. I hadn't bothered to remind him of our encounter a few years ago and a few yards away. He'd kept up the pose throughout the conversation with a consistency that had me almost doubting myself. I took a deep breath, scrolled my notes, and looked up.

'The ramjet component or, uh, aspect of the Rammie,' I said, 'seems to be getting plenty of attention, for obvious reasons. So I'd like to look more carefully at what everyone's calling "the balloon". It isn't strictly a balloon, is it? It's a very big version of the flying spheres that BAS developed.'

'That's right,' Baxter said. 'It's similar, but in very different proportions. The skin is literally inflated and functions as a balloon, lifting the payload. The ionisation engine is in the centre of the sphere, and obviously with such a large surface the thrust developed is less than in the spheres we tested, but more than enough to counteract the wind.'

'I'm afraid it's not obvious to me why the thrust is less over a larger surface. In effect the entire surface is covered with tiny jet engines, actively moving air in or out. Why shouldn't the thrust be *more*? For that matter, why bother with any kind of shaped shell – wouldn't a single sheet of the stuff move through the air just as well?'

306

'I suppose so,' Baxter said. 'Some kind of closed surface, and sometimes streamlining, is a convenience. As for the lesser thrust, larger surface question – you're quite right, in theory a large, say, sphere could move as fast as a smaller one, if not faster, but the size of engine and power source required would be quite impracticable, as well as prohibitively expensive. The whole point of the Rammie is that it isn't all that costly, and that it saves an immense amount of fuel in just lifting the payload the first twenty miles or so up.'

'OK,' I said, 'I'm clear on that, thanks. But just out of interest – why do the new craft move so slowly?'

'I beg your pardon? Slowly? Sixty to a hundred knots is a respectable enough clip, if you ask me.'

'Yes,' I said, 'if you compare the craft to balloons or blimps, which because of their shape we naturally do. But that's not the relevant comparison, is it? They putter about the sky like light aircraft or even drones or microlights. Their precursors used to keep pace with airliners and jet fighters, and could zip along faster than the speed of sound.'

Baxter looked puzzled. 'Precursors? You've lost me, I'm afraid.'

'You know,' I said, in as casual a tone as I could manage, making a few half snaps of my fingers as if trying to remember something trivial, 'when they were still secret military aircraft and secret drones, and when BAS was test-flying prototypes or whatever.'

'The BAS prototypes?' said Baxter. 'These were . . . what, a couple of years ago? They were slower, if anything.'

'I know,' I said. 'I saw the first one in Orkney. No, I'm talking about the ones you were flying secretly ten years and more ago.'

'BAS never did anything of the kind,' said Baxter. He gave a short laugh. 'Not in my time, anyway. And I would have known about it.'

'Oh, you probably did,' I said. 'I saw one of those things over ten years ago. More than saw it, actually. It fell out of the sky on me and a friend and knocked us out. Burned a big circular patch in the heather around us. I had some very weird and terrifying dreams that night – and for years afterwards, I can tell you.'

Baxter's lower lip twisted. 'Sorry to hear that.'

'I'm sure you are, because you came to see me the week after it happened, posing as a minister—'

'Oh!' cried Baxter. He shook a finger at me, half laughing. '*That's* who you are! I *knew* I'd met you before. Of course! You had an altercation with me on the steps outside during the Forum. Yes, it's all coming back now.' He shook his head sadly. 'You made the same accusation then. And again, I'm sorry, but I'm completely baffled by this story of yours.'

'Don't worry about it,' I said, waving the matter aside. 'Water under the bridge, as far as I'm concerned.'

His eyebrows shot up. 'Really?'

'Seriously, yes.'

'So why bring it up?'

I shrugged. 'Just so you know where I'm coming from. But

let's leave that aside for a moment, and talk hypothetically. That OK with you?'

Baxter made a show of looking at his watch. 'I have half an hour to spare, if you have half an hour to waste.'

'Good,' I said, ignoring the barb. 'Hypothetically, then. Suppose the new propulsion system that BAS rolled out recently had existed for years or decades before as a secret military technology, black budget, black programme, all that. What any ordinary observer would see when one of these things flew over would be, precisely, an unidentified flying object.'

'That's a truism,' said Baxter.

'Uh-huh. But here's my hypothesis. The ionisation engine produces a powerful electromagnetic field; ionised air has an electric charge; and between them they do very odd things to people's brains. Not everyone's, and the pilots and crews of these aircraft can wear metallic helmets and suits – flexible Faraday cages if you like – to counter the effect. For ordinary civilian use, that would be a bit of a nuisance to say the least, but hey, not a problem really, no civilians are going to be on board, and any who do encounter the machines up close can attribute any weird experiences they have then or afterwards to alien Greys or just hallucinations. Even so, you'd want to check up on as many of these civilians as possible, just to be sure they weren't saying or doing anything too awkward. You've got the whole UFO mythos working for you, not to mention the Men in Black mythos. As long as people believe that it's all about the government

309

covering up its knowledge of aliens, you needn't worry for your military secrets. And by monitoring their reactions, you gather some interesting data on the physiological and psychological effects of the fields. So far, so good.

'Eventually, though, your secret propulsion system and your advanced metamaterials are superseded by something new – could be just the sheer ubiquity of surveillance satellites and drones, could be a new stealth system or cloaking device, it could even be some breakthrough technology out of the blue-sky section of the black budget. Anti-gravity, space warps, whatever. Doesn't matter. Your hitherto top-secret technology is obsolete. So what do you do?

'Well, for a start you can just reward your loyal defence contractors and sub-contractors who've kept your secrets all those years by letting them roll out the ionisation engine and the metamaterials for civilian use. Strange fabrics flap on catwalks, silvery globes flit through the skies at air shows. And here we have a problem. A significant fraction of the population will have a noticeable reaction to the electro-magnetic fields, a smaller fraction I think will have no reaction at all, and most will be somewhere in between and just not feel good about the whole experience. You can't have random passengers and crew seeing visions, or having an uneasy sense of unseen presences, or even just a feeling of being watched, every time they ride the shiny new flying machines. I suppose you could issue everyone with special suits or helmets, but come on, that's inconvenient and it doesn't build confidence.

'So what do you do? You limit the engines' output to a level that doesn't affect people, at least not in such a drastic way. The civilian selling point of your new machines isn't speed, after all – it's manoeuvrability, dirigibility, silence, vertical take-off and landing, et cetera. They don't need engines powerful enough to run rings round MiGs and startle airliner pilots.

'But still . . . let's think of the future. You might want to have faster and more powerful machines. You might want to compete with the airlines. Heck, the airlines them-selves might be interested. The freight market looks very inviting. So there's a continued pull towards more powerful engines. Wouldn't it be handy if you knew in advance who was likely to have a bad reaction? And who could be sure not to have any reaction at all? And suppose you knew the genetic basis for these differences? That would open the way to isolating the biological mechanism – and then maybe the whole problem could be circumvented by something as simple as a pill, like a seasickness pill. Wouldn't that be worth having?'

Baxter looked at his watch. 'Are you finished?'

'Not quite,' I said. 'Still in the spirit of letting bygones be bygones . . . like I said, I and a friend had an encounter with one of these machines ten years ago, and I had some very unpleasant and vivid experiences afterwards. My friend didn't. I've traced his family history, and I've found evidence of a lineage of people who form an almost isolated reproductive group within the population. It ties in nicely with other evidence of speciation within humanity, from infertility studies

311

and so on. I've made a family tree, with notes. I think you might find it interesting.'

I picked up the file from my pad and flicked it onto Baxter's desk. He frowned, looked down at it, and poked about with his fingers.

'Hmm,' he said. 'I'm not sure I'd be interested in that sort of thing. Why do you think I would be?'

'Apart from the value of the genetic information to BAS?'

'Yes,' said Baxter. 'Apart from that. The value isn't much in any case. It's an interesting speculation to be sure, but even if there's a genetic basis for different reactions to electro-magnetic fields – which I'm sure there is – it's of very little practical use to an avionics company. Even a drug company would pass it up. Going from genomic information to medical treatments takes years, as you must know, and frankly I don't see such a minor projected benefit passing muster with the regulators, or being of much interest to investors. And apart from that . . . what?'

'Well,' I said, 'it might be of interest that there's a new race of people emerging who would, if you could identify them, make ideal pilots for the new aircraft if the companies ever do want to go in for heavy lifting.'

'"A new race"?' Baxter's voice was heavy with disdain. 'I don't like hearing talk about *race*. I don't even like hearing Africans referred to as "the Pure Race". I know, it's meant to be flattering, in a way, a sort of compensation for past prejudices and worse, but it still reinforces the old racial thinking. In a global market we literally can't afford that sort

of thing. And what does it imply about people of mixed race
– that they're of *impure* race?'

For some reason, Sophie's face flashed in my mind, adding
weight to the hint of reproof.

'No, no,' I said. 'I don't think like that at all.'

'I should hope not,' said Baxter. 'And I'd be offended if you
thought I did.'

'Of course,' I said. 'But . . .'

'But what?'

'I think what I've identified here is an actual human
speciation event.'

Baxter shrugged. 'So what? Humanity isn't a species, it's an
achievement. There have been several co-existing human
species in the past. Maybe there still are, though it's a little
unlikely now we can peer into every thicket. If new species
emerge among us, what of it? They'll still be human, and so
will we.'

'It doesn't bother you that the medical and genetic
professions are keeping very quiet about this. even though
they know it's going on?'

'Not much, no,' said Baxter. He stood up and stepped to
the window niche, and turned around with the daylight
behind him, a shadowy figure. 'In my line of work and to be
blunt in my line of politics, I get my sleeve tugged every so
often by sad little people who think I share their obsessions
over statistics on IQ and crime and what they call "race".
They assure me the correlations are all kosher, so to speak,
and that scientists are playing it down for political reasons.

And you know what I tell them? I tell them I don't know if what they're saying is all true, and I don't care. In a free society it has no public policy implications. And good day to you, sir, or madam.'

'Yeah,' I said. 'It must be annoying, getting pestered by racists.'

'Indeed,' said Baxter, dryly. He stepped away from the window. 'As for the matter you raised earlier. Let me put to you a point you may overlooked. I was for many years an employee of a defence avionics company. I rose to a position of some responsibility. In general, someone in such a position is required to sign the Official Secrets Act. Please note, I am not saying that I signed it. Now of course, the constitutional situation has changed since the days when someone such as myself might have done that. But it has been common knowledge for several generations now that persons who have signed the Official Secrets Act take their obligations under that Act very seriously. Unless a specific exemption is granted, nothing covered by the Act may be divulged. The commitment entered into is for life. It is inviolable.'

'Are you saying that's why you can't tell me what really happened?'

Baxter sighed. 'No. I'm not. I'm saying that someone who could tell you, speaking hypothetically as you put it, would be unable to answer your question. In my case there are two possibilities. One is that I don't know. The other is that I do, and have solemnly sworn never to breathe a word of it. I am not saying which, but in either case you are wasting your time badgering me about it.'

314

I thought about this.

'Well, I think that's just about everything covered,' I said. 'Thanks very much for your time, Mr Baxter.'

'Call me Jim,' he said, as if by reflex. He sat back behind his desk and looked at a diary panel, genuinely this time.

'That door handle's a bugger,' he said, barely looking up. 'Close it firmly on the way out.'

I took the hint.

My article took the rest of that week to write, and was worth every minute. After a bit of editorial back-and-forth it was accepted by *Sci/Tech World* and syndicated elsewhere, and it did indeed lead to a few minutes of earnest discussion on one late-night news channel. The payment came through on time. The Rammie project featured the piece in its own publicity, and sent me an invitation for the Holyrood press conference scheduled to coincide with live coverage of the ascent on the day (whatever day that turned out to be). The whole thing was a win at every level, until the last.

PART SIX

24

On the day of launch I woke early and checked the news. The balloon with its controversial payload had lifted from Machrihanish on schedule at dawn. The day was calm with high cloud and what little wind there was coming from the east, weather fronts almost stationary far to the west. Conditions for the experiment were ideal. I knew the controversy inside out and I had no need or wish to follow the commentary on the craft's remaining hours of uneventful ascent. I rattled out a few responses and then, feeling like a creep as usual, watched Gabrielle go to work.

Gabrielle had been gone over half a year. A dozen pairs of her shoes were under the bed. Dried-out cosmetics and jewellery clutter made the top of the dressing-table a dusty shrine.

Every so often I'd think of sweeping the lot into a black bag. Sometimes I'd get as far as taking a bin-liner into the bedroom. I'd stand there, half-crouched, my arm drawn back to swing across the surface.

The Scottish Parliament building at Holyrood overlooks a terraced plaza of concrete and grass, designed as a place for crowds to gather and demonstrations to culminate, and opens out to Holyrood Park and the lower slopes of Salisbury Crags. The effect, perhaps intentional, is to make any gathering there seem insignificant. The only one I've seen that didn't was the Forum, all those years ago, and that was unique in its scale and purpose, overwhelming its surroundings like a great flood. The morning of the launch the space dissipated rather than contained a couple of hundred protesters, with the usual placards and banners and – high above earnest, angry faces – the more original gimmick of a bobbing fleet of silvery balloons, from which hung carefully and aptly safety consciously designed cardboard and plastic mock-ups of dangerous-looking bits of old ironmongery and deadly-looking missiles, nose-cones pointed down.

Under high cloud and a watery sun the chant went up: 'Nae tae the Rammie! Nae tae the Rammie!' With open space behind and beside and a complex facade in front, the sound died away amid its own distorted echoes, but it persisted. I forbore to sneer, but I didn't spare the demonstration more than a glance before I ducked into the Media Tower. My face has long been on the list so that was no problem. Security scan is an automated archway of short-range radar and sonar, and always gives me a creeped-out feeling, a sort of shudder as I pass through, but that's probably psychosomatic. I took a right and hurried up the stairs to the journalists' pen in the lobby of the press conference hall.

At barely ten twenty I was early but the pen was buzzing, at least in a relative sense. The woman from the BBC was talking to the Member of the Scottish Parliament for Aberdeen, who was arguing against the Rammie on behalf of all the North Sea's wind farmers, oil workers, ferry passengers and remaining fish. Karl from the *Guardian*, alarmingly younger than me, waggled his fingers in the air with an occasional pause to swig from a plastic cup. Two young women from a station in Jakarta were walking around wearing antique recording gear like tiaras over their hijabs, boom cams and mikes projecting from the sides of their heads. The dozen or so drones parked on a shelf had all been booked by agencies or channels. A couple of tables had been set up with company and project reps behind them and freebie clutter on top. I hung about for a minute, taking all this in on my glasses, and then checked in at the project table to pick up a badge. After a chat I moseyed into the cramped kitchen with its familiar smells of microwave and instant. A tallish guy with his back to me was moodily waiting for a kettle to boil.

He turned, looked up. It was Calum. Black hair fashionably collar length and wavy; three-piece suit. His face thrust forward, leading with the strong forehead and jaw; his bright inquisitive eyes under bushy black eyebrows looked momentarily startled. I could see the wheels turn, then he plastered on a grin and stuck out a paw.

'Ah, Sinky! Good to see you, man!'

His voice rang with insincerity. I returned him the quickest handshake consistent with politeness. Calum had good reason to feel awkward and a bit guilty towards me, and he knew I knew. I had two entirely different, and each equally good, reasons to feel awkward and guilty towards him, but he didn't know this, at least as far as I knew. Hence a certain froideur in our interaction. I tried to keep it out of my voice.

'Hi, Calum. How's things?'

'Fine, fine.' He poured hot water into a cup, added milk, fiddled with a sachet of sugar.

'And what brings you here?'

'We're covering the weather.'

I already knew that Calum's employer, StrathSpace, had that contract and/or sponsorship deal: hyper-local meteorology for the balloon ascent and the payload drop. I bloody well should have not just known that but expected him to be there, having a fortnight or so earlier written the article that had given today's experiment its modicum of global publicity.

'We're daein the live feed as well, obvs,' Calum added.

I hadn't noticed, but now that I looked again at the display – a barely changing view of the darkening sky, the balloon and the suspended payload, whose central shaft and paired side pods had drawn an online flurry of schoolboy sniggers – I saw the SkEye logo in the lower corner. The view was from

322

directly below, from a camera on the end of a needle-thin carbon-fibre boom extending from the payload's nose-cone.

'Ah, right,' I said.

Calum stepped aside; I lurched for the kettle, then had to stand politely aside myself as Josie from the *Herald* made an entrance. Like a Dr Who companion striding from the 1850s to the 1890s between one footfall and the next she deftly shrivelled her modish metafabric meringue to a crinkled column of pleats, but even so there wasn't enough space in the galley for all of us. I delicately edged my hips past her now-bustled butt, and let her in to take care of her tea. There was a triangular exchange of pleasantries. I got back to the kettle as Josie shimmied out. Coffee at last. Calum was standing just outside the doorway.

'Kindae funny looking at that thing,' he said, gazing apparently at nothing but actually at the SkEye feed of the steadily ascending silver sphere. He glanced round, and dropped his voice. 'Given, you know. Our previous.'

'Arr,' I said, in that generic Scottish imitation of an English rural accent from some phantom shire between the Dales and Devon, all straw-chewing yokels and soot-smeared cloth-capped barefoot dole-fed blacklisted miners' waifs, 'when we were lads, like, we called them tharr shiny flying things Yow Eff Ows, we did.'

'And if owt said 'e'd seen inside 'un,' Calum fell in, 'we'd string t'bugger oop fer a witch.'

This didn't release the tension between us, but it cracked us up. It was close to the bone. Things got closer to the bone a moment later, as we both shifted from the kitchen doorway and saw the Shadow Minister for Technology arrive with a researcher and an adviser. Baxter noticed us noticing, then looked quickly away.

'Fuck me,' Calum muttered, still staring, 'the gang's all here.'

Anyone overhearing might think this referred to the politician and his retinue, but I knew it didn't. We're the close-encountered and he's the Man in Black, is what it meant.

'You know Sophie's company supplied the metafabric?' I remarked, by way of swerving from the subject.

'Yeah, course I know,' Calum said. He looked around. 'Fuck me, she's no here too, is she?'

'No,' I said. 'Why? Oh, I see. Then the gang really would be all here.'

'Aye,' said Calum. 'Think ae all ae us being involved, eh?'

At this I had a moment of panic that he was on to me, then I realised he meant us old school pals all having different involvements in the Rammie. Or was this all he meant? Luckily for me, the actual Minister for Technology arrived flanked by the Rammie project director, Hayley Walters, and her PA, so I didn't have time to wrap this particular rope any more turns around the bollard as I joined the crush for quotes and pics.

The Technology Minister, Simon Nardini, held up his hands and called out, 'OK, OK, everyone, plenty of time for questions when we get started. Ten minutes!' He disappeared into the press conference hall with Walters and the PA. I spent the ten minutes trying not to catch Baxter's eye, which wasn't too difficult because he was deep in conversation with the Indonesian lassies, and avoiding Calum, which again was easy because Calum was minding the StrathSpace table. Nobody else but Karl and Josie knew me anyway, and they were chatting to Baxter's adviser. Just as I finished my coffee and was looking for a place to dispose of the empty cup the doors opened and we were all invited in. I hung back as everyone trooped through. The drones whirred into the air and followed, leaving a vacant shelf and solving en passant my problem about where to leave the cup.

The Holyrood press conference room has a few disorderly rows of plastic chairs in front of a stage with a podium in front and a 3D HD screen behind. The screen isn't strictly necessary but it's dramatic and kind of traditional. Here and there in the room, like misplaced coat trees, are perches for drones. Most drones these days can hover unobtrusively and silently for hours, but the ones available to hire in the Media Tower aren't among them. The logos of their current users were flagged in my glasses, and this morning they were (rather aptly considering the hardware) heavyweight: Popolare, al-Jazeera, Xinhua, Frente, Zeit.

I grabbed a seat beside Karl and behind Josie, both of whom gave me the quick dismissive glance that's more or less a contractual obligation for staff to give freelance, at least in public. Chairs scraped, gear clicked, everyone settled down.

The screen lit up with the same view of the ascent we'd all been keeping track of in glasses or phones. A column at the edge gave the package's altitude and location, which a map app on my glasses translated to safely over the Atlantic, off the coast of Donegal. Now and then the view from the tiny nose-cone boom camera cut to a downward view. You could see the curve of the Earth and the white cloud layer far below. Then it cut again to the silver sphere and the blue-black sky, and stayed there. From the wings Nardini bounded to the podium, while his shadow and Walters took up flanking seats on stage.

'Good morning,' Nardini said, 'and welcome to this final stage of a great Scottish project, a giant step towards a bold and visionary method of affordable access to space, achieved by partnership between the Scottish Government and Scotland's engineers and entrepreneurs. I now turn you over to one of them, an engineer as well as an entrepreneur, Ms Hayley Walters.'

He stepped back from the podium as Walters stepped up. She tweaked her glasses, wiggled her fingers, grasped the sides of the lectern, and leaned forward.

'Thank you, Mr Nardini, and thank you all for coming. I know you're here to ask questions, and I'm ready to answer, but to tell you the truth we've answered a lot of questions over the past few weeks. Ground control at Machrihanish have just confirmed that the Rammie has reached its test altitude, the air and shipping lanes below are clear and everything is good to go. So, without further ado . . .' She turned to the screen, and – no doubt in synch with her own feed from ground control – called out: 'Five . . . four . . . three . . .

two . . . one . . .' Dramatic downward sweep of the arm, then, 'Release!'

The silver sphere shot upward as if snatched away. The camera stayed trained on the central rocket and the ramjet pods to which it was attached until the sphere had dwindled to a bright speck, then cut to the downward view. The screen showed white cloud. The altitude and air pressure numbers were a blur, the latitude and longitude stable but for a flicker to the right of the decimal points. Back to the package.

'Any second now for the ramjets,' said Walters, voice steady.

Paired flares erupted above and merged. The view became one of three black overlapping solid circles – one large, two small – and the two projecting straight lines of the wings on a background of orange and red fire.

I added my, 'Yay!' to the general spontaneous cheer.

Cut to the downward view. The white cloud had become ragged, leaving black by contrast gaps here and there.

'Flaps deployed,' said Walters. 'Thrust vector reversal sequence initiated.'

The view didn't change, except that the texture of the cloud layer became more evident.

'Any moment now.'

Nothing happened. The dark gaps became visibly larger. I heard everyone breathe in at the same moment.

'Mission abort,' said Walters, still calm. 'Cut fuel to ramjets, repeat, cut fuel to ramjets.'

The view flicked upward. The orange fire still bloomed.

'Ramjet fuel supply control malfunction,' said Walters. Her voice steadied. 'On course for fail-safe sea-level failure mode.'

Cut again to the downward view. The colour in the gaps was now brown and green. There was the sound of everyone leaning forward at once.

'What the fuck!' said Walters, not calmly. The sentiment appeared general. Her voice steadied again. 'Automatic fuel dumping initiated.'

Quick cut upward – no change – and back down. A shape familiar from maps and satellite-pic apps filled the screen. My glasses reinterpreted what was in front of my eyes at the moment my brain did the same. Right in front of us, right below the rocket, was Edinburgh. Meanwhile the telemetry rolled on, reporting a location far to the west. This was impossible, but we were seeing it.

Someone screamed. Hands went to heads. I thought to do what no one else did: I wrenched my gaze from the screen, and looked up, blinking to EyeFly. The floors and roof became transparent. In a patch of clear blue directly overhead I saw the flare, brightening. The Rammie was coming down right on top of us. I needed no technological enhancement to hear that people outside had noticed too and were making their feelings known. The noise of pandemonium battered through the walls of the Media Tower like royal cannon fire through a baronial castle. When I looked back at the screen I fancied I could see the upturned open-mouthed faces as tiny spots of white.

At the last second the looming mass of the city, its main

roads and great basalt outcrops already distinct, swung away. My quick upward glance took in a fireworks display, like a skidding turn in a shower of sparks. The screen went white, then blue. Everyone breathed out.

'Main engine firing,' said Walters.

The blue blackened by the second. Minutes passed in tense silence. I could feel my palms sweat.

'Full detonation abort,' said Walters.

The screen went black.

'Downrange confirms safe detonation abort,' said Walters. 'Debris falling clear of coasts and shipping.'

There was a moment of shaking silence. Walters took a deep breath, pulled her shoulders back, and faced forward.

'Well,' she said, 'I'm afraid there's no getting around the fact that what we've just seen is a catastrophic mission failure. However, I should say even at this point that the thrust reversal worked albeit with some delay and that the mission failed safely without casualties or significant property damage, and . . . and . . .'

'I think perhaps you should sit down,' said Nardini, taking her elbow and guiding her to one of the bucket seats on the stage. She sat, glasses on, staring straight ahead, mouth working silently.

Nardini sighed and took the podium. 'Questions?'

Clamour followed. Nardini cut through it with a pointed finger.

'Yes – BBC?'

Josie stood up.

'Mr Nardini, I've just received confirmation from ground control at Machrihanish that as well as continuous downlink telemetry they had full radar tracking of the Rammie's location at least until the drop. How do you account for the project's being so far off course that it dropped its payload above Edinburgh?'

As I listened to the question I had a flash of what felt like sheer inspiration as the answer clicked into place. I shot my hand up at once.

'Ms Thompson,' Nardini said, 'we're all a little shaken and trying to get our heads round what we've just witnessed. But my first response is to say that I have full confidence in the competence of the project director and her team, as well as in the Scottish Government's scientific and technical advisers. There is no question in my mind that we're faced here not with mere miscommunication, accident or malfunction but something altogether more deliberate and sinister.'

'Do you mean sabotage? Surely that would imply a shocking lapse of security and dereliction of duty?'

'I think it would be premature at this stage to say sabotage, precisely, but . . .' He spread his hands.

'Anyone else wish to comment?'

Baxter, who'd been as transfixed as the rest of us by the unfolding catastrophe and had sat jabbing at his phone in smouldering silence since, sprang to his feet.

'Excuse me, Simon. I wouldn't think it premature at all to call this sabotage. In fact, I would go further. We all saw where the payload was headed. We all felt it was headed directly at us, did we not? I've just run a sim of its precise trajectory, and can say with some confidence that had it not pulled out of its dive at the last moment it would have crashed on the main building of the Scottish Parliament.' He paused, and flashed a smile. 'Quite possibly, everyone here in the Media Tower would have survived.' Another pause, then a lower pitch and more solemn tone, 'In the main building, not so many. What we have just seen was an attempted terrorist attack on the government and people of Scotland.'

'Terrorist?' Josie sounded incredulous. 'We haven't had terrorist attacks in a generation. Who do you imagine could be responsible?'

Baxter's smile was thin, his voice suave. 'Ms Thompson, even someone of *your* generation may recall, if only from childhood, the many, many outrages – power cuts, traffic disruptions, net collapses, fires and explosions, to mention but a few – that the revolutionaries inflicted on us during the troubles. What was that but terrorism? To be sure, the media called it sabotage, but that was because the word "terrorism" was too closely associated with, ah, issues arising from the Middle East conflicts and of course with the war. But terrorism it was, by definition. I suggest this may be the first shot – perhaps a warning shot, perhaps a merciful failure in execution – in its return, and from the same source.'

By now he was in command of the press conference, and therefore at the front of a sensational story that was topping more and more news agendas by the second all round the world. I had to admire his despatch and panache, his ability

to think on his feet. He'd planted terrorism and the revolutionaries at the forefront of speculation; out of the corner of
my eye which I was keeping on the less respectable strands
of the net I could see the hare he'd started up running, and
an army of hitherto torpid conspiracy theorists bestirring
themselves in their basements to shamble in its trail, all
windmilling arms and wheezing halloos.

I waved my hand and stood up, but the attention was –
sensibly enough – all on the big hitters.

'Gentleman from Xinhua?' Nardini indicated, trying to wrest
the joystick back from his shadow, evidently so rattled he
couldn't read Leung Yi's name on his glasses.

'Ah, a question for Mr Baxter. Sir, the so-called revolutionaries to which you refer dissolved their organisation many
years ago. They admitted defeat. They have not been heard
from since. Does it not seem more likely that this spectacular
but limited action is designed to discredit the New Improvement
and with it the new economic policy as a whole? And which
political forces and economic interests do you think would
benefit from that?'

Oh, very good, I thought. Can't beat the professionals in
the conspiracy-theory game . . .

'Well played, Mr Leung!' said Baxter. 'Your expensive
cadre schooling wasn't wasted, I see. For the benefit of
anyone who doesn't get it – Mr Leung is hinting darkly
that those who've argued against the unsound economic
policies foisted on the world by the Chinese communists
may benefit from this outrage. To this I say quite frankly

that we may very well benefit. So what? We should. I hope we do. Next.'

With this, as so often before, Baxter over-reached. The reaction in the room and in the ever-expanding shockwave of news and comment radiating from it turned hostile or indifferent as the shadow minister saddled his familiar hobby-horse. I could see it happening, in the room and online.

Nardini took back the initiative, and my outstretched arm caught his eye.

'Mr Sinclair, from, ah . . . Mr Sinclair, the freelance.'

I tried hard not to let my voice shake.

'I just want to raise a . . . an obvious possibility. Maybe someone here already has the answer, but – before we get too worked up shouldn't we make sure that what we've just seen wasn't exactly what it seemed? The telemetry and radar showed the Rammie coming down over the sea, and the nose camera and the view in glasses showed it coming down over Edinburgh. Isn't it possible that it's the radar and telemetry data that were correct, and the camera and glasses views that were false? And therefore falsified, obviously, and a serious situation but not as bad as we—'

I could see heads shaking all around me. Calum was glaring; Karl was looking at me and making 'cut, cut' gestures.

Nardini frowned and turned to Walters. 'Perhaps you could answer that?'

She stayed seated. She fiddled with her glasses for a moment, then took them off and leaned forward. She spoke with a sad smile in her voice.

'I see that in the past ten minutes there has sprung up a "5/15 Truth" website that has already had thirty thousand views and climbing . . .' She shook her head, as if in disbelief, and continued in a sharper tone. 'No doubt my answer will go down as part of the cover-up. Let me start by saying unreservedly that my initial comment was unduly defensive – though entirely true it missed the point. I'm an engineer, not a politician. OK. First off, the real failure was of the control system – the turn was initiated far too late. If the Rammie had been where the telemetry and radar showed it to be, over the Atlantic, we'd all be terribly disappointed and indeed embarrassed but no one would have seen this as anything but an accident or an operational failure. For any shortcomings that may have led to that failure I as project director take full responsibility.

'It was of course the descent of the Rammie above Edinburgh and the very real possibility of catastrophic loss of life that has most shocked us all and raised the questions of sabotage and conspiracy. No one would be more happy than I to say that Mr Sinclair's speculation is correct. Unfortunately it is not. I can now clarify what was for all of us a confusing complex of events. The lifting device, the self-propelled balloon, was well above the cloud layer and beyond visual tracking for much of its ascent. It was however tracked by radar, and its position was confirmed by the telemetry. Even the drop itself showed up on the radar, though the package fell out of view and the balloon rose more slowly out of range. At that point all attention was on the camera images and instrument telemetry from the package, and was further focused on the . . . the delay of the thrust reversal manoeuvre. It was only when the camera images showed not sea but land below, as breaks in the cloud became visible, that we all realised that something was even more wrong than we'd thought.

'The telemetry continued to give false readings throughout. Interestingly they were a precise inversion of the true location. They showed a hundred miles or so west and a little south of Machrihanish, rather than the real location the same distances to the east and north. The package fell into Edinburgh airport radar view, and that of airliner onboard radar. The subsequent trajectory was tracked by civilian and military radar to the final detonation, which was visually confirmed almost immediately. Witnesses on the ground in Edinburgh also saw the descent and the turn, and I should add many saw it with the naked eye.'

'So why wasn't the off-course balloon picked up on radar?'

Walters stared at me. 'I see you are accredited as a technology correspondent, Mr Sinclair. You should know that there is no routine ground radar coverage at such altitudes. As it turns out, it was spotted by a passing airliner at one point, and logged as a UFO. In the precise technical sense, I hasten to add! And it may have been spotted by anti-missile radar, but no defence significance was attached to it. Will that be all?'

'Yes, thank you,' I said, with as much aplomb as I could muster. I sat down thoroughly shamefaced.

Walters took a few technical questions, and the press

335

conference broke up in some confusion as journalists stampeded outside for vox-pops and hopefully fragments of debris, which were (I saw) already appearing on sale across the Central Belt.

I didn't join the rush. All I wanted to do was head for a café, rattle out a think-piece spiced with my own on-the-spot (virtually speaking) reportage, and try to figure out how the false telemetry and its radar tracking confirmation had really been done. Calum had made himself scarce, not to my surprise. I walked out, head down, toking on the sly. Baxter caught up with me on a corner of the stairs.

'You!' he barked. 'Sinclair!'

'Sir?' I felt for a moment as if I'd been caught vaping behind the bike sheds, as in a manner of speaking I had.

'Don't "Sir" me, you insolent tyke!' Baxter poked a forefinger at my sternum, hard enough to hurt. 'I *know* what you're up to! I'm *on* to you!'

'What?' I said, drawing myself up to full frontal injured innocence for the benefit of the stairwell, busy as it was with security cameras and curious glances.

'You know very well what,' he said. 'You're mixed up in this. You came to my office six weeks ago to spin me a cock and bull story about secret races hiding among the Travelling People in the hope I'd swallow it and come out with some racist outburst and discredit myself and my party in advance. And you've just fuelled all the stupid conspiracy theories that what we saw was all a clever illusion or augmentation hack or whatever. Nice bit of disinformation, that! I don't know if you're a dupe, a pasty, a tool or a player, but I'm going to make it my business to find out. You already know which I am, Sinclair. Let me tell you, you have no idea how deep is the shit you are in.'

He was off down the stairs before I had time to think of a reply.

I thought of several on my way out, but they don't call that sort of thing *l'esprit d'escalier* for nothing.

25

In what he said to me on the stairs Baxter, of course, was right on every point. Maybe not absolutely – my story about the hidden race was entirely sincere and well-evidenced as far as I could see – but I had told it to him with ulterior motives, of which one was indeed that he would take it up and discredit himself. He didn't know what I was up to, he was going to do his best to find out, and I did know he was a player.

And I had no idea how deep was the shit I was in.

At first I thought I was under suspicion of a taste crime. It does happen. Some people affect surprise to learn that the aesthetic offence laws are still on the books. Dating from the early and militantly self-righteous phase of the New

Modernity, widely suspected of being the unintended outcome of an undergraduate guerrilla art criticism project that went too far and got taken up by an exceptionally dim-witted and self-righteous Liberal Democrat MSP and passed into law on the ensuing ripple of moral panic, the anti-irony restrictions are seldom enforced, and when they are it's more in the nature of a shakedown than anything else. You pay the fine, you promise not to do it again, and everyone goes on their way in the full understanding that you will, and that the enforcers won't be back.

So when two middle-aged guys turned up outside my flat the evening after the Machrihanish incident, wearing clean, sharp-pressed boiler-suits and brandishing council-official ID that my door camera confirmed as genuine right down to the thumbprints and retinal scans, I was annoyed but not unduly concerned. I let them in. People say they won't, but they always do. What else are you going to do? Call the police?

Willie McCormick and Ron Humphries – these were the names they gave – were solid, dependable-looking men in their mid-fifties. They sidled past me in the hallway with exactly the manner of electricity meter readers, and that air of vague apology for invading your privacy they radiate as they hunker down to read a meter in the back of the ironing cupboard. These two stood in the middle of my living-room floor and waved their scanners about. There was a ping like a microwave timer going off.

'Ah,' said McCormick, in a tone of disappointed surprise. 'Here's one.'

He reached into a bookshelf, pulled out an old DVD, and turned it over in his hands. Humphries looked on, nodding gravely as he saw the cover.

'"*Anachron*, Complete Season Two",' McCormick read out. 'On a digital video disc, and all. Takes me back, Mr Sinclair. My own kids used to watch it every Sunday evening. The law's the law, though.'

'Yeah, OK,' I mumbled. 'It was kind of a cult thing when I was in high school.'

Anachron, for those of you too young to have enjoyed that guilty pleasure, was a popular if somewhat niche television series whose high concept or inspiration must have flashed into the mind of its maker while he was watching a re-run of the genuinely classic 1976 BBC TV series *I, Claudius* and it struck him that what was missing from the frequent banqueting scenes were cigarettes and smartphones. All those upper-class Romans lolling around pretending to enjoy listening to Horace recite his poetry – or whatever sorry excuse for live entertainment the rulers of the world had to endure that week – and sipping wine, spitting out grape pips and eating dormice on sticks, just obviously needed to have a smoke and to update their relationship statuses to give them something to occupy their hands. Once the thought's got your head in its grip it won't let go. You can never see *I, Claudius* on screen again without noticing that everyone in it is just dying for a cigarette. No doubt when the series was made back in the 1970s nearly everybody *did* smoke, and the actors really were aching for their fix – that's why the frequent flashes of bad temper are so authentic – but that doesn't account for the equally conspicuous once it's pointed out lack of smartphones, which hadn't even been invented in late imperial Britain, let alone early imperial Rome, and for which everyone's thumbs are itching in vain to twitch.

The genius of *Anachron* was that it was played absolutely straight, with no suggestion of comedy or camp. It was a historical drama set in an ancient Rome where most people smoked, everyone but slaves had smartphones, and everyone including slaves watched scenes from the Colosseum on television. The regular characters even had favourite series of their own, particularly the reality TV series *I'm a Martyr, Get Me Out of Here!* in which terrified Christians and traitors and captives were thrown to the lions or hacked up by gladiators or hurled from hovering helicopters week after week. *Slave Idol* was another big hit, but its sadism was so gratuitous that the game-show was summarily axed by senatorial decree in the third or fourth episode. A particularly clever aspect of *Anachron* was that the imperial wars that appeared on the news channels and involved some of the characters happened in exactly the same places as the real imperialist wars that were going on at the time, and you could watch Romans watching their legions pacifying Persia, Mesopotamia, Cyprus, Libya and Palestine and getting attacked by bearded, robed, turbaned religious fanatics and understand exactly what it was all about.

'You do know that possessing copies of this filth is illegal, Mr Sinclair?'

'Yes,' I admitted.

Humphries chipped in, 'Do you know *why* this particular series falls foul of the law?'

I nodded. Even in the circumstances, I felt a little smug that I knew.

'It isn't the content,' I said. 'It was the marketing.'

'Aye,' said Humphries. 'The stealth marketing campaign. Legendary, that was.'

'Legendary,' McCormick agreed, still looking down at the plastic square jewellery-box cover, still turning it over and over in his hands. He looked up, as if suddenly snapping into focus. 'It was all true, you know.'

'No, it wasn't,' I said. 'That was the point.'

He cocked his head. 'Explain. Go on, Mr Sinclair. Impress me.'

'Why should I?' I shrugged. 'You know it as well as I do.'

McCormick sighed theatrically. 'An awful lot of people don't seem to comprehend the seriousness of the offence. They give me lip about censorship and that – which really ticks me off, to tell you the truth. It gets me in the mood to throw the book at them. And we wouldn't want that. So tell me.'

'All right,' I said. 'The marketing campaign was a rumour that the series inside the series, the *I'm a Martyr, Get Me Out of Here!* thing, was real. Like, it was real jihadists and shaheeds and war on terror prisoners getting torn apart by lions and all that. And the surface point, if you like, was that the British Government and the MoD and MI6 didn't deny it. The Prime Minister herself even actually winked once when she was challenged about it in an interview. The real point was that everyone went on watching it, even though they thought it might be true. But of course it wasn't, it was, uh, postmodern irony.'

'Aye,' said Humphries. 'Postmodern irony. That was the point, all right. That's why it fell foul of the law.'

'But,' said McCormick, 'the real twist is that it *was* all true.'

'Oh, come on!' I said. 'If it had been true, it would have been exposed years ago.'

'It was,' he said, sounding bored with the topic. 'But of course, that was taken to be another twist of the irony. Or maybe a conspiracy theory.' He shrugged. 'Doesn't matter, I forget. But I remember the way the prisoners screamed when we threw them out of the chopper. The dust the blades kicked up and the red splashes. That's not the sort of thing you forget.'

I stared at him, sick with the unwanted, gloating reminder of just how bad things used to be. 'You're winding me up. Look, let me just pay the fine and get this over with.'

'How do you know I'm winding you up?'

He sounded serious, and curious, like he really wanted to know.

'Well,' I said, remembering a point Baxter had made to me, 'if you were involved in something like that you wouldn't be able to talk about it, because of the Official Secrets Act, and anyway you'd be confessing to a war crime, which seeing as you know I'm a journalist and you don't know how wire-lessed this room is would be a really stupid and careless thing to do.'

'So it would,' said McCormick, 'if I gave a toss about the Official Secrets Act, or about investigative journalists.' He spun the DVD into a cluttered corner, without looking. I think the cover cracked. 'Or if we were council officials.'

At this point I realised I was in deep shit all right and made a lurch for the door, but Humphries had anticipated my move and blocked it with two expert blows, one just above the elbow and the other to the hip. I collapsed quite neatly onto the sofa. I tried to get up but my leg and arm let me down, not gently and not painlessly. I fell again in a huddle, clutching, curling up.

I looked up at them.

'Take what you want,' I said.

McCormick grabbed my glasses off my face and my phone from my shirt pocket.

'Not much use to you,' I pointed out.

'Oh, we're not *criminals*,' said Humphries, in a tone of one trying to set my mind at ease. 'We're secret police.' He glanced at McCormick. 'Are we allowed to say that?'

'I think so,' said McCormick. 'We just can't give him the name or initials. Which raises a delicate problem. How to explain?' He frowned down at me, then brightened. 'Mr Sinclair, I'm given to understand that you have been under the impression that James Baxter is or was a Man in Black.' He laughed. 'Baxter isn't a Man in Black. We are.'

'Ah, fuck off,' I said.

Without a flicker of change to his expression, Humphries

kicked the knee of my hitherto undamaged leg. I howled and doubled up, then fell apart again.

'We can keep this up all night,' said McCormick. 'Don't push your luck. As I said, I was in the helicopters.'

'What do you want?' I moaned.

'Ah, that's better,' said McCormick. 'We just want to talk, really.' He glanced over his shoulder. 'Mind if we sit down?'

'Be my guest,' I said, with as much dignity as I could muster while blinking back tears and sniffling up snot.

Humphries dragged in a couple of chairs from the kitchen. The two men sat facing me across the coffee table. I wasn't going anywhere. I tried to convince myself that if they had been criminals I would have fought back. That thought wasn't going anywhere either.

'You may well be wondering,' McCormick said, 'what you've done to bring us down on your head. You may even be feeling rather pleased with yourself that you have at least done something of significance; that you must be on the right track, that you have touched a nerve. I see you've spent the afternoon and evening digging into today's unfortunate incident. You may speculate that after we leave, you will resume your investigations and uncover the truth. I must disabuse you of that notion. If that were the situation, you would already be dead.'

He let that sink in for just long enough, and continued, 'Luckily for you, that is not the situation at all. There is no possibility of your discovering, or even touching on the truth except by accident, and even if you did, it wouldn't matter in the slightest. Let me tell you the truth about today's events. It was obvious straight away that the Rammie flight was deliberately sabotaged. By assiduous investigation, you may find – may already have found, for all I know – that this was done by overriding the controls to send it east instead of west, and to falsify all the downlink telemetry. The radar echoes were spoofed, or a decoy device was used – I don't know, and it doesn't matter. Logically, something of the sort must have happened, wouldn't you agree?'

'Yes.'

He leaned forward, elbow on knee, didactic finger pointing. 'Now, whatever the method used, it was far beyond the capacity of one person. Therefore, it was done by more than one person. Therefore a conspiracy, likewise a logical necessity. The only question remaining is: how do we find out who the conspirators were? And once again, the answer drops out with tedious predictability. We apply the time-tested principle of *cui bono?* – who benefits? And there, my friend, is where your troubles begin.'

I shook my head, or tried to. 'I don't get it.'

'Oh, you get it all right,' said McCormick pleasantly. 'But allow me to elaborate. At the press conference you heard two distinct suggestions in that respect. One was Baxter's, that the revolutionaries are coming out of sleeper mode. The other, from the local eyes, ears and mouth of the Red empire, was that what you – what he, anyway – might call *counter-revolutionaries* were behind it. People opposed to the new order, the Big Deal, the New Improvement. People, in short, like Baxter. And, not to beat about the bush, people like me and my colleague here.' He glanced sidelong at Humphries, and smirked. 'We, as you'll have gathered from what we've told you, are men of the old order, kept around by the new for our general usefulness in dirty work, but with who knows what real allegiances and values and resentments and what have you. Securocrats. Are you familiar with the term?'

'Yes,' I said.

It was first used, if my Modern Studies Higher hasn't let me down, during the Northern Ireland peace process. Some republicans saw the new settlement as a defeat and a betrayal. Most saw it as a victory, or as a step to victory, for the republican cause. The latter view was shared by many in the security forces who'd spent their lives fighting the very same terrorist bastards who were now posturing as legitimate politicians and in due course posing as elder statesmen. And the bitter old spooks did their best to undermine the peace process, along with, of course, the hard-line dissident republicans and the old-guard Unionists and die-hard Loyalists, all of whom got well and truly played by the securocrats.

McCormick shrugged, almost apologetically. 'Here we are, having to accept that the revolution we fought against has happened in a different form, one that some of the revolutionaries themselves didn't accept and still reject. But, you know, that ship has sailed. Now, it doesn't take a genius to join the dots, seeing as there are only three dots. Baxter and us, obviously – a right-wing politician is easy to link with the likes of us. Less obvious, taking maybe another minute's thought, is a connection between us and the third dot: the revolutionaries.'

'What?' I hadn't joined these dots at all.

'Who knew them more intimately, back in the day, than us? Some of us spent the best years of our lives spying on, infiltrating and disrupting the revolutionaries. If we were even minimally good at our job, we'd have had assets in place. Some of the revolutionaries would be spooks. Uh-huh?'

'I suppose so,' I said.

'Now, we all know who won that round. The revolutionaries admitted defeat, dissolved their organisation, quit their pranks, and dispersed. But, as they used to boast, they didn't go out of business, they went *into* business. They resumed the middle-class careers that their youthful enthusiasms had so rudely interrupted. Some of them will have changed their ideas to suit their circumstances, exactly as their own theory would predict. Being determines consciousness, except when it doesn't. Isn't that how it goes? Great fucking insight, that. It explains those who fall away, as well as those who don't. The ones who hang onto their ideas become, in effect, sleeper agents within the system they despise. Who knows what they're waiting for, or what they intend to do? Or indeed what they're doing now?' He coughed modestly. '*We* do. Not all of it, but some. Because some of these revolutionary sleepers are *our* sleepers. And by a high probability, some of *our* sleepers are *their* sleepers.'

'Wait a minute,' I said. 'Let me get this straight. You're saying there are outwardly respectable business and professional people who are secretly revolutionaries, that some minority of these are secretly working for the security services, and that you suspect a minority of *that* minority are assets of the revolutionaries, either infiltrated or turned?'

'Spot on,' said McCormick. 'Again, I'm not telling you anything that can't be figured out. What complicates matters further is that some personnel of the security services, namely old securocrats like us, are of dubious loyalty to the new order and would be quite happy to see it undermined. So if, let's say, someone wanted to make one of the new order's prestige projects screw up very publicly and spectacularly, almost literally blow up in the faces of its sponsors, the question of whether it's the revolutionaries or the counter-revolutionaries, the ultra-left or the ultra-right, behind it becomes indeterminate, irrelevant and moot.'

The didactic finger wagged with emphasis. '*Particularly* when we consider that the net of *cui bono?* can be cast far and wide. Competing space business interests, other states, the entire freaking menagerie of non-state actors, and last but not least, the new brooms of the security services, setting up a provocation to lure any disloyal elements out from the woodwork and chop their heads off.'

He sat back and sighed at the unfairness of it all. 'Fucking wilderness of mirrors, man.'

'I can see that,' I said. The pain was beginning to ease if I didn't move too much. By way of perverse compensation, my head was beginning to hurt.

'There will of course be an investigation,' McCormick said.

'Fingers will be pointed. Heads will roll. Hidden enemies will be dragged into the light of day. Small unpleasant creatures will be found under upturned stones, scuttling for the dark. The journalistic clichés just roll off the tongue. Don't they, Mr Sinclair?'

'Yes,' I admitted. Some of them had rattled off my keyboard already that day.

'And there, as I said, is where your troubles begin. Because you've been pointing some fingers of your own, haven't you, Mr Sinclair? And, if you'll forgive another cliché, you should always remember that when you point a finger, three fingers point back.' He demonstrated.

'I haven't pointed a finger at anyone,' I said.

'Or maybe it was like this.' He raised a hand, extended two fingers and crooked a thumb, and brought them down: the pistol gesture. 'You took a shot at Mr Baxter. Why?'

'I was trying to divert his attention.'

McCormick shot a pleased glance at Humphries. 'Aha!'

'I know why I'm in trouble,' I said.

'You do?' Despite having earlier implied as much himself, McCormick sounded sarcastic. 'In your own words, then, please.'

'But not in your own time,' added Humphries, in a menacing tone.

'Oh, we have all night,' said McCormick, in an emollient manner that seemed to be directed, scarily for me, at Humphries. To me, 'Please go on.'

'You know about my, uh, UFO encounter years ago?'

McCormick snorted. 'Yes!'

'And Baxter's, uh, pastoral visits?'

McCormick looked amused; Humphries sniggered. 'Yes.'

'Oh, right, fine,' I said. 'Well, when I was researching for an article about the Rammie, I had an idea about what might have been really going on. It came up because I saw the new flying globes, and Baxter's name, and a company called Fabrications, all on the same screen as it were. An old school friend works for that company. Her name's Sophie. You can check her out, she has nothing to do with all this, but she does in a way, that's the point.'

'You've lost me there,' said McCormick.

'Sorry. OK. Look, the thing is, we weren't supposed to be on the hill.'

'For fuck's sake!' snapped Humphries, half rising. McCormick laid a hand on his forearm. He sat back, glowering.

'Go on,' said McCormick. 'Pull yourself together, man.'

'All right,' I said, trying again. 'What I noticed when I started thinking back was that every time I saw Baxter, it was *after* I'd seen Sophie or been in touch with her. Right at the start, me and my friend Calum set out from Sophie's house for a walk on a hill above Greenock. We left our phones behind so our parents would think we were still at Sophie's. We walked up to a microwave mast at the top of the hill, and on the way we saw a police drone and a civilian drone from some strikers who were blockading the main road. Then a mist came down, and after it lifted we saw this light in the sky that came down more or less on our heads

351

and knocked us out. A few days later I was chatting by phone with Sophie and Calum; I was on my own and shortly afterwards Baxter came to the door. A few years later when I was at university I was talking to Sophie, who I hadn't seen since we were at school, and Baxter turned up again and we had a long conversation. And finally, at the big Forum, Calum and I met Sophie and an hour or two later bumped into Baxter, who by now was an MSP and claimed never to have seen me before. So when I thought back, there it was, staring me in the face all along.'

'What?'

'What this was all about. What this has *always* been about. It had nothing to do with the UFO in itself, even if it was some secret early version of the things we see flying around now. The real question was what it was being used *for*, and *why* it came down on us in the first place. I think it was being used as a drone, and it came down on us because – well, there were all these troubles going on, remember, the police at full stretch, and two lads who've left their phones behind so they can't be tracked are spotted walking up to a microwave mast overlooking the Firth of Clyde. Maybe they're there to plant a bomb and bring down the mast. Communications disrupted over a strategic area, God knows what else could be in the works. The mist covers up everything, makes normal drone work impossible. It's an emergency, this secret drone gets scrambled or is maybe on station anyway, and it's called down or called in. It arrives within minutes – not in time to prevent us but in time to catch us, scan us for explosive traces or whatever, and nothing's found. We're left with ash stains and bad dreams.

'But I and Calum and Sophie remain persons of interest from then on. Baxter checks me and Calum out, no doubt having a bit of fun with the MiB act. He finds we have no clue. But when Calum, me, and Sophie get together in later years, a flag goes up. Baxter noses around. He duly finds there's *still* nothing going on, but what does that mean? Like you said, you don't know who's a revolutionary and who isn't. And we all fit the profile. I'm a journalist, Sophie and Calum are doing well and climbing fast in two industries related to the new aviation and old UFO thing.'

'Interesting speculation,' said McCormick. 'You haven't answered the question, though.'

'Oh! Right. Well, that's simple. You see, *I* knew we weren't revolutionaries. I *knew* we hadn't set out from Sophie's house to blow up the mast. And when all this occurred to me, I'd just rung up Sophie to ask her who I could talk to in the company about the new aviation metamaterials. I guessed that this contact would be pinged to Baxter, or he could find out if he was given a reason to enquire. So I decided to give him a reason.'

'You what? Why?'

'Look,' I said, 'Baxter's been messing with my head half my fucking life. For years I had nightmares arising from that fucking flying object descending on me. So yeah, I wanted to give him some payback. I rang up Calum, whom I haven't been speaking to since he ran off with my ex-fiancée, and asked him some innocuous question about StrathSpace's involvement in the Rammie project. Then after a wee wait to let that sink in I set up a meeting with Baxter, who agreed right away. When we met the following morning I told him—'

'We know what you told him,' McCormick interrupted. 'And why you told him – so he'd take up that ridiculous theory of yours and discredit himself for racial demagogy.'

'No, no,' I said. 'That was what I *wanted* him to think was the reason I told him. The *real* reason was that I wanted him to think he was being messed with by the revolutionaries. Well, by the supposed revolutionaries me, Calum, and Sophie.'

'Why?'

'To mess with his head, to see how he liked it. And also . . . I suppose part of it was I wanted to see if he would take the bait. To test him, you know? But mainly I wanted him to feel that just for a change he was the one being watched and having his chain jerked.'

'I see that,' said McCormick. 'Oh, aye, I can see that. But if he were to take this seriously, it would bring the attentions of the security services to bear on your friends.'

I shrugged, and immediately regretted it. 'They're being watched already. I couldn't see it doing Sophie any harm, because she's not involved in anything of defence significance, she's just a frock-fabric designer.'

'That doesn't apply to your friend Calum. He's in the space industry. Having any suspicions against him – I'm not saying there are any – hardened could have quite serious consequences.'

'He's not my friend.'

'Ah,' said McCormick. 'So *that's* what this is about! Personal revenge against Baxter for – as you put it – messing with your head, and against Calum for running off with your girlfriend. And if Baxter were even privately to take seriously your tale about a secret race, and pass the evidence on to his supposed handlers or superiors, then maybe your girlfriend's family would face some unwelcome attention themselves. That about it?'

'Yes,' I admitted.

'You really are a piece of work.'

I had to agree.

'And now your little ploy has come down on your head, just like the Rammie nearly did on everyone's.'

'Yes.'

'Because suddenly it's not a game any more. Suddenly you have a lot of powerful interests scrambling to find, or hide, the truth about what happened today. Suddenly any trace of an advance diversionary operation by the revolutionaries – or anyone – becomes a matter of grave significance. Your friend Sophie works in the company that supplied the meta-fabric. Your former friend Calum works in the company that supplied the telemetry. And you've done your little bit to make sure that today's events had a global audience, you've been feeding disinformation to Mr Baxter, and you blurted out a theory at the press conference just plausible enough to look like a deception operation. Your little ploy doesn't seem like such a clever idea now, does it?'

'No,' I said, miserably.

'Baxter is raging,' McCormick said. 'Without in any way endorsing your, ah, interesting theory about what he's been up to, he's a well-informed and astute politician, and well versed in the ways of people like us. He knows all about sleepers and double agents and false-flag ops and all the rest. He might think – he might very well think – that it's not the revolutionaries but elements in the security services themselves that are behind the sabotage, and behind your diversion.'

I couldn't help but laugh, hurt though it did. 'You mean Baxter thinks *I* might be a spook?'

McCormick nodded. 'The thought has crossed his mind. He feels that his chain has been jerked, all right. As he told you, privately he was most enthusiastic about the Rammie, so he takes its sabotage quite personally. Even if – especially if – it's what you might call his own side that's behind it. He's in no mood to believe anything coming from inside the state, no matter who tells him. He feels betrayed. He's ranting to everyone who will listen, stomping the corridors of Holyrood and prowling the bars of the Royal Mile. As far as we're concerned, he's off the reservation.'

'Good,' I said, finding at last a flicker of defiance and hope. 'I've got nothing to hide. Neither do Calum and Sophie.'

'That won't prevent their lives and yours being turned upside down by people who want to make damn sure of that, and by people who *do* have something to hide and who are quite capable of framing people who don't.'

'Speaking of lives being turned upside down,' said Humphries. 'Did you know the lassie's three months pregnant?'

It was like a dash of cold water on my chest. 'What lassie?'

'You know fine what lassie. The lassie you're stalking.' He snapped his fingers. 'Gabrielle.'

I felt a surge of guilt and self-loathing at the jealousy and vengefulness that had let me smirk at the thought of Gabrielle, Calum and their families becoming objects of malign attention.

'Shit,' I said. 'Shit, shit, shit.'

'Wouldn't want her to lose another, would you?' Humphries said. 'Even if the bairn's no yours this time.'

I was on my feet without being quite aware of how I'd done it. Humphries jabbed me in the solar plexus without leaving his chair, caught my shoulders as I doubled up, and shoved me back. I toppled again onto the sofa and spent the next couple of minutes gasping and groaning. The two spooks watched in silence until I sat back up.

'Let's get back to business,' said McCormick, with an expression of mild distaste. 'There is another possible outcome to this imbroglio. One that would be very much in your interests, as well as in ours. Because there's one other place where the Rammie project might have gone pear-shaped, one simple alternative explanation of what went wrong. A single point of failure that bears an innocent, if embarrassing, interpretation. Well, to be precise that plus one ad hoc, shit-happens freak event that can be shuffled out of sight in the general relief at finding the main explanation. One that gets Baxter off our backs, the big players off the case and you and your . . . acquaintances off the hook. And above all, one that gets

357

us off the hook. Leaves our activities uninvestigated and leaves all the other serious players – agencies, companies and states – satisfied that there's nothing to see here, move along.'

'Aren't you forgetting something?' Humphries asked.

McCormick gave him a puzzled look. 'What?'

'The aliens,' said Humphries.

McCormick smacked his own forehead with the heel of his hand. 'The aliens! Of course! I was forgetting. Funny that, how one can forget about the little Grey bastards for long stretches of time. Must be a psychological coping mechanism, or something.' He stared into space for a while. 'Nah,' he said at last. 'I reckon they'll be happy with it too.'

His attention snapped back to me. 'Interested?'

26

In the morning everything still hurt: knee, hip, elbow, chest, and all the muscles I'd contorted trying not to lie on any of the bruised parts. The whisky I'd downed after the two spooks had left me to it had dulled the pain enough to let me get undressed and into bed, but it had come round like a loan-shark's heavy to take repossession on that unpaid debt. I rolled out of bed, knocked back painkillers, vaped Bliss and drank juice while I brewed coffee and burned toast. After a while I began to feel more able to face the day, or at least the daylight. The sun was bright and the sky was blue.

The time was nine thirty, a late start for me. I checked the news. It was all Rammie this and conspiracy that and investigation the other. My own articles were clocking up the page-views, which made me no money directly but should count for something next time I pitched a story. I set that aside, and laid out a plan.

I called Baxter and got through to his office. He wasn't in. I left a message. He took his time about calling me back. I'd allowed for that, and got on with working through my encrypted email folder, whose contents had more than doubled at around six that morning. By eleven I had pulled together enough evidence to sway him. It was good evidence, or so I hoped. It had damn well better be, I thought. It had been faked and planted by professionals. But as I well knew, mistakes could be made in any rushed overnight job, however skilful.

The phone flashed. Baxter. I picked it up. He didn't waste time.

'What do you want?'

'First of all, Mr Baxter, I want to apologise for what I did a few weeks ago. I'm very, very sorry about that and if we could talk privately I could explain what it was all about, even if I can't excuse it.'

He made some kind of inarticulate snorting noise that was difficult to interpret on the phone. I took this as encouragement, and ploughed on.

'And, ah, rather more pressingly I've received some information about what happened yesterday which I think might concern you and that in all fairness I think you should have the chance to comment on before it goes further.'

'Why does it concern me?'

'It's about BAS, Mr Baxter.'

'I have no connection with BAS any more.'

'Yes, I appreciate that, but all the same I think it might be of interest because it relates to the area you worked in and some of your former colleagues. There's . . . quite a bit of documentation going back to when you were there yourself.'

'Documentation?' Now he sounded interested, and suspicious.

'Yes,' I said. 'I really think you should see it.'

Long pause. I could imagine him racking his brains and scrabbling about online.

'Very well,' he said at last, as if making a huge concession. 'Why don't we meet for lunch in an hour and a half, at the pizza place? Outdoors, if the weather holds?'

'Very good, Mr Baxter,' I said. 'Thank you. I'm on my way.'

'You're walking?' He sounded surprised and amused.

'Yes,' I said. 'I need the fresh air.'

Confess everything, they'd told me. Except about our visit, obviously. Breathe a word about that and . . .

You're dead, Humphries had said. No one will believe you, McCormick had said, rather more credibly. Either way, I assured them, I had no intention of talking about it. And I haven't. Until now, of course, but I think they'll let that pass.

As I hirpled up Leith Walk and over the Bridges and down the Royal Mile to Holyrood, I accepted the pain in my knee and hip as penance. I resolved to confess everything, not just to Baxter, but to the others I'd dragged into this and endangered: Calum, Gabrielle and Sophie. Even if my approach to

Baxter failed – and the spooks had warned me that its success was in no way guaranteed – the others deserved to know why whatever was going to happen to them was happening. They would at least know whom to blame.

I quite liked and had often used the pizza place with the courtyard beside the Tun on Holyrood Road. Just beside the BBC and across the road from the *Scotsman*'s offices, and a few minutes' walk from the Parliament, it's convenient for politicians and journalists alike. Although far from private, the al fresco dining area is at busy times noisy enough to make any but the most blatant eavesdropping difficult. Surveillance, of course, is a given.

Not that I cared who might overhear me this time. I grabbed an aluminium outside table for two, ordered juice and plenty of water, and waited. The sun was high, the air was warm, the place was busy. I sipped, vaped, and people-watched. Baxter turned up on the dot of 12.30 and sat down with barely a nod for acknowledgement. His face looked more haggard than mine had been when I woke up. He hadn't shaved or put on a tie.

He looked blearily at the menu, then looked up.

'Two bruschetta, antipasto to share, two peroni – does that work for you?'

I thought about it, especially the beer.

'Hair of the dog, bit of grease to restore the stomach lining,' Baxter coaxed.

'Seeing you put it like that . . . Yes, thanks.'

'Oh, we'll split the bill,' Baxter said. 'Rules.'

'Fine,' I said.

He tapped the order onto the menu, and sat back. A waiter shimmered up with the beers.

'Ah,' Baxter said, after a sip. 'That's better.'

'Yes.'

He jerked the bottom of his bottle towards me in an ironic token toast. 'So. Out with it.'

Though I told him more than I'd told the spooks, I got through the gist before the food arrived ten minutes later. The encounter, the abduction experience, the dreams, Baxter's first visit, the UFO obsession, Calum's claims about a secret race, my private conspiracy theory about electrical stimulation of the brain, how I'd lost faith in it under Sophie's mild questioning, and my subsequent meeting with Baxter. I told him about my inability to conceive with Gabrielle, and how she and Calum were now together. I told him about how I'd connected meetings with him with meetings with Sophie, and my theory of why he had done this. I left out the whole thing about watching Gabrielle, but that was just too embarrassing and in any case not germane.

Baxter listened without comment, beyond the occasional interjection to ask me to clarify something. Now and again his eyebrows twitched, but that was as much of a response as he gave.

The food arrived. Baxter looked at the waiter, waited for a nod from me, and signalled for two more beers.

'Well, well,' he said, ripping a chunk of bruschetta and

cramming some salami into a fold. The rest of the conversation took place between bites, which at least gave me time to think. 'I had no idea. No idea at all.'

'About what?'

'About any of this. Especially of course the abduction experiences, and the dreams and the strange lines of thought they led to.' He shook his head. 'I'm sorry to hear of what you went through.'

'It wasn't your fault. And I shouldn't have—'

'No, but I can see now . . . It never crossed my mind,' Baxter said, 'that you or any of your friends were revolutionaries. When you came to me with your story, I was suspicious of course, but I suspected some little sting might have been set up by a news outlet or by one of the other parties – you know, I wouldn't put it past half the people around us at the moment. It was only when you came out with that nonsense yesterday that I suddenly saw it in a more sinister light.'

'So what were you doing when you were "Reverend Baxter"? I know you won't admit that, but . . .'

'All right,' he said, 'all right. I've examined my conscience, I've examined the rules, and – I won't go on the record, or even off the record, but I think I can couch a satisfactory answer in hypothetical terms. You OK with that?'

'Let's hear it,' I said, not willing to concede any advance acceptance.

He sighed. 'All right. Let's suppose that, some unspecified time ago, in some unspecified country an unnamed company was carrying out unspecified R and D towards a type of device whose precise nature shall be left to the imagination. Let's suppose, furthermore, that they're alert for possibilities that the competition, to put it very generally, might be a little more advanced in that research than them. One fine Monday morning – I think it's safe to be specific about the day – the said company receives confused, fragmentary reports of an incident that weekend on the other side of the country, reports that suggest the involvement of . . . a more advanced form of the imagined device. Worse, two young male civilians have had . . . some physical interaction with it.

'Now, this company has friends in high places, among them an institution whose name we dare not breathe and whose very initials are classified information. Let us call it the Non Existent Agency. This NEA can sift millions of messages and images in moments, and do far more with their content than users of keyword searches and semantic parsers can dream. It has no difficulty in identifying the two individuals involved. From their web searches and conversations it has no problem at all in recognising that the hapless lads are interpreting their unfortunate experience in the classic template of a close encounter. The company is fully briefed, and left to sort the matter out, resources being limited, as always. So a certain young engineer, whose name we need not mention, and who happens to have the appropriate clearances if not quite all the acting talents one might ideally wish for, is sent to investigate and, not to put too fine a point on it, to sow confusion.

'You can imagine how he might have gone about it, and what conclusions he might have drawn. He could, you may imagine, have exploited the Man in Black scenario. He could have used his real name – any searches on his name and his face, or even his face alone, would have shown who he really was, but that didn't matter, because the searcher might conclude that the advanced machine was in fact a product of our unnamed company, which in the circumstances is itself useful disinformation. Some years later, one of the subjects – still under low-level surveillance by the NEA – is heard broaching some interesting topics in conversation. The engineer, now somewhat older and wiser, is hurriedly despatched to have a word, and to see whether or not the subject seems likely to do or say anything embarrassing, or indeed to have something useful to say. As it turns out, he doesn't.'

'And why,' I asked, 'might this hypothetical engineer urge the subject to study Divinity, of all things?'

Baxter frowned and looked down at his plate. 'The engineer might have genuinely have had the subject's interests at heart, perhaps because his own conscience was troubling him. He might have thought that he owed the subject some . . . reduction of confusion, shall we say? And that same troubled conscience might, just possibly, have later induced the engineer to go into politics in the cause of the small state and open government.' He looked up, grinned, and spread his hands. 'And that's the end of the scenario. I can't say more about that. I can say this, though: your seeing me outside the Parliament during the Forum was a complete surprise and happened by sheer coincidence, and not too improbable a coincidence at that.'

'Oh, I can believe that,' I said. 'And your scenario sounds plausible enough.'

'Do you believe it, though?'

I hesitated. Baxter looked, at that moment, so open and honest that I had to remind myself not just that he was a politician, but of what the spooks had told me. He knows, they'd told me. He knows. That's why he might accept our story. And that's why you have to confess and apologise first, to set him up for that.

'I can accept it,' I said. 'It more or less fits what I thought was going on at first, before I made all these other connections.'

Baxter smiled. 'Good. Well, I'm glad we've got that cleared up. No hard feelings on either side, I hope. Now – you have something more urgent to tell me?'

He knows. He knows. I had to keep reminding myself of that. Just as I'd been confident in telling him what had happened and what I'd thought had happened, because I *knew* Calum and I hadn't had any sinister purpose in walking up to that microwave mast, so how Baxter responded to what I had to tell him now hinged on what he knew. What he knew and hadn't said – hadn't so much as hinted at – and that I couldn't hint at either.

'Yes indeed,' I said. 'It's probably best if . . .' I took my phone out, thumbed up the document folder, and looked at Baxter. He nodded, took out his phone and laid it on the table. I picked up the folder from my phone and placed it on his.

'Have a read,' I said. Our plates were clear and waiters were nowhere in sight. 'I'll get coffees.'

'Cappuccino,' he said, not looking up. 'Chocolate on top, no sugar.'

We touched phones to split the bill, and waited for our coffees to cool. With a stirrer stick Baxter doodled patterns in the chocolate powder on top of the foam.

'Ah, well,' he said, as if to himself. 'So this is how it's going to be. I should have known.' He looked up. 'You're going to publish this?'

'Yes. I can't not.'

'And if you don't, somebody else will.'

'I guess so,' I said. 'I mean, I have no idea who sent it.'

'Some public-spirited whistle-blower, of course,' Baxter said, with heavy sarcasm. 'No, I reckon you know as well as I do who's behind this.'

'If I did,' I said, 'and I'm not saying I do – do you think I could tell you?'

His cheek twitched. 'Same problem as I have, eh?'

'Maybe.'

'So . . . this certainly clears up why the Rammie ended up in the wrong place.' He pointed overhead, with a dark chuckle. 'It doesn't explain why the radar showed it in the place where it was expected to be.'

'No,' I admitted. 'It doesn't. But . . .' I found my hand was rubbing the back of my neck. 'There are other cases on record of that sort of thing. False echoes caused by temperature inversions, instrument unreliability, all that . . .'

'Indeed there are,' said Baxter. 'Hell of a coincidence that it should happen just then and there. Or maybe not. Peculiar weather conditions that day. Unusual reflective properties of the metafabric, which in any case was being used at altitudes it was never designed for. I've seen that sort of thing before, of course.'

He gave me such a quizzical look that I felt sure he knew I knew he knew.

'Maybe you could mention that,' I said, 'if you want to make a statement.'

He wiped foam from his upper lip and stood up. 'Let's get this over with.'

Not sure what he meant, I walked along with him as he headed back to the Parliament.

'Funny thing,' he said, as we turned into the High Street. 'Funny thing. I checked you out last night, trawled up everything I could find. I admit I was looking for something to use against you if I had to. I was a bit surprised to find you have a long-standing interest in UFOs – even spoken on the subject. As a sceptic, naturally. Now I see why.' He laughed self-consciously, and lowered his voice. 'You know, I understand the fascination myself. Even if there's nothing there, there's so much there, so to speak. Psychology, perception, meteorology, astronomy – ufology can be quite educational if you approach it in the right way.'

'Like an atheist might study Divinity, you mean?'

He shot me a glance. 'Aha! You don't catch me out like that. But what I meant to say was – don't worry about the dreams. They're real all right, but they're not *about* anything real, if you see what I mean.'

'I'm afraid I don't.'

'They're a manifestation of something that has been with us since before the ice. Since Africa, perhaps. They'll always be with us. We'll take them with us to the stars.'

'I'll not ask how you know that.'

He laughed. 'A wise decision. Oh, and by the way . . .'

'Yes?'

'If you should ever feel the temptation to go over to the dark side . . .'

'Which dark side would that be?'

'Making the news rather than reporting it. I have a research assistant vacancy coming up.'

'You're offering me a job?'

'Yes, if you want it.'

'I'll bear it in mind, thanks,' I said, less than graciously.

'Do,' he said. 'Seriously.'

We walked to the steps of the Parliament, and then to the far corner with the hill behind it. Baxter turned and faced me.

'Good location?' he asked.

'For what?'

'A recording.' He smiled thinly. 'Get your phone out. You want a scoop? I'll give you a scoop.'

When we had finished, he shrugged and said, 'Do what you want with it. Bung it to the Beeb, I'd say. They're near enough. Meanwhile, I've got work to do. See you around – or see you again soon, perhaps?'

He shook hands, then walked briskly off into the building. As I watched him disappear behind the doors I felt elated at having such a story in the cam, and at the same time heard a small voice in my head reminding me: he knows.

I took my interview with Baxter to Josie Thompson in the BBC office in the Media Tower. She edited it so as to put herself in the reaction shots asking the questions, with my full permission, because it increased the credibility and didn't diminish my credit, Baxter having mentioned me by name several times as having dug out the documents. I gave Josie a copy of the folder, so she could check the details herself.

The folder contained documentation of a tiny error in the instrumentation system manufacturing area of BAS. The component in question was one that the Rammie project had bought off-the-shelf. Its normal use was in the control systems of drone copters. Its function was feeding navigational readings from the GPS into the control system, from whence they were passed to the telemetry. Its tiny flaw was an internal counter connected to the altimeter that returned to zero when its value in metres passed 9999. As drone copters can't fly at anything near ten thousand metres, this wasn't a problem. Nor was it a problem that if the altitude read by that counter incremented to zero, a cascade of unpredictable but inevitable consequences ensued, one of which was that the system inverted its other positional co-ordinates: north became south and east became west. It only became a problem when the system was used in, say, a self-powering balloon ascending to thirty thousand metres.

The documents were, of course, virtual: they existed only in the company's computers. The copy of the folder that I gave to Josie held copies of all the documents except one dated seven years earlier: an inspection docket confirming that the design passed quality control, and screen-signed by James Baxter. I hadn't told Baxter I was going to do this, but I felt I owed him that, especially as I knew that the document, like all the others in the folder, had been forged the previous night.

I wasn't entirely sure if he knew that, too, but I did know why he was so emphatic that – while the error in the control system was an inexcusable screw-up for which he took full responsibility, it having happened on his watch – the false radar location could be dismissed as one of those things that happen from time to time.

That night I had a new dream. It was as vivid as my first abduction experience. I was in a spaceplane that was some future fulfilment of the Rammie project: a sleek arrowhead that was lifted high by a silver sphere and dropped, to swoop around and up and away to orbit.

That first time, I woke in the initial terrifying drop. In later recurrences of the recurring dream, I wake from further stages of the journey.

I still wake falling.

PART SEVEN

27

Saturday, mid-morning. I emerged from Kelvinbridge underground station into bright sunlight, ran up the steps to street level and walked across the green iron bridge over the Kelvin and on up Great Western Road, then turned left into one of the side streets. I knew exactly which door to go to, though it was odd seeing everything from ground level; odd, too, to wonder what lenses, if any, were this time watching me.

In the past couple of days the Rammie near-disaster (as it was now being called, symptomatically) had slipped from global sensation to local topic. Baxter's retraction of his conspiracy accusation, and his revelation of the instrumentation flaw, had been accepted by everyone except the inevitable conspiracy theorists. As McCormick had predicted, the puzzle of the radar anomaly had been brushed to one side in the general relief that Scotland, Britain, Europe, capitalism, socialism, civilisation, or whatever the putative target had been, wasn't in fact under attack.

I stood at the foot of the familiar short flight of worn stone steps, took a deep breath, bounded up, and rang the doorbell of Calum's flat. The power light of the camera in the top right corner of the doorway winked on, a red bead like the gaze of a lab-rat's eye. The speaker grille crackled.

'Hello?' I said. 'It's me – Ryan.'

'Oh, right, Sinky.' The voice was Calum's. 'Just a minute.'

More than a minute passed. The grille crackled again.

'OK, Ryan,' said Gabrielle. 'You can come up.'

She didn't sound welcoming. I pushed the door as the lock buzzer sounded and went up three flights of stairs within, past the usual parked bikes and scattering of car rental and fast-food flyers. Calum opened the flat door halfway and looked at me round the side.

'Morning, Sinky.'

'Hi, Duke.'

'What are you here for?'

'I just wanted to see you and Gabrielle and, uh, explain and apologise for a few things.'

'"A few things"?' He snorted. 'We havnae got aw day, you know.'

'I didn't say everything.'

He cracked a smile, and opened the door wider.

'Ah, come on in then.'

He looked not long up, barefoot and in jeans and an old T-shirt. Gabrielle, similarly dressed, sat curled up in an armchair in the small front room. She smiled but didn't get up, and motioned me to the couch.

'Coffee?' Calum offered, from the doorway.

'Yes please. Black, no sugar.'

'I remember whit yi take.'

The room looked like it was still very much Calum's, apart from the pictures on the walls, which as I'd noticed months ago showed Gabrielle's taste. The carpets were as worn as I expected and the bookcase in a niche in the corner had only half its shelves occupied by books: casual collectors' items by the look of them, more for decoration than for practical use. The other shelves suggested Gabrielle's hand at work: shells, feathers, odds and ends of old crockery, some with small cut flowers in them; glass paperweights with fossils inside, instead of the random dusty clutter the shelves would no doubt have accumulated when the place was Calum's alone.

Gabrielle watched me with a wary eye.

'How are you?' I asked.

'I'm fine,' she said.

'Everything going, uh . . .'

She sat up a bit. 'How did you know?'

Her pregnancy wasn't showing under what she was wearing at the moment: one of Calum's old T-shirts.

'Someone told me,' I said. 'I'm happy for you.'

A flicker of a smile. 'Fingers crossed.'

Calum returned bearing a mug of coffee. He handed it to me and sat on the arm of Gabrielle's chair, fingers lightly playing with her hair in what struck me as an unduly possessive manner. She didn't seem to mind.

'OK, Sinky,' said Calum. 'Shoot.'

'Well, there's two things I want to apologise about,' I said. 'First of all I want to apologise to the two of you for being such a dickhead about your being together. I mean, I knew it was all over with me and you, Gabrielle, and I know it was my fault or anyway not your fault, and, well, fuck, I'm sorry.'

'Oh, I'd have been miffed if you'd not been jealous,' Gabrielle said.

Still wounding, still teasing, still winding me up. I tried to rise above it.

'Yeah, I understand that, but still I should have been a bit more mature about it. I shouldn't have called Calum . . . all the things I called him.'

'You called me things?' Calum shook his head. 'Cannae remember. Forget about it yirsel, OK?'

'Yes,' I said. 'Thanks. Well. The other thing is . . . a bit more awkward.'

Gabrielle laughed. 'More awkward than harassing me and slandering Calum?'

'Well yes, actually. And, uh, sorry about all that, too.'

At that moment I was thinking about what I hadn't confessed and had no intention of confessing. I must have looked impressively guilty and ashamed of myself because Gabrielle shrugged one shoulder and said, 'All right, apology accepted. A note to my parents wouldn't be out of place either, by the way.'

'I'll do that,' I said.

'Grovel a bit,' she advised.

'Uh, that won't be hard,' I said, 'because the other thing kind of concerns them, as well.'

'It does?' Gabrielle looked less lazily sensual, less accepting of an apology that was nothing but her due, wary again and more alert. 'What's it about?'

I took a fortifying puff of Zip and sip of coffee. 'Do you have your glasses handy?'

With a faint snort of irritation, Calum heaved himself up, padded out, and returned with two sets of glasses. I took out my phone and thumbed up the genealogy file, and flicked it across. They examined it.

'Jeez,' said Calum, when he saw what it was. Gabrielle shot me a look of anger and disappointment. They turned the structure over and pulled it about as I explained why and how I'd compiled it.

'And that's not the worst of it,' I said.

'Not the worst?' Gabrielle asked, sounding shocked.

I drained the mug. By now the coffee was lukewarm. 'No,' I said. 'There's more.'

I then told them how I'd taken it to Baxter, and why, and what had happened – including about the spooks' visit, and the aftermath.

'Jesus, Sinky,' said Calum, 'You are a bit of a shit.'

'I know,' I said. 'I'm sorry.'

'No, really,' said Gabrielle, voice shaking, her face white to the lips, 'this is the most spiteful, vindictive, stupid thing you

379

could have done. Didn't you even *think?* What if Baxter really *had* been a fascist? Did you not think about that? Or *did* you? Did the thought of me and mine getting identified and investigated and maybe even persecuted give you a little smirk of quiet satisfaction?'

'No!' I said. That was exactly what it had given me; even though I hadn't taken the possibility seriously I'd entertained the fantasy. The guilty memory added heat to my denial. 'No, nothing like that! I *knew* it wouldn't come to anything like that. I knew Baxter would treat it as a provocation, that was the whole point. I knew he'd be suspicious of it.'

'Oh, you knew, did you?'

'Yes, and anyway this is all public, it's all on the databases, and you said yourself about the speciation thing being known—'

'Oh, fuck you, Ryan, grow up. It may be out there but it takes a – an evil ideology or an evil mind to pull it all together like that.'

'I don't have *any* ideology,' I said. I raised both hands, and half a smile. 'An evil mind, OK, I'll admit to that.'

'It's no fucking joke, Sinky,' said Calum. 'I mean apart fae whit Gabrielle's saying, there's yir other disturbing wee admission that what yi were really trying tae dae wis finger me and Sophie as revolutionaries, for fuck's sake.'

'And myself as well,' I pointed out.

'Aye, but *you're* aw right,' said Calum, leaning forward and shaking his finger at me. 'You ken fine yir no a revolutionary. The fucking spooks could rake through yir entire fucking life and no find a scrap ae evidence against yi.'

'Well, they could,' I said, still trying to be reasonable, trying to make light of it. 'I still have a copy or two and a zip drive of *What Now?* somewhere.'

'Aye, and so has every cunt that ever had a spark ae curiosity or rebellion back in their teens. They'd be mair suspicious if yi didnae! The point is, Sinky, you only know for sure about yirself. You don't know for sure about me and Sophie.'

'Oh, come on!' I cried. 'This is ridiculous. I know *you* all right – you and me were practically fascists ourselves when we were at school, hoping for a military coup and all that, and to this day you bang on about how we're living under socialism already – just like Baxter does, come to think of it. And as for Sophie, OK I don't know her so well, but she's no revolutionary. She makes cloth for *frocks*, for fuck's sake! I've never heard a political word out of her.'

This was not strictly true, I realised as I said it, remembering her alarming reflections about the ethics of taking the long view. But that was too abstract a consideration to count.

'Disnae matter,' said Calum. 'It was no your call tae make.'

I'd come here to confess and to apologise, but I'd thought of it more in the nature of clearing up a misunderstanding. Only now did the enormity of what I'd done come home to me. McCormick had been right about me. I really was a piece of work.

I found myself sitting with my head in my hands. I didn't know how long for. I sat up straight and looked at Calum and Gabrielle, that perfect Neanderthal couple, at this moment almost literally joined at the hip, who regarded me from across the room with silent scorn.

'I've done you wrong,' I said. 'You and a lot of other people. I'm sorry.'

Gabrielle and Calum looked at each other, and each, almost imperceptibly to me, nodded. Then they faced me again.

'Good,' said Gabrielle. 'Now, what are you going to do to put it right? You've convinced Baxter that it was all nonsense, you've come and told us everything, and I guess you're going to tell Sophie.'

'Yes,' I said. 'That was the plan.'

'It's not enough. You have to keep an eye on Baxter and his lot from now on, and you have to convince us you're never going to pull a stunt like this again.'

I felt relieved that this was all she demanded.

'Oh!' I cried. 'I know how I can keep an eye on Baxter. I can take him up on his offer of a job.'

Gabrielle smiled thinly. 'Getting a proper job would do you good, as I used to tell you over and over. But how can you convince us you'll be loyal to your friends?'

So we were still friends. That was something.

'I don't know,' I said. 'I don't have any hostages to offer you. I could swear, if that would help.'

'You swore tae me once,' said Calum. 'By God and Darwin, I seem tae recall. Didnae make any difference, did it?'

'It did!' I protested. 'I never said a word about the book to anyone. That's what you swore me to silence about. The book

382

you told me about and that you faked the evidence for and that didn't exist anyway.'

'The book wisnae the main point,' said Calum. 'But OK, I'll gie you that. And Gabrielle got you thinking about the family secret and made out it was no secret and no big deal apart fae the, uh, the personal aspect ae it. So I'll let yi off on a technicality. But this time, I just want you tae swear tae stay loyal tae yir friends, like Gabrielle said.'

'Of course,' I said. 'I'll swear.' Giddy with relief, I essayed a smile. 'What do you want me to swear on this time?'

Calum slid off the side of the armchair, stalked over to the bookshelf niche, pulled down a book and gave it to me, from both of his hands to both of mine. It was bound in ancient, furred leather with faint remnants of gold tooling, and lay heavy in my hands and across my knees. I opened it, and saw within the striking, surprising white of vellum; turned over the leaves, and saw the incomprehensible words in an unfamiliar alphabet, and the text divided in the easily recognisable form of gospel and epistle, chapter and verse; and the weird, crabbed, violent illustrations throughout. I turned to the last book, and its ninth chapter, and saw the locust picture.

I closed it, hands shaking, and looked up at Calum.

'You can swear on this,' he said.

PART EIGHT

28

The big frocks blazed in jewel shades in the window panel on the front of the Fabrications office in Hope Street. The illusion of an old-fashioned formal dress shop window was perfect until one of the mannequins morphed to a model with a catwalk scowl and twirl, or a gown changed shape and colour more radically than even metafabric garments actually could. I watched several cycles of such transformations before I nerved myself to go in. Behind the door, it was a normal front office, apart from the wall pictures, which were more of the same, and the receptionist likewise. The juxtaposition was bizarre. She looked as if she'd stepped from a Winterhalter or Sargent painting into a 1970s office-furniture ad, to park her bustle on a swivel chair behind a compressed-pine desk.

I'd originally intended to visit Sophie the following week, but Calum and Gabrielle had pointed out that she often worked on Saturdays, and insisted I go straight to her workplace from their flat. Perhaps they suspected that my resolve would falter with delay, or that I'd come up with some scheme to evade the issue and mitigate the confrontation.

'Good afternoon, sir. Can I help you?'

'Ah, is Sophie Watt in today?'

The receptionist eyed me. 'Do you have an appointment?'

'No, I'm an old school friend. I just dropped by on impulse.'

'I'll see.'

She rang and spoke, listened, nodded.

'Second floor,' she told me. 'Third door on the left.'

I smiled, thanked her, and trudged up the four flights of stairs. The third door opened silently to a big studio space. Bolts and swatches of fabric lay on long tables, weighted by scissors and metal rulers, alongside complex bits of laboratory apparatus and synthetic biology tanks and tubes. Prototyping machines and 3D printers jostled for space with industrial-grade overlockers and sewing machines. In one corner stood a small tent, and overhead hung what looked like the wing of a man-sized bat. Sophie stood in front of a big tilted screen, light-pen in hand, caught in thought. She was wearing narrow jeans, long boots, and a protective smock spattered with vari-coloured splotches of plastic and paint like a kindergarten child's art-class tabard.

She must have heard my step, or seen a shadow flicker. She turned from her work and smiled.

'Oh, hi, Ryan! Good to see you.'

She threaded her way through the clutter, and indicated two stools by one of the long tables.

'Have a seat, watch your step.'

'Thanks. And thanks for making time to see me. Hope I'm not interrupting anything.'

'Only the most totally brilliant idea for a new fabric that I've ever had.' She put the heel of her hand to her forehead. 'Then the phone rang. It's gone now.'

'Oh, Christ, sorry about—'

She laughed at the look on my face. 'Honestly, Ryan! Of course not. I'm just dealing with stuff I should have got done during the week. Come to think of it, that really is your fault. We were all agog about the Rammie business. Thank goodness it wasn't our material that was the problem. Nice bit of investigation you did there! I saw you mentioned on the telly.'

'Oh, yeah, well, I got a leak from inside BAS. Just luck in a way.' I stopped myself from spinning yet another lie as if I'd already forgotten why I was there and what I'd so recently sworn to do. 'Actually, no, it wasn't. That's . . . kind of why I'm here. I've got something to tell you.'

'Really? Go on.'

She raised her eyebrows and widened her eyes, as if expecting some delightful surprise. I was still rattled, still shaking inside from the response I'd got from Calum and Gabrielle: a response I should have expected, and would have if I'd applied the smallest gumption to forethought. A minute's thought would have set me right; but, as someone once said, thinking is painful and a minute is a long time. Was I now about to stray into another minefield, having expected nothing more than a patch of rough ground?

'Well, it's kind of a long story,' I said, floundering, 'and it concerns you because . . . well, a few weeks ago I sort of suddenly realised or at least thought I did that, well, when I looked back it was all *about* you, that it's *always* been about you, and—'

She slipped off her stool and flung her arms around me, damn near knocking me off my seat.

'Oh, Ryan! That's so sweet!'

Her misunderstanding was so unexpected, so perfect, and so welcome that I was tempted then and there to say nothing more, or at least to delay telling her the truth. I returned her hug, and then put my hands on her shoulders and gently pushed her away.

'Yes, Sophie,' I said. 'There's that, yes. But there's a lot more, and you really have to hear it, and maybe when you've heard it all you won't even like me.'

She stepped back and sat up again, with a frown that was more puzzled than angry or wary.

'Try me,' she said.

And oh, how I tried her. I held nothing back. Well, almost nothing. After what I'd learned about myself in my conversation with Calum and Gabrielle I was in no shape to repeat the various evasions that had smoothed my confession to them. I told her nearly everything, including things I hadn't told any of the others, and things I haven't told you.

It wasn't as one-sided as it sounds. Sophie had plenty of questions and interjections and expressions of disbelief. This took some time. It took the rest of the afternoon and half the evening, and the conversation that began in the studio continued through a long walk, up Hope Street and along Sauchiehall Street, across Kelvingrove Park. It ended at last in the Aragon, an old and oft-renovated pub on Byres Road.

'And that's it,' I finished.

I faced her across a table in an alcove, our small eddy in a swirl and roar of students. Half a shared platter of chips was getting cold on the table between us, reeking of vinegar. I wiped my mouth and fingers with a tattered paper napkin, and took a swallow of Glasgow Pride and a long draw on my pipe.

'That's it?'

'Everything,' I said.

Well, nearly everything. And what I'd left out was nothing that need concern her, anyway.

'Ryan, you are one devious, shifty, thoughtless, heartless, worthless, obsessive, perverted, voyeuristic, neurotic, idiotic, selfish, self-centred, cowardly, pathetic excuse for a human being.'

'That sounds fair,' I said. 'Mind you, I'd have put it a bit more harshly myself.'

'I still like you.'

'You do?'

'I've always known what you're like,' she said. 'But I've always liked you anyway.'

'You did?'

'Yes. Liked you and lusted for you.'

'Damn. I wish I'd known that years ago.'

'When we were both free and single?'

'Yes.'

'Oh, wait,' she said. 'We *are* both free and single.'

I hadn't thought of myself in that way at all. I had fancied myself still besotted with Gabrielle, nobly sacrificing my passion to her decision, still carrying a torch for her while she went off with Calum and had children with him – the one thing I couldn't do for her. Even when I'd apologised to them that morning for my behaviour and said I knew and accepted that it was all over between me and Gabrielle, I'd been lying my arse off as usual.

I'd still hoped to win her back, somehow. Eventually. When the kids had grown up, or at least were old enough to take the disruption without lasting trauma. Or when she saw through Calum, a fine chap and a good pal but probably not great husband and father material, being far too engrossed in his work, or when . . . but there even I have to stop. Some things are just too embarrassing for words.

At that point I did the first really brave and sensible thing I'd done all day, and in many a day. I reached across the table with both hands and clasped Sophie's as they rose to meet mine and said, 'Not now, we're not.'

29

And not now. We're still not free and single, and Sophie and I are both happy with that.

I arrive at the office about twenty past ten on my late mornings, bringing with me coffee and tea in cardboard cups from the machine. Baxter may or may not be in his office, but his secretary Safiyya is always in the office we share at the front. She takes the tea, thanks me; we exchange a few pleasantries and get on with our work. If Baxter is in he calls out for a coffee for himself, and I go and get one for him, and take it in.

'Morning, Ryan,' he says. 'Found any flying saucers yet?'

'Nope.'

'Keep looking,' he says.

It's a ritual, a running gag that's got old and tired but that we both keep flogging along. We talk for a bit about whatever the real science or technology issue of the day is, and I go back to the front office and crack on. Contrary to what the now-stale joke implies, UFOs aren't a big part of my research for Baxter. No more than one per cent. A watching brief.

There are far more interesting things going on, in space, in Africa, in China, in the labs and factories of Scotland itself. For some of them we have to come up with a response – a comment, a reaction, a policy. There are constituents to help and surgeries to hold and caucuses to plot and votes to carry, or to lose. That's the day-to-day stuff, the routine; and then there's the longer term, the strategic picture.

What I watch for most intently, and report to Baxter at once, are any signs of strain and stress: advance tremors of the crisis we both for different reasons expect. Nothing much so far: the Big Deal holds, the New Improvement continues. We've had a few false alarms. I usually manage to talk Baxter out of talking them up. Not always, but I can't protect him from himself all the time. He's quite the Cassandra, the economic and political drama queen. Maybe that's not such a bad reputation to have when the crunch comes, as we know it must. All our generation know. Baxter's ten years older than me, a little too old to be part of my generation, and Safiyya – in her early twenties, just out of university – is too young. I recognise my kind.

We're a strange generation, a peculiar cohort: those of us who were just young enough and just old enough to have lived the moment of the Big Deal as part of our conscious youth. We all have a sense of insecurity, of possibility, arising from certainty; from the sure knowledge we share, that the world can turn on a penny. Any stability is apparent, and can flip from one day to the next. All that is solid can melt into air. We all know that in our bones.

I sometimes find myself thinking about what that spook who called himself McCormick said. The revolutionaries dissolved their organisation and went into business, and now there's no way of telling who is a revolutionary and who is not. Because everyone knows everyone is watched, and everyone watches, no one knows, really, deep down, what any other thinks. All understandings are unspoken.

In that long Saturday of long conversations that changed my life, Sophie never did tell me she wasn't a revolutionary. Nor did Calum. Nor Gabrielle. I've never asked. All I know is that I'm not, and that I know what Baxter knows. That's enough.

Baxter's wryly liberal about office hours; a certain employment law he noisily objected to and voted against is kind to parents; and with glasses and phones everyone's always on call anyway. So most days, even days I haven't watched Gabrielle go to work, I can watch her go home. She picks up her little girl from the nursery where Calum left her in the morning on his way to work, at around the same time as I pick up our little girl from the nursery where Sophie left her in the morning, on her way to work. Out of the corner of my eye I can see Gabrielle holding Tanya's hand as she skips along University

Avenue, at the same time as I hold Angela's hand as she skips or trudges or otherwise drags her cheery or weary way up Dalry Road beside me. I try not to look too much.

Sophie has a longer day than I do, but much the same commute: five minutes to Haymarket, twenty minutes on the new-improved train to Queen Street, ten minutes' walk to Hope Street, and the same in reverse coming back. For me going home it's fifteen minutes from Holyrood to the Mound, five minutes by tram or fifteen minutes by foot to Haymarket, then five minutes' walk to the flat. Vary each of our journeys by the time it takes to leave or to pick up Angela.

Angela and I get in before Sophie most days, and most days I get the dinner going before Sophie comes in. Sophie's work is too much like cooking for that to be recreation for her, and it's the other way round for me. Sometimes, while I'm in the kitchen and Angela's parked in front of children's telly and Sophie's verifiably on the train home, I send a message to Gabrielle. It's always the same message: nothing to report. Gabrielle sends me a :-) and a X back.

It's all innocent. Sophie knows I watch Gabrielle. She doesn't know I text her. Calum does. It makes me feel a bit guilty sometimes, but it doesn't keep me awake at night. Not even the dreams keep me awake at night. What sometimes does, as Sophie snores beside me – she denies this, but she does snore – and I slip my glasses on and gaze up through the ceiling and the floors above and the roof and the clouds at the real stars, is remembering what the spooks told me about what Baxter knows.

It was why, they told me, he'd accept the story about the manufacturing flaw, even though he'd probably suspect it was false, and why he'd insist that the radar reading was nothing very important.

'What Baxter knows,' McCormick said, 'is that whatever it was that fell from the sky and knocked down you and your pal, *it wasn't one of ours*. And whatever it was that made the false echo on the radar at Machrihanish wasn't one of ours either.'

0.02222 Recurring

Sometimes I find myself, as it seems, lying awake at night and looking at the stars, and I realise I don't have my glasses on, and I know I'm in the dream. Usually I wake up before it completes its course. Now and then I'm in it to the end.

This is how it ends.

I peer out of the tiny round-cornered thick-paned window beside me, the left temple of my forehead pressed to the glass, and see the blue curve of the Earth below, and ahead of us, approaching – the space station. It's far bigger than any of the space stations that are really up there in low Earth orbit, a huge spinning torus straight out of Kubrick and von Braun, and quite impossible to miss with the naked eye from the ground. It's like nothing we have yet. But I don't feel as if I'm in the future. I feel as if I'm in the present. In fact, in the dream I *know* I'm in the present. This space station has spaceships docked round its hub. Some of them are drop-jet spaceplanes like the one I'm in, and others are like nothing I've ever seen: gnarly old vessels pockmarked with micrometeor impacts and ablated by solar wind, bristling with vanes and blades and spikes, like mailed fists in the face of the night.

Of course I know what they are.

They're starships, they're ours, and this is now.

There are sharp kicks of deceleration as course and speed corrections are applied in brief burns of the main and secondary motors. The delicate ballet of ship and station concludes with the shuddering embrace of docking. The view from the window is of steel plate and rivets. One by one, the passengers' seat-belts are unlocked and retract, and one by one, hand over hand, we float down the cabin to the exit through an airtight concertina connection and out to the station. There's no processing to go through here, no security checks; all that has been done at embarkation far below and hours ago. Every passenger knows where they're going, or is meeting someone who does.

Following the rest, I swing into a long tube with a continuously rolling ladder. Foot on a step, hand on a grip. My weight increases as I'm carried down toward the rim of the spinning station. At the bottom I'm in one gravity. I stride confidently away, along a long wide corridor that curves up in front of me and behind. It's a busy place; people are hurrying, this way and that. I know there is somewhere I have to go, someone I have to talk to, someone who must know everything, and who will decide my fate. I know that I'm in some kind of trouble, but I'm not afraid. I've reviewed my life so far on the way up, I have all the evidence I need stored in my glasses, and I'm confident that everything can be explained and justified.

My pace quickens. I'm keen to get this over with. I'm already looking forward to getting back. And then—

Always this happens. Always it surprises me. In the quick-flowing crowd of strangers from all over the world going the other way, I see two faces that give me a jolting shock of recognition. A man and a woman, both tall and good-looking, both in a uniform that looks out of place here but that no one looks twice at, except me.

It's the Space Brother and the Space Sister. Between them and with them walks a shorter figure, a lad in his mid-teens. His skin is a little paler than theirs. He's a fine young man, not full grown yet. I can see the family resemblance: there are elements of his features that resemble the Space Sister. There are others that remind me of my own face.

The Space Brother and the Space Sister recognise me at the same moment as I recognise them. Their faces light up. Their heads turn to the lad between them, and nod towards me. He gives me a searching look, and a warm but watchful smile as they approach. All three nod and smile as they come level with me, and then express with a subtle twitch of eyebrows and lips some chagrin or mild regret: they have to keep going, they have somewhere to go. The crowd carries them past, and me on.

I push against the flow, stumbling and apologising, and join the stream in the opposite direction. The three I'm following are already about five metres ahead of me, heads bobbing above the crowd. I weave and dodge through, trying to catch up, but they stay ahead of me. I know I'm going the wrong way.

We pass the chute I came down, and several others. The look and feel of the corridor has changed. The surroundings have a naval cast. The steel walls are bare; the air has a tang of rust; there's a metal grille rather than pliant plastic floor tiles underfoot. There are fewer people around, and they're stranger than the strangers I saw earlier. These are no aliens, no Greys, just people, but they look as if they come from countries and continents that aren't on any map. Some of them give me curious glances. The exits and entrances of the chutes with their rolling ladders have notices in languages I don't know, in letters I can't read, that remind me of some strange alphabet I've seen before.

I know what the inscriptions mean. They are the names of destinations, of worlds and stars.

Behind me, I hear shouts. I hear my name called. I don't look back. I quicken my pace. I've almost caught up.

The Space Sister looks over her shoulder, sees me and frowns and shakes her head. I shake mine, negating her negation. She looks forward again, then back; smiles and shrugs. On your own head be it, she seems to say.

The three reach the hatchway that leads to a chute. One by one they step inside, grab on and get carried up. The Sister is the last. She looks over her shoulder again, and nods, and rises away.

I follow. I step into the chute and look up. On one side a rolling ladder ascends, on the other it descends, in endless belts. I know where this one goes. It goes where I must and cannot follow, to the starship dock.

I grab on, and rise, and fall.

Acknowledgements

Thanks, as always, to Carol for love and support.

I wrote most of this book while in the post of Writer in Residence on the MA Creative Writing course at Edinburgh Napier University. Many thanks to the course and the university for providing a congenial and stimulating place to work, and especially to Sam Kelly for all her help, advice and encouragement.

Thanks to Sharon MacLeod, Sam Kelly and Farah Mendlesohn for reading and commenting on the draft.

Ken MacLeod graduated with a BSc from Glasgow University in 1976. Following research at Brunel University, he worked in a variety of manual and clerical jobs whilst completing an MPhil thesis. He previously worked as a computer analyst/programmer in Edinburgh, but is now a full-time writer. He is the author of thirteen previous novels, six of which have been nominated for the Arthur C. Clarke Award, and two which have won the BSFA Award. Ken MacLeod is married with two grown-up children and lives in West Lothian.

Find out more about Ken MacLeod and other Orbit authors by registering for the free monthly newsletter at www.orbitbooks.net.